A DETECTIVE INSPECTO

WHISPER FOR THE REAPER

NEW YORK TIMES #1 BESTSELLER **TONY LEE** WRITING AS

JACK GATLAND

Hooded Man
MEDIA
INSPIRATION • PRODUCTION • PUBLICATION

Published by Hooded Man Media

First Edition: April 2021

PRAISE FOR JACK GATLAND

'This is one of those books that will keep you up past your bedtime, as each chapter lures you into reading just one more.'

'This book was excellent! A great plot which kept you guessing until the end.'

'Couldn't put it down, fast paced with twists and turns.'

'The story was captivating, good plot, twists you never saw and really likeable characters. Can't wait for the next one!'

'I got sucked into this book from the very first page, thoroughly enjoyed it, can't wait for the next one.'

'Totally addictive. Thoroughly recommend.'

'Moves at a fast pace and carries you along with it.'

'Just couldn't put this book down, from the first page to the last one it kept you wondering what would happen next.'

Before LETTER FROM THE DEAD...
There was

LIQUIDATE
THE PROFITS

Learn the story of what *really* happened to DI Declan Walsh, while at Mile End!

An EXCLUSIVE PREQUEL, completely free to anyone who joins the Declan Walsh Reader's Club!

Join at bit.ly/jackgatlandVIP

Also by Jack Gatland

COVERT ACTION

COUNTER ATTACK

STEALTH STRIKE

DAMIAN LUCAS BOOKS

THE LIONHEART CURSE

STANDALONE BOOKS

THE BOARDROOM

For Mum, who inspired me to write.

For Tracy, who inspires me to write.

CONTENTS

PROLOGUE

CRAIG RANDALL LED A DOUBLE LIFE.

That's what he told everyone that he spoke to; it made him sound like a secret agent, some kind of exciting, enigmatic hero rather than what he really was; a fifteen-year-old bully with a Walter Mitty fantasy.

Craig's double life *wasn't* fake though; it just wasn't what you'd expect to see when asking someone about it. During the week, Craig was just a Year 10 loser, picked upon by the bigger, stupider kids in his year because he wasn't a fan of the same football teams, a teenager who spent a lot of time on his own, and who didn't have that many friends. He wasn't that academic; he wasn't that sporty. In fact, he wasn't that... anything. If you looked up the words *academically average* in a school guidebook, you'd probably find a photo of Craig Randall smiling out at you. Or, at least scowling, annoyed that he was being made fun of again.

But on the weekends, oh yes the weekends, he was a *God*.

For Craig Randall spent his weekends somewhere else. Not in South East London like the other losers in his class, no; Craig and his family would spend every weekend from Easter until October at a camping and caravan park in Hurley Upon Thames.

It'd started when he was eight. His parents, sick of the estate they lived in and desperate to escape from the city, if only for a day or so borrowed a frame tent from a friend, and, with a minimum of camping equipment and experience had muddled their way to Hurley after seeing it mentioned in the back of Camping and Caravanning magazine. They'd arrived late on a Friday evening in May and, as Craig and his dad wrestled with the tent, realising very early in the process that they didn't have a manual explaining which pole went where, Craig's mum and his sister Ellie went to visit the camp shop, and picked up some fish and chips from a van that had arrived just outside it.

They'd been cramped back then; eight-year-old Craig and five-year-old Ellie had to share one of the two 'bedrooms', nothing more than a cloth divider between their manky sleeping bags on cheap air beds, and their parents' double air bed, with equally battered sleeping bags.

They'd had a BBQ on the Saturday and cooked from a single camp stove the other days. They'd played football. Although they had a small TV to watch things on, they didn't really bother. There was a small boat ramp that led into the Thames, which you could get to by following a path from the first field, or by making your way across a rickety, home made bridge created from wooden pallets over a stream beside the third, furthest away field, and then following the Thames back to it.

He played there a lot. And he built the bridge, too.

It had been a break in every sense of the word; a break from the artificial normality of the world, and a return to an easier time. From that day onwards, the Randalls were born again weekend campers, updating their equipment piece by piece while travelling down every Friday evening, often from the moment Craig left school, and returning mid afternoon on the Sunday, just in time for him to prepare for school the following day.

They weren't the only people who did this and over the weeks and months that they lived this double life, Craig had recognised other people, other families, other *children* who also travelled to Hurley on the weekends. And, they met new families who were just starting the journeys.

Families and children who didn't know Craig, and had no context of what he was truly like.

And thus the *second* Craig Randall was born.

This Craig was a cool one. He was captain of his school's football team, had a girlfriend who was super hot and two years older than him, and he was doing these new visiting children a favour by hanging out with them. He was the experienced one, the veteran of the camp; he knew the coolest places to play in the woods that surrounded the campsite, the best places to swim, and he always had a story of something amazing that'd happened in the past which was always a story that made him look as equally brilliant. In fact, as the years went on and Craig reached his teenage years, he'd spend the weeks waiting for the weekends, when he could go back to Hurley and gain adoration from the smaller kids there, annoyed when the camping season ended in October and he had to wait almost half the year to return.

He didn't explain what he did while camping to his weekday friends. They weren't that important to him. They didn't see him in the same way.

They'd adopted a spaniel named Scamper, named after

some book dog his dad had loved as a kid a couple of years into this. Craig wasn't a fan of the spaniel, mainly because he ended up as the de facto dog walker, but that said, it seemed to attract girls to him, all wanting to stroke Scamper; and Craig had by then reached an age where girls were very *interesting*.

And then it'd all gone wrong. His parents now had a caravan, and although Ellie still slept with them inside it, they allowed Craig his own three-person tent, which he'd had to save up for. It was like having his own place; he had a double mattress inside it, even if his sleeping bag fitted one person, and a small radio that played CDs. But for the fifteen-year-old Craig, this was a bachelor pad. He was finally becoming a man.

And his attitude to the other kids on the site changed.

He wasn't bothered about playing in the woods like he was five years earlier. He wanted to kiss girls and look cool. He'd just finished his Year 10 mock GCSE exams. You were effectively a grown up when you did that.

He bullied the smaller kids in the campsite, mainly because he could. That, and it was revenge for the bullies who still attacked him at his own school. He'd also realised that he was no longer the 'veteran' who could show the coolest places to other kids; that was now a position given to his sister, or even other younger children who, arriving years after he had claimed the role were now looking at him as some kind of weird hanger on. And this had angered him.

He'd acted out by hurting the smaller kids; not physically, but mentally.

He'd take things of theirs, left outside the tents at night and throw them into the Thames or break them, leaving them back outside the tents for the owners to find the following morning.

He'd tell stories of the *Grey Lady,* a ghostly woman who hanged herself in Medmenham Abbey, a stately home across the Thames and historically infamous as the location of Sir Francis Dashwood's The Hellfire Club, who used it for "obscene parodies of religious rites" in the mid-1700s, her ghost walking the banks of the Thames late at night, stealing children's souls.

He'd even pretended to become possessed by Dashwood, terrifying the younger children until they cried, now and then finding an intrigued teenage girl who wanted to know more.

He'd never gone too far with that, except for the one time.

But now it was summer, school was over, and the Hurley campsite had become a prison for Craig. After seven years there, he had built a reputation; one that his parents had often argued with him about. *They were one strike away from being banned because of his antics,* they'd say. He'd laugh and tell them that the ghost of Francis Dashwood had done the terrible things, not him, and then walk out before they could reply. In fact, he'd just done that, walking with Scamper eastwards along the Thames, towards Hurley Lock, a mile or so away.

The Thames was to his left, strangely quiet for the time of day; nobody was fishing, there weren't even any kids playing in the water. It felt wrong, odd, somehow. The bank of the river became an open field to his right, and about fifty yards away a bank of trees showed the woodland copse that bordered the campsite. This was where Scamper was running to, as Craig tried to get his battered old iPod Nano to work. If he'd charged it earlier, he wouldn't have heard the barking.

And that would have changed everything.

As it was, he hadn't charged the iPod, and therefore it wasn't playing music and he heard Scamper barking at something somewhere near the edge of the woods. The bloody dog wouldn't come back after being called, and Craig almost continued on, convinced that Scamper would just follow him, or just do him a favour and leave forever, when he heard the barking cut off abruptly with a *yelp*.

Turning back to the trees, Craig could see that Scamper had run over to the rickety bridge. And, walking towards it, frustrated that Scamper had most likely run into the trees, he stopped about twenty feet away from it, as a man appeared the other side, emerging from the woods.

He was old, maybe in his fifties. He was slim, had short brown hair in a buzz cut, and wore a green Barbour jacket. His face was pale, like he didn't get out into the sun that much. And he was smiling.

'Have you lost your dog?' he asked, his voice showing the slightest hint of a European accent. 'He is right here. Come and get him.'

'Nah, it's okay,' Craig said. There was something about this old man that unnerved him. 'I'll just wait.'

'I think he is tangled in nettles,' the man replied. 'You must come and help him.'

'It's cool, I'll wait until you've moved on,' Craig tried to smile, but it came out as a leer. The man however nodded at this.

'Understandable,' he agreed. 'I am a stranger. You are right to be wary. But we are not strangers, are we *Craig*?'

At the sound of his own name, Craig felt an icy wind

blowing down his spine. He'd never seen this man before, and he'd sure as hell not given his name away.

'Who are you?' he asked. 'How do you know who I am?'

'I know everything about you,' the man continued to smile as he spoke, and Craig found himself irrationally angry at this. 'I know you have been coming here for years. I know you are a bully. I know what you did to that girl.'

'I didn't assault her,' Craig snapped back. 'She came on to me. I didn't do anything.'

'I'm sure you did not,' the man replied, stepping back from the bridge, beckoning Craig in. 'But perhaps we should talk more about this together, rather than shouting it loudly across a stream?' The old man watched Craig, still not moving.

'Your dog is in pain,' he said. 'You will not save him?'

Now terrified, Craig shook his head. The man thought about this for a moment and then pulled something out of his jacket pocket, tossing it over the stream, the item landing at Craig's feet. As Craig bent down to look at it, he could see it was an ivory handle. Picking it up, he realised it was a wickedly sharp cut-throat razor.

'See?' The man smiled. 'Now you have a weapon. If I attacked, you could hurt me. Please, come in, Craig. Come and play a game with me.' And as Craig watched, the man walked back into the woods.

With the blade now in his hand, Craig felt more in control of the situation. The man was right; he *could* hurt him and hurt him badly if he tried anything. And, as he crossed the rickety bridge and entered the wooded copse, he saw Scamper, a rope loosely tied to his collar and secured to a tree, wagging his tail with delight at this strange game they were playing. The dog wasn't in pain or in distress at all.

Craig looked to the man, angry that he had lied to him, and found him sitting on a fallen tree trunk, with another fallen trunk facing him.

'Sit, please,' the man indicated the other trunk. 'We have much to talk about.'

Now more curious than scared, Craig ignored the dog and walked to the tree, sitting down on it, blade still in his hand, ready to defend himself. Noting this, the man reached into a pocket and pulled out a hip flask with two small metal cups, made of metal bands that clicked into shape when flicked. Into these, he poured a liquid, offering one to Craig, who shook his head.

'And I thought you were almost an adult,' the man sighed, drinking one cup. 'See? Not poisoned. But you will need to drink this, Craig Randall of Gleeson Road.' He held the offered one up again. 'Drink.'

Craig didn't mean to, but the man's voice was so commanding that he couldn't help himself, taking the metal cup and downing the liquid with a cough. It was a sweet, strong taste, like apples.

'Good, yes?' The man smiled. 'Schnapps. With a little benzocaine added to numb the pain.'

Craig coughed as the man pulled out a small, silver coin.

'You know what this is?' the man asked, not waiting for an answer as he explained. 'This is a solid silver East-German Mark.' He twirled it in his fingers. 'See? A number *one* is on this side, that is *heads*, while on the other side is a compass and a hammer; *tails*. I have had this for many years now.' He looked up from the coin now, staring intently at Craig.

'We play a game now,' he explained as he reached into his pocket again, pulling out another cut-throat razor. 'I will flip it. If it lands heads, I will take this razor, this very sharp blade and slash my throat open. If it shows tails, however, you will do this instead, yes?'

'No!' Craig rose now, angry. 'You're mad! I—' he stopped as a heaviness overcame his legs, sending him back to the tree trunk. 'What did you do?'

'I told you,' the man replied. 'Schnapps. With a little benzocaine.'

'I don't want to play,' Craig whined, realising that this was a terrible place to be right now.

'I understand, it is scary,' the man nodded sympathetically. 'But you have been a wicked man, Craig. As have I. And as such we must face repercussions.' He rolled the coin over his fingers. 'And you might not get tails. I might lose.'

'I'll scream,' Craig insisted. 'I'll call for help.'

'And that is your right,' the man nodded calmly. 'But know that if you do, I will be gone before anyone arrives. And then, at some point very soon, I will enter your house while your mother, father and dear little sister Ellie are asleep and I will slowly and painfully skin them all alive. And then I will find you and make you watch as I slice pieces off you with this straight razor.'

Craig was crying. 'Please, I'm sorry,' he said. 'I don't want to die.'

The old man smiled.

'Maybe you will not,' he said as he flicked the coin into the air, watching it lazily flip before landing on the back of his hand. 'Let us see, shall we?'

DI FREEMAN CLIMBED OUT OF HIS BMW AND LOOKED AROUND the campsite. It was right after the school holidays had started, and there were families and children everywhere. A nightmare to keep a crime scene contained.

There was a perimeter already placed around the entrance to the copse; a couple of police officers ensuring that the small crowd of onlookers couldn't enter.

This was good. They really didn't want to see this.

One onlooker, a young dark-skinned woman with frizzy black hair, waved to him as he approached the police officers, catching his eye. Forcing a smile while silently swearing, Freeman walked over to her.

'Kendis,' he said amiably. 'I didn't think you worked for the Maidenhead Advertiser anymore?'

'I don't,' Kendis Taylor replied, pulling out her voice recorder. 'But I'm visiting mum. It's the Olympic opening ceremony tonight and my cousin's in it. Saw the blues and twos as I was driving to the house.'

Freeman wanted nothing more than to escape. 'You needn't turn that on. There's no story here.'

'You sure?'

Without answering, Freeman walked away from the annoying reporter, showing his ID to the nearest officer and passing under the incident tape, entering the woodland clearing. Here he found more officers, mainly forensics, working the case while other officers kept the public out of sight. Recognising one officer through the white PPE suit she wore, he waved to gain her attention. Regan was a solid SOCO, and he didn't want to piss her off if he could help it, so he kept as far away as he could.

'What've we got?' he asked. Regan walked over to him, glancing back as she did. On the floor, lying on his back, his arms outstretched and his throat slashed, was a teenage boy.

'Craig Randall, fifteen years old, throat slashed from right to left,' she said, making the motion with her hand. 'Went out with the dog two hours back. Dog arrived back in the camp-site about an hour ago. Family went looking for him, couldn't find him, tried calling his phone, no answer. Eventually that caravan there heard the ringing and entered the woods, thinking someone had lost a phone. Instead, they found this.'

'Nice,' Freeman stared at the body. 'Cause of death?'

'We think it's some sort of razor,'

'Think?' Freeman looked back to Regan. 'No weapon found?'

'None yet,' Regan admitted. 'But then he could have slashed his throat and then thrown it into the bushes or even the stream.'

'You think this was self inflicted?' This surprised Free-man. Regan waved for him to follow, moving a little closer to the body, but not close enough to contaminate the scene.

'See there? The cut is from right to left,' she explained. 'It's jagged, so it wasn't committed; almost like he started, stopped and then continued through.' She pointed to the left hand, currently against the ground. 'Blood started spurting out on the right-hand side, then spurts to the left as he continues to cut, where it splatters all over his fist and arm. But his palm is absent of any sign of it.'

'Because he was gripping the blade,' Freeman nodded. 'Any reason he'd do this?'

'Apart from the fact that he's apparently a little shit with a bit of a rep for being a bully?' Regan shrugged. 'Better ask the parents.'

'No note?'

Regan pointed to a tree where, on the bark, was etched one word.

SORRY

'That do for you?' she asked.

DI Freeman sighed. 'Anything else?'

'Actually, yes,' Regan waved to an assistant who passed over a clear plastic bag. In it was a piece of card the size of a business card, blank except for one image; a little red man with what looked like a hat on, arms out to the side, and holding a scythe. 'We think this is some kind of collectable—'

'It's *murder*,' Freeman said, his face draining of all colour. 'This wasn't suicide. I need to call Walsh.'

'Walsh? Why does he need to get involved?' Regan was irritated now, aware that she'd missed something, but unaware of what it was.

'Because we've seen that picture before,' Freeman replied, pulling out his phone and dialling. 'Yeah, it's me,' he eventually said into it. 'Get Detective Superintendent Patrick Walsh on the line, now.'

He looked back at the body.

'Tell him we have another *Red Reaper*.'

1

KIDNAPPED

DECLAN DIDN'T KNOW HOW LONG HE'D BEEN IN THE VAN FOR. All he knew was that he'd been sedated immediately after they had thrown a bag over his head.

And that pissed him off.

The van was driving straight; he knew this because even though he was hooded, he couldn't feel the sway of the van as it turned corners, only the occasional slight movement that was comparable with changing lanes on a motorway. Was he heading into London down the M4? It'd make sense. He went to pull at the hood, but realised that he couldn't move his hands. Not that they were restrained, but that they simply weren't responding.

Some sort of nerve agent.

Okay, so he was in a van, hooded and restrained. But at the same time it was one that was connected to Trix, and she'd recently helped him escape custody, so there had to be a reason for this. What it was, though, he had no idea.

Declan leaned back in the seat; to be honest, it was a comfortable seat, and there was a seatbelt on, as he could feel it pressing against him. They'd wanted him to be secure, but not uncomfortable. He concentrated on the sensations he could feel. The hood had a slight ammonia smell to it, but that could be remnants of whatever sweet smelling sedative was used on it, back in Hurley.

Hurley.

He'd been at a funeral, that much he could remember. That was to say, he wasn't at the funeral, but watching it from afar. Kendis Taylor. A woman he'd loved for over half his life, even if a lot of that was spent doing it equally from afar. A woman who was now dead, a death that he'd avenged.

A death that he'd caused, as well. If he'd kept Kendis from the Andy Mac case at the start, she wouldn't have continued on with it. She wouldn't have—

No. She would have done it either way. That was what Kendis did. That's why he had admired her so. She was always destined for this, no matter what Declan did to save her.

He'd been so angry, convinced that this was folly when he had last spoken to her. He should have stayed with her. Ensured that she didn't go to Brompton Cemetery alone.

But he didn't. And she did. The past was written, and he had to move on, think about the present. Which, currently, was in the back of a van with a hood on his head.

He could feel his fingers now as life crept back into his extremities. Outside the van he could hear traffic; it was busier; the van moving slower. Central London, perhaps? A swing to the right. *Heading southwards now? Possibly.* He thought about what he'd been wearing. What did he have on his person? He had keys, a small *Leatherman* utility tool that he always carried, and the tactical pen he wrote his notes with. In his inside jacket was a USB with the word WINTERGREEN written on it; ever since he'd returned to the house after Westminster, he'd kept that on him, like some kind of good luck charm.

Fat lot of good luck it'd given him so far.

There was a dip; the van was moving downwards. An underground car park, perhaps? A swing to the right, the van moving slower now confirmed this. Declan attempted moving his hand; it tingled as he tried, but it moved a little. He moved onto his arm—

The hood was pulled off, and Declan saw Trix, her face a mask of concern as she peered at him, checking his eyes as she did so.

'You're awake?' she asked. 'Good. Thought as much. Here, smell this.' She cracked open a phial in front of him, allowing the smell to waft up Declan's nose. It made him gag with the stench, but within a couple of seconds he found he could move his muscles again.

'Neat trick,' he muttered, flexing his neck, allowing the kinks to release. 'You'd better have a damned good reason for that.'

'She didn't know I was going to do it,' a male voice said as a young man, dark-haired and in his late thirties, leaned around from the driver's seat. 'I thought it was the best way to get this done. We couldn't let you see where we took you, see. It's a secret.'

'Sorry Declan, but believe me when I say it's for your own good,' Trix stepped back now, out of the van, through the sliding side door and into a nondescript, half-empty underground car park. Declan didn't follow; instead he looked back to the young man.

'And you are?' he asked calmly.

'Tom Marlowe,' the man replied. 'And yeah, I'm not commenting on if that's a real name or not.'

'And you work with Trix?' Declan continued. Marlowe shrugged.

'In a manner of speaking,' he replied. 'I work with her in a specialised department. We're actually taking you to our boss, though. She's been wanting to chat to you for a while now.'

'Oh yeah?' Declan asked. 'Why's that?'

'Because you've been making a bloody noise looking for her,' Marlowe climbed out of the van, indicating for Declan to follow. 'Her name's Emilia Wintergreen.'

Declan hadn't expected this. Quietly and suspiciously he clambered gingerly out of the van, the after affects of the drug still in his system, making him unsteady on his feet. He wondered if this was how Monroe had felt a week earlier when the man with the rimless glasses had attacked him, but he put that thought aside as he followed Trix and Marlowe to the car park doors.

'So you're a spook?' he asked conversationally. Marlowe decided not to reply, pressing a button on the elevator and waiting beside it.

'I'm guessing you're a spook because of the hood and the covert shit you seem to employ here,' Declan continued, warming to the task. 'I mean, I know I'm in Central London, and I think we came up the M4, maybe the A40. I'm thinking down into London somewhere near Euston, so we're maybe in Holborn or somewhere near Soho.'

'You learn that in copper school?' Marlowe entered the elevator as the doors opened.

'Military Police,' Declan replied as he followed him.

'Look, Declan, I told you. You're toxic right now,' Trix

explained as the doors closed. 'You've pissed a ton of people off recently, and we can't walk you in through the front door.'

'But you won't even tell me where the door is,' Declan replied. Trix shrugged.

'Until we know if you're an asset or a threat, we'd rather play on the side of caution.'

'So I'm a threat now?' Declan chuckled as the elevator stopped at the third floor. 'If I pass your tests, do I get to know where we are?'

Trix glanced at Marlowe, who stared at the doors, waiting for them to open.

'Above my pay grade,' he said.

'And what *is* your pay grade?' Declan asked, but the doors sliding apart interrupted him. The elevator had opened up into a corridor, and Marlowe and Trix walked Declan left, towards a pair of old looking blue double doors, each with small windows embedded in the middle. There was a faint smell of what seemed to be curry powder, which didn't fit the location and as Declan entered through the doors behind Marlowe, he felt like he'd fallen into the eighties, with the decor of the office space that he'd now entered looking older than the offices of Temple Inn.

The office floor was open plan, with brown carpet tiles leading to grey cork walls. It was filled with rows of desks; cheap wooden ones, placed in lines of two so that each desk faced another, with the surfaces comprising cheap looking computer monitors, phones and a page of telephone numbers beside each one. It reminded Declan of a summer telemarketing job he'd had when he was sixteen, selling carpet cleaning services to people who obviously didn't want them. Marlowe, seeing his expression, smiled.

'All for show,' he explained. 'Management is up the stairs.'

'What is this place?'

'Whatever we need it to be.'

They continued to the end where another painted door led them to a set of stairs that continued upwards to a second, more intimidating door. This one was steel and had no window. A fingerprint scanner was to the side; Marlowe placed his own into it and, as it opened, he waved Trix and Declan through. On the other side was a security area; a metal detector and a rolling conveyor that led to an x-ray machine, just like the ones that airport security had. Marlowe meanwhile moved once more to the left, bypassing this by taking Declan through a door to the side.

Now the room was more modern; monitors on the walls and desk unit setups made this look more like mission control than a telemarketer's office. As Declan glanced around, taking in the people at their stations, most of whom ignored him, he realised that this wasn't a world he was used to. This wasn't a world of justice by arrest. This was a world of justice by whatever worked.

'In here,' Trix said, knocking on a door. A moment later she opened it, bringing Declan into what seemed to be a windowless boardroom, sound insulation panels along two of the walls, as if to deaden the noise made in the room, ensuring it didn't leak out to the outer offices. Declan hoped this wasn't so that people outside didn't hear screaming.

'Sit, please,' Marlowe pointed to a chair at the table as he walked to a coffee machine on a side cabinet, one of the posh ones that took small plastic pods, nestled beside one of the walls. 'White, no sugar, right?'

Declan nodded. He didn't need to ask how Marlowe knew this; Trix had made enough coffees while pretending to be a part of the *Last Chance Saloon*. Reluctantly, he sat at the table and waited.

He didn't wait long, as a minute later a door at the other end opened and a woman entered. In her late sixties she was slim, attractive and wore her white hair short. Declan laughed. She did indeed look like Helen Mirren.

'Something amusing?' The woman asked, her voice showing the slightest twinge of an accent. Maybe Scouse. Maybe Geordie.

'I was told you looked like Helen Mirren by a friend,' he replied. 'It amused me to see that he was right.'

'Ah, the elusive Karl Schnitter,' the woman said as she sat across the table from Declan, placing a folder on it beside her. 'I assumed he'd been watching me. Old habits and all that.'

Declan didn't ask what she meant; instead, he pulled out the USB stick with WINTERGREEN on and pushed it across the table at her.

'Here,' he pointed. 'I'm guessing that's for you.'

Emilia Wintergreen took the USB, nodding as she looked at it. 'Did your father leave a note with it?' she asked. Declan shook his head.

'Didn't even know you existed until I was researching the Angela Martin case,' he replied. 'Learned then about a Detective Sergeant who took money from the Lucas Brothers.'

In a similar fashion to when Declan didn't reply to the comment about Karl, Wintergreen didn't reply to this, instead taking the USB drive and rotating it in her hand as she examined it.

'You've seen what's on it? she asked. Declan shook his head.

'Can't,' he replied. 'Don't know the password.'

Wintergreen frowned. 'Well, I don't know it either,' she muttered, sliding it across to Trix, standing near the other door. 'See what can be done with this.' As Trix took the drive and left the boardroom, Wintergreen looked back at Declan.

'You have questions, I'm sure,' she said. Declan shrugged.

'Not as many as you might think,' he replied. 'Trix alluded to me who she was working for when she came by about a week back. I'm guessing that you moved from the Met to Whitehall, from Detective Sergeant to, well, 'M', in the process scrubbing your past, turning you into a ghost. How am I doing?'

'It's Control, not M,' Wintergreen smiled. 'But you're pretty close.'

Declan nodded at this. 'Was my dad a spook?'

'What makes you ask that?'

'Secret studies with bookcase doorways and cryptic USB drives are a bit of a giveaway,' Declan replied.

Wintergreen didn't reply for a moment, as if weighing up how much she could really say.

'He helped us, but he wasn't an agent, nor was he an asset,' she simply stated. 'To some, he was a threat, even.'

Declan looked around the windowless room. 'And which am I?' He asked. 'An asset? Or a threat?'

'That depends on you,' Wintergreen replied. 'If you're an asset, we'll discuss whatever you want, you'll be shown where you really are, and then you'll be taken home by Tom there. If you're a threat, this ends now and it'll be the hood and the van again.'

Declan leaned back in his chair, considering this. 'If my father trusted you, then I suppose I should,' he said. 'So why don't you tell me what this is really about.'

Wintergreen mimicked Declan, leaning back in her own

chair. 'You wanted to speak to me, remember,' she smiled. 'I have nothing to gain here.'

'Yeah, not buying that,' Declan leaned forward now, steepling his fingers together as he rested his elbows on the table in front of him. 'You could have used Trix as a middleman and never seen my face. You could have taken your time, decided whether I was a threat before bringing me in. Instead, you kidnap and drug me, to ensure I'm here right now. So how about we cut all the spy bullshit and get to the point? If you hadn't gathered, I'm having a pretty rotten day right now. I've buried a friend, had a fight with her husband, I'm likely fired from my job and I'm still seen as a terrorist by half my village, no matter what BBC News says right now. So lady, friend of my father or not, my patience is really running thin right now.'

Wintergreen went to reply, then stopped, nodding.

'You're in an office in Seven Dials, in London,' she replied. 'Just off the Donmar Warehouse theatre and down from Cambridge Circus, where the original Whitehall spies used to work. And you're right. I brought you in for a reason.'

She paused before continuing, as if worried what the answer to her next question would bring.

'What do you know about the *Red Reaper?*'

2

COLD RED CASES

OF ALL THE THINGS THAT WINTERGREEN COULD HAVE ASKED, Declan hadn't expected that question. He thought for a moment as he tried to dredge through his memories for something. He remembered snippets, partly from the television, but also through conversations later with his father.

'Some kind of sick suicide cult,' he replied. 'All linked by a card with a red man, in the shape of a cross, holding a scythe. Dad ran the case about ten years back.'

'Did he ever talk about it?'

Declan shook his head. 'I'd just started in Tottenham with DI Salmon,' he explained. 'Derek and dad didn't get on that well, as you probably know. Things were a little strained until mum died. And after that, although we spoke, he didn't talk business.'

Wintergreen pulled the folder on the table closer, but didn't open it. 'A dozen people died between 1990 and 2012,' she began. 'None of them had any kind of defensive injuries, all seemed to take their own lives in a variety of different ways. Hanging, shooting, injecting, slashing at their throats. The only thing that linked them together was a single white card with this image on.' She pulled a business card sized piece of card in a small, clear plastic bag out of the folder, showing it to Declan. One side was blank, but the other side had a small red man, wearing a hat, arms outstretched, one hand holding a red scythe.

'Every one of them had this. And every one of these had only the victim's fingerprints on it, right here.' She held the card through the plastic by the corner, with her thumb and index finger.

'As I said, a sick suicide cult,' Declan repeated. 'I remember something; weren't they all people with secrets, or who'd done wrong too? The one in Hurley was a rapist, right?'

Wintergreen pulled a file from the folder, reading it.

'Craig Randall,' she said, holding up the image of a fifteen-year-old boy. 'Visited Hurley with his parents every weekend. Believed to have assaulted a fifteen-year-old girl at the campsite, but nothing was ever proven. Found dead in the woods, having slashed his own throat. No sign of a struggle, blood spatter proved it was a self-inflicted wound.'

'But my dad believed it was murder,' Declan replied, remembering snippets of the case. 'Something about the blade never being found.'

Wintergreen nodded at this, opening the folder and scattering other files across the table. Women, men, all ages and sizes faced Declan. All dead, all found with the Red Reaper card.

'None of them were found with the item that caused their death,' she said, showing them. 'The ones that hanged them-

selves had the noose but at the same time didn't show what
the victim could have stood on to gain the height.'

Declan worked through the files, arranging them into
chronological order.

'First one is in Berlin, in 1990,' he said, reading through
them. 'Then Bruges, then Paris... The rest are all in Britain
from 1996, and over a sixteen-year period.'

He considered this.

'If it was a killer, then they came from Germany to the
UK, most likely settled...' he stopped, and then nodded.

'This is why you have an issue with Karl.'

'How much do you know about Karl Schnitter?' Wintergreen asked, as if confirming this.

'Not much,' Declan admitted. 'Came from East Berlin
when the wall fell, was an apprentice to a mechanic, worked
in London for a bit and then moved to Hurley, opened up a
garage in Marlow, with a smaller one in the village.'

'What would you say if I said that Karl hadn't just been a
mechanic?' Wintergreen watched Declan. 'What if I told you
that before the wall fell, he'd been a border guard on the East
Germany side?'

'I'd say it wasn't my business, and if my dad vouched for
him, then so did I.'

'And how do you *know* your father vouched for him?'
Wintergreen raised her eyebrows as she asked this, giving the
impression of an elderly schoolteacher, asking a question
that she already knew the answer to. Declan bit back his
immediate reply and considered this. How much *did* he
know? He knew that as a child they'd been friendly, but in
the last twenty years he'd only visited home a scattering of
times, even less after his mother had died. Karl was always

around, but never there. And it was only after Patrick Walsh's funeral that Karl attempted to befriend Declan.

'No,' he replied staunchly. 'I'm not playing this game. This is what spooks do. Make you doubt yourself. If dad had believed that Karl was a potential murderer, then he'd have damn well proved it.'

'Maybe he did,' Wintergreen smiled, 'and placed it on an encrypted USB drive?'

The room was silent for a moment.

'Look, this is interesting, but still circumstantial,' Declan continued. 'And I'm still waiting to see what this has to do with me.'

'Everything,' Wintergreen said, looking to Marlowe, who passed her a second folder. 'The victims, because that's what they were, they were never given justice. They were simply classed as strange but acceptable suicides.' She picked up the card with the red image and tossed it across to Declan. 'What do you make of this?'

Declan picked the clear bag up, but the moment he turned it around, Wintergreen raised a hand. 'There,' she said. 'Right there. If you were holding the actual card, how many fingerprints of yours are now on it?'

Declan considered this. He'd turned it, using two fingers and his thumb. He'd held the corner, but now the thumb was along the side.

'Every card,' he intoned. 'Every card had the same place-ment of the fingerprints?'

Wintergreen smiled, as if watching a student coming to the same conclusion.

'Yes,' she replied, pulling out of the second folder a blank business card; the only things visible on it were two fingerprints, one on each side at the corner, as if she'd placed ink on her index finger and thumb to create it. 'Just like this.'

She watched Declan.

'You're the detective, and Patrick always said you were a better one that he was. So tell me, DI Walsh. What does your gut, your detective instinct, say now?'

Declan worked through the files in front of him, slowly checking the details of each before moving on.

'Going on the hypothetical situation that these are all murders, and that these are all by the same person, we have someone who's male, or at least an incredibly powerful woman.'

'Why?'

'The bodies,' Declan replied, still reading. 'They're positioned. Also, the killer has to stay with them throughout the death.'

'Why?'

'The fingerprints,' Declan continued. 'Sure, there's a chance that they could make the victims hold the card while alive, but this is too precise. Far easier to wait until the victim is dead, then simply use the dead hand to place the prints. So the killer watches the victim kill themselves, waits, places the prints on the card and then secretes it away before leaving. That's someone with a firm belief that they won't be disturbed.' He stopped, going through the files a second time. 'What I can't work out is why they listen to them. Hypnosis? No. There're drugs in several of the systems, but nothing that would make someone suggestive. For the victims to kill themselves, there must be some kind of emotional trigger, a psychological reason. Blackmail?'

'What kind of blackmail?' Wintergreen was leaning closer now as she watched Declan work through the options.

'All the deaths are quick, painless,' Declan considered. 'Well, mostly. Craig Randall slit his own throat, but the autopsy shows that he had benzocaine in his system. That's a topical pain reliever, so probably numbed the immediate pain. And by the time it broke through, it was too late. So the killer isn't in it for the pain, the trauma. They're in it for the death. The finality, perhaps.'

'You still haven't explained the blackmail.'

Declan looked up.

'I'll give you a choice,' he said calmly, as if considering his words. 'I can slowly cut your arm with a dull blade, or I can quickly stab the arm with the sharp point instead. Which do you choose?'

'The stab,' Wintergreen replied.

'Why?' Now it was Declan's turn to ask the question.

'Because it's quicker.'

'Exactly,' Declan mused. 'You go for the path of least personal discomfort. It's one reason people jump off buildings. There's no pain until the very end. So what if the killer gave them a choice? They kill themselves quickly, or he, or she, whatever the killer is, does it to them slowly? Maybe even add the family as a bonus into it. Now the victim knows they're going to die, but they can choose to decide how.'

Wintergreen smiled. 'That's what your father believed, too.'

'But my father never caught the Red Reaper,' Declan continued. 'After Craig, the killings stopped.'

Wintergreen looked at the second folder. 'Actually, that's not quite true,' she said. 'There was one more murder.' She opened the folder and passed a file over to Declan.

CHRISTINE WALSH

'My mum died of cancer,' Declan said as he looked down at the folder. 'She was terminal. In hospital.'

Wintergreen nodded at this. 'I know,' she replied, pulling out a clear bag from the folder, one with a card in it. A now familiar card. 'However, there's more to that. Your mother was sick, and she was fighting a real bastard, but the doctors still believed that with new treatments, they could extend her life-span. She was in hospital, but they expected her to be released within the week. Your father went to the cafeteria to grab a coffee, and when he got back, your mother had passed away in her sleep.'

'I know this,' Declan was getting angry now. He didn't want to relive this moment. 'What are you getting at here?'

Wintergreen tossed the bag over so that Declan could look at it. 'That was found under her when they moved the body,' she explained. 'There was no reason for Christine to have one of these, and again, the fingerprints, once the nurse who found it was removed from the suspects, were the same two fingers in the same location.'

'The Red Reaper killed mum?' Declan shook his head. 'No, that's not the way he works.'

'Your mother didn't die in her sleep,' Wintergreen continued, tapping at a line in the file. 'She gave herself a fatal morphine overdose. It's exactly how the Red Reaper worked. And this was a personal message. Your father was Chief Superintendent by this point, and this took the wind out of his sails. He never spoke of the case publicly again.'

'Publicly?' Declan looked up. 'So he still worked it?'

Wintergreen shrugged. 'Where do you think we gained these files from?' she asked. 'He had duplicates of everything. Once he retired, he started working on this. Claimed he was working on his memoirs, but actually this was his entire life.' She sighed. 'The USB drive was supposed to tell us everything. But the day before he was to meet with me, he had a car accident. The one you believe was murder.'

'Was it?' Declan almost didn't want to know the answer. Wintergreen didn't reply. Instead, she looked to Marlowe, who passed her another clear bag, with yet another Red Reaper card.

'This was in the glove compartment of his car when it crashed,' she explained. 'The police assumed it was evidence from a case that Patrick had taken, but we snaffled it before they tossed it aside. Can you guess what was on it?'

Declan looked from Wintergreen to Marlowe. 'So what, you want me to avenge his death?'

'You *don't* want to?' Wintergreen watched Declan closely. 'Think about it, Declan. You're damaged goods right now. You need to get yourself back in the police's good books. Solving this could help you.'

'More cold cases,' Declan muttered but stopped as Wintergreen held up a hand.

'I never said this was a cold case,' she reached into the folder and pulled out another file, sliding it across. 'This is why we had to use such an unconventional route to get you here. Nathanial Wing. Sixteen years old, moved into Remenham four years ago with his parents, worked as an intern for a web designer in Henley while he did graphic design at college. Found yesterday morning on the sixteenth green of Temple Golf Club, in Hurley. Poor bastard had slit his wrists open and bled into the hole. No blade located.'

She leaned closer.

'He knew your father was hunting him. He sent him a

message by killing your mother. And then at the end he killed Patrick as well. Now, he's free to do whatever he wants.'

'Why the sixteenth hole?' Declan started moving through the cases again. 'It should have been the fifteenth.'

'Why?' Wintergreen frowned at this. Declan started counting on his fingers.

'Twelve murders. Then mum and dad. If that's correct, then that's fourteen. So this should be the fifteenth.'

'Maybe the sixteenth was an easier hole to get to?' For the first time, Marlowe spoke. Declan shook his head.

'It's not,' he replied. 'It's right next to the road, which means although it can be reached easily, it's also more visible. Fifteenth is far easier, if you want privacy. They've gone out of their way to do this. Which means...'

'Which means that there's a body out there that nobody's considered,' Wintergreen leaned back in her chair. 'Your father was right about you.'

Declan went to reply to this, but stopped. A moment from a couple of weeks earlier came to mind now. When he'd sat in the local pub with Karl, they'd toasted to his parents.

'*He never got over her loss. He was never the same after her murder.*'

'*What?*'

'*Her death. He was never the same after her death.*'

'*You said murder.*'

'*Apologies, sometimes words for me merge when speaking in another tongue. Death and murder, they are very similar in German.*'

No. This couldn't be. Karl couldn't have done this.

Karl was a mechanic. He serviced Patrick Walsh's car. What if that was why the car had run off the road? He could have placed the card in the glove compartment way before the drive.

'I know you're working this through,' Wintergreen continued. 'I can see that in your eyes. You're wondering whether Karl Schnitter could have done such a thing. Could do it again, even. Do you know DCI Mark Freeman?'

'I knew him briefly when he was a DI under dad,' Declan replied. 'Why?'

'He's running the case in Maidenhead,' Wintergreen gathered her folders together now, rising from the chair as she did so. 'You should reach out to him. Offer your services.'

She stopped, as if deciding whether to add anything to this. Eventually she looked back.

'There was no Karl Schnitter before the fall of the Berlin Wall, by the way,' she ended. 'We looked. There was a Karl Meier, who worked as a guard on the wall near Bernauer Street, who disappears from history the day that Karl Schnitter arrives in 1990. Two weeks after that? The first Red Reaper body is found in Potzdamer Platz.'

'Possibly coincidence,' Declan replied. 'And we can't prove that they're connected.'

'Bar one thing,' Wintergreen walked to the door. 'Schnitter is a German word. It translates in English as *Reaper*. Mister Marlowe will drive you home. And we'll be in touch once we decrypt your father's USB drive.'

Declan sat silently in the boardroom, trying to take in everything that had been thrown at him. His parents were both killed? Karl Schnitter, the mechanic who'd not only been a friend of theirs for years, was an East German guard who not only changed his identity but also picked a name to match the image on these cards? And there was something about the image too, a memory from years earlier, but Declan just couldn't picture it yet...

'She's a piece of work, isn't she?' Marlowe smiled. 'Come on, let's get you home.'

Rising from the chair, Declan followed Tom Marlowe out of the boardroom and back to the car park. It'd be late by the time he arrived back home, but he didn't see himself sleeping anytime soon.

3

DISCIPLINARY DATES

DS ANJLI KAPOOR WAS ALREADY WAITING IN TEMPLE INN WHEN DC Billy Fitzwarren phoned.

'Where are you?' he asked.

'Where do you think?' she replied irritably.

'I'm entering from Fleet Street,' Billy said, the sounds of traffic heard behind him as he walked through the north entrance into Temple Inn. 'Give me a moment.'

Anjli disconnected the call and looked up at the red brick building that she faced. Four storeys high, it was once the offices of the Temple Inn Crime Unit, otherwise known as the Last Chance Saloon. Now, however, it was a building site; Bright yellow tubes ran down the frontage, held in place by scaffolding that ran across it and ending in large orange rubble tips, where contractors on the upper floor could throw pieces of broken and ripped apart plasterboard and brick-work, saving them from having to carry the pieces downstairs.

Anjli didn't really know what was going on here; they'd

told her it was a renovation of the offices, but the Temple Inn offices had only operated on the lower two levels of the building. This was a full scale build of the entire thing.

This was also a plausible way to remove the Last Chance Saloon quietly.

She'd expected this, if she was brutally honest. After the problems with Declan going on the run and Monroe hiding for his life, there had been rumours of the unit being too autonomous. Most units like this had uniformed officers, cells and even a Detective Superintendent in charge of everything. And although Chief Superintendent David Bradbury had helped the Last Chance Saloon in their last case, he controlled the City of London's police force and was technically Anjli's boss's *boss's* boss.

Maybe they'll promote Monroe, she thought to herself. That would be a good thing in her books; promote everyone up. Declan could become DCI, she'd become DI... But she knew that this wouldn't happen. They'd painted too many targets on their backs, actively shaken too many wasps' nests to expect a simpler life. After the fallout, when the unit was temporarily disbanded considering an enquiry, they relieved both Declan and Monroe of duty on injury-related accommodations. That one had been recently branded a terrorist and had gone rogue, while the other had gained help from *organised crime* were ignored publicly, but Anjli knew these were tallies that were about to be counted. There was still every chance that Monroe could be invalided out of the force altogether, while Declan would be quietly dumped somewhere rural to finish out his years. Meanwhile, Doctor Marcos had gone on sabbatical, DC Davey was working in Tottenham for DCI Farrow, Billy was dumped into the central Cybercrime

Unit and Anjli was back in Mile End, working in the same unit that had fired her almost a year earlier. Granted, there wasn't a DCI Ford there to make her life hell, but it wasn't exactly the joyous homecoming you'd expect.

The Last Chance Saloon was, for all intents and purposes, ended.

There was a tap on her shoulder, removing her from this melancholy train of thought, and Anjli looked around to see a smiling Billy Fitzwarren, still wearing his trademark three piece Saville Row tweed suit. Although he was effectively disowned by his family, Billy still came from money, and you could see it simply by looking at him from the expensive and trendy haircut his blond head had, to the watch on his arm. Anjli, with her black hair pulled back and her off-the-shelf, store-bought grey suit, cheap and misshapen, felt very poor when standing beside him.

'They let you in yet?' he asked. Anjli shrugged.

'Haven't even tried, to be honest,' she replied. 'Feels a bit ghoulish, you know?'

Billy nodded, looking up at the construction workers, currently walking along the scaffold gantries. 'Any hot ones up there?' he enquired with a cheeky grin. Anjli sighed, linking arms with Billy and guiding him towards the exit. And a nearby wine bar they both knew.

'Your libido will get you into trouble one day,' she muttered as, looking back to the contractors, Billy protested feebly.

Neither of them saw the man across the courtyard, leaning on his cane, stroking his short, white beard as he watched them leave.

DCI Alexander Monroe knew that he should have gone to

them, spoken to them, seen how they were doing, but it would just start more conversations on how he was, what he intended to do, whether there were proceedings about to occur, and how they could help him. And the fact of the matter was that Monroe didn't know any of this. He didn't even know if he wanted to stay in the force. There was a certain convenience in letting himself be invalided out to take an early retirement.

He'd never be attacked again.

He'd never be drugged or face death again.

Taking a deep breath to shake away the sudden memories that crashed into his thoughts, DCI Monroe turned and slowly limped back out of Temple Inn.

He could always speak to Billy and Anjli next time.

Yes.

Next time.

THE DRIVE BACK TO HURLEY WAS FAR COMFIER THAN THE ONE there; this was because Marlowe's usual car was a black BMW i8 Coupe, and he drove it with the skill of a man that not only knew how to drive a car well but also knew how to fit in with the surrounding cars; which meant that the drive was quick, yet safe.

'How did you work for Wintergreen?' Declan asked as they cruised along the middle lane of the M4. 'Or is that, you know, classified and all that?'

'It's classified,' Marlowe replied. 'But, as she trusts you, I trust you. Ask what you want.'

Declan wondered which *she* Marlowe mentioned,

whether it was Wintergreen or Trix that he spoke of, but he left that for the moment. 'Same question then.'

'I was a Royal Marine,' Marlowe replied. 'Went for SAS selection, but didn't get in.'

'I thought all spooks were ex-SAS trained and all that?' Declan asked.

Marlowe grinned.

'Oh, I'm SAS trained, I just never joined their ranks,' he replied. 'Did a few special ops with them, eventually moved into the Secret Service. Did a year in Vauxhall, utterly hated it. It was all *James Bond* wannabes and filing cabinets. Wintergreen turned up on one mission, we had mutual friends and after that she met me for a pint. Gave me the hard sell.'

Declan chuckled. 'Monroe did the same thing when he recruited me.' He changed subject. 'Trix said that Wintergreen was running a similar thing to the Last Chance Saloon when she visited me,' Declan looked out at the motorway. 'Was it your last chance too?'

Marlowe nodded. 'She saw it frustrated me, she knew I had strikes against me. Did Trix tell you what we're called?'

Declan shook his head. 'Just that you work for Charles Baker.'

'Sometimes,' Marlowe confirmed. 'Usually it's more the suits in Whitehall. We're known as *Section D*.'

'As in D-Notice?'

'You know the term?'

'I was in the *Special Investigations Bureau*. Military Police,' Declan explained. 'We had our share of targets who had D-Notices slapped on them, stopping the public from seeing the crimes.'

'That's an old term,' Marlowe replied. 'These days it's a

DSMA Notice. Stands for Defence and Security Media Advisory Notice.'

'So it's not that then?'

Marlowe grinned. 'No. It's for Disavowed.' He indicated left, moving into the slow lane in preparation to turning off at the upcoming junction. 'Wintergreen takes the misfit toys and makes her own little play set out of them.'

He glanced at Declan.

'You know, she was going to come for you,' he said. 'After you punched that priest. She called your old man, asked if he'd be okay with you swapping badges.'

'And he said?'

'She never told me,' Marlowe watched the road as he spoke. 'Monroe recruited you and she lost interest. She does that. Hey, how did you deal with Trix?'

'What do you mean?' The question slightly threw Declan. Marlowe glanced over.

'She does my head in,' he admitted. 'Bloody girl won't shut up.'

'Wasn't my experience with her,' Declan replied with a smile. 'Maybe she's got a crush on you.'

'Well, she's only human,' Marlowe sighed mournfully. 'It's a curse.'

Declan laughed. He liked Marlowe and found him easy to talk to. But he wondered how much of this was the spook training, the ability to make anyone feel at home.

'Will she really send me the contents of the USB when she opens it?' He asked. Marlowe didn't answer immediately.

'If she doesn't, I will,' he eventually promised. 'I don't like it when people don't keep their word.'

'Is that a thing with her?' Declan turned to face Marlowe,

trying to garner anything from his micro expressions, but the driver stared expressionless.

'Here we go,' he said as they turned left, off the A404. Declan looked to the right, past Marlowe and out of the driver's window. They were on the Henley Road now, the open driveway of the Temple Golf Club passing on the right as they carried on north. Declan wondered whether it was worth stopping now, having a look at the murder scene while there was still light, but there was a voice at the back of his head that suggested that *this wasn't a good idea*. He knew how pissed he'd be if a rival detective encroached on his patch. No, he'd contact DCI Freeman in the morning, see what he could find out. Tonight would be an early night. What with the funeral, the confrontation with Peter Taylor at Kendis' graveside, the abduction and consequent return from London, he was wiped out. All he wanted was a takeout and his bed.

Unfortunately, that wasn't going to happen.

As the car pulled off the High Street into the small housing estate where Patrick Walsh, and now Declan lived, he saw that his living room light was on. It hadn't been when he left for the funeral earlier that day.

Marlowe had also seen this as he pulled up across the road.

'Problem?' he asked, nodding towards the window. 'You expecting guests?'

'I wasn't,' Declan unclipped the seatbelt. 'But to be honest, only a couple of people have a key.'

'Just because the light's on, doesn't mean they came in through the front door.' Marlowe was already shifting, and Declan knew that somewhere on his person was a gun, likely a Glock 17 or similar. Bloody spies and their toys.

'I'll be fine,' Declan opened the door, exiting the car. 'If there's a problem, you'll know soon enough.'

He was about to continue when the door to his house opened, and a woman emerged.

No, not a woman. A girl, on the cusp of becoming a woman. Fifteen years, coming on sixteen, and as far as Declan was concerned ten years older than she should be. Her hair was jet black; last time he'd seen her, it had been blue. Or red, he couldn't keep track now.

'Dad!' She exclaimed, coming out to meet Declan, grabbing him in a wide embrace, but peering into the car as she did so. 'Who's that? He's cute. Is he coming in?'

'He's leaving,' Declan nodded to Marlowe and closed the car door. Before they'd even stepped away, the BMW i8 had already accelerated off, Marlowe on his way back to London. Watching the car retreat into the distance, Declan looked back to his daughter.

'What are you doing here, Jess?' he asked. 'Last I heard, you weren't happy with me.'

'Yeah,' Jess replied as they walked back to the house. 'It annoyed me that we had to go into hiding because of you. But then I realised I was being petty, and that you'd had a way worse time than me, and I should give you the benefit of the doubt.'

Declan stopped in the driveway, staring at his daughter for a moment.

'Your mum sent you here, didn't she?'

Jessica Walsh grinned widely. 'She wanted to make sure you're doing okay, now you're, like, suspended all over again,' she walked into the house now, Declan following. 'And between us, I think she wanted some *alone* time, you know?'

Declan went to ask what Jess meant by that, but then

remembered that only a week ago, Lizzie had mentioned to Declan that she was looking to date again. Considering what had happened between Declan and Kendis, he couldn't really be angry at this development.

'How long do I have you for?' he asked as he pulled off his jacket, tossing it on a chair as he walked into the kitchen. 'Tea? Coffee?'

'I brought my own,' Jess followed him in. 'Matcha green with oat milk.'

Declan shuddered, and Jess smiled. 'Wait until you try my bulletproof coffee.'

'I don't know what that means, and have no intention of learning,' Declan solemnly informed. 'Again, how long are you here for?'

'A week if you'll have me?' Jess filled the kettle. 'We can work on granddad's crime board. Oh, and Mister Schnitter came by to make sure you were okay after the funeral? I didn't even realise it was today.'

Declan stopped at the fridge.

'Did he say anything else?'

Jess shrugged as she took a half teaspoon of green tea, placing it into a metal bottle with a whisk on the end of the cap. 'Not really, just that he'd catch you later. Why, is there a problem?'

Declan looked back to Jess. 'Do me a favour,' he replied, his face calm, but his voice obviously forced. 'If you see him, keep away. Just for the moment. I need to speak to someone tomorrow, and then we'll discuss that.'

Jess stopped now, watching her father.

'What aren't you telling me?' she asked. 'And is it something to do with the cute guy in the cool car?'

'I'm your father, kiddo,' Declan forced a smile now.

'There's a ton of stuff I'm not telling you. But first I need to check granddad's study for some files. And after I make a call tomorrow, I'll tell you everything.' He looked to the sideboard as a realisation struck him. 'I almost forgot,' he continued. 'I was going to give it to you when I saw you next, but I got your phone back. The one Frost stole.'

'That's okay, dad,' Jess replied. 'I have a new one now.'

'I know,' Declan walked over to the sideboard. 'It's just that you might have some photos on here that—'

'*I said that's okay!*' Jess shouted. Declan turned to his daughter, seeing her visibly shaken.

'It's...' Jess couldn't find the words. 'It's just that he stole my bag, dad. I didn't even realise he was there. He... he could have taken me. I could have been killed.'

Declan nodded. He knew what Jess was feeling; a form of survivors' guilt.

'I thought you'd died,' he whispered. 'Your mum didn't call, and then Frost phoned me from the number. I couldn't breathe. The world was ending. It was only your mum phoning later that saved me from doing something rash.'

He walked over to Jess, holding her tight.

'He took out both me and Monroe when we weren't expecting it,' he admitted. 'But he's dead now. He's dead and he won't be coming back.'

'You promise?' Jess looked up at her father, eyes brimming with fearful tears. Declan nodded, holding her even tighter.

'I promise,' he said and, as he spoke, he felt his own bottled up emotions burst out. The anger at Kendis's death, the devastation at losing her, the frustrations of the closure of Temple Inn, the uncertainty of Monroe, all of these fears and worries came forth in a stream and, as Jess cried into his chest, Declan wept silently into her shoulder.

And then the moment was over.

Smiling faintly, wiping an eye, he looked down at her.

'Chinese or Pizza?' he asked. Because tonight was going to be a father and daughter night. A night of fast food and cheesy film watching.

He could start hunting serial killers *tomorrow*.

4

THE THIN BLUE LINE

ANJLI HAD STARTED HER CAREER AT MILE END COMMAND Unit, but she never expected to end it there. Walking back into the office, she was unsurprised to find the place half empty; there was always something happening around here, and there were always officers walking in or out, finishing up or starting on the next big problem that had landed on the doorstep.

The last time Anjli had worked here though, it had been DCI Ford who controlled the teams; now she was gone, drummed out of the force on conspiracy to fraud, attempted murder and a ton of other charges. She'd always been a degenerate gambler, in hock to a variety of criminal empires including The Twins, *Johnny and Jackie Lucas,* who ran the East End like it was their personal playground, and when everything came crashing down around her, primarily because of Declan Walsh before he even met Anjli, the powers-that-be in the Met had attacked this with a 'clean sweep' and 'new broom' mentality. Everyone had been assessed, and either moved up, moved on or moved out. The only reason that Anjli hadn't been caught up in this was because she'd already left by that point, joining Alexander Monroe after she beat the living crap out of a wife beater with links to the Twins.

And now she was back here. Like she'd never left.

A middle-aged man, tall, lean and dark-skinned with his black hair parted on the right, while at the same time left to its own devices, leaned out of the door to his office.

'Oh, you *do* work here,' he muttered before popping back into his office. Anjli sighed. DCI Esposito was a good detective, and definitely the one to clean up the shit that had been left for him, but he was also a pain in the neck jobsworth. Walking to the office, she leaned in.

'Sorry Guv, just meeting an old colleague for lunch, and then spent the afternoon patrolling my new area, getting a feel for it,' she explained. Esposito didn't look up from his computer screen.

'Crime doesn't take lunch breaks,' he replied. 'Crime waits for detectives to take lunch breaks and then strikes.'

'Did anything happen while I was out?' Anjli asked, looking back into the office. It didn't seem like anything big was going on out there.

'No, but it could have.'

Anjli grinned. 'Maybe crime took a lunch break today then, Guv.'

Esposito looked up from the monitor. 'Sass, DS Kapoor? I don't know how things were when you were at Monroe's kindergarten, but here we work professionally. We don't go out on wild adventures, or play out hunches, regardless of the consequences.'

'No, Guv.'

Esposito sighed. 'Go down to Victoria Park,' he ordered. 'There's been a spate of vandalism there. See if you can't nip it in the bud.'

'Surely that's a uniform job?' Anjli groaned inwardly at this the moment she spoke. She knew she'd said the wrong thing even before Esposito rose from the chair.

'If you'd prefer to be in a uniform when you do it, *Miss* Kapoor, I'm sure that can be arranged,' he snapped.

Anjli nodded.

'Very good, sir, I'll go right away, sir.'

Anjli left the office of DCI Esposito and without even stopping at her desk, she continued out of the office and out into the late Mile End afternoon. Feeling the sun on her face, she fought back the urge to scream. Most of her lunch with Billy had been complaints about this new secondment, and she'd spent the last couple of hours trying to find reasons not to return. She wanted nothing more than to leave, to return to Temple Inn and the insanity that she'd got used to.

But the more she thought about it, the more she realised things would never be the same again. And if she stayed at Mile End, she'd end up killing someone.

Maybe it was time to consider alternate careers.

FOR THE LAST SEVEN YEARS, ALEXANDER MONROE HAD LIVED IN a small detached house in Bexleyheath. It wasn't much, as police salaries were never that high, but he was alone in it, and had all the space that he needed. Besides, he spent more time in the office than at home, so in effect it was nothing more than a posh and more lived in hotel room; a place where Monroe would return only to eat, watch TV and sleep.

Although there hadn't been a lot of sleeping recently. The nightmares saw to that.

It had been a week since DI Frost had tried to murder him. A week, more to the point, since DI White drugged him in Birmingham, and he'd been dragged to a manor house in the middle of nowhere and tied to a pillar, expecting to be executed by an insane gang lord. To be brutally honest about this, it hadn't been the best of weeks. And the days that had followed hadn't been kind either. He still suffered from migraines connected to the head wound he'd received at Temple Inn, and he hadn't slept over three hours in a night since then either.

They had placed him on sick leave; signed off to 'get better', but he was very much aware that this was office talk for *'signed off until we know what to do with you'.* His relationship with East End crime lords, one that had existed for several decades now was finally brought out into the open after he'd turned to them for help. Internal Affairs were already digging into that, seeing what else could be found. And Monroe knew there was a lot down there that could be dredged up about him.

And so he'd kept a low profile. He'd visited the Temple Inn building earlier that day on a whim, but had chickened out of approaching Anjli and Billy when he saw them there. They had enough to deal with without him arriving and ruining their day.

He'd already ruined their careers.

There was a knock at his door; he was in the kitchen, pouring out a mug of tea when he heard it and, mug in hand, walked to the door, opening to reveal Doctor Rosanna Marcos in the doorway.

'I didn't realise it was Halloween yet,' he said, nodding at her wild and frizzy black hair. 'Trick or treat happens at night.'

'You're a funny man,' Doctor Marcos ignored the jibe, walking past Monroe, taking the mug of tea as she did so. 'Don't listen to what everyone else says.'

Monroe shut the front door and walked back into the living room, where Doctor Marcos was now sitting on the sofa, sipping at the tea.

'Ugh. No sugar,' she complained. 'You know I like sugar.'

Monroe bit back the urge to reply, instead walking into the kitchen and returning with the pot of sugar and a spoon, placing them both onto the coffee table in front of her.

'Is there a reason for your visit?' he asked, a little too politely.

'You're having nightmares,' Doctor Marcos sipped at the tea, nodding at the correct taste. 'You're shouting out names in your sleep. You're reliving moments.'

Monroe stopped at the door to the kitchen. He had indeed been having nightmares, but he hadn't spoken about them to anyone. 'And how would you know this, lassie?'

'First off, I'm not anyone's 'lassie',' Doctor Marcos replied. 'And secondly, I used your sleep app.'

'The one you told me would monitor my heart rate at night?' Monroe asked, appalled. 'You used it to spy on me?'

'Of course I did, you bloody idiot,' Doctor Marcos snapped. 'I'm worried about you. You've got multiple cases of Post Traumatic Stress Disorder, and you're not doing anything to fix it. So when you sleep, the app also records noises you make in your sleep. You're quite vocal these days.'

Monroe walked to the sofa and slumped down onto it. 'It's the same dream. I'm in the office,' he admitted. 'I see Frost. And I know what's going to happen and I try to change it, but my body won't listen.'

'I know,' Doctor Marcos replied. 'And it'll probably get worse before it get's better. And it doesn't help that you're stuck here with nothing to get your teeth into.'

'I went out yesterday,' Monroe argued. Doctor Marcos shrugged.

'You want a medal for that?' She picked up the mug of tea again, blowing on it. 'You need to decide what you want to do, Alex.'

'And what's that supposed to mean?' Monroe was defensive now, his body language altering as the conversation changed.

'I mean, I know what you were doing the night Frost attacked you,' Doctor Marcos said softly, keeping her gaze on the mug rather than at Monroe. 'I know you were writing a resignation letter. And sure, you can keep on with this lie that you can't remember, but we both know that you can.'

There was a long moment of silence.

'Bloody Billy,' Monroe muttered.

'Don't be harsh on Billy,' Doctor Marcos looked to him. 'He's worried about you.'

Monroe nodded slowly. 'After Birmingham, with everything that happened, I thought I'd lost my edge. That I shouldn't be out there. It wasn't a resignation letter, more an 'I'd like to consider early retirement' letter.' He looked at Doctor Marcos. 'But then everything happened so quickly, and I realised that my job, all this, it was almost taken from my grasp without my permission. And I realised I needed it, Rosanna. I needed to be on the thin blue line, working cases, solving them. And you can't do that when you're retired.'

He rose now, pacing as he continued.

'But it's out of my hands now. Chances are that they'll can me. And even if they don't, there's talk of the Temple Inn unit being expanded. We've shit the bed a couple of times, to be honest, but we've nailed some pretty bloody big scumbags. They can't just remove us. But they're sure as hell not going to promote us.'

'You think they'll bring someone in above you?' the comment surprised Doctor Marcos. 'A Detective Superintendent?'

'I'd say so,' Monroe stopped pacing as he thought. 'It'll be too big for a DCI to run. What I need to do is find someone to take the spot who we can work with.'

'Why don't you go for it?'

Monroe grinned now. 'Christ, woman. I'd hate it,' he said. 'Once you wear the uniform, and sit in the office, you never get to play outside.' He thought for a moment. 'Did you ever watch *Star Trek*?'

'Of course,' Doctor Marcos replied haughtily. 'Doctor McCoy was the reason I chose my profession. Why?'

'Captain Kirk,' Monroe explained. 'He was a great Captain, you know? He saved the universe loads of times. And then the show ended and a few years later they did the movies. But now Kirk? They promoted him. He was an Admiral.'

'I'm loving the fandom here, but I have no bloody idea where you're going with this,' Doctor Marcos sipped at her tea as she watched Monroe.

'Because now the movies had a problem. Admirals don't captain star ships.'

'But it's made up.'

'Bear with me,' Monroe held a finger up. 'Kirk couldn't captain the Enterprise. So they give him a reason, as Admiral Kirk, to be there. And lo-and-behold, during the film he ends up taking the Captain's chair again. They do it again in the second movie. And in a way they do it in the next two.'

'So?'

'So, the story's biggest flaw was that Kirk needed to be out there, but they promoted him out of the chair. In the end he's rewarded for saving the universe again by being demoted back to Captain. Getting him back out there.'

'You're Kirk in this scenario,' Doctor Marcos suggested.

'I'm a man who needs to be where the action is,' Monroe admitted. 'Not behind a desk all the time. I saw that happen to Patrick, Declan's dad. Once he was out of the field, he lost all interest.' His eyes brightened. 'But we could get anyone we wanted in there, I'm sure of it. We need to convince Bradbury that the best candidate is someone we don't want.'

'Because then he'll promote them into the position, and let you carry on in a more reduced role,' Doctor Marcos nodded at this. 'So who do we want as your new boss?'

Monroe grinned. 'I already have that in hand,' he finished.

BILLY WALKED UP FLEET STREET TOWARDS THE CITY. HE'D FELT bad lying to Anjli about his role in the central Cybercrime Unit; but at the same time he knew she wouldn't understand. She was a dyed in the wool beat-cop turned detective, while Billy had grown up in the world of code monkeys and developers.

Now passing St Pauls and heading into Cannon Street, he stopped at the entrance of a large chrome and silver building. Taking a deep breath, he entered, walking up to reception and giving his name. They passed him a small paper printout with his name and an image of his face on it and, after sticking it to his lapel, he followed directions to the fifth floor and the offices of Harrington Finance.

Rufus Harrington was waiting for him as the elevator doors opened, a smile on his face. Wearing an expensive Ted Baker suit, Rufus wore his brown hair shaved at the sides and slicked back, the amount of gel in it making it look like a Lego hair piece as he nervously played with the large masonic signet ring on his left middle finger.

'Excellent, you made it,' he said as he led Billy past the reception desk and into an expensive-looking day trader's office, banks of monitors all showing graphs, stock prices and company profiles as the men and women at the desks talked animatedly into headphones.

'Look, I said I'd chat, but I'm not sure if I'm cut out for this,' Billy admitted as they walked into Rufus' office. White walled with a full-length window looking out onto London, it had movie posters in black frames contrasting with the brown leather and black wood of the decor; 300, Inglorious Bastards and The Wolf of Wall Street, all with Gerard Butler, Brad Pitt and Leonardo Di'Caprio staring down at Billy as he sat on a brown leather sofa, Rufus now lounging in a similarly designed armchair facing him.

'You haven't told anyone you left?' he asked.

'Not yet,' Billy admitted. 'It's easier to move on and then explain.'

'I must admit, it surprised me when I got your call.'

'I don't know why,' Billy replied. 'You were the one that told me to get out.'

'Sure, but then you didn't,' Rufus laughed. 'I meant to get out before the shit hit the fan, not after they covered you in the bloody stuff.'

As if a switch was pressed, Rufus went from amused to serious in the blink of an eye.

'We could use someone like you in our cybersecurity department. I'd give you your own team, stock portfolio, whatever you needed.'

Billy looked to the side, out of the window, looking over London. 'It's nothing personal, you understand?' he asked. 'It's not that I don't want to be a police officer anymore. It's just...' he paused for a moment, staring blankly out of the window before turning back to Rufus.

'I have these dreams,' he said. 'But they're memories. I'm standing in a warehouse, about to be shot. I'm standing outside a Manor House about to be shot. Always about to be shot.'

'But you weren't.'

'Yeah, but only by the grace of God,' Billy admitted. 'Declan jumped in front of the bullet, taking it in the shoulder. If he hadn't, I'd be dead right now.'

He shivered.

'I came from the Cybercrime office. I was a DC rank, but I wasn't a copper in the same way that Declan and Anjli was. And then what I did with Frost and Sutcliffe, how I played them, pretended that I was on their side while gathering information...'

Rufus nodded. 'I'm afraid that this could be quite a boring job for you then,' he pulled out a piece of paper, passing it across to Billy. 'However, stock options included, this would be your yearly salary.'

Billy took the paper and opened it, glancing at the number. He swallowed visibly, and then looked back to Rufus, smiling now.

'When would you like me to start?' he asked.

5

RURAL CRIME

EVEN THOUGH HIS FATHER HAD BEEN A METROPOLITAN POLICE Chief Superintendent, that had worked primarily out of Maidenhead before his retirement a couple of years earlier, Declan had never visited Patrick Walsh at his place of work. Which meant that as he arrived at the Maidenhead Control Unit, he didn't know what he should expect.

He'd woken up earlier that day with a hangover, even though he hadn't drunk anything; he assumed that whatever they had sedated him with had caused this, but it still turned him into a bear with a sore head who had an equally apathetic teenage daughter in the house. To her credit Jess, already showered and dressed, had taken one look at Declan and taken the hint, retreating to her room with toast and a glass of orange juice as Declan half-heartedly tried to eat a bowl of cornflakes. The previous night they'd opted for Chinese in the end, and Declan had picked something stupidly spicy for his choice, probably because he had some deep-seated need to punish himself. Jess meanwhile had ordered some kind of Cashew related tofu dish, pointing out repeatedly every time that Declan took a mouthful of his own tongue-burning mistake of a meal, that Veganism was actually incredibly healthy, and that by looking at her father, she could see that he really needed some health right now.

He'd never felt so old.

He had spent the night with dead friends and nightmares keeping him company; Kendis was there, obviously. Derek Salmon came to visit, and his dad made an appearance, waving business cards with Red Reapers on. Private Tooley, a junior engineer that Declan knew back in the SIB even appeared; the first time that Declan had even considered her for close to fifteen years.

His subconsciousness was really working overtime here.

In the end he'd woken grudgingly, made his way down to the kitchen and tried to eat some cereal, in the end deciding that it was a lost cause, pouring the remaining, frequently stirred yet not eaten mulch into the bin.

Cereal killer.

Declan chuckled at the joke, although the sudden remembrance of the previous day's conversation with Emilia Wintergreen put a stop to that. And with a new determination he showered and dressed, picking a suit but no tie. He wasn't officially entering Maidenhead police, and he wanted to show he was a little more 'relaxed'. A lack of a tie wasn't much, but it was better than turning up in a pair of jeans and a sweatshirt.

Jess had seen Declan walk past her bedroom door and leaned out, calling down the corridor.

'Job interview?' It was meant in jest, but as he looked back to her, Declan could see that Jess already regretted making the joke.

'I'm popping to Maidenhead nick,' he replied with a

smile, trying to defuse the situation before it even began. 'Seeing an old friend of dad.'

'Can I come?' Jess's eyes sparkled with interest. It was no secret that as the daughter and granddaughter of detectives, Jess had decided at an early age to plant her future career prospects on the police force. Declan thought for a moment. It wasn't procedure, but it could help defuse any uncomfortable situations. And the fact of the matter was, if Declan decided to investigate, he'd most likely bring Jess in to help him, anyway.

'Sure,' he replied. 'But I need to speak to DCI Freeman alone, so bring a book.'

Jess eagerly ran back into her room to grab a jacket and a backpack and, her items gathered together, she followed Declan out of the door. Glancing at the backpack, Declan could already make an educated guess what was in it; a notepad and pen, maybe a pencil, a book, a small bottle of water, maybe a protein bar in case the day meant that lunch was missed, maybe even an iPad or similar to check things on.

His daughter was probably more prepared than he was.

'Is this to do with the body at the golf club?' she asked as they reached his Audi. Declan stopped at the driver's door, looking at her.

'What do you know about that?' He replied. Jess shrugged.

'I stopped off in the High Street before coming here yesterday,' she explained. 'Grabbed a drink and a packet of crisps from the shop. They were talking about it in there. Something about a kid found on one of the greens.'

Declan clambered into the car, Jess joining him on the passenger side.

'I'll come back to you on that point,' he said as he started up the car. Pulling out of the drive, he started towards the end of the road, glancing down the alleyway that ran beside his house as he did so.

Karl Schnitter was standing in the alley, watching the car as it drove past.

Declan couldn't help it; an involuntary shiver ran down his spine. He didn't want to believe that Karl was anything but a friend. He'd actively assisted Declan when he was on the run.

But Wintergreen's warning rang in his head and, rather than stopping the car, he pressed on to Maidenhead.

THE DRIVE TO MAIDENHEAD HADN'T TAKEN LONG; IT WAS A straight route down the A308 into the centre of the town and the offices of the Thames Valley Police were to the north, off a four-way roundabout that gave a police station and a fire station to the north, and a retail park and fast food area to the south. Parking up, Declan looked to Jess.

'Best behaviour,' he warned. Jess smiled in response as they emerged from the car and walked to the main entrance.

Declan was City Police, and before that had been Metropolitan Police, covering Greater London. The Thames Valley Police, although still connected to the others, was a more rural force, directed into local areas. Maidenhead however would cover Hurley and the surrounding areas, and there was a constant thoroughfare of officers from all Police areas, so Declan wasn't worried about any territorial issues with his appearance there. That said, he still felt a little nervous as he walked up to the front desk, behind clear, thick

Perspex. There was a Duty Officer there; a desk sergeant in his late fifties, bald and bearded, peppered with white throughout the deep ginger curls. He wore metal framed glasses, but these seemed only for reading as when he looked up to Declan and Jess, he took them off.

'Can I help you?' he asked politely. Declan pulled out his warrant card; although he'd been suspended from duty, it had been an injury related one because of his shoulder, and therefore he'd been able to keep this when he returned home.

'DI Declan Walsh,' he said. 'I'd—'

'Bloody hell! Paddy Walsh's boy!' the desk sergeant exclaimed in delight. 'I haven't seen you since you were a lad!' The smile was genuine on his face as the desk sergeant patted his bald head. 'I lost all this, but when I saw you last I had a full head of hair, and the beard was just a dream.'

'Sweeney?' Declan could only remember one red-headed officer from around the area. Although Patrick Walsh had been a Metropolitan Police detective for most of his career, by the simple fact of living in Hurley, he always seemed to know every police officer around, and often they'd visit when the Walshes held summer BBQs in the house. Desk sergeant Sweeney grinned.

'Guilty as charged,' he said as he looked to Jess. 'And is this the next generation of Walsh detectives?'

Jess grinned in return at this.

'My daughter, Jessica,' Declan introduced. 'Jess, this is Sergeant Sweeney. You know the story about how I locked myself into a pair of handcuffs when I was a teenager? They were his.'

'The key wouldn't work,' Sweeney explained. 'We had to drive to Henley nick, pretend that Declan did it himself, and ask them to cut through with a hacksaw.' He looked back at Declan. 'Christ, it's good to see you up and about,' he replied. 'We didn't feel right about wandering around your house.'

Declan nodded at this. Sweeney was referring to the events of a week or so back when DI Frost had broken into his house, bringing in seemingly the entire Thames Valley uniformed contingent to hunt for Declan, who at the time was hiding in Patrick Walsh's secret study.

'Water under the bridge,' he replied. 'You were doing your job.' A thought came to mind. 'The poor bugger I hit with a plank,' he continued. 'Is he around? I probably need to apologise to him.'

'Forey? Yeah, I think he's about,' Sweeney leaned closer to the window. 'Between us, he's a bit of an arrogant bastard. Better off licking his wounds.' He looked at Jess. 'Pardon my language.'

'I've heard worse—' Jess started, but stopped at a glance from Declan. 'I mean, I've never heard such language in my incredibly cloistered existence.'

'She'll go far,' Sweeney said, tapping into the computer. 'You here for a visit, or is there anyone in particular you want to see?'

'Mark Freeman, if he's about,' Declan replied. Sweeney tapped into the phone and waited a moment.

'DCI Freeman? Front desk. We've got DI Declan Walsh here, wanted to... Absolutely.' He disconnected the call, looking at Declan. 'You been here before?'

Declan shook his head, so Sweeney leaned back. 'De'Geer!' He shouted. 'Get your scrawny arse to the main door!'

There was a moment of silence, and then the door beside the sergeant opened out to reveal a police constable who was far from scrawny. A tall, obviously muscled man with what looked to be some kind of Scandinavian heritage down the line, he looked like a Viking who'd had his beard trimmed, his hair cut and had then been given a uniform. Declan was sure that he'd seen him before, but couldn't think where.

'Sergeant?' He asked, looking back to Sweeney through the glass.

'Take DI Walsh up to DCI Freeman, if you please,' Sweeney replied. 'And then look after his daughter while they talk. Take her for a tour of the station. She'll be gunning for your job in a few years.'

Staring at the blond, bearded officer, Jess's smile widened.

'I'd like that,' she said. 'I'd like that very much.'

Declan wanted to refuse, to tell Sweeney that he'd rather an older, less attractive officer do that, but then realised that actually, having his daughter have a crush on a police officer was far better than the usual suspects that he saw hanging around her school on the few times that he'd picked her up.

As they walked through the back corridors, Declan finally stopped De'Geer.

'Look, I'm sorry to ask, but have we met?' He asked. 'You're really familiar, and no offence, but I think I'd recognise you.'

'No, sir,' De'Geer replied. 'I only started here last year, straight from Hendon. I'm Morten De'Geer.'

'Morten as in...'

'Yes, as in *a-ha*.'

Declan didn't comment on that, but something was still niggling...

'You were in my house!' He suddenly exclaimed. 'You were knocking on doors and were the first responder, right?

You spoke to Frost about the loft. I knew I recognised your voice!'

'How did you know that?' De'Geer's expression was suspicious now as he watched Declan. 'We searched everywhere. You weren't there.'

'You didn't search everywhere,' Jess muttered.

'I'm superb at hiding,' Declan continued. 'You wouldn't enter the house. I appreciate that.'

'Thank you,' De'Geer said, still confused by this. He pointed at a door to the right. 'That's Freeman's office. Is there anywhere in particular your daughter would like to—'

'The morgue,' Jess suggested eagerly.

'Anywhere she can't get into trouble,' Declan smiled. 'I shouldn't be long.'

'You can tell me all about Hendon,' Jess said as they walked away. 'Also, what do you bench?'

Declan sighed and knocked on the door. There was no answer, so he opened the door and entered.

He'd never met DCI Freeman before. He'd been at Patrick's funeral, but Declan hadn't gone to the wake afterwards, so hadn't spoken to him. Freeman was sitting at his desk when Declan entered the office; it was sparse, a little *too* sparse, nothing more than a small bookcase, a desk with chairs either side, a laptop and phone on it, and an uplighter in the corner. It gave the impression of an office where someone had just moved in, or was expecting to move out very soon.

'Declan,' Freeman shook Declan's hand as he waved for him to sit. 'How are you doing?'

'Shoulder twinges still, but the doctors say it'll take a few weeks to knit together.'

'And the job?' Declan knew that Freeman would have

been told about the suspension. This was his polite way to ask if Declan was looking for a transfer.

'Don't worry, I'm not hitting you up for a reference,' Declan smiled, trying to defuse an already awkward conversation. 'I'm here on a semi-official basis.'

'Oh yes?' Freeman leaned forward. 'Do tell.'

'The Red Reaper.'

'Oh Christ, Declan,' Freeman moaned. 'Not you as well? Is it some kind of bloody family curse?'

Declan shrugged. 'Old friend suggested I should look into it while I'm off sick,' he replied casually. 'Heard about the body at the golf course, I'm guessing it'll be classed as a suicide, like the others?'

'For the moment,' Freeman was more cautious now, realising that this wasn't the casual catch up that he'd considered it to be. 'There's not a lot to go on.'

'No leads?'

'Not for murder, no.'

Declan considered this. 'Who's taking the case?'

'Nobody,' Freeman replied. 'It's a poisoned chalice, Declan. Your father tried for years to find the so-called killer, and if he couldn't do it, then nobody can.'

'I'm at a loose end at the moment,' Declan continued. 'Let me have a shot at it.'

This threw Freeman. 'You want to work here?' He asked. 'I thought you were on injury leave, effectively suspended?'

'From the City of London police,' Declan nodded. 'But not from the Thames Valley police.'

'You want to be seconded here?'

'No need. Just allow me to consult,' Declan now leaned closer. 'Look, we both know dad was fixated on this. And that it's happened again within months of his death seems a little convenient. I'm wasting away in his house and could do with something to take my mind off it. Let me look into it.'

'Alone?'

'Maybe. Depends if anyone else is stupid enough to assist me,' Declan smiled. 'You can provide me with a liaison to the station. That De'Geer chap could do it.'

'De'Geer's an excellent choice, actually,' Freeman was musing as he considered this. 'Used to go out with Ellie Randall as a kid.'

'Craig's sister?'

'Yeah. They were about the same age. Summer romance. I think it was what made him want to be a copper. Bloody idiot.'

There was a moment of silence.

'You're a loose cannon, Declan,' Freeman finally admitted. 'I heard the stories of your time in the SIS, told by your father. You have a reputation for killing your suspects. That's if you're not punching them out.'

'That's harsh,' Declan protested. 'The priest deserved it. Ford was corrupt. Derek Salmon was murdered, and Susan Devington killed herself. The Beachampton incident was because of a ton of gangsters trying to kill each other, and SCO 19 killed DI Frost after he shot me...' he paused.

'Yeah, okay, there's a lot,' he admitted. 'But, if this is a serial killer, he's a vicious, sadistic bastard and needs to be put down. And who's better at doing that than me?'

Freeman looked out of the window, considering this for a moment.

'Loose cannons escape their mountings,' he said. 'They fall out of the ships and sink to the bottom of the sea. I don't want to see that happen to you, if only for your late father's sake.'

Declan nodded. 'I can't promise I'll be an A-student, but I'll do my best. And if I can't work it out, I'll give it back and walk away,' he replied. 'It's win-win for you. If we succeed, you take the credit for bringing it in. We fail? You never backed it. I also know from my dad's notes that you believed these were suspicious as much as he did.'

He waited, let the moment stretch, letting Freeman warm to the idea before he continued.

'So how about we go through what you have so far, and I go catch us a serial killer?'

6

THE GAME IS AFOOT

It was half an hour later when De'Geer and Jess entered the briefing room to see Declan and Freeman sitting at a table, a selection of files distributed around them.

'Good, you're here,' Freeman rose from the table, looking at De'Geer. 'I'm putting you under DI Walsh's remit for the moment. Do what he says, unless it's bloody stupid.' With that, Freeman nodded to Declan and left the room.

'What's this?' Jess was already sitting at the table, working through the files. 'What's a Red Reaper?'

De'Geer stiffened at this. 'You're hunting the killer?' he asked. Declan nodded at this.

'You have a problem with that?'

'No,' De'Geer stood beside the table but made no attempt to sit. 'I was one of the first on scene at the golf club.'

'And you knew Craig Randall,' Declan added. 'Back in 2012.'

'I knew his sister,' De'Geer corrected. 'Craig just happened to be there. I was also twelve.'

'Can you tell me what happened?' Declan asked. De'Geer

glanced nervously at Jess. 'Don't worry about her,' Declan continued. 'She's been going through dad's old records for weeks without telling me.'

Jess looked up, surprised at Declan's knowledge of her surreptitious activities, as De'Geer finally relented and sat down.

'My family moved here when I was about eight,' De'Geer started. 'We lived in Aldershot before that, and my father worked in a rare book shop in Henley Upon Thames. I didn't know that many people, and I was already tall for my age, so I started hanging out in the campsite a mile up the road. It was an easier time back then. And children, especially ones on holiday, make friends quickly.'

Declan nodded at this. 'I used to do the same thing,' he admitted. 'Probably before you were even born.'

'That's likely,' Jess replied as she read through the files. 'He's in his twenties and you're a hundred and two.'

'We're being professional right now,' Declan chided. Jess looked up in horror.

'Sorry, I wasn't thinking,' she apologised. 'A hundred and two, *Guv.*'

'Tell me about the Randalls,' Declan ignored this.

'Nothing to tell,' De'Geer explained. 'They were regulars. Came almost every weekend for years. I got to know Ellie, the daughter, when I was nine. Craig was twelve then, I think. He'd been coming to Hurley every summer for years. He would show us all the cool hiding places, or the best places to leap into the Thames. Kid stuff. But then by the time I was eleven, maybe twelve, he changed.'

'How?'

'He turned fifteen.'

'Troubling age, fifteen,' Declan watched Jess as he stated this. She smiled but kept reading.

'Yeah,' De'Geer, not getting the joke continued. 'He was darker now. More vicious. He would help small children climb high into the trees near the campsite and then leave them. He'd take out tent pegs of other campers at night, or pour water onto sleeping bags when nobody watched.'

'Sounds like a darling,' Declan muttered. It wasn't the word he really thought, but he was trying to be polite.

'Everyone knew it was him, but they couldn't prove it,' De'Geer looked around the room as he tried to remember events of a decade earlier. 'He started harassing girls at the campsite. He'd started doing it to locals, but some bigger boys had cottoned onto this and gave him a beating. The campsite girls were often new and didn't have that sort of support. There was one; I can't remember her name, but he really fell for her. Stopped any other boy talking to her and one night he tried to kiss her.'

'Did she kiss him back?' Jess looked up now. De'Geer nodded.

'He was attractive and confident. It was a holiday romance, nothing more. I was doing similar with Ellie by then, but it was different. We'd known each other for years then. We were best friends. To Craig, this girl, I think her name was Sheryl? She was a trophy. They fumbled around, played the part of a lovey couple all week long, but then near the end you could see that Craig realised that soon she'd leave. And he hadn't had what he wanted.'

'And what was—' Jess stopped as realisation took over. 'Oh. That.'

'He took her into the woods, and later on there was crying

and shouting. I wasn't there, but I heard that her father had gone looking for her and found her in tears. Craig had tried to make her... do things. She was fifteen. Eventually he'd shouted at her and left. The father then argued with Craig's father, while Craig claimed that it was a misunderstanding and she'd come on to him... it was word against word. Nothing happened, and the next day her family left, never to return.'

'What about the Randalls?'

'They carried on for a couple more weeks; this was July now. But people talked, and everywhere the family went, they heard the insults, the rumours. Then, one Sunday afternoon, Craig was found dead. I never saw the family again. I never even said goodbye to Ellie.'

'Do you think he did it?' Declan asked. 'The crime report states he cut his own throat.'

De'Geer shook his head. 'Craig was too arrogant to be apologetic,' he replied, going silent once he'd finished. Declan considered this for a moment.

'So he had a reputation,' he asked. De'Geer nodded in confirmation.

'And this new body?' Declan asked. 'Nathanial Wing?'

'I don't know much about that case—' De'Geer started, but it was Jess that continued.

'Sixteen years old, was doing an Art and Design diploma at Henley College,' she said. 'Worked part time as a web design intern in Henley while doing the course. I think they paid for the college. Found on the sixteenth green of Temple Golf Club with his wrists slit, but no sign of a blade.' She looked up at Declan. 'You think that's why it was the sixteenth green? Because he was sixteen?'

'It's a possibility,' Declan replied. 'I'll be having another look at the golf club with PC De'Geer here later, if that's okay with him.'

De'Geer nodded. 'If this is a killer, then he needs to be stopped.'

'If this is a killer, then he knows his subjects,' Declan continued. 'To control someone to make them take their own life isn't something you gain on a first appearance. We might need to have a look into the weeks leading up to each case.'

'They're not all local,' Jess looked back at the sheets. 'There're cases in London, in Reading, even Dover. They go on for years.'

'And we'll be looking into all of them,' Declan insisted. 'But first we need to ensure we have the capabilities to do this. I need to make some calls. PC De'Geer will take you home. I need to go to London.'

'I've got a motorcycle,' De'Geer replied. Jess grinned.

'That's totally fine. I'll hold real tight.'

Declan sighed and, taking one last look at the table and the files, he rose from the desk.

'Take the most recent folder with you,' he suggested. 'I have a feeling we'll find copies of all the others in dad's filing cabinet.'

Jess nodded, smiling at De'Geer with the look of a slightly hungry shark.

Declan almost felt sorry for the poor man.

THE BIGGEST PROBLEM THAT ANJLI HAD WITH THE MILE END secondment wasn't that she disliked DCI Esposito, nor was it the fact that she was back at a place where she thought she'd finally moved on from; it was the simple fact that she wasn't with the Last Chance Saloon. She'd only been there a few months in the grand scheme of things, but at the same time she'd gained more friendships and solid work connections there in that short time than she had anywhere else. And, as she sat at her desk scrolling through social media, she leaned back in her chair, wondering whether this was truly the career for her anymore. If the Temple Inn office didn't open again, would she stay in the force? Or would she go corporate, like so many others would?

There was a *ding* in her email. Switching from the browser, she frowned as she looked at the message.

There was a temporary problem delivering your message to
w.fitzwarren@city.police.uk

Why was there a problem? Anjli had used that email address countless times, and the only way it'd fail was if the email had changed, or if they'd deleted it. She couldn't help herself, she actually chuckled at this.

The Cybercrime expert had a faulty email address.

Grabbing her phone, she sent a message to Billy, letting him know of the issue, and leaned back again, staring up at the ceiling.

She was bored.

There was movement at the door to the office, and Anjli looked up to see Declan entering carefully, as if expecting to be stopped at any moment. Which was probably likely, considering that the last time he was here, he'd caused the arrest of not only a Detective Constable but also the then Detective Chief Inspector.

Seeing that Anjli had seen him, Declan motioned for her to join him outside, retreating through the doors. Looking to

Esposito's office, Anjli saw that there was no movement; the DCI hadn't noticed Declan's brief appearance. Rising, she looked around the office at the other officers. Not one of them looked back at her, all involved in their own personal cases.

She didn't look back at them as she left the office.

Declan was leaning against a waist height wall as she walked out of the main entrance.

'Are you supposed to be here?' she asked. Declan grinned.

'Christ no,' he replied. 'That's why I was so cautious. Worried that I'd be hit by lightning just for considering it.' He looked at Anjli, as if evaluating her. 'How's it been?'

'You've worked the spot,' she replied. 'How was it for you?'

'I was here a couple of days, and in that time I uncovered two corrupt cops and solved a murder,' Declan smiled. 'Probably an uncommon situation.'

'Fair point,' Anjli shrugged as she joined Declan on the wall. 'There's something off, here. It's not the people, they're all perfectly fine. Even DCI Esposito's doing his best to make me feel at home, although it's obvious he'd rather I buggered off elsewhere. He had me sorting out vandalism in a park yesterday.'

'That an option?' Declan asked. 'To go elsewhere?'

'Dunno,' Anjli sighed. 'Don't even know where I'd go. I spent most of my career here and then went across to Monroe. Feels like a massive step backwards.'

'I might have an answer,' Declan smiled. 'You got any holiday time?'

'Even if I didn't, I reckon Esposito would give me something, just to get me out of the way,' Anjli chuckled. 'Why do you ask?'

'Because I need your help as much as you look like you

need mine,' Declan replied. 'And with you beside me, it'll be easier to get Monroe on board.'

'On board what?' Anjli frowned. Declan rose from the wall.

'I'm hunting a serial killer that might have killed my parents.'

Anjli went to speak, stopped, and then started again.

'Let me go speak with HR,' she suggested.

MONROE DIDN'T KNOW WHY HE KEPT COMING BACK HERE; probably because he had nothing better to do. But here he was again, standing on King's Bench Walk in Temple Inn, staring up at the building that had once been the offices of his baby. A child that had grown so tall, taken down some of the worst people possible, and might now be kept from him forever.

His phone vibrated; pulling it from his pocket, he saw it was Declan, again. Monroe groaned, staring down at it until the call went to voicemail. Not that he didn't want to speak to Declan, it was the fact that he didn't know what to say to him. You can't give advice when your advice has been proven wrong.

Another call now; this time from Anjli. Sighing again, Monroe let this do the same as the first. However, as it also moved to voicemail, a message from Declan appeared on the screen.

Answer your phone you stubborn bloody idiot it's important

As Monroe read this, the phone started vibrating again; a

second call from Declan. Looking to the heavens in exasperation, Monroe connected the call, putting it to his ear.

'Declan,' he said, forcing a smile. He'd been told once that if you smiled when you talked, the voice would sound warmer. He didn't know if it worked, but it was worth a try. 'Sorry, I missed your call. I'm in the shops.'

'Signal's always bad in shops,' Declan replied. 'Which one are you in?'

'Supermarket.'

'Yeah, it's the steel in the construction,' Declan was walking as he spoke. 'Always a problem until you get outside.'

'If you want, I can call you when I get out,' Monroe suggested.

'Not a problem, Guv,' Declan said down the phone. 'I'll just come to you.'

Monroe went to reply again, to lie once more, but something didn't feel right here. Looking around, he groaned as he saw Declan and Anjli walking across the Temple Inn car park towards him.

'In fact, I see you right now,' Declan continued down the line. 'In the produce section.'

Monroe silently swore as he disconnected the call, waiting for Declan and Anjli to approach.

'How did you know?' he asked.

'Marcos,' Anjli replied. 'We called her before you, Guv.'

'Bloody woman,' Monroe muttered. 'Can't keep a secret.'

Declan looked up at the building. 'How long until it's operational again?' he enquired. Monroe shrugged.

'Week, maybe two.'

'And will we be back inside?' Now it was Anjli's turn to talk. Monroe went to reply, but found he didn't have the words.

'I'm not sure,' he eventually admitted. 'I genuinely don't know.'

Declan was watching Monroe as he spoke. 'How bored are you? On, like a scale of one to ten? One being usual day at the office and ten being you'll do anything to get out of this rut?'

Monroe considered this carefully.

'Twenty seven,' he smiled. 'Christ, I'm going mad, laddie. Finally ready to get back on the bike and someone nicked the wheels.'

'I might have a different bike for you to ride,' Declan replied. 'Putting together a team. Been given the go ahead to hunt a serial killer. Very off the books, unpaid, and possibly even uncredited. But at least it'll give us something to work on together.'

'Is it going to be a ball-ache of a job?'

'Most likely.'

Monroe smiled. 'Can we bring Rosanna too?'

Declan laughed. 'She's already examining the body.'

'Aye, so there's a body?' Monroe slapped Declan on the arm. 'Why the hell are we standing around here chatting, then?'

And with that, DCI Alexander Monroe gained his next case.

FUNCTIONING ROOM

THEY DECIDED THAT NOTHING COULD BE DONE UNTIL THE NEXT day, so Declan gave both Anjli and Monroe details of where to meet him and then took his leave, returning to Hurley before the evening rush hour traffic became too much of a problem.

Once in the village and parked up, Declan walked over to The Olde Bell pub. He was very aware that arriving at Maidenhead with a full team would turn heads, and currently that was exposure he didn't need. And at the same time, he didn't want to turn his house into a police unit, especially with Jess around.

Although, to be honest, she'd probably fit right in.

There was another alternative; one that he considered as he walked to the bar. The landlord, a young man in his early thirties, was cleaning glasses as Declan approached. Declan knew that the glasses would have been washed en mass in a glass washer under the bar, and that this was more a drying of the glasses, but the traditional imagery wasn't wasted on him.

'Declan,' the man nodded, taking the pint glass he was drying and placing it on the bar. 'Guinness?'

'Make it a half, Dave,' Declan replied, looking around the bar, freezing when he saw Karl Schnitter sitting in the corner, reading a newspaper.

Realising he was staring, Declan looked back to Dave the landlord.

'You using the function room at the moment?' he asked casually. 'I'm looking for a place to have a couple of meetings.'

'How many meetings?' Dave poured the Guinness as he spoke. 'Ongoing usage or a couple of parties?'

'Police business,' Declan leaned in, speaking softly. 'Got a team coming up from London.'

'Oh aye, is that about the Chinese lad on the golfing green then?' Dave passed the half pint over and Declan returned a five-pound note across as payment.

'You know I can't talk about an active case,' he replied.

'Your dad talked about them all the time.'

'Dad talked about a lot of things that he shouldn't have.'

'Your dad was more fun than you, it seems,' Dave grinned.

'Maybe I'll tell you about it when I'm further down the line,' Declan took a sip of the Guinness and sighed. He wasn't a drinker, and had avoided alcohol since the night with Kendis, but there was something to be said for a nice pint of Guinness. 'Maybe you have a meeting room to hand? Just a few days, so anything you're not using.'

'We've got meeting rooms in the Malthouse, next door,' Dave suggested. 'Library's not being used, it's smaller than the rest but I'm guessing you won't be paying corporate rates.'

'What *would* I be paying?' Declan didn't really want to ask, but Dave thought this over for a moment.

'If it's only a couple of days, I'll let you have it for free, civic duty and all that, on the condition that all food and drink is bought here. No sneaky lunches down at the Rising Sun.'

'I can do that,' Declan smiled, shaking Dave's hand. 'We'd need it from tomorrow.'

'That can be arranged,' Dave leaned closer, so that the other drinkers at the bar couldn't hear. 'Do you want me to let the Germans know?'

Declan stared at Dave in confusion for a moment. 'The Germans?'

'Well, I'm guessing it's all connected, considering that they're in the same business?'

Declan shook his head. 'I have no clue what you're talking about.'

'Ah, so not then,' Dave tapped his nose. 'Well then, a word to the wise. Couple of weeks back we had a German couple arrive. Booked an open-ended stay, brother and sister, they claim, took a twin room. In their thirties, he said he was LKA, some sort of German police.'

'*Landeskriminalamt*,' Declan replied. 'I worked with them twice when I was stationed in Germany. They're like German CID.' He looked around the bar. 'I wonder why they're here though?'

'Well, the girl said that they were hunting someone,' Dave was warming to the role of informant now. 'Wondered if it was the same thing as you?'

'Maybe,' Declan mused. 'Do me a favour, let me know if they pop in here. I ought to have a word with them, police to police and all that.'

He looked back to the corner of the pub now. Karl was

staring up at him, the newspaper now placed on the table in front of him.

'Give us whatever lager Karl's drinking these days,' Declan said, looking back to Dave, who pulled out a bottle of Belgian ale from the fridge, opened it and passed it across with the altered change from the five-pound note.

There wasn't much.

'Lucky I didn't order a pint for myself,' Declan mused as he put the change away. Dave had already moved on to the next customer, the conspiratorial conversation now over, so Declan took the half pint glass and the bottle over to the corner table.

'Mind if I?' he asked. Karl smiled, waving to a seat.

'Only if that is for me,' he motioned at the bottle. Declan nodded and passed it across as he sat.

'I wanted to thank you,' he started. 'Again. For trusting me when nobody else did. When I was on the run for terrorism, you were pretty much the only person who helped.'

'You would have done the same,' Karl sipped from the bottle, smacking his lips and sighing with pleasure. 'And I knew you were innocent. I know you. It is difficult to believe someone you have known for decades could be capable of such a thing.'

'I know exactly what you mean,' Declan replied, watching Karl. He couldn't believe that Karl could be a killer. He'd known him all his life. But at the same time, there were questions that needed to be answered. He must have worn these worries on his face because Karl, noticing Declan's expression, leaned in.

'Are you alright?' he asked. Declan leaned back; not intentionally backing away from Karl, but more so he could take in the man sitting opposite him.

'Germans,' he started. 'I spent a lot of time with them when I was in the Military Police. Mainly helping them arrest pissed squaddies. I always found Germans to be blunt in conversations. Not as comfortable with the fancy language of a more British conversation.'

'Is this a way of saying that Germans are rude?'

'Not at all, the opposite in fact. I always found Germans to be refreshing. You can be blunt with them. You don't need to dance around topics. You can just talk about them.'

'And what topics are you dancing around now, *Detective* Walsh?' Karl's voice was softer now, the emotion drained out of it. Declan knew he was wary now, not sure where the conversation was going.

'When I came to you that night, on the run and scared, you took me at my word,' he said. 'You knew I wasn't lying. Or, at worst, you trusted me enough to believe that even if I was lying, there was a reason.'

Karl didn't reply. Instead, he made a curt nod at this.

'So, in return, I'd like you to tell me the truth. And know that no matter what, that if there is a reason for you to lie, I trust you enough to understand that.'

'I see,' Karl wore the expression of a man who really *didn't* see.

'What was your job in Berlin before the wall came down?' Declan asked.

Karl stopped, as if frozen, the bottle of beer halfway to his mouth.

'I was a mechanic,' he eventually whispered. 'I have said this already.'

'Let me rephrase that,' Declan replied carefully. 'I might not have explained it correctly. What was your job in Berlin before the wall came down, *Mister Meier*?'

To his credit, Karl didn't bluff his way out of this, or stammer that there was some kind of mistake. Instead he nodded, placed the bottle down onto the table and looked directly at Declan.

'Your father's notes?' he asked. Declan shook his head.

'Helen Mirren.'

'Women. They will be the death of me,' Karl replied calmly. 'Yes, my name was Meier. And yes, I was, as you probably already know, a *Grenztruppen*, a border guard on the Eastern side of the Berlin Wall.'

'Why lie about this?' Declan sipped at his drink as he observed Karl. Karl shrugged.

'This was the end of the eighties,' he explained. 'Less than forty-five years since the Second World War. My father had been a German soldier during the war. He was young, and even though he did not follow the teachings of Hitler, it did not matter as they conscripted all Germans. However, he was a soldier, and thus became called *Nazi*. After the war, there were trials.'

'Nuremberg.'

Karl nodded at this. 'Many soldiers were arrested, charged with terrible crimes. All of them had the same excuse. *I was just following orders.*'

'And how does this relate to you?'

'I too was just following orders. And my orders were to stop people escaping from East Germany to West Germany. I patrolled the Bernauer Strasse section; if you have visited the Berlin Wall memorial, you see that they have kept a section just as it was back then, showing the two walls and the kill zone between. There is a watchtower there. I was in that, and several nearby.'

Declan nodded. He had indeed seen that section of wall before.

'I was led by a Hauptmann, a Captain in the Grenztruppen by the name of Wilhelm Müller,' Karl continued. 'He was a monster of a man and followed the GDP orders to shoot at fugitives with great happiness. In fact, he would walk the land between walls slowly, listening, feeling vibrations, from where the tunnels were being built. Then, he would mark a line in the sand where he believed the tunnel was, and then order us to machine gun the line. Tunnels were very close to the surface sometimes, and occasionally bullets would get through, injuring builders. And when he was not doing that, he was tempting dissidents to run, convincing them of weaknesses in the wall, so that when they attempted, we would shoot them.'

He took a swing of ale.

'He claimed it was all by chance though, and he would flip a coin. An East German Mark. If it landed number side up? They would survive, and Müller would let them try for freedom. If it came up on the other side though, then they would be killed.'

'So he claimed the universe was killing them, not him?' Declan shook his head. 'Hell of a guy.'

'A liar,' Karl added. 'One of the other guards told me once that Müller dropped the coin once, when tossing it. When the guard picked it up, Müller snatched it back angrily before he could look at it. But he'd see enough. He'd seen that the coin had two sides the same. What you would call 'tails'. He would show a coin, make this big speech about chance and destiny, and then palm it for one that gave him the outcome he needed. That way he looked like he wasn't consciously deciding to kill, when at all times he was.'

They sat silently for a moment.

'Movies make it seem like crossing the wall is simple,' Karl added. 'It is just two walls, after all. Not even that high. But hundreds of people died trying. And they hated our unit for what Müller did.'

'You expected another Nuremberg after the fall?' Declan asked. Karl nodded.

'Müller was known. He had his own nickname, *The Reaper*. And as such they named us *The Reapers,*' he said, looking at the bottle as he spoke, not seeing Declan flinch at the name. 'When the wall came down, we knew they would come for him. For *us*. I wanted to leave too, as I hated what I had done. I had a passion, repairing cars, and decided that I would start a new life somewhere far away. But Grenztruppen didn't find it easy to do that. I had to create a completely new identity.'

'Why did you pick Schnitter?' Declan asked. Karl chuckled.

'It was not of my choice,' he replied. 'Hauptmann Müller heard I was trying to leave, to escape, and came to me. He said that for a year's salary, he would create a new life for me. He had a friend, an Oberst in the Stasi who could do this. I agreed, I paid the money, everything I owned to do this. And in return, he names me 'Reaper'. A reminder that I will always owe him for my new life.'

Declan nodded. He didn't know what he would have done if placed in the same situation.

'You think I am the Red Reaper,' Karl continued. 'I can see how you would consider that. Especially with the image.'

'What do you mean?' this threw Declan. Karl's eyes widened in surprise.

'I thought you knew?' he replied. 'The image, the man with the hat, with the scythe? It is an *Ampelmännchen*.'

Declan recognised the name, but couldn't remember where from. Luckily Karl was still talking.

'Your little stop go men on traffic lights?' he continued. 'Green man is go, red man is stop? In East Germany we had different images for the little men. They still exist even now. A green man with a hat walking, and a red man with a hat, standing still, arms outstretched. Ampelmännchen.'

He looked to the bottle again.

'Müller created the image of the man with the scythe,' he explained. 'Red man meant stop, and that was what the Reaper did. He stopped escapees. He even made this into a badge, forced us to wear it when on duty with him, when he flipped that lie of a coin to satisfy his conscience, as he fed his lust for blood.'

'Wait,' Declan was confused now. 'Are you saying that Wilhelm Müller is the Red Reaper?'

Karl nodded. 'Was,' he replied. 'I learned years later, through your father in fact, that Müller had followed me across Europe, and had killed people. Patrick showed me the cards, and I was living here when Craig Randall and Dorothy Brunel died.'

Declan understood this; he'd seen Dotty Brunel as one of the victims when Freeman had shown the files to him earlier that day. She'd died in 2010, two years before Craig.

'Did you know either of them?'

'Yes,' Karl replied sadly. 'I knew both. Dorothy and Craig's father had both used my garage. In fact, all the people who died had crossed my path over the years. It was as if Wilhelm had decided that anyone who spoke to me, who befriended me, had to be punished.'

Declan leaned back at this. 'People like my mum.'

At this Karl's eyes started to tear up. 'I knew I had said the wrong thing when we toasted your parents,' he replied. 'That I said murder. Because that was what it was. Patrick was away for ten minutes and that monster ended her life. That was when we decided that the law would fail in stopping Wilhelm Müller. That was when we took matters into our own hands.'

'You and my father became vigilantes?' Declan was shocked at this.

'None of the victims could be linked to him. None of the victims could be proven even as murder. Your father was angry, frustrated, and now his wife, who was already dying, was taken from him rather than passing at her time. The police would not help us.'

'Why not?'

'First, because there was no proof of murder. But also because Wilhelm Müller was untouchable, a ghost.'

Declan shook his head. 'I don't get what you mean.'

'I heard, years later, that Müller also changed his name when he left Berlin,' he explained. 'But it wasn't the Stasi that gave him a new identity. It was the Americans.'

'But why would—' Declan stopped himself. There was only one real reason the American government would give someone like Müller a new identity. 'He became an informant for them.'

Karl nodded. 'More than that. He gave testimony, provided documents that took down many prominent people. He was given a new life, and more importantly, he was given a kind of diplomatic immunity. Müller was no diplomat, but if they accused him of any crimes, his documents would ensure that rather than going to trial, he would disappear once more, under another alias.'

'Christ,' Declan swirled the last of the half pint of Guinness in his hand as he considered this. 'The ultimate get out of jail free card.'

'And if the Americans refused, he still had paperwork on people who had risen up over the years, enough to ensure that they would also ensure his survival,' Karl muttered. 'As Stasi officers burned folders, he was collecting as many as he could.'

He looked up.

'Patrick could not stop him by legal means. However, there were always other options.'

'I'm guessing that before he could do this, Müller killed him,' Declan replied. Karl frowned.

'What do you mean?' he asked.

'My father's car accident,' Declan stated. 'They found a card in the glove compartment, complete with his fingerprints on it. And the body at the golf club, Nathanial Wing? He also had a card. Looks like Müller has returned to carry on this, well, whatever this is.'

Karl shook his head. 'That cannot be,' he exclaimed. 'These murders, if truly a Red Reaper? They have to be of a copycat, or someone else.'

Declan leaned forwards, intrigued. 'Why would you think that?' he asked.

Karl looked him in the eyes, and Declan almost shuddered at the coldness within them.

'Because we killed Wilhelm Müller and hid his body five years ago.'

8

ORGANISED FOR CRIME

Jess was in the living room, working through piles of A4 printouts, when Declan arrived back home.

'You sort out what you needed to sort out?' She asked, looking up briefly before returning to the organisation of sheets of paper. Declan took off his jacket as he walked over to join her, sitting on the sofa as he watched his daughter at work.

'Monroe and Anjli are in, and Doctor Marcos is already checking through the autopsy of Nathanial Wing,' Declan sat back in the seat, moving his neck to loosen his shoulder. It was aching after overexertion. When preparing the bullet wound, the doctors had told him to be careful when using it, and he'd been driving a lot recently. 'Can't get hold of Billy though.' He was still watching Jess. 'Get home okay?'

'Morten brought me here on his bike,' Jess replied.

'So it's *Morten* now, is it?' Declan grinned. Jess's crush had been obvious; as obvious as the reddening of her cheeks as she realised what she'd said.

'I mean PC De'Geer,' she blustered. 'Don't worry, he didn't come in.'

'You want some dinner?' Declan reached for the phone. 'I could call in pizza?'

'Sure, as long as it's Vegan,' Jess was now moving to a stapler, binding the small piles of paper together. 'Can I get this done first though? I don't want to get tomato sauce on any of the pages.'

'What are you doing, anyway?' Declan leaned over now, picking up one of the piles. It looked very much like the case files that Freeman had showed him earlier that day.

'While I was waiting for you, I went and had a look around granddad's study,' Jess explained. 'I remembered you saying that he always kept copies of his cases and assumed that it'd be the same here. I found them all under R for *Reaper.*'

Declan flicked through the pages. All twelve crime reports, mostly half investigated and believed to be suicides, all with his father's familiar penmanship scrawled beside them.

'It's not all of them,' he muttered. When Jess looked back questioningly, Declan realised he'd spoken out loud and forced a smile, waving to the sheets.

'How did you print them?' he asked, changing the subject. 'Dad's iMac was stolen a week and a half back, and I had my laptop with me.'

'I'm not a Luddite, dad,' Jess chided him. 'I have my iPad. There's's a scanning app on it. You take a photo of every page and it turns them into PDF copies. I then wirelessly printed five copies of each one.'

She frowned.

'Will five copies be enough? I have it as a digital file too.'

'I didn't even know dad had a printer here,' Declan ruffled Jess's jet black hair as he read through the report. 'Did you read these?'

Jess nodded. 'Every two years,' she said, pointing at the first crime report. 'If these are all correct, he started in 1990 and killed someone every two years from then, all the way to 2012 and Craig Randall.'

'You believe he killed them?'

'You believe it, and I believe you. And granddad did too.' Jess almost jumped as she remembered something. 'Oh, mum called. She said you need to remember that I have exams this year and I'm not to sit around doing nothing.'

'She has a point,' Declan looked at the paperwork. 'As much as I appreciate this, you need to finish your schoolwork first.'

'It's half term,' Jess started piling the piles of sheets together. 'And I've already done everything they gave me. And besides, this is *on-the-job experience*, isn't it?'

Declan watched his daughter as she hurriedly bundled the paper together. 'What's really the matter?' he asked softly.

Jess stopped and audibly sighed; the sigh of a teenager was something that only a parent truly understood, and this was a sigh that Declan had heard many times over the years.

'I don't think I like Robert,' she admitted. Declan nodded at this; Robert, or 'Robbie' Brookfield was an old friend of Declan and Liz's, and a couple of weeks earlier Robbie had contacted Declan out of the blue, primarily to ask for Declan's permission in asking Liz out on a date. It wasn't phrased as such, but Declan knew what it was.

'He's just dating your mum,' Declan said, putting an arm around Jess. 'When he wants to be called 'dad', you can hate him. He's genuinely a good man.'

He frowned.

'What is it you don't like about him?'

'He's not you,' Jess muttered. 'You weren't supposed to stay away, you were supposed to both realise that you couldn't live without each other, and get back together.'

Declan laughed at this. 'I love your mum, and she loves me,' he replied. 'But, sometimes that's not enough for a marriage. The job kept me away for long hours. And when I had to make a choice, I made the wrong one.'

'Yeah,' Jess muttered again; a judgement more than a response.

'If you want this life, Jess, it's a choice that you too will have to make at some point,' Declan continued. 'This isn't a career. It's a vocation. A calling.'

Jess nodded, understanding this even if she wasn't happy about it.

'Are you dating anyone?' she asked. Declan had a twinge of regret at the question; there had been someone, but she was dead now. How did he explain this to his daughter?

'No,' he replied. 'I'm not currently dating anyone.' It wasn't a lie, just a response that kept to the rules of grammar. Jess, however, had noted the slight delay and pressed on.

'Were you dating anyone?' she asked again, adjusting the question. 'Kendis Taylor, maybe?'

'Why would you think that?' Declan asked. Jess shrugged.

'Maybe because you were plastered all over the news as her terrorist handler?' she continued. 'Maybe because her husband apparently punched you out beside her grave a couple of days ago?'

Declan groaned inwardly. *Of course Jess would hear about that.* The whole bloody village was probably still going on about that. 'It wasn't beside her grave,' he corrected. 'It was beside your granddad's grave.'

'Oh,' deadpanned Jess. 'Because that makes it totally different.'

Declan sighed. She was right. And she had a right to know.

'I love your mum, and I always will,' Declan started. 'But Kendis was my first love. We had a bond, of sorts. But then I didn't see her for years. Down the line I married Liz, we had you... Life went on.' He thought before speaking, phrasing his words now. 'Kendis was working with granddad, on his book, and that's how we got back into contact. But I passed her information on a case and that led her down a rabbit hole, one that eventually ended with her death.' He knew it wasn't a complete lie, but Jess didn't need to know about the one-night stand right now. She didn't need to know that Kendis was considering leaving Pete for Declan, and that she was torn between two loves. Or, more likely, that she wasn't leaving Pete, and had played Declan like a fiddle for one last roll in the sheets.

'Pete punched me because I caused her death,' he finished. 'And I deserved it. I deserved more.'

There was a moment of silence as Jess stared at her father in surprise.

'I thought you were having an affair,' she eventually said. Declan forced a smile, ignoring the voice in his head.

It was an affair. And you bloody well know it, you hypocrite.

'I know,' he replied. 'And you're old enough to know the truth.' He stopped. She was old enough to know the truth; all of it.

'I have something else to tell you,' he leaned forward now, taking Jess' hand, stopping her from bundling any more sheets of paper. 'But it's between us, okay? No telling mum. She'll only worry, and you don't want that.'

Jess turned to face her father now, her face a mask of concern. 'What is it?'

Declan took a deep breath and, over the next half hour told his daughter about the conversation he'd had with Karl Schnitter earlier that day, including the information he'd been passed about the possible murders of his parents, her grandparents, and what had eventually happened to the murderer.

When he finished, neither of them were in the mood for pizza anymore.

'TWO CATCH UPS IN ONE WEEK? I AM FEELING SPOILED,' BILLY smiled as he sat down opposite Anjli in the upstairs bar of The Old Crown on Fleet Street. 'I got the impression from the text that something important was going down.'

'You'd know if you'd read your email,' Anjli sipped at her drink as she watched her friend's reaction. 'But it seemed to bounce from your City Police address. Any reason?'

'They're changing the emails,' Billy lied smoothly. 'More of a cybercrime domain. Your email must have got lost in the moving.'

'Awesome,' Anjli pulled out a notebook and pen, passing it over to Billy. 'Write your new email down then, please.'

Billy stared at the notebook as if it was a poisonous viper and, with no comment coming from him, Anjli continued.

'I mean I'd love to see how you have an email considering you gave in your notice and walked out,' she said, crossing her arms. 'All ears.'

Billy groaned. 'How did you find out?' he asked.

'Monroe tried to contact you,' Anjli's expression didn't waver as she faced her friend. 'Christ, Billy, what the hell are you playing at?'

'I don't think the force is for me,' Billy muttered, looking out of the window beside them, looking out onto the lamp-lit street. 'I'm just not the running, jumping, climbing trees type, you know?'

'But that's why you asked for cybercrime!' Anjli exploded, finally unable to hold back her anger. 'When they said we were being seconded, you *asked* for it!'

'I asked for it because I needed space!' Billy snapped back.

'Space from what?'

'Space from *you!*'

There was a silence in the upstairs bar. The other drinkers were now looking at Anjli and Billy, their drinks paused mid rise. Anjli pulled her warrant card out, waving it around before speaking.

'Anyone want to comment on our conversation? Happy to have a chat.'

The other drinkers returned to their own conversations, and Anjli looked back to Billy, who looked appalled at his own outburst.

'I didn't mean it like that,' he explained. 'I mean all of you. The Last Chance Saloon. I... Look,' he leaned forward. 'I came from cyber, I was a desk jockey. And then, under Monroe, I'm out in the field. That's fine, but then I have SCO 19 rifles aimed at me outside Devington House, we're racing red lights to save Monroe from an execution, I'm going undercover with a murderer, one that tried to shoot me and was brutally shot down in front of us...' His voice trailed off.

'I could have died, Anjli,' he whispered. 'Frost wanted to kill me. I was so cocky, so 'ah gotcha' and he was going to execute me. He could have killed Declan. He almost did.'

'Don't be a drama queen,' Anjli smiled. 'He grazed Declan's shoulder. I've had worse playing rugby. Well, obviously not worse than a gunshot, but you get the idea.' She grabbed at Billy's hand, holding it tight. 'You're a good copper, Billy Fitzwarren. You're an excellent copper, even. Nobody I know is better than you with a laptop and a wireless connection. We need you.'

'Who's the *we* here?' Billy murmured. 'Mile End still looking for a computer whizz after Sonya Hart was arrested?'

'Actually, I'm not at Mile End anymore,' Anjli replied. 'I'm taking some time off for personal reasons.'

'Wait, is your mum okay?' Billy looked concerned for Anjli; he knew that her mother had been battling cancer for a while now. Anjli patted his hand.

'She's super fine,' she assured Billy. 'We think the chemo did its job. I owe... well, let's say that I owe some people for getting her the best care, but we look to be kicking it into remission.'

'So why the personal reasons?'

'It's a term I could use when talking to DCI Esposito and guarantee him not asking questions,' Anjli replied. 'I'm heading up to Hurley tomorrow to help Declan with a case.'

'Declan has a case?' Billy leaned back now, confused. 'I thought he was suspended? Or on some kind of injury list that was as good as being suspended?'

'For City Police duties, but not Thames Valley,' Anjli picked up her drink again, sipping at it. 'He's got an old serial killer case of his dad's that's come back. The police are claiming it's some kind of suicide game, not murder, but they've allowed Declan to get a small team together and look into it.'

'Let me guess,' Billy chuckled at this. 'The team is basically the Last Chance Saloon?'

'Pretty much,' Anjli nodded. 'And his daughter, Jess. Don't ask.'

Billy looked around the bar in realisation. 'This isn't a drink, is it?' he asked cautiously. 'This is a sodding recruitment session! You knew I wasn't with the police anymore and you're trying to poach me back!'

'I'll admit, we could use you,' Anjli admitted. 'Declan and Monroe are one step above primates when it comes to computers.'

'I'd love to, but I can't,' Billy looked away. 'I can't go out in the field. It's too much to ask.'

'Actually, I didn't want you in the field,' Anjli shrugged. 'To be honest, I'm always holding your bloody hand. I was thinking you could hold the fort at the hotel, maybe use the spa—'

'Hotel?'

'Well yeah, we're using a meeting room at The Olde Bell on the high street,' Anjli continued. 'More of a vacation than a crime unit, if I'm being honest. And we don't need you on the beat, as we have some kind of hot viking for that. Some PC named De'Geer?'

Billy sat up at that name. 'I met him last week,' he said. 'He was there when we searched Declan's house.'

'Well, it's just a shame that you won't be meeting him again,' Anjli looked down at her nails, forcing herself not to smile as out of the corner of her eye she could see Billy squirming. She knew he wanted to come, to help, but she also knew that this irrational fear of his would stop him. She needed to pull out all the stops here. 'Apparently he rides a motorbike.'

'Fine, I'll come and help you,' Billy threw his hands into the air in mock despair. 'But not because of De'Geer. Because Declan saved my life and I owe him.'

'Great,' Anjli smiled. 'Can you pick me up tomorrow? I still don't have a car. And I'll need to be brought back in the evening.'

Billy felt that something was missing in this story. 'You're commuting there?'

'Not all of us can afford a few days in a swanky country hotel,' Anjli replied. 'And you're unemployed and cut off from your rich family, remember?'

'I'm not that cut off,' Billy was already looking at his phone. 'Ooh. The rooms look nice.' He looked back to Anjli.

'I'll come if you stay with me,' he said. 'As in I'll pay for your room. But you buy me dinners. Deal?'

Anjli shook Billy's hand.

'Deal.'

9

FIRST BRIEFING

THE FOLLOWING MORNING, DECLAN AND JESS WALKED INTO The Olde Bell with a slight feeling of trepidation. The bar wasn't open, but the dining room was for guest breakfasts, and as Declan entered, looking for someone who could direct them to the meeting room, he spied a couple at one table. A man and a woman, both in their thirties, they ate sparingly at a full English breakfast, glaring distastefully at the food as they did so.

This, Declan assumed, had to be the Germans.

'Wait here,' Declan said to Jess as he made his way through the tables towards the couple who, as he approached, patted their mouths with their napkins and placed their cutlery on the plates, almost in unison.

There was something a little bit creepy about the act, but Declan tried to move past it, stopping at the table.

'I'm so sorry to interrupt your breakfast,' Declan said. 'I'm—'

'Detective Inspector Declan Walsh, City of London Police,' the male interrupted. 'Yes, we know you well.'

Declan took a moment to examine the man sitting at the table as he planned a reply. Both the man and woman were brown haired, maybe late thirties; the man's hair was cut short at the sides but was left longer on top and allowed to curl naturally. He wore small, round framed glasses that perched on the end of his hawk-like nose and wore a grey wool blend suit over an open white shirt. He was slim, maybe some kind of runner or gymnast in build.

His sister however, was the polar opposite; her hair was long and wild and dyed blonde at the tips. Her face was round and friendly, overdone with blue shades around the eyes and she was more shapely than her brother, which made Declan wonder whether his slightness was deliberate rather than genetic.

One thing was for certain though; they were definitely related in looks, no matter how they differed.

'Should I be flattered or concerned?' Declan asked. The man shrugged noncommittally at this.

'Your village, they like to talk,' he said simply. 'They talk of you, the terrorist who is not a terrorist who has armed police turn up once a month to visit, so it seems.'

'My job is a bit all over the place,' Declan admitted.

'Or you are not good at your job?' The man suggested. Declan fought back an urge to snap back at this, instead preferring to smile.

'I'm sorry, I didn't get your names,' he replied.

'I am Kriminalkommissar Rolfe Müller of the Bundeskriminalamt, in particular the Schwere und Organisierte Kriminalität,' Rolfe explained. 'A Kriminalkommissar is the same as your Detective Inspector rank. And the Schwere—'

'The Schwere und Organisierte Kriminalität means Serious and Organised Crime,' Declan added before Rolfe could continue. 'I worked with them when I was in the Military Police.'

Rolfe nodded, as if he'd expected Declan to reply, showing his sister. 'This is Ilse, my younger sister,' he explained. 'She is my... How would you say it? My secretary?'

'You have a secretary?' Declan forced a smile. 'Maybe we should start doing that over here. Would be great with reports.'

'Yes, you should,' Rolfe sniffed. 'You would make fewer errors. But Ilse is here because she has a much better grasp of your language than I have. She is here to ensure I make no communication mistakes when talking to your police.'

Declan's smile stayed, but there was no humour behind it. He really didn't like this man, and that his surname was Müller hadn't gone unnoticed.

'Are you here on holiday?' He turned to Ilse now, asking her instead.

'We're on a case,' she replied, looking to her brother in case she'd overstepped by speaking.

'We hunt a war criminal,' Rolfe had picked up his cutlery again and was now frowning at a sliver of sausage on the end of his fork. 'It is international crime, not rural, like yours.'

'I see,' Declan nodded at this as if genuinely caring. 'If we can help in any way—'

'I will not need help,' Rolfe stared at the sausage still. 'Especially from one such as yourself. I read about your father. He was poking his nose into the wrong things. He died carelessly driving, yes? You should have better driving examinations.'

Declan was really fighting the urge to punch this arrogant little shit, but wondered if this was a deliberate attempt to taunt him, to gain a rise.

Well, two could play at that game.

'Rolfe Müller,' he said, rolling the words around his tongue. 'I've heard of several Müllers before, but only one Rolfe. He was a Nazi in *The Sound of Music*.'

There was a moment of silence, and Rolfe tore his eyes from the sausage, turning his face and round framed glasses to stare at Declan.

'Did you call me a Nazi?' he asked in an almost hissed tone. Declan smiled.

'No, he was *a* Nazi. Rolfe. In *The Sound of Music*,' he said. Before Rolfe could reply, Declan looked at his watch. 'I'm sorry, but I'm late for a meeting,' he said, glancing back to Jess, across the room. 'Enjoy Hurley, though. It's a beautiful, quiet village.'

'It is maybe not that quiet though, yes?' Rolfe smiled. 'I mean to say, you have a body on a golf course, your own house was broken into, and your father's computer stolen? And your terrorist adventure last week? As I said, we know all about you.'

Declan looked around the room, idly wondering how many witnesses would see him punch Rolfe, before deciding against this and looking back down.

'Don't worry about the body,' he smiled. 'We're looking into that. Hunting a serial killer, in fact. German chap. And we'll catch him. I'm sure if we have questions you'll be around, right?'

And with that line left hanging, Declan walked back to Jess, motioning for her to follow him out of the dining room.

'What was that all about?' she asked. Declan shrugged.

'Inter police relations,' he replied, noting that PC De'Geer was standing by the main entrance. 'You lost?'

'They sent me to find you,' De'Geer said. 'They were worried *you'd* got lost.'

'Making friends,' Declan subtly showed Rolfe and Ilse Müller. 'What do you know about them?'

'The German police? They arrived two weeks ago, and have been pissing everyone around off royally since,' De'Geer replied. 'Why? Do you want them arrested for something? Half of Maidenhead want them arrested.'

'Just find me all you can on them,' Declan watched Rolfe and Ilse talk; it was a heated exchange. 'There's something more there. And their surname is too exact to be a coincidence.'

'Sir?' De'Geer, having not yet been informed of Declan's meeting with Karl, or the contents thereof, looked confused at this. Declan turned back to him.

'Were you involved at all in the break in at my house a week or so back? The one through the back window?'

'No,' De'Geer shook his head. 'But I know of it. Your computer was stolen.'

'*My* computer?'

'Yes,' De'Geer looked to Jess. 'Is that wrong?'

'No,' Declan replied. 'The report said my iMac was stolen, but it was actually my dad's computer.' He looked back to Rolfe, now attacking his breakfast with military precision.

How had he known that the iMac was Patrick Walsh's?

Jess nudged him and, returning to the present, he smiled, leading De'Geer and Jess out of the dining room.

'I'll explain everything when we're all together,' he said. 'Now, where's the bloody Library?'

THE LIBRARY TURNED OUT TO BE A CHARMING LITTLE ROOM IN the Malthouse; oak-panelled walls gave way to bookshelves and a fireplace complete with white marble mantle, surrounding a large table in the middle. Half of the Library was lower than the other, obviously built onto the side of the unit at some point.

Wide, open windows, built into the wall above the drop in height shone light into the room, and two leather chairs sat beside a side cabinet and additional window that looked out into the garden. The hardwood floor led to the corner where a hand painted cocktail cabinet was positioned, and beside that were coffee and tea-making facilities, a plate of biscuits placed carefully beside the white cups.

'I like this better than Temple Inn, laddie,' Monroe smiled from one of the chairs by the window, the sun hitting his face as he basked in it. 'I think we need to do some extra redecorating when they're done.'

Declan grinned as he looked around the room at Monroe, Billy, Anjli and Doctor Marcos. 'No Davey?' He asked.

'She's at Maidenhead for me. Checking the body,' Doctor Marcos replied. 'Who's the big chap?'

Declan introduced both PC De'Geer and Jess to the group, and then motioned for everyone to sit around the large, rectangular table in the middle.

'Thanks for coming,' he started as he stood at the end, facing them all. 'We don't have a fancy plasma screen or anything here, so Jess has made copies of the files. We have them as digital versions, if you prefer. I know Doctor Marcos already has them.'

Jess passed the papers around, and emailed the digital version to Billy, who'd already set up what looked to be a small computer system at the end of the table. As the group looked through them, Declan continued.

'I'll give you the cliff notes version before you get too deep,' he said. 'From 1990 to 2012, a dozen people died across Europe, from Berlin in Germany all the way to Hurley. Every other year, a body turned up.'

'But the police didn't think it was a serial killer,' Billy asked as he read through the sheets on his screen. 'I'm guessing because the evidence didn't go that way.'

'Exactly,' Declan replied. 'Forensic evidence seemed to reveal that each victim inflicted their own wounds. There were never signs of a struggle, and each victim, when checked into, had some kind of secret that could cause them to take their own life, whether it be something embarrassing, financial debt or even a crime.' He looked through the pack at his side, showing a scan of a card, a red Ampelmännchen holding a scythe.

The calling card of the Red Reaper.

'There were two things that stood out on each of these cases though,' he continued, looking back to the team. 'First, the weapon used was always missing. A gun, knife, even the chair the victim stood on to place the noose around their neck. All gone. And secondly? Each of them had one of these cards on them. An Ampelmännchen, an East German crossing man. And, each card was completely devoid of fingerprints except for the deceased, and always the same two prints in the same location.'

'So it's a German we're looking for?' Anjli asked.

'Possibly,' Declan replied. 'My dad worked with Karl

Schnitter, a German mechanic who lives in the village. They believed it was a man that Karl had worked with back in Berlin during the fall of the wall. Hauptmann Wilhelm Müller.'

'That's the same surname as the two Germans in the dining room!' Jess exclaimed. 'Sorry, thought I'd seen a clue.'

'You did,' Declan smiled. 'But, all things in the correct place. My dad and Karl hunted Wilhelm Müller for years, and it ended in blood.'

'What sort of blood?' Monroe asked. Declan paused, looking at everyone at the table before speaking.

'There's a reason I took this case,' he started. 'My dad believed Müller killed my mum.'

'Your mother was terminally ill,' Monroe was quieter now, as if shocked by this revelation. Declan nodded.

'So we all thought,' he replied. 'But when they moved the body after her death, they found the same calling card. Dad was away when she died, grabbing a coffee. There was every chance that she was killed.'

'So we hunt Müller,' Anjli nodded at this. 'Nail the bastard good and proper.'

'Yes and no,' Declan made a faint smile at Anjli as she threw up her hands in exasperation. 'Karl Schnitter told me they caught Karl after my mum's death and, rather than arrest him, my dad took him somewhere and executed him, hiding the body.'

'Hiding it where?'

'Probably the bottom of the Thames, knowing dad,' Declan shrugged. 'But Karl was convinced that Wilhelm Müller was dead, never asked my dad about it and life went on.'

'Until three days ago,' PC De'Geer muttered.

'Not quite,' Declan corrected. 'There's one more. I spoke to Emilia Wintergreen a couple of days back—' he stopped as Monroe rose in anger.

'*You spoke to that bloody woman?*' he exclaimed. '*You only now mention this?*'

'Yes,' Declan replied calmly. 'And we'll discuss her later.'

'Who's Wintergreen?' Billy asked. 'I feel like I walked into a film halfway through.'

'She was a DS who worked with Monroe, my dad and Derek Salmon back in the day,' Declan explained. 'She's in Whitehall now.'

'Of course she is,' Monroe mumbled angrily.

'Anyway,' Declan returned all eyes to him. 'She showed me proof that I'd been looking for, proof that my dad didn't die in an accident. That he was murdered several months back. And in the glove compartment was a Red Reaper card, with only his fingerprints on.' Before anyone could comment on this, he continued on. 'And then, as PC De'Geer mentioned, three days ago Nathanial Wing was found on the sixteenth hole with a card that matched.'

'Copycat,' Billy suggested. De'Geer shook his head.

'We thought that too,' he replied. 'But when the original cases came up, nobody ever mentioned the cards. There was talk it was some kind of sick suicide cult and nobody wanted the press fallout. If they're using the same cards, they have to know about them from another source.'

'It's worse than that,' Doctor Marcos chimed in now, checking her phone. 'Joanna texted me earlier. She compared Wing's card to Randall's one, as they were both still in Maidenhead evidence. It's the same ink, paperstock and age. Which means they were on the same print run. If Wilhelm

Müller is dead? Then someone else knew where he kept his toys.'

'What do you mean *is*, Doctor Marcos?' Jess asked, curious. Doctor Marcos shrugged.

'We have no body, and only the word of your grandfather that he did what he said,' she explained. 'He could have scared Müller off, threatened him with something, who knows. And now he's back.'

'Who does Wintergreen think it is?' Monroe asked.

'She thinks it could be Karl Schnitter,' Declan replied. 'And he's a suspect, no matter what he said to me. But we need to work on several things at the same time here.' He looked to Anjli. 'Take De'Geer and go see the Randalls. See if they missed anything when they gave their statements back in 2012.'

'Sure,' Anjli wrote in her notepad. 'Will they want to see us though?'

'That's why you're taking De'Geer,' Declan smiled. 'He used to date the daughter, and nobody's going to argue with you if he's beside you.' He turned to Billy. 'Find out anything you can on Rolfe and Ilse Müller. In particular, if Daddy Dearest was a murdering Hauptmann.'

'Already on it,' Billy tapped on his keyboard. Declan turned to Monroe.

'If it's okay with you—' he started, but Monroe waved him silent.

'For god's sake, laddie, it's your call,' he said. 'I might be DCI to your DI, but I'm here assisting you, so lead the bloody thing.'

Declan grinned. 'You, me and Doctor Marcos will check out Temple Golf Club and Nathanial Wing. With my dad's death and the name of the club, I can't help but think this is some kind of message to me.'

'Because it's always about you,' Anjli mocked.

'And me?' Jess asked. Declan looked to her.

'I need you to go undercover,' he smiled. 'Everyone got their roles? Good. Let's get to work.'

10

PAR THREE

Temple Golf Club was situated just off the Henley Road, or the A4130 to give it the proper name, a country lane that ran north to south from Hurley down to the A404 junction and the eastern suburbs of Maidenhead. Built around 1909, it had once been land owned by the Knights Templar, although knowing things like that didn't really help you when you were stuck in the rough and two strokes over par.

Declan drove Monroe and Doctor Marcos there in his Audi, even though it was effectively less than a mile to walk across the fields. Although Declan now had wellington boots that fit him, a purchase that came in the last week after various mud-filled wood visits to both Epping and Savernake Forests over the last three cases, visits that had destroyed his favourite brogues, neither Monroe nor Doctor Marcos had a pair, and it was simply easier to drive.

They didn't enter the main building; the manager of the club was already waiting for them outside when they arrived. A tall, slim, balding man in a red, V-neck jumper over a blue polo neck, he looked like he'd just finished a round of golf, which, in all actuality, he probably had.

'Thought I'd save you the hassle of trying to find me,' he said, shaking their hands. 'Alfie Bates. I'm the manager here. I got a call, saying you wanted to see the green?'

'If possible,' Monroe said, before looking sheepishly to Declan. 'If that's what you were thinking?'

Declan nodded, annoyed at Monroe. Not because he'd spoken, but because he kept looking to Declan for orders. They'd have to chat about that later.

'You'll be unimpressed,' Alfie explained, already walking to the right of the building, expecting them to follow. 'It rained last night, and we've had sprinklers on. There's nothing left to see.'

'It's more a case of getting a feel for the place,' Declan explained. He'd already seen the crime scene photos of Nathanial, laid out on the green, arms outstretched either side, one wrist bleeding into the hole while the other puddled around the flag, held in Wing's left hand. Declan hadn't missed the fact that he was laid out in a representation of the Red Reaper.

'Do you have any CCTV of the night?' Monroe asked. Alfie nodded.

'We do, but it's not great. We only have a couple of camera light things and they're not HD. It's mainly for insurance reasons. Not many people want to rob a golf club, and it's not like we're gated or anything.'

'I saw that,' Doctor Marcos looked back to the main road. There was no fence, no wall, nothing. 'Why is that?'

'We can't withhold access to the public,' Alfie explained as he led them across the car park towards a gap in the hedge. 'There's a public footpath that goes across the course, between the twelfth and thirteenth greens. Bloody annoying, to be honest. Comes out on a dirt track that goes under the A404, and continues out of the entrance, across the road and then around the fields towards Prospect Hill. Ramblers are a sodding nuisance, always walking across just as someone's about to tee off.' He paused. 'You're not ramblers, are you?'

'Love it,' Declan deadpanned. 'Do it all the time.'

'Ah, well, there's a time and a place in my opinion,' Alfie's face reddened. 'Anyway, this is the seventeenth hole, a tough one that doglegs left, and usually sees people trumped by that beech tree. Once past it, we'll see the sixteenth. It's a par three for the men, but a pretty standard par four for the ladies. It has a two tiered green, so expect a couple of puts to sink though.'

Declan glanced to the right, where the top of a building could be seen through the trees.

'What's that?' he asked.

'Apple Hill Nursing Home,' Alfie replied, continuing on. 'They back onto the first leg of the seventeenth. And they're walled and gated, for about fifty yards. Then it turns into standard country fencing.'

Monroe looked to Declan at that. 'He means three bar wooden fences, about chest high,' Declan explained.

'Easy to get over then,' Monroe nodded. 'We should check the home to see if they have CCTV.'

'There's a hotel across from them with a car park, too,' Declan mused. 'Might as well check everyone.'

'About CCTV,' Doctor Marcos interrupted. 'You were originally telling us about yours?'

'Oh, yeah,' Alfie stopped, looking sheepish. 'We saw the boy, Wing? Yeah, he walked into the main entrance about eight, nine pm, clear as day on the video.'

'Anyone with him?'

'Nope,' Alfie turned a corner on the fairway, and the sixteenth green came into view. 'To be honest, he looked like any normal person. He walked to the right, like we did, stops, picks up something from the floor and then he was gone, out of frame.'

'Anyone follow?'

'Nope, clear footage for a good twenty minutes. And then it's only Frank Peters turning up to drop a sheet off.'

By now they were standing on the green, and Declan could see that the water had mostly washed away the blood, although the white edge on the inside of the hole was still rimmed with a scarlet tint. Doctor Marcos, who had examined the images thoroughly, was now kneeling at the hole, looking up as she did so.

'He was laid here,' she said, opening a small compass app on her phone and looking at it. 'North to south, arms outstretched, east to west.'

'What do you mean, laid?' Alfie frowned. 'Lad killed himself, right?'

'You've been a great help,' Monroe walked over and shook Alfie's hand warmly. 'We can take it from here.'

'Well, alright then,' Alfie replied, backing away slightly as if realising he was intruding on police business. 'Any questions, just let me know. And, if you want a round on me, just holler. We're not starting players until Saturday, so there'll be no balls landing around here.'

And, with a last look at the flag, now pulled out and placed onto the green as Doctor Marcos shone her torch deep into the green's hole, Alfie turned and almost fled from the scene.

'Thoughts?' Monroe asked. 'First one is that you shouldn't

keep deferring to me,' Declan chided. 'You're DCI. You have experience in these. I'm only running this because I asked first.'

Monroe nodded, smiling. 'Understood, laddie,' he said, looking across the green and towards the road, the other side of the trees. 'So, the green can be accessed from the road over there. We're shielded by the trees from the road, the care home, the clubhouse and the A404. If you're looking for somewhere quiet while out in the open, it's not that bad a place.'

'There's a lay-by down the road, too,' Declan mused. 'You could park there and no CCTV would catch you.'

'So how do we catch this guy then?' Monroe was staring down at the flag now. 'We have nothing that proves that Wing was murdered, or even coerced to take his own life.'

'Wing sliced both of his wrists open,' Doctor Marcos was still peering down the hole. 'There's no blade of any kind. But there is something down here...' She reached into the hole with a pair of tweezers, pulling out a folded and damp piece of paper.

'The police who arrived on scene didn't know this was a murder. They took it as a suicide, and the CCTV of Wing alone confirmed it. Only when the body was examined at Maidenhead, did they find the card in Wing's pocket.'

She placed the paper on the green as she reached into her jacket, removing a pair of blue latex gloves and pulling them on.

'I know that they positioned the body, but the blood from the right wrist cut went straight into the hole, so the hand was over it. The killer, or at least the enabler, would have positioned the body, but likely kept the hand there and missed this.'

The paper was covered in dried blood, dampened by the rain that had entered the hole over the last couple of days. It was folded and only an inch in size.

'Wing could have held this in his hand,' Doctor Monroe carefully opened the letter up as she spoke. 'It took us a good couple of minutes to walk here from the car park. If our mystery man was waiting here, having sent Wing through the front entrance while climbing over the fence, Wing could have written a note, folded it up and held it.'

'Why not run for help instead?' Declan crouched beside Doctor Marcos now as she finished opening the paper. It was a sheet of paper, around A5 in size; on one side was scrawled writing, while the other side was a half filled Temple Golf Club score sheet. The paper itself was stained and blooded, the blue ink slightly smudged, but the message on it was still visible, written in capitals.

IF I DON'T DO THIS THE GERMAN WILL KILL MY PARENTS.

'Not much to go on,' Declan said.

'Probably didn't have time to say anything more,' Doctor Marcos pulled out a clear plastic evidence bag and carefully placed the sheet into it. 'He must have found it on the ground in the car park, realised it was his chance. We'll need to check it for prints.'

'Poor wee bugger,' Monroe looked across the fairway as he spoke. 'No wonder he did this. If I thought that my family would suffer instead, I might do the same thing too.'

Doctor Marcos rose. 'We're done here,' she said, her voice clipped with anger. Declan understood the emotion; he felt the same way too.

'Back to Maidenhead?' He asked. Doctor Marcos however shook her head.

'Not yet,' she replied. 'We have a crash scene to look at first.'

Declan felt a cold wind slide down his spine. He hadn't visited the site where his dad had died since it'd happened.

There was a first time for everything, he supposed.

THE RANDALLS HAD LIVED NEAR ERITH, IN SOUTH EAST London when their son Craig had died, but two years after the event they'd split, the father disappearing abroad with work, and the mother and Ellie moving nearer relatives in Basingstoke. And, six years later, it was at this Basingstoke house that PC De'Geer and DS Anjli Kapoor arrived on a police motorcycle.

'Not gonna lie, that's pretty awesome,' Anjli said as she pulled off the helmet, placing it on the seat. 'Used to have a Suzuki Marauder when I was a teenager. Only 125cc, but it looked like a Harley.'

'And sounded like a hairdryer,' De'Geer grinned as he turned off the bike's engine, the smile fading as he looked towards the house.

'I haven't seen her since Craig died,' he admitted.

'Not even to check in on her? Like, later in life?'

'She knew where I lived, while I only ever knew her caravan,' De'Geer admitted. 'She could have looked for me, but never did. Life moves on.'

The door was already opening as they walked towards it; the sight of the police motorcycle pulling up outside was enough to spark curiosity from the young woman who now stared at them as they approached her along the path.

'Ellie Randall?' Anjli asked. 'Are you—'

'That's Ellie,' De'Geer said, his voice softening. Ellie Randall stared at Anjli, and then De'Geer... And then her eyes widened.

'Morten?' she asked. De'Geer smiled, but it seemed forced to Anjli.

'Hello, Ellie,' he said warmly. 'Can we come in? We need to talk about Craig.'

———

ELLIE SAT IN AN ARMCHAIR SIPPING AT HER TEA AND STARING across at De'Geer as Anjli pulled out her iPhone, turning the voice memo app on and placing it on the table.

'Do you mind?' she indicated the recorder. 'It's easier than writing notes.'

Ellie shook her head. 'I don't know what I can give you though,' she replied. 'I told the police everything.'

'Did Craig have any enemies?' Anjli started. Ellie nodded.

'Loads by the end,' she said. 'He pissed off pretty much everyone.'

'What happened here?' De'Geer asked. 'Your parents—'

'Dad left us about two years after it happened,' Ellie explained, while sipping at the mug. 'Mum and me came here. Aunty Bev lives nearby. Mum's at work right now.'

'Do you work?' Anjli asked. Ellie shook her head.

'Laid off a month back,' she said. 'Cutbacks.'

'Can you tell me in your own words what happened that day?' Anjli continued. Ellie however shook her head.

'We try not to think about it.'

'Please, Ellie,' De'Geer leaned closer. 'There's been another one.'

Ellie's eyes widened. 'So he *was* killed?' she whispered. Anjli nodded.

'We believe so,' she replied. 'A monster of a man who forced his victims to kill themselves. So anything you can give us would be incredibly helpful.'

Ellie was silent for a moment, and Anjli could see that she was weighing up her options here. Then, nervously, she nodded.

'We had a fight,' she started. 'The camping site had been getting complaints about Craig again. We were one strike from being banned. We'd been going there for years, and dad was right royally pissed about this. I was told later that they fought again, and Craig stormed out with Scamper. He was our dog,' she explained to Anjli, who nodded.

'You said you were told later?'

'I wasn't there,' Ellie replied. 'I was on Hurley Lock Foot-bridge when they fought.' She glanced at De'Geer as she spoke. Anjli looked to him also, curious why Ellie had deferred to him.

'It's a place for teenagers to meet,' he explained. 'It's a romantic place. Many have their first kisses there. We had our first kiss there.' He smiled at Ellie, who smiled back. Anjli nodded at this; she'd been told that De'Geer and Ellie Randall had a history.

'I came back to the campsite via the Thames entrance,' Ellie continued. 'Thought nothing was wrong. About an hour later someone found the phone, and then... then they found Craig.'

'Was there anyone around that seemed off?' De'Geer asked. 'Anyone who didn't look like they should be there?'

'Why, you suddenly *care* now?' Ellie snapped.

There was a moment of silence before she continued.

'Sorry, it's just I told the coppers back then, and they did nothing.'

Anjli frowned at this. 'What do you mean?'

'I mean I saw something that day and I told the coppers but they ignored me,' Ellie continued. 'When I came back, walking along the Thames, I looked to the woods by the makeshift bridge that was by field three. I could see Craig and some man.'

'What were they doing?'

'Sitting,' Ellie shut her eyes as she brought the image back in her head. 'I didn't say anything, as we weren't talking. Brother and sister stuff, you know. But when they found the body, I told the police, and they ignored it.'

'What did you tell them?'

'That I saw Craig and the man together, talking, and then the man flipped a coin or something,' Ellie opened her eyes. 'Then I saw Tracey, my best friend by the main gate and I forgot all about it.'

'Well, this time we'll use it,' Anjli pulled out a card, passing it to Ellie. 'If you remember anything, let me know, okay? Can you remember what the man looked like?'

'White, with brown hair?' Ellie was reaching now. 'Honestly, it was years ago, and it was at a distance. Sorry I can't help any more.'

'That's more than enough to go on with,' Anjli said as she rose. De'Geer, seeing this, followed suit. Walking to the front door, Ellie glanced shyly at De'Geer.

'You've definitely grown,' she smiled. De'Geer nodded.

'Not the scrawny kid I was,' he agreed.

'If you're ever around, we should catch up,' Ellie opened

the door as De'Geer and Anjli walked through. 'You know, a drink or something.'

'Now I know where you are, I'll remember it,' De'Geer smiled and, with Anjli following, he walked to his motorcycle, pulling on the helmet.

'That was a little cold, wasn't it?' Anjli asked. 'I mean, you were childhood sweethearts, torn apart by trauma, and now you're ignoring a blatant *come on*?'

'We *were* childhood sweethearts,' De'Geer sadly replied. 'And we shared our first kiss on the Hurley Lock Bridge.' He climbed onto the bike, starting it up.

'But I wasn't with her that day, and I sure as hell wasn't at Hurley Lock Bridge with her.'

'Oh,' Anjli replied before realising. '*Oh.*'

Climbing onto the pillion, Anjli took one last look at the house. Ellie Randall was watching from the window as De'Geer revved the motorcycle and sped off towards Hurley once more, his mind now focussed on teenage love and betrayal.

11

MOVING PICTURES

WHEN HER DAD HAD TOLD HER SHE WAS GOING 'UNDERCOVER', Jess hadn't exactly known what he meant, but had nodded and agreed to do whatever she could to help the investigation.

Unfortunately, that meant doing what her dad had asked for; go undercover at the Henley College where Nathanial Wing had studied, find his classmates and gather whatever she could from them. Apparently Wing's parents had been very vocal about the police and were refusing to speak to any of them. This was the only way to get any advantage.

The problem with this was the same issue that allowed Jess to be in Hurley in the first place; it was half term. The college wouldn't be open. Still, undeterred, she caught the 239 bus from outside the Malthouse and travelled the five miles to Henley-Upon-Thames, deciding that as the college was closed, she'd look into the web company that Wing had apparently been interning at, *Bardic Design*. In Adam Court, off Bell Street, it was a small boutique firm with only about three full-time staff. Someone there should be able to help.

When she arrived, however, she found it was smaller than she had even imagined, with one woman sitting at a reception desk, and a lone man, no older than thirty working at a computer in a glass walled back room.

'Can I help you?' the woman asked, smiling as she looked up at Jess.

'Actually, yeah,' Jess walked up to the reception desk, trying to match the woman's smile. 'I was hoping someone here could speak to me about Nathanial Wing.'

The smile faltered at this.

'Ah, Nathan,' the receptionist said. 'So sad. Expected, but sad.'

'Expected?' Jess frowned. 'You knew he was going to do this?'

'He was troubled, let's leave it at that,' the receptionist replied, now all business. 'What's your business with Nathan, anyway?'

'I knew him,' Jess lied. 'That is, I met him a couple of times.'

'Let me guess,' the receptionist sighed. 'He owed you money.'

'Why would you think that?'

'He owed everyone money,' the receptionist replied, looking back to the other office where the man still worked at the computer. 'Clive didn't even pay him, and yet we ended up being owed a couple of hundred. But I shouldn't talk ill of the dead,' she looked back to Jess. 'Nobody's paying you back, love. Class it as lost money.'

'Did he have any other friends?' Jess asked. 'I was at least hoping to speak to people who knew him.'

'Try the college,' the receptionist suggested. 'Or if not

there, the Regal Picturehouse on Boroma Way. There's a downstairs cafe that they all liked to meet up at.'

Jess thanked the receptionist and made her way down Bell Street, towards the Picturehouse while she considered what she'd learned. Nathanial Wing was a debtor. Could someone have cashed in their chit? Demanded payment and, when he failed to do this, killed him? It certainly made better sense now why Nathanial Wing was classed as a suicide. And a son hideously in debt was one of the worst insults that parents who were incredibly traditional could endure. It was probably why they wouldn't speak about it, too.

The Red Reaper had chosen wisely. If it hadn't been for her dad stepping in, this would have gone as unsolved as the others.

Just like the ones involving her grandparents.

Jess shook away the thought as she turned down Boroma Way, and entered the cafe on the ground floor of the Regal Picturehouse. It was a warm, open space, with a pale, wooden hard floor, under brightly painted yellow chairs around small tables, the white walls and windows contrasting against the emerald green wallpaper behind the counter. There was a young woman at the counter, a barista currently pouring an espresso for a customer, and the cafe was quiet apart from a small group of four teenagers sitting in the cafe's corner, huddled together. Two boys and two girls, they seemed deep in some kind of debate, so Jess decided to start with the barista first. Walking up to the counter, she tried the same smile she'd attempted at the Web Design company. The barista smiled back.

'What can I get you?' she asked.

'Lemonade, please,' Jess looked around the cafe again,

breathing in, taking in the smells of coffee and fresh cakes. It was glorious and calmed her instantly while giving her a conundrum.

How could a teenager who hung around such a place kill himself? How had nobody considered foul play?

The barista placed a glass of lemonade in front of Jess, and she passed across a couple of pound coins. 'Hey, did you know Nathanial Wing?' she asked conversationally. The barista paused, watching Jess carefully.

'He owe you money?' she replied. Jess shrugged.

'I think he owed everyone money,' she said, as if this was a well-known situation. The barista nodded at this.

'You should join the club,' she pointed at the four teenagers in the corner. 'They have badges and everything.'

Thanking the barista, Jess took her lemonade and walked over to the table. The four teenagers were all around the same age; mid teens, maybe sixteen, seventeen at a push. The two girls were both Asian; one was slim and stunningly beautiful, her makeup on point and her clothing obviously expensive, while the other was larger and more relaxed in her look, wearing a denim hooded jacket and jeans over a band tee shirt. Opposite her were two boys, one Caucasian and blond, as equally manicured and dressed as the first girl, while the other one was Mediterranean in looks, olive skinned, his long black hair pulled back into a ponytail, his piercing green eyes looking up at her as she approached.

'Hi,' she said nervously. 'The barista said you were all friends of Nathanial Wing?'

'How much did he owe you?' the boy with the piercing eyes muttered.

'That obvious?' Jess tried to smile as the blond boy

reached across to another table, pulling a fifth yellow chair to the table.

'Please, sit,' he said. 'I'm Leon, that's Bino, the princess is Meena, and the lesbian is Prisha.' He ducked a half eaten muffin as Prisha threw it with surprising force at him.

'I'm Jess.'

'So, go on then, how much?' Meena asked, pointing at Bino. 'So far Bino's in the lead with three grand.' Jess's surprise at this was obvious, because Prisha started laughing.

'See, boy?' she said to Bino. 'Nobody's as stupid as you.'

'I loaned him a couple of hundred,' Jess lied. 'I didn't know—'

'That he was a serial debtor?' Leon interrupted. 'Yeah, that was his modus operandi. We all took the same class as him, and none of us knew that anyone else had loaned him money.'

'You think that's why he killed himself?' Jess enquired carefully, hoping that she wasn't overstepping. Leon shrugged.

'If he did.'

He leaned into the group, lowering his voice.

'I heard he was offed by a loan shark. Owed him ten grand.'

'I heard you were full of shit,' Meena responded. 'Loan sharks don't kill the debtor. They'd take all of his stuff first.'

'You can't retrieve a debt from a dead man,' Prisha agreed.

'What kind of loan shark?' Jess asked. Leon shrugged.

'I dunno,' he admitted. 'But I was with Nate when he took a call, yeah? Scared the crap out of him. Seems he'd run out on someone, and they were telling him that if he didn't fulfil his end of the bargain, the debt would pass to his parents.'

'He told you this?'

'I could hear it,' Leon shrugged. 'The phone was close by. Nate grabbed his stuff and ran shortly after. Next thing I hear, he's dead.'

'Yeah, but that just sounds like he had nowhere to run and took the coward's way out,' Bino replied. 'If some gangster called me up telling me I'd screwed up like that, I'd be on the phone to my parents immediately. His mum and dad could easily cover a ten grand loss.'

'Just saying what I heard,' Leon held up his hands. 'The German seemed pissed, that's all I'm saying.'

'German?' Jess looked to Leon, who nodded sagely at his one believer.

'Voice on the phone had a strong accent. Couldn't miss it.'

'So Nate was owing German loan sharks money and ended up being offed on a golf course,' Prisha chuckled. 'You get many German loan sharks around here?'

Leon leaned back, sulking, aware that his great revelation was being mocked.

'I just didn't think he was the sort of guy to kill himself,' Jess muttered, as if surprised.

'He didn't,' Leon insisted. 'I said what happened.'

'Leon's bullshit aside, I agree,' Meena spoke up now. 'Nate wasn't a quitter. Christ, he kept trying to get out of the hole he'd got himself into.'

'By borrowing more money,' Prisha added.

'Sure, but he was trying,' Meena replied.

'What did he need all the money for?' Jess asked the group. 'He never told me.'

Leon laughed at this. 'Nothing,' he replied. 'He was sticking it into crypto, trying to make the big pot, you know?

Screwing around on Uniswap and DeFi groups, talking it big about the next solid moonshot coin.' He looked to his cup of coffee, sighing.

'Prick never had a clue how it all worked. Listened to the wrong people, screwed over a lot more online, shilling coins that had no value, rugging a lot of investors by default and walking away with sod all.'

Jess nodded at this. It was a common scam in crypto to create a coin that was similar to a big selling name coin and then, once it had made a ton of money to sell everything, grabbing a great profit but dumping the price at the same time, pulling the rug out from under the investors' feet.

Rugging.

The problem was, it also gained people who shilled it, people like Nathanial Wing, desperate investors who needed the coin to rocket in price, telling people how great it was, not knowing that the coin was soon to disappear. And, having done the developers own work for them, they would lose their own money, and their reputations, when it died.

Rising, Jess thanked the four teenagers for taking the time to speak with her and, placing the empty glass on the counter, she left the cafe and started back towards Hurley.

She didn't like being undercover. They were good people, and she'd lied to them.

She needed to get back to her dad's house and take a shower.

DECLAN HAD PULLED OVER AT THE SIDE OF THE ROAD, allowing Doctor Marcos and Monroe to emerge on the passenger side while he opened the door carefully, ensuring no speeding maniacs were going to take it off as he climbed out of the Audi. Honey Lane was a narrow country road, one lane in width that ran south from Henley Road, a mile north from them, down to the T junction that Declan and his team now stood at where Honey Lane continued to the east, while a lane equally narrow and no more than a bridleway to the west led to the Dew Drop Inn, a pub that claimed a heritage that not only went back to the 1600s but also a connection to noted Highwayman *Dick Turpin*.

Declan chuckled to himself. What with Epping Forest and Ambresbury Banks also being linked to him, Declan and Turpin seemed to spend a lot of time together. The man was as busy as Charles Dickens for the amount of pubs that claimed he'd visited.

As you drove down Honey Lane to the junction, directly ahead of you was a public footpath that led into dense woodlands, part of the Berkshire Loop of the Chiltern Way; but before that, and on either side were more trees and a ditch on the left-hand side, a ditch that followed around to the left, and the route east.

'So let me get this right,' Doctor Marcos was already pacing the scene. 'Where was your father's car found?'

Declan pointed to the ditch. 'Down there,' he said. 'I got hold of a set of copies of the case notes from a friend in the pathology office.' He walked to the ditch where even now, a couple of months later, you could still see small glints of broken glass in it from the windscreen and side windows. The car was long gone. 'It claimed that dad apparently died when his car, caught in terrible weather and en route to Maidenhead spun out of control at the corner, flipping over as it clipped the edge of the road, and coming to a rest, on its roof around here.' He took a deep breath as he remembered the report.

'Dad, smashing his head against the steering wheel with enough force to shatter his nose apparently died instantly as his heart gave way.'

'And you think it was murder.'

'I know it was murder,' Declan snapped. 'People said he had the heart attack first. Maybe the road was wet and slippy. But look. We're going *up*hill. How does that even happen?'

Monroe was walking west, towards the bridleway. 'Why was he driving down here anyway?' he asked. Declan considered the last conversation that he'd had with his dad. It had been while he was investigating the Bernard Lau case, at the moment when Declan had learned that DCI Ford had lied when she had told him that Patrick Walsh had asked her to bring him onto the case.

'Look, I've got an event to go to in Maidenhead right now. Let me make some calls and I'll come back to you.'

It was the last thing that his dad had ever said to him. An hour or so later, while in Victoria Park, Declan had been given the news of the accident.

'He had an event that he was going to,' he whispered. Monroe shook his head.

'I don't mean *that*, laddie. I don't live here and I've only visited a few times, but even I know that this isn't the best way to Maidenhead from Hurley. The Henley Road is way better and much safer. These country lanes are dangerous at the best of times, let alone in a bloody storm.'

Declan had wondered the same thing over the last few weeks. Patrick had worked in Maidenhead as a Chief Superintendent for years before he retired. He knew these roads like the back of his hand, but he'd still go the quickest route. And this wasn't the quickest route.

'Impossible,' Doctor Marcos looked up from the impact site. 'Physically impossible to come from there, turn here and end up there.'

'Are you saying that he was struck?' Declan asked. Doctor Marcos was looking to the west, and the sign that showed the Dew Drop Inn.

'What car was he driving that night?' she enquired as she crouched down beside one tree at the side of the road.

'A Mondeo or a Peugeot, I think.'

'Colour?'

'Metallic blue.'

Doctor Marcos nodded to herself.

'Then I'm saying your father didn't come that way,' she replied. 'There's damage to the tree on the left up here. Metallic blue scrapes, around a foot, maybe eighteen inches high, and coming from the west. It looks like a car swerved, clipped itself on the passenger side. That could have spun the car, causing it to roll...' she followed the road, as if imagining the rolling car passing her. 'And then ended up in that ditch.'

'What are you implying?' Declan followed her gaze. 'That dad wasn't going to Maidenhead?'

'Oh, I think he was definitely going to Maidenhead,' Doctor Marcos replied. 'But he wasn't coming from Hurley when he crashed. He was coming from that direction.' She pointed at the Dew Drop Inn sign.

'Maybe he met someone at the pub before he carried on,' she said. 'Someone who maybe caused him to crash and placed a Red Reaper card in his car at the same time.'

Declan looked up the bridleway. If Doctor Marcos was

right, then Patrick Walsh had stopped off at a pub in the middle of nowhere for a clandestine meeting in the middle of a thunderstorm, moments before he died in a fatal car accident.

The question was, though, with who?

12

ADDING UP

DECLAN RETURNED WITH MONROE AND DOCTOR MARCOS TO The Olde Bell just after one in the afternoon, and pretty much as the lunchtime rush was starting. Anjli and De'Geer were in the Library, both eating pub-bought lunches on the table; Anjli was eating some kind of curry of the week with basmati rice and a naan to the side, while De'Geer was polishing off a roast beef baguette, dripping with horseradish sauce.

'I hope you saved some for us,' Monroe muttered. Anjli slid a bar menu across the table to him.

'Order at the bar,' she said through mouthfuls. 'Vegan is VG, vegetarian is V.'

As Monroe picked up the menu and examined it, Declan looked around. 'Anyone seen Jess?'

'She's just popped to the bar to order herself a black bean burger,' De'Geer replied. 'Says she has some information on Wing.'

'And Billy?'

'He's on a lunch date,' Anjli grinned. 'Seems that after we

all left, that German guy, Rolfe turned up at the door, flashing his own badge and demanding to see all the crime stuff we had in here, as if we were all beneath his remit or something. Anyway, Billy plays dumb, says he's just the tech guy, brought in from Marlow and can't let anyone in or it's his job. Rolfe stomps off, but an hour later Ilse turns up, all smiles, and invites him to lunch.'

'So they want to gain intel from our weak link?' Declan almost chuckled. 'By the end of the first course he'll have everything on them instead.'

'Or they'll be dating,' De'Geer muttered.

'Not likely,' Anjli replied, looking across to him. 'She's not his type. Plumbing's all wrong.'

De'Geer's eyes widened slightly at this revelation, but then returned to his baguette. Monroe threw the sheet back to the table.

'Sod this, I'm having a small and a large plate,' he said. 'And maybe a dessert. I didn't eat before I travelled here today. Salt and pepper squid, and a sausage and mash.'

'Because they'll go so well together,' Doctor Marcos wrinkled her nose at this.

'Well luckily, you won't be eating any of it,' Monroe sniffed.

'You sure about that?' Doctor Marcos smiled and almost winked at Monroe, and for a moment Declan almost wondered if the two of them had finally revealed to each other how they actually felt. But then the moment passed, and Declan realised it was nothing more than accidental flirting. He pulled out a twenty-pound note and passed it to Monroe.

'If you're going to the bar, get me a pint of coke and a chicken and bacon salad, yeah?' he asked.

'When did I become your bloody servant?' Monroe protested.

'When you told me to stop deferring to you and take charge,' Declan smiled. 'And make sure it has the honey mustard dressing on it, too.'

Monroe huffed irritably, but with the hint of a smile he turned to leave the Library as the door opened and Billy and Jess walked in, Billy beaming with pride as he did so.

'You know, I thought I'd had enough of being undercover, but it's actually quite invigorating,' he said. 'I'm Billy Myers, IT Support.'

'It's not quite *Bond, James Bond*, but it suits you, laddie,' Monroe replied. 'I take it you got some tea for us?'

'Oh, I hadn't ordered—' Billy's face fell.

'He means gossip, news for us,' Doctor Marcos interrupted. 'As in *spill the tea*. He's been watching a lot of reality TV of late.'

'Well, in that case I have an entire pot of it,' Billy said as he walked to the table.

'Hold on it until we've ordered,' Declan suggested. 'If we miss the lunchtime cut off, the Guv will be miserable as sin all day.'

Monroe left for the bar to order a round of drinks and food, and Declan looked to Jess.

'You did okay?' he asked. Jess nodded.

'I have information on Wing,' she replied. 'But it can wait until after food.'

And wait they did for the food to arrive. During that time, with Anjli and De'Geer now finished eating, they spent the minutes finally catching up, the matters of the case placed on hold until after lunch was consumed. Anjli brought them up to date on the state of her mother's cancer, pointing out that it was now effectively in remission, while Monroe talked about some television show he'd been binging about very rich Asians in Beverley Hills. After ten minutes DC Joanna Davey finally arrived, having finished up in Maidenhead and was surprised at the boos and annoyance her arrival brought, until it was pointed out that this was because she wasn't bearing their food, which turned up five minutes after her arrival.

Eventually lunch arrived, and they ate heartily, possibly the most relaxed that the Last Chance Saloon had ever been. And, once they'd all finished, Jess and De'Geer were sent to take back the dirty plates, purely because of their time on the team.

Once they returned, it was time to catch up on what they'd all learned.

'Ellie Randall hadn't told the police everything,' Anjli started. 'By that I mean she had tried to tell them something she'd seen, but it didn't fit their narrative, so they ignored it. Apparently, when she was playing with some friends, she saw Craig in the woods with a man. Just sitting there, as if talking. She didn't pay it any notice until later.'

'Did she describe him?'

'Caucasian, brown haired,' De'Geer added. 'But it was at a distance and she was distracted.'

'There was one thing she was sure of,' Anjli continued. 'The man was flipping a coin.'

Declan looked up at this. 'You sure?' he asked. Anjli nodded.

'Why?'

'Something that Karl Schnitter had said to me,' Declan replied. 'When he was in the Grenztruppen, Müller would tempt dissidents to run, so that when they tried it, they'd be shot. But he would flip an East German Mark to give them a sporting chance.' He considered this for a moment. 'Karl reckoned that the coin was faked, so that the "tails" was on both sides. Bastards never had a chance.'

'So what, Müller's returned, and he's doing it again?' De'Geer asked. 'Tosses a coin, convinces the victim that they're getting a fighting chance? That's shitty.' He paled. 'Pardon my language.'

'No, you're right,' Davey replied. 'It's shitty.'

'Jess? What did you find?' Declan asked. Jess pulled out a small notebook. It wasn't police issue, but it was as near as you could get. Declan felt a little swell of pride. She was really taking this on board.

'So Nathanial Wing owed everyone money,' she started. 'Family was well off but Chinese and owing money was a no no. One of the kids I spoke to said he'd lost it all on crypto but was trying to build it back up.'

'Like Bernard Lau?' Declan asked. He knew Jess understood crypto, because she'd assisted him in understanding it when Bernard Lau had died in Mile End, before he'd even joined Monroe's team a few months back.

'Yeah but I got the impression that Wing was more like a gambler betting on horses because he liked the name,' Jess replied. 'He owed everyone, it seemed, in particular someone they thought was a loan shark with a German accent. One of his friends heard him on the phone to him, and said that the guy basically told Wing that if he didn't fulfil his end of the bargain, the debt would pass to his parents.'

Declan looked to Doctor Marcos at this.

'Do you have the paper?' he asked. Doctor Marcos nodded, pulling out the plastic bag holding the Temple Golf Club scorecard.

'Did Wing have a pen when they found him?' she asked Davey, who nodded.

'Blue pilot G2,' she replied. Doctor Marcos examined the words on the back for a moment.

''Yeah, that could be this. Definitely blue,' she said. 'We found this in the hole where Nathanial Wing died. We think he entered the club through the main entrance while our killer slipped over a fence down the road and away from CCTV. Because of this, Nathanial had a moment or two to himself, and wrote a note on a discarded scorecard, folding it and holding it in his hand. When he died, it fell into the hole on the sixteenth green where it stuck to the side of the plastic hole tube, and was missed because of the amount of blood. Only reason I saw it was because there'd been rain the previous day.'

She showed it to the group.

IF I DON'T DO THIS THE GERMAN WILL KILL MY PARENTS.

'So, we have a German owed by Nathanial, although we don't know if it's money or not yet,' Declan mused. 'We also have a German Hauptmann who was believed to be the earlier Red Reaper, who used to flip a coin to decide someone's fate, and a Caucasian male who was seen flipping a coin with Craig Randall.'

'Then we have two suspects,' Monroe spoke up. 'The first is Wilhelm Müller.'

'Who's dead,' Declan replied.

'That we know of, and based on something your father told someone else,' Anjli nodded. 'What if he wasn't killed, but was warned off? Then came back, killed Patrick Walsh and then realised he enjoyed doing this?'

'Until we find a body somewhere with his DNA, then we need to class him as a suspect,' Davey added. Declan nodded.

'Then we have suspect two, Karl Schnitter,' he continued. 'I know he's an old family friend, but Wintergreen suspected him, and he was around Müller at the start.'

'He also claims that Müller performed the original murders to get at him though,' Billy said, looking up from the laptop. Declan nodded.

'True, he's claiming the victim here, and he probably is. But I'll only be happy with that once we discredit that theory. He was the mechanic who worked on my dad's brakes, he would have easily been able to visit my mum before she died, and he knew both the Randalls and Dotty Brunel. We have to hold him as a potential.'

'There's a third,' Billy said, leaning back. 'Rolfe Müller.'

'You've got something?' Monroe asked. Billy shrugged.

'Maybe,' he replied. 'I played it dumb throughout the lunch, and Ilse was more than happy to talk. I think she needed more of a soundboard, a therapist than someone to gain information from.' He picked up his notebook, where he'd scrawled some notes. 'Not that easy to write notes while there, but I put down the salient facts of the matter.' He smiled. 'You were all too busy working out your lunch orders.'

'Says the guy who had his lunch paid for,' muttered Anjli. Billy grinned.

'So, Ilse told me that Rolfe is her older brother, he's thirty-seven, she's thirty-four. They were both born before the fall of the wall, in East Berlin. Their father was a border guard Captain, but they didn't say where.'

'*Captain* is the same as *Hauptmann*,' Monroe added in. 'Could be the same Müller. We need to check into that.'

'Yeah, I think so too,' Billy continued. 'I got the impression that Ilse and daddy weren't close, but Rolfe was as a toddler. Daddy also disappeared during the fall of the wall. Their mum died a few years back, so it was just the two of them. She used to be a PA in a pharmaceutical company, but lost her job and Rolfe hired her to be his assistant, mainly I think to monitor her.'

'Are they close?' De'Geer asked.

'No,' Billy shook his head. 'There's some kind of issue with either Ilse or Rolfe being an affair child? I couldn't probe any deeper, but there was definitely some kind of half-sibling issue. And I couldn't really go 'I know a great DNA person, and we could find out for you', you know.'

'You could,' Doctor Marcos muttered. 'You totally could.'

'So brother and sister don't get along,' Declan mused. 'We might be able to use that. Did she say why they're here?'

'Yeah,' Billy looked back to his notes. 'They're hunting a war criminal.'

'That's what they also told me,' Declan replied. 'Any particular one?'

Billy shook his head.

'She didn't say, but I felt there was some kind of familial thing going on.'

'How do you mean?' Doctor Marcos asked. Billy turned to her as he spoke.

'I got the impression, and it could be because of poor translations, that Rolfe is ashamed of something this guy did, they've been looking for him for a while and it's more than just a standard case.'

'Maybe they're hunting Müller senior?' Anjli suggested. 'Or, it's your mechanic friend.'

'They've been here two weeks though,' Declan frowned. 'They're literally drinking in the same bar that he does. If they're hunting him, they're doing a piss-poor job of it.'

'Unless they're waiting for something,' Jess suggested. 'Maybe it's like you have with arrests, you need to see the crime being performed before you can arrest?'

'I think you've been watching too much TV there, lassie, but I get your point,' Monroe nodded. 'They want Karl, or maybe their daddy, or maybe someone else to expose themselves somehow. But how?'

'Maybe by being the Red Reaper,' Declan walked to the sideboard and poured himself a sparkling water as he thought. 'We said there was possibly a missing murder, and we know that the first one we know of is in Berlin. Maybe there's something here we don't know about?'

'I'm going to have to become besties with Ilse, aren't I?' Billy moaned. Declan smiled.

'Your undercover days are not over yet, William,' he replied. 'And while you're on it, see if she knows anything about the break in at my house a couple of weeks back.'

Billy pulled out a folded piece of notepaper from his pocket. 'She gave me her number and email address, told me to contact her at any time,' he explained. 'I was going to throw it away...'

'But now you're going to email her back and arrange another meeting, lonely IT technician that you are,' Monroe grinned. Billy sighed, tossing the note to the table where it landed next to the laptop.

'I hate undercover,' he muttered. 'And I hate Billy Myers, IT Support.'

'You think they might have done it?' Anjli was surprised at this. She'd been there with Declan when he'd arrived at the house to find the back window broken and the iMac removed. 'Why?'

'I have a list of suspects who could have stolen my dad's computer, and one by one they're being struck off,' Declan shrugged. 'About time I put some more people on it.'

He looked around the table.

'We've had a good day today, and we've gained some positive leads. But we've also gained more questions than answers.' He looked to Monroe. 'What would you suggest we do next?'

The DCI thought about this for a moment.

'Interview anyone else we know connected to the previous murders,' he suggested. 'Dotty Brunel had a husband, I believe? He might still be in town. We also need to look into Berlin and see why Rolfe is even here—'

'I can answer that,' a voice said from the door, and Declan turned around to see Tom Marlowe standing in the doorway.

I hadn't even seen the door open, he thought to himself. *That guy's good.*

'Guys, meet Tom Marlowe,' Declan said. 'Likely not his actual name, so don't bother remembering it. He works for Emilia Wintergreen.'

'I've got news from London,' Tom said. 'We cracked the USB cypher and opened up Patrick Walsh's file.'

Monroe rose at this.

'Spook,' he almost spat the word in disgust.

Tom grinned.

'Hello, Uncle Alex,' he replied.

13

FAMILY FEUDS

WITH MARLOWE'S ARRIVAL, THE AFTERNOON'S PLANS WERE scrapped, as Billy worked through the files that the probable spy had brought with him. Many of them were doubles of the files that Jess had found and collated from Patrick Walsh's secret filing cabinet, but there were some German files, and more than a few redacted CIA numbers that had caused a buzz of interest.

'It looks like there was another murder,' Billy announced as he flicked quickly through the files. 'Or something similar.'

'What do you mean?' Monroe asked, walking over to Billy to read the screen. Marlowe, now sitting in a chair by the coffee machine, stretched.

'In 1988, two years before the fall of the wall, there was an attempted murder,' he replied. 'I read the files. Sorry if I wasn't supposed to.'

'Define attempted,' Declan asked. Marlowe shrugged.

'One that didn't happen,' he replied. 'Basically, there was an eighteen-year-old woman named Eva Mencken who claimed that a border guard had attacked her and tried to force her to commit suicide after she'd helped two East Berliners escape to the West. Apparently she didn't play along, and then a week later her parents were brutally murdered in a knife attack. She refused to speak to the police after that, and a month later she disappeared.'

'She wasn't killed though,' Billy added as he read from the screen. 'She went into hiding and only appeared when the wall fell.' He leaned back. 'Died of cancer though about fifteen years ago. Apparently raised a complaint about Wilhelm Müller in 1996, but they quashed it.'

'Why would it be quashed?' Declan asked.

'Because someone high up wanted it stopped,' Marlowe replied. 'Müller had very high up friends, it seems. On both sides of the Iron Curtain.'

Monroe looked to Billy, who'd paused scrolling through the Eva Mencken file, pointing to a line on the screen.

'When she raised the complaint, she said that Müller flipped a one mark coin,' he whispered. 'She says he flipped a coin to see if she would live or die.'

'A game he kept playing after the fall,' Declan muttered. 'Interesting though that they stopped it before she could continue.'

'No proof,' Monroe replied. 'Her word against a Hauptmann? Needs more than that. And we already know Müller had high up friends.' He looked to Billy, still scrolling. 'Anything else?'

'Most of this we already have,' he admitted, 'but I can go through it over the afternoon.'

With this agreed, Anjli and De'Geer had left, going to visit the Brunel family, while Doctor Marcos and DC Davey worked through the forensics reports that Patrick Walsh had encrypted, on the off chance that something might appear.

With nothing else to do for the moment, Declan and Jess decided to take a break back at the house, see if there was anything missed in Patrick Walsh's secret study before returning in the evening, while Monroe and Marlowe returned with them; Monroe because he still hadn't seen the secret room, and Marlowe because he simply didn't seem to want to leave for London just yet.

———

'So, tell me about Monroe being your uncle,' Declan said as he passed Marlowe a coffee. Monroe was upstairs, being shown the secret study by Jess, playing the role of an eager tour guide, and this gave Declan a chance to talk alone with Marlowe, something that he felt the spy had wanted since he'd first arrived.

'He's not an uncle by blood, so to speak, but he was close enough to the family to be called that,' Marlowe explained. 'Wintergreen too, although she's told me that if I call her Aunt Emilia one more time, she'll ensure when I'm next out on ops, she'll have someone whack me in the back of the skull.' He mimicked a gunshot motion. 'And to be honest, I believe her.'

Declan nodded at this. He'd only met Wintergreen once, but he could easily believe that she was cold enough to do such a thing.

'Anyway, my mum was in Military Intelligence,' Marlowe continued. 'Around 9/11 there was a lot of fear that something similar would happen in London, mainly Canary Wharf or the City, so the police were doing a lot more of the anti-terrorist thing, you know? One team was Patrick Walsh's one. They'd just finished the Davies murder and were on a bit of a winner's lap. Special Branch moved them onto the patch, and they liaised with Olivia, my mum.'

'Wintergreen too?'

'All of them,' Marlowe counted on his fingers. 'Walsh, Salmon, Wintergreen and Monroe.' He looked back at Declan. 'It was very much an 'any means' kinda remit. They were playing with terrorists who didn't read the rulebook, so they had to be innovative, make deals with people they wouldn't usually work with.'

'The Twins,' Declan nodded, finally understanding how his dad and Monroe had found themselves in league with Johnny and Jackie Lucas, the gangland kings of the East End of London. Marlowe nodded.

'Yeah, that mad bastard was top of the list. He knew everything that was going on, and so they did a little quid pro quo with him.' He sipped at the coffee. 'That said, once you start down that route, you forget where the *quid* starts and the *pro* ends. You start turning your head, looking the other way. Maybe take a little wad of cash for your problems. You've been told to do this by your bosses anyway, so why not make a little scratch?'

'My dad?'

'All of them, mate,' Marlowe nodded. 'For a good couple of years.'

Declan sat for a moment as he digested this. 'And then what happened?' he asked.

'My mum died,' Marlowe replied as if it was the most normal thing in the world. 'During the 7/7 attacks in 2005. She was following intel on one of the bombers, and followed him onto a train, intending to eradicate the threat.'

He sighed.

'She got to him just after they left Kings Cross Station,

and right as he detonated his bomb, killing her and twenty-six others. They didn't add her to the victim list because she wasn't officially there, but everyone knew. After that, it became a little personal for Wintergreen, and she accepted a role in the same department, mainly to avenge my mum's death.'

'Where were you then?'

'I'd just started training at CTCRM Lympstone,' Marlowe replied. 'They didn't even tell me about this until after I finished.'

'Commando training?' Declan was impressed. He'd known that Marlowe had trained with the SAS but hadn't been accepted; this had been stated when they drove together to Hurley, but Declan had faced a few commandos in his years as an SIB officer, and they were no slouches. Marlowe though, shrugged.

'I intended to work the route to get in with mum,' he said. 'Never happened though. And then a few years later I was headhunted by Wintergreen.'

'Yeah, I still don't get that,' Declan mused. 'How she went from DS in my dad's squad to basically M in James Bond.'

'Blame Monroe for that,' Marlowe replied. 'They were married.'

'What?' Declan almost dropped his mug. Marlowe smiled.

'That's a conversation for him to explain,' he said, rising from the sofa as he placed his mug back onto the table. 'I need to head back. But I wanted to give you something.' He pulled out a small USB drive, passing it across to Declan. 'Your dad didn't just have folders on the Red Reaper on the drive you gave us,' he explained. 'There were some other things, about...' he looked up the stairs, as if looking at Monroe.

'...other people,' he finished. 'Things you should look at and know.'

Declan stared down at the USB drive, wondering what secrets he'd find on it.

'She really wanted you for the team,' Marlowe walked to the front door. 'You were going to be asked at your dad's funeral. She was there, you know. But she saw Monroe in the car park and decided not to. And by the next day you were with him.'

'They really hate each other then?' Declan asked. Marlowe shrugged.

'I don't think it's hate, but when you're married to someone one day and then the next you allow the government to remove every scrap of identity about you, effectively saying that not only does the marriage no longer exist, but you yourself no longer exist, that's probably a bit of a marital punch in the balls for the other half.'

With a last nod and a wave, Marlowe started down the path towards his BMW, currently parked on the verge.

'Take care, Tom,' Declan finished with a smile. 'Don't ever end up in my crosshairs.'

'It's when you end up in mine, you need to worry,' Tom smiled back as he climbed into his car, and Declan felt that this was more a warning than a jocular reply. And as the car drove off, back towards London, Declan entered his house, closing the door behind him.

Monroe was on the stairs.

'He gone?' he asked. Declan nodded.

'He explain who he was?' Monroe continued. Declan nodded again.

'If you want to talk about it, I'm here,' he replied. 'Especially the marriage part.'

Monroe groaned at this. 'Bloody rumour'll be all over the Met by tomorrow, with your sodding knack for keeping secrets,' he muttered. 'Thank God Kendis is gone, or it'd be on the front—'

He stopped, his eyes widening.

'God laddie, I'm sorry.'

'It's okay,' Declan picked up Marlowe's mug of coffee, walking it into the kitchen as he spoke. 'But I do want to know what the hell happened.'

'Just what you think happened,' Monroe followed him into the kitchen. 'Me and Emilia fell in love on the job. We had a fling, ended up getting married. We were seeing things every day that made us wonder how long we had on this earth, seeing people snap out of existence like that. And then one day she was gone.'

'What do you mean, gone?'

Monroe poured himself a glass of water from the tap and sipped it before replying.

'Marlowe's mother was a spook that we worked with. She died.'

'At the 7/7 bombings. Marlowe mentioned that.'

'Emilia and Olivia were close. Very close. With hindsight, I'd even say they were having an affair, but I didn't see it. And then when Olivia died, Emilia changed. We had problems, but then name me a marriage that doesn't. We were in too deep with Lucas by then, and Derek Salmon was off the rails big time, we had a massive barney about this and then the next day Emilia was simply gone.'

He finished the glass, as if using the time to plan the next sentence.

'I learned later that she'd accepted a Whitehall position to run a deep-ops organisation, effectively replacing Olivia, and in the process had her entire identity scrubbed. To keep her loved ones safe, if you can believe that spook bollocks. I came home to find everything connected to her gone, even the photos. She didn't turn up to work, and when Patrick checked in to why, he was told we'd never had a DS Wintergreen working with us. Even the file notes were altered. And just like that, I was un-married.'

He looked to the sink.

'Spooks,' he spat the word like a curse. 'A pox on the lot of them.'

Declan wanted to mention the USB drive, but Jess entered the kitchen at that point.

'Have you asked him?' she asked Monroe, who forced a smile back at her.

'Not yet,' he said, looking back to Declan. 'I was going to go home, as unlike every other bugger here I didn't book a room at the resident bloody hotel, and now the rooms are all gone.' He filled the glass again. 'And I'll be honest, I'm finding it hard to be here. I'm still not sure that I want to stay on once this all finishes. Even if the Last Chance Saloon continues after this case, we're higher profile now. They'll want someone in above me, a Detective Superintendent, and I don't play well with others.'

'If you need to leave, I totally understand,' Declan replied, but Monroe shook his head.

'I'm going to help, but at a distance,' he explained. 'Get out of your way. I've booked a flight tomorrow to Berlin, and I'm going to check into our German cop friend, his mad bastard dad, and your mechanic buddy.'

'Are you sure?' Declan frowned. 'I mean, you had a concussion—'

'Christ, laddie, I'm not an invalid!' Monroe snapped. 'And besides, I won't be alone. I've called for backup.'

Monroe didn't elaborate, and so Declan didn't ask any further questions.

'As long as you're sure,' he finished. 'What time's the flight?'

'Stupidly early in the morning,' Monroe smiled. 'I'll take my leave tonight and be there by first thing.'

'Well, you can stay for dinner first,' Declan insisted. 'If only to tell me what you gathered from my dad's secret study.'

'I'll tell you what I gathered,' Monroe laughed. 'I gathered that Patrick had some serious trust issues at the end.'

Declan laughed back at this, but at the same time there was a weighing down of the USB drive in his pocket.

What was on it, and what did it say about Monroe?

BILLY WAS ALONE IN THE LIBRARY WHEN DAVE THE LANDLORD walked in.

'Don't mind me,' he said as he gathered up the dirty plates. 'Just cleaning up the lunch rush.'

'No worries,' Billy smiled as he carried on working. Dave walked around the table, picking up plates and glasses, but paused as he reached Billy, staring down at the file on the table beside him. A photo of Nathanial Wing stared up at him.

'That the kid who died on the golf green?' he asked. Billy looked up.

'I'm sorry, but we can't talk about active investigations,' he replied apologetically. 'Unless you have anything that can be used—'

'I might, actually,' Dave had placed the plates down now, picking up the photo and staring hard at it. 'Yeah, it's him.'

'What do you mean?' Billy, now interested, turned to face Dave who placed the photo down.

'That lad was in the pub a few days back,' he replied.

'You remember everyone who comes into your pub?' Billy was impressed, but Dave shook his head.

'Not like that,' he said. 'I mean, I remember watching him as he didn't look eighteen, but he didn't order anything. It was more who he met with.'

Billy felt like he already knew the answer to the next question, but he asked it anyway. 'You're telling me that a day or so before his death, Nathanial Wing met with someone in your bar?'

'Yup.'

'Who?'

Dave had grabbed the plates again and was already walking to the door as he spoke.

'The German police officer, Müller,' he finished. 'They met for a couple of minutes, and then the kid left after some heated words. I didn't hear what they were, but the German shouted out something as he left. Something like *tag send gezalt*.' He smiled. 'I don't know what it meant, but I remember thinking he'd sneezed on the last word.'

As Dave left with the dirty plates, Billy started checking the words through a German to English filter on his laptop. After a few tries, he found what he was looking for.

Tage Sind Gezählt

Billy stared in shock at the translation next to the three German words.

Days Are Numbered

His hand trembling, Billy picked up his phone and called Declan.

'Guv?' He said when it was answered. 'I think you need to come back to the Library. I think we have a lead.'

14

WHEELER STEALER

By the time Declan, Monroe and Jess had arrived back at the Library, Billy was already deep in conversation with Doctor Marcos.

'What do we have?' Declan asked. Billy showed his screen, and so Declan and the others joined Doctor Marcos at the table. On the screen was CCTV footage of the bar.

'Our landlord friend was kind enough to give me this footage,' Billy said as he returned the footage to the start. 'Taken the night before Nathanial Wing died, so we're looking at around twenty-four hours before his murder.'

On the screen was the bar, and several tables were in view. At the bottom right however was Rolfe Müller, sitting on his own, and reading a book.

'He's like that for about fifteen minutes,' Billy explained. 'Doesn't order a drink, just sits and reads. And then around seven twenty...' he slid the viewing slider along, and the scene jumped slightly as Nathanial Wing now walked into the bar in the top left-hand corner.

'Watch,' Billy said as, on the screen, Wing walked directly over to Rolfe's table.

'He knew exactly where to go,' Monroe mused. 'Didn't even look around.'

On the screen Wing and Müller exchanged words, Wing still standing. Then, after about twenty seconds, Wing sat down opposite the German detective.

'We don't have sound, but we have body language,' Doctor Marcos added here. 'Nathanial Wing is nervous, agitated. Even through this camera we can see that he's fidgeting, filled with nervous energy. Müller on the other hand is calm, relaxed. He's not surprised to see Nathanial.'

'They know each other,' Declan rubbed at his chin. 'Why do they know each other?'

'Maybe Müller is the German that the other kids heard talking to him?' Jess suggested. Absently, Declan nodded as, on the screen, the two men leaned in, deep in discussion. And then, as quickly as it started, it was over as Nathanial Wing rose from the chair, still talking to Müller, slamming something down onto the table.

'What's that?' Declan asked. 'Can we zoom in?'

'We've had this talk before,' Billy admonished. 'We're not the movies. All I can make out is that it's a chit, or a coin of some kind.'

'Maybe we should get one of the movie guys then,' Monroe muttered.

'Go wild,' Billy replied as on the screen Nathanial Wing walked off as Rolfe Müller shouted after him. 'They cost way more than me. Oh, here's where he shouts out in German that Wing's time is numbered.'

On the screen Ilse Müller appeared in the bottom right

corner, walking to the table as Rolfe quickly pocketed whatever Nathanial Wing had left. She sat facing her brother as Declan paused the footage.

'Go back,' he ordered. 'To where Wing rises.'

Billy did so, and on screen Nathanial Wing did the same as he had before, but this time Declan noted something else.

'There,' he paused the recording. 'He's looking off to the bottom right before he rises and leaves. I think he sees Ilse entering and leaves before she can speak to him.'

Playing the recording again, the team watched as Nathanial Wing rose, placed the whatever onto the table and left, as Ilse returned.

'They sit together for five minutes and then she too leaves,' Billy said, speeding through the footage until on the screen Ilse rose, walking away from the table.

'She's angry with him,' Doctor Marcos commented. 'Body language is tight, tense. She's expecting a fight.'

There was a moment as Rolfe watched her, and then he picked up his book and read—

'Stop,' Declan snapped, tapping the space bar to do just that as he spoke. 'Look.'

In the top right corner, another figure could be seen walking after Ilse as she left.

'That's Karl Schnitter,' Declan hissed. 'I'd recognise him anywhere. And I know he drinks in there most nights.'

'Could be coincidence,' Monroe pursed his lips as he considered this. 'Or, there's something more going on.'

'We need to speak to Karl,' Declan looked to the door. 'I could get Anjli to—'

'She's already interviewing,' Doctor Marcos said. 'And we need to speak to Müller too.'

'I'll do that,' Monroe inserted. 'From what we've already seen, Müller's arrogant and a stickler for rules.'

'How do we know that?' Billy asked.

'He believed we should share everything with him, but wouldn't force the issue when you said you couldn't,' Declan replied. Monroe nodded at this.

'He sees himself as an equal to Declan, as he's the equivalent in rank. So let's see what he does when a Detective Chief Inspector has a word.'

'You talk to Rolfe, and I'll go talk to Karl,' Declan suggested, already texting the German mechanic to see where he was right then.

'*We'll* go talk to Karl,' Doctor Marcos interjected. 'He's an old friend of yours, and you might find yourself swayed by that. If I'm there, we'll ensure it's by the book.'

Declan almost went to contest this, but stopped himself. He knew Doctor Marcos was right.

'Anything from Anjli and De'Geer?' He asked. Billy shook his head.

'I'll keep you updated,' he replied. 'Go on, get out there and be detectives, while I tell your daughter that she really needs to reconsider her career choices.'

'Good luck with that one,' Declan laughed as he moved to the door.

KARL SCHNITTER HAD TWO GARAGES, BUT OFTEN WORKED OUT of the smaller one in Hurley Bottom, towards the Henley Road. And it was here that Declan and Doctor Marcos went to. It wasn't that far from the pub, but Declan still drove the Audi, mainly because he was too tired to bother walking.

'Did you know Monroe was married once?' he asked Doctor Marcos as they pulled up outside the garage.

'He's been married a couple of times,' Doctor Marcos replied with a smile. 'But then again, maybe I have too.'

'Have you?'

'You'll never know, my dear.'

Declan grinned as they walked towards the main entrance. 'More than once? Twice? Are you a Black Widow? I mean, if anyone knew how to off husbands without people knowing, it'd be—' he stopped as he pushed at the main door. 'That's odd. The door's usually open.'

Doctor Marcos pointed at the closed garage doors. 'Maybe he's not working here today?'

'I suppose so,' Declan said as a *crash*, the kind of crash that a toolbox of spanners tumbling to a concrete floor would make echoed around the inside of the building. Declan walked to the doors to the garage, hammering on them.

'Karl!' He shouted out. 'It's Declan! Open up!'

There was still no sound, and Declan banged on the door again. Hearing nothing, he looked around for something to gain height, so he could look through one of the top windows in the garage doors. Rolling a tyre to the door, he clambered up on it to peer through the window.

'Christ!' he shouted as he almost fell from the tyre, jumping down and running to the door. 'Help me get it open!'

He shoulder barged the door, but yelped in pain as his gunshot wound tore. Before he could try for a second time though, Doctor Marcos ran over with a crowbar and, jamming it into the space between door and frame, cracked the lock out of its mounting, smashing the door open.

'Come on!' Declan ran into the garage, and for the first time, Doctor Marcos could see what had caused his panic.

The garage had two ramps, with hydraulic lifts, so that they could lift cars over a dip in the ground. Here, mechanics could move freely underneath the cars as it held them in the air. And, on the left-hand side, a SUV had been placed onto the hydraulic lift and raised up to its full height, the top of the SUV almost scratching the top of the high garage ceiling. From wheels to floor, there was a height of about eight, nine feet.

And, at the back of the car, in his overalls, with a ratchet strap around his neck and hanging a foot off the ground, was Karl Schnitter.

'Quick!' Declan grabbed Karl's legs, taking the weight as Doctor Marcos ran to the control box, pressing the DOWN button. As the SUV lowered, Declan saw that someone had tied the small ratchet strap around the rear towbar of the SUV and, as it'd risen, it had pulled Karl up with it until he was hanging off the ground.

Declan saw the toolbox, the contents scattered across the floor.

'The killer might still be here!' he snapped as Doctor Marcos grabbed a length of pipe and looked around.

To Declan's surprise though, as they pulled the strap off Karl's throat, the German's eyes opened and he drew in a thick, raspy breath of air.

'*Huh-huh-huh*' was all he could say though as he grabbed at his throat, wide eyed and looking around, a mixture of relief at surviving and fear as he realised that whoever did this could still be here.

'It's me!' Declan said as Karl locked eyes. 'You're lucky we found you. A minute or two later and you'd be dead.'

Karl leaned over and coughed onto the concrete, the coughing bringing up bile and a small amount of liquid as he vomited. Eventually he lay back on the ground, staring up at the ceiling. Doctor Monroe was already on the phone, calling an ambulance as Declan rose, looking around. The back door to the garage was open, leading into the back corridor.

'Where does that go?' he asked urgently. 'Stay with me, Karl. Where does that go?'

'Buh-back door,' Karl croaked. Declan left Karl on the floor, grabbing the largest wrench that he could find and running to the door, moving into the back corridor and, more slowly now, inching his way to the right-hand turn at the end—

Which led to an open door, leading out to a space at the back of the garage. There was a ten foot high wire fence around the property, but there were enough palettes and parked up car chassis for someone to use one of them as an escape ladder. Whoever had run out of the door was long gone by now.

Returning to the garage, Declan saw that Doctor Marcos had opened the main doors and was now tending to Karl.

'You're bloody lucky,' she muttered as she examined the bruises now appearing around the throat. 'It'll hurt for a while but you'll survive. The ramp rises slowly, so your neck didn't have the sudden crack that most hangings have, and the ratchet stopped the strap from tightening all the way. So you still gained some amount of oxygen,' she said. 'But mark my words, you'd have died in minutes if we hadn't arrived, Who did this?'

'I do not know,' Karl croaked. 'I was kneeling, taking off the wheel of the SUV. I heard a noise, and then I felt something strike me, here.' He rubbed at his head. 'Next thing I know, I am laying here and Declan is about to give me the kiss of life.'

'Well, let's not go too far,' Declan smiled. 'I like you. But not that much.'

Karl laughed, but started to cry, large wracking sobs as the realisation of what happened finally connected with his brain. 'I almost died.'

'You should have died,' Declan looked around. 'Made to look like a suicide. They even kicked over the box there, to make it look like you kicked it away from you.'

He paused, looking back at Karl.

'Empty your pockets,' he ordered.

'They are overalls,' Karl whispered. 'I keep nothing in them.'

'Please, for me,' Declan insisted. In the distance he could hear the faint sound of ambulances approaching the garage. Slowly and with great effort, Karl checked his pockets, one by one, but stopped as he reached into his left side chest pocket. Slowly, and with great care, he pulled out a business card.

One with a Red Reaper on it.

With a yelp of fear, Karl tossed the card across the floor, where it was scooped up carefully by Doctor Marcos.

'Looks like the Red Reaper wanted you dead,' Declan said as he watched her examine it.

'It's the same as the others,' she confirmed as she placed it into a plastic bag. 'Looks the same cardstock and everything.'

Declan looked back to Karl.

'We're going to take you to hospital,' he said gently. 'We'll post a guard—'

'That will not stop him!' Karl snapped. 'He killed your mother in a hospital, remember?' He looked around. 'He's dead! We killed him!'

'Best not to say that to anyone else, yeah?' Doctor Marcos forced a smile. 'We'll be the ones checking whether that's true, but people might get confused with the whole 'I committed a murder' theme.'

Karl looked to Declan.

'Rolfe Müller and his sister,' he croaked. 'They have been following me.'

'And we're following them,' Declan said as the ambulance pulled up outside the garage. 'But you need to get better, okay?'

The EMTs moved into the garage now, kneeling either side of Karl as Declan stepped back. To the side, Doctor Marcos was already placing the ratchet and strap into a second clear bag, and examining the up and down controller.

'We need the fingerprint guys to check this,' she said, pulling out her phone. 'And by that I mean Joanna.'

As Doctor Marcos called DC Davey, Declan looked back to the open door at the rear of the garage. There was something about it, something he saw but didn't connect as he was running through. Now, with Karl being placed into an ambulance, an oxygen mask over his face and his eyes now shut, Declan walked to the door once more, being careful not to touch it, aware that he could contaminate the crime scene more than it had already been contaminated.

Now in the back corridor, he looked down to the end, where the corridor turned to the right and the outside. To his right were metal shelving racks, filled with a variety of items; five litre cans of oil, wheel hubs, even an alternator were placed randomly on these shelves. However, at the back of the top shelf, something caught his eye, and he grabbed a wooden step, most likely used by Karl to put things up on the shelf in the first place, moving aside some items to gain a better look at the item he'd seen briefly.

It was an iMac computer.

More specifically, Declan was pretty convinced that it was his *dad's* iMac computer. The one stolen from his house a couple of weeks ago.

Why the hell was it on Karl Schnitter's top shelf?

15

UNDERGROUND, OVERGROUND

MONROE THOUGHT THAT HE'D PICKED THE EASIER OF THE TWO jobs; after all, how hard was it to find a German police officer in a tiny village; but it turned out that this was far harder than he'd expected, as the man was a literal ghost.

Eventually, he gave up hunting for Rolfe Müller, deciding that he'd simply wait for the man to return to the hotel, but by now he was outside St Mary The Virgin, and so he went to visit an old friend.

'Sorry I didn't come to the funeral,' he said to Patrick Walsh's gravestone. 'I didn't think you'd really want me there, what with how we ended on things.'

He paused, as if expecting a reply from the grave itself.

'I'm doing my best with the boy,' he continued, looking out across the churchyard. 'He's a damned good detective, you know. He's done you proud. Better than the pair of us. Better than me, definitely.' He paused, taking a deep breath of the clear afternoon air.

'I saw your secret room,' he continued. 'Jesus, Patrick, you should have called. You knew I'd help you if you needed it.

You should have told me about Christine.' He lowered his head, looking to the older gravestone to the left, that of Christine Walsh.

'But I can understand why you wouldn't,' he said softly. 'We're trying to find who killed you, and we will bring them to justice, but if you are up there, watching down on this, we could do with a little help. In particular, finding a runty little German chap who's given me the bloody slip.'

He sighed, looking out across the churchyard again. The last time he'd been in here was Christine's funeral, years earlier. He hadn't entered the churchyard during Patrick's funeral, he'd simply waited for Declan in the car park, ambushing the grieving son as he left his father's last resting place.

'A sign would be great right now,' he whispered.

There was a movement out of the corner of his eye, towards the south-eastern corner of the churchyard. Looking up, Monroe couldn't believe his eyes.

It was Rolfe Müller, heading towards the remains of the old priory next door.

'That was bloody impressive,' Monroe said to the gravestone as he left it, following Müller at a distance, passing through the hedgerow that led to the grounds next door, and the remains of Hurley Priory; in particular the crypt that was not only once underneath it, but still in existence, hundreds of years later. It was more commonly known as Old Ladye Place Crypt, and it was where the ghost of the Grey Lady was supposed to haunt. Well, *one* of them, anyway. The village seemed to be infected with bloody Grey Lady ghosts.

Entering the crypt itself was easy; the building that had been above it was long gone now, and the ruined crypt, although covered, was open to the elements in several places.

It was built as most crypts were; pillars in the ground arched up to the ceiling, creating effective and open arched passages, about eight feet high at the apex. Once known as 'the vault', there were several spaces, all connected by pillars, with gaps of around twelve feet or more between them. It smelled of mildew, of wet stone, and Monroe had to force himself not to sneeze as he entered it. He didn't need a torch, as the light from outside was shining through, and it was easy to see about. In fact, this felt more akin to standing under a bridge than it did standing in a crypt.

In the corner, Rolfe Müller was watching him.

'I come here twice a day,' he said. 'Such a forgotten place, with such history. It is beautiful, is it not, *Detective Chief Inspector Monroe?*'

Monroe was impressed at Rolfe Müller's knowledge of his identity, but assumed that this had come from simple homework rather than anything else. 'I don't know the history here,' he admitted.

Unsurprised, Müller waved a hand around.

'This was where they plotted to bring William of Orange to England, to create a new king in a bloodless coup,' he said. 'It is also where Princess Edith, sister of King Edward the Confessor was buried, when this was a Benedictine Priory.'

'Oh aye?' Monroe was mildly impressed by this. 'Do we know where?'

'No,' Müller shook his head. 'Maybe where you stand right now. There is supposed to be a tunnel here too, one that goes directly to The Olde Bell.'

'Why would you need a secret tunnel here?'

Müller shrugged. 'If you plan to overthrow a king, perhaps you need to keep your arrival secret?' he looked around. 'I have searched here several times, but cannot find the tunnel. I think it is a myth, a joke to play with tourists. Is there a reason you followed me here, Detective Chief Inspector?'

'Aye,' Monroe nodded. 'We have some questions for you. I know you've been interested in our case, and by now you know what we're doing.'

'Investigating the death of Nathanial Wing,' Müller replied. 'I assume you want to know why I met with him a day before he died.'

This surprised Monroe. He'd expected Müller to be evasive, not jump directly to the point. 'Aye, I would laddie,' he said. 'Maybe we could leave this bloody place too while we talk? It damn near gives me the creeps.'

Müller smiled and left the crypt with Monroe, walking back into the churchyard.

'It was to do with my case,' he explained.

'And what exactly is your case again?' Monroe pressed. 'I heard something about a war criminal.'

'That is correct,' Müller seemed unconcerned still. It was irritating Monroe. 'A man who killed many people during his time as a border guard.'

'Border guard, or border *Captain*?' Monroe asked. 'I mean, I believe your father, Wilhelm Müller, has been missing for a few years now. Are you hunting *him*?'

This shook Müller, and Monroe saw the slight twitch of an eyelid as he stayed silent.

Aye, you wee little bugger; we do our research too.

Encouraged, Monroe pushed on. 'And are you really on an international case, or are you just AWOL? Absent without leave, eh, laddie? You gone off the reservation here? If I was to speak to your superiors in Berlin, would I find you were on administrational leave, or holiday perhaps?'

'Good luck with that,' Müller simply stated. 'It is very hard to speak to my superiors by phone or email.'

'I wouldn't worry about that,' Monroe grinned. 'I'll be in Berlin myself tomorrow, so I'll go speak to them personally.'

Müller hadn't been expecting this answer, and he faltered as he replied. 'I am no threat to your investigation.'

'Yeah? Then prove it,' Monroe snapped. 'Tell me why you spoke to Nathanial Wing, and more importantly told him that his days were numbered, less than a day before he died.'

Rolfe Müller thought about this before replying.

'You are a superior officer, and I respect that,' he spoke carefully. 'So I will explain, as I can see why that could look incriminating. But, be aware that my investigation is different to yours.' He stopped, as if working out the words. 'I had been led to Mister Wing by a source that claimed that he was a computer expert. A man who could hack into hard drives. And I had a hard drive that needed to be unlocked.'

'Whose?'

Müller ignored the question. 'He promised repeatedly that he could do this, but constantly let me down. On the night we spoke, he demanded more money, and told me he had another buyer. I said he would get it, only if he hurried with the task in hand. I told him he was running out of time, because we return to Germany soon.'

Monroe considered this.

'And where were you and your sister the night Nathanial Wing died?' he asked.

'I was in my room, reading,' Müller replied calmly. 'My sister was out. She likes to walk along the Thames. She finds that this soothes her.'

'So neither of you have alibis or witnesses?'

'Are we suspects here, Detective Chief Inspector?' Müller was still calm as he asked. Monroe nodded.

'Aye, laddie. I think you both are,' he said. 'And your whole reason for being here seems a little suss.'

'Let me give you a hypothetical situation then,' Müller replied. 'Do you have a father who is still alive?'

'I do,' Monroe answered. 'Lives in Glasgow. We don't see each other much, he's in his eighties, doesn't travel well. Phone calls every couple of weeks, Christmas cards and birthday wishes, nothing more really. Why?'

'Imagine that one day, your father disappears. Not die, but simply vanish. And now it has been years. You learn that he may have taken a new identity, maybe even been murdered, and they give you names to investigate. Would you do it?'

'Of course.'

'Say your superiors tell you not to, that there is no case. Would you take matters into your own hands?'

'Well, yes,' Monroe replied. 'But let me give you another hypothetical question. Your father disappears, and when you look into him, you learn he was a monster, a serial killer who would force people into killing themselves. Would you still investigate this?'

'My father was not the Ampelmännchen Killer,' Müller stated. 'That is what we call him in Germany.'

'Are you sure?' Monroe insisted. 'The world's filled with sons and daughters who didn't know the truth about their parents. Perhaps your sister disagrees with you on that?'

'Why would you think that?'

'You're often seen arguing.'

Müller shrugged. 'So we argue, that is not a crime. She and I, we learned when my mother died that we are not brother and sister, that our mother had an affair. She told us on her deathbed.'

'That's harsh.'

'That was our mother, Detective Chief Inspector.'

'So which of you's the bastard?' Monroe asked more jovially than the words suggested.

'We never found out,' Müller replied, staring down at a gravestone. 'We chose to live with the ignorance. That way our father is still our father.'

'Did your father know about this?' Monroe leaned against a statue of an angel as he spoke the question. 'I mean, if I found out my wife was having an affair, I'd be pretty pissed off.'

'My father was a good detective,' Müller replied. 'I would assume he knew.'

Monroe thought about this for a moment. 'Was Karl Meier the man she had the affair with?'

Rolfe Müller nodded. 'I believe so.'

'Jesus,' Monroe exhaled. 'That's a bloody tangled web right now.' He pulled out his phone as it beeped. Reading the message, he looked up.

'I know you couldn't give an answer to your whereabouts when Wing died, but what about an hour ago?' he asked. 'And, for that matter, your sister?'

'I was in the church, praying,' Müller calmly announced, as if this act would obviously make him seem more innocent. 'And I am not my sister's keeper.'

'Shame,' Monroe tutted. 'We'll need to find her. And you'll need to sit down and have a proper chat with us.'

'And why is that?' Müller was rattled. He didn't know what had been on the text message, and that he was in the dark here obviously affected him. Monroe placed his phone away.

'Because someone just tried to hang Karl Schnitter,' he said.

DECLAN HAD FOLLOWED THE AMBULANCE INTO MAIDENHEAD and St Mark's Hospital, with Doctor Marcos staying behind at the scene of the crime. He knew she was still banned from active crime scenes as a forensic examiner, but technically she was a witness, and she could tell DC Davey where to look.

He'd paced around the waiting room for a good half hour before the nurse had appeared informing him that Karl Schnitter was now stable, had a bruised larynx but wanted to speak to him. Declan followed her into a ward where, in a quiet side room, Karl was lying in a bed.

'He's sedated,' the nurse explained. 'Not, like *sedated* sedated, but enough to take the edge off.'

'Like he's high?'

'A little, yes,' the nurse continued. 'So he might be a little more relaxed than you'd expect from a man who recently cheated death.'

Entering the room, Declan saw Karl smiling at him from the bed.

'My saviour,' he croaked, the voice barely audible. There was nobody else in the room, but Declan moved to the side of the bed, pulling a chair behind him so that he could sit close to Karl.

'Can you remember anything else now?' He asked. Karl shook his head.

'I did not see my killer,' he whispered, and then giggled. 'The attempted killer, anyway. For I am not dead.'

'Karl, I need to ask a serious question, and I need a serious answer,' Declan continued, already regretting not waiting until Karl was clearer headed. 'In your garage, there was an iMac. My father's iMac. What were you doing with it?'

Karl shook his head. 'No, no, no,' he whispered. 'That was not the computer. That was the shell.'

'Shell? You mean outer casing?'

Karl nodded, his eyes closing as he spoke. 'Yes, casing. The hard drive, the computer itself was removed. I found it in a skip off the High Street.'

'Why did you have it then?'

'Because I wanted to find the hard drive,' Karl whispered. 'I thought the shell might help me find it. I guessed it was stolen by Rolfe.'

'Rolfe Müller? Why him?'

'Because he was hunting your father and I,' Karl's voice was softening, as if he was falling asleep. 'He believed your father had information on the Reaper.'

'And why would he think that?'

'Because I told his sister that,' Karl replied lazily. 'When she visited me two months ago.'

Declan raised his eyebrows in surprise at that. Rolfe and Ilse Müller had only been in Hurley a couple of weeks. If Ilse had arrived months earlier than that...

She would have been here the same time that his father died.

'Why did she visit you?' Declan asked. 'What did she want?'

But it was too late. The sedatives had performed their task, and Karl Schnitter was now snoring gently in the hospital bed. Declan leaned back, annoyed. If Karl had been telling the truth, then Rolfe and Ilse Müller could have been the ones that stole his father's computer. But more importantly, why had Ilse Müller visited Karl months before this arrival?

Declan rose from the chair and left the ward. Karl wasn't going anywhere, and he sure as hell wasn't going to be awake for a while. There were other places to go, and other people to interview.

But first he had to go visit some grieving parents.

16

NEW LEADS

'I'M VERY SORRY,' DECLAN SAID AS HE SAT ON THE WING FAMILY sofa. 'But I needed to ask questions.'

Nathanial Wing's parents looked uncomfortable as they sat opposite him. They'd been like that for five minutes now, since Declan turned up on their door, waving his warrant card and demanding to speak to them, informing them he didn't really care about public personas, and that hiding wouldn't solve anything.

'What sort of questions?' Wing senior, a Chinese man in his late thirties, his hair already thinning and shaved down to a two-length asked as he wrung his hands. Declan knew that they would have been worried about their son's shame getting out; that he'd killed himself over debt.

'Look,' he said, leaning forward. 'I'm not supposed to talk about active crime investigations, but you deserve the right to know. Your son didn't kill himself. That is, he committed suicide, but someone forced him to.'

'What?' Nathanial's mother, a slim, petite woman in a flowery dress looked horrified. 'Who did this to him?'

'That's what we're looking into,' Declan continued. 'We believe it's a killer who has struck before and has a long history of attacks across Europe.'

'But why our son?'

Declan shrugged. 'It could have simply been that he was in the wrong place at the wrong time,' he said. 'But, our investigations have brought up two lines of enquiry. The first is that your son was in extreme debt.'

The Wing parents looked at each other at this, and Wing senior started wringing his hands again. Declan continued on.

'The second line is that before he died, he was talking with a German, someone who was pressuring him.'

'The police officer,' Wing senior replied. 'He was here several times, talking with our son.'

'Müller?' Declan asked, surprised. 'He was here?'

Mrs Wing nodded. 'He would visit Nathanial in his room,' she explained. 'Nathanial was trying to open a hard drive for him.'

'Do you know what the hard drive had on it?'

Wing senior shook his head. 'Nathanial would never talk to us about it. He just sat in his room, working on it.'

'I'll need to see this,' Declan insisted, and Mrs Wing rose, indicating for him to follow, leading him up the stairs and to Nathanial Wing's room.

It wasn't a traditional teenager's room; Declan remembered his own bedroom from his youth, and his walls were covered with pop star and footballer posters, and shelves of videos and books over a homework desk. Declan knew video cassettes were mainly a thing of the past, but the scarcity of the bedroom surprised him.

The walls were white, the bedclothes pale grey. The desk

was pine, with a PC gaming tower under the right-hand side. There was a large monitor on the desk, but not much else. There were no posters on the wall; instead there was a single framed print, a painting of a man, staring out over a foggy landscape. Declan recognised this. It was *Wanderer above the Sea of Fog* by the German artist Caspar David Friedrich. He'd owned a print of this himself when he was younger.

On the desk was a keyboard, a hard drive connected to a wire, with a small soldering kit beside it. Declan assumed that this was the hard drive that Nathanial' had been told to hack.

'Do you know how far he went with this?' he asked. Mrs Wing looked back down the stairs, as if scared her husband would hear.

'He opened it,' she replied softly, so as not to carry her voice downstairs. 'He told me a couple of days before he...' she broke off in a sob.

'Then why did he tell Müller that he hadn't?' Declan asked, confused now.

'Because the other German told him to keep quiet,' Mrs Wing added. 'Even paid him to keep silent.'

'Other German? You mean Karl Schnitter?'

Mrs Wing shook her head. 'No, the woman.'

Declan stared down at the hard drive. 'Did she take a copy of what was on the drive?' he asked. Mrs Wing nodded. 'In that case I'll need to take that with me.'

Carefully, he pulled the hard drive from the connecting cable, holding it gingerly in his hand. He didn't know if shaking it or even moving it would cause damage, so until he passed it to Billy, he would hold it with kid gloves.

'Did the woman visit often?' he asked as they walked down the stairs. Mrs Wing shook her head.

'Just the once,' she replied. 'The day before he disappeared.'

So, the same day that Rolfe shouted at him.

'Thank you for all your help,' he said to the grieving parents as he stood in the doorway. 'We will find who did this, and we will bring them to justice.'

'It won't bring back Nathanial,' Wing senior muttered, and Declan nodded. He understood the anger. The Red Reaper had taken their son, just like they'd taken his parents.

But now he had even less of a clue who the Red Reaper was.

BILLY HAD TAKEN THE HARD DRIVE FROM DECLAN AND PLACED it onto the table, pulling some cables from a bag beside his chair and connecting it to the laptop. As he did this, lines of numbers ran up the screen in the terminal app as he typed furiously. Declan felt he was in *The Matrix*.

'The drive is wiped,' Billy said as he worked through the boot drive. 'It's an iMac OSX, but I can't find any personal information on it. It might have been your father's, it might not. We can compare it to the iMac, see if that gives us any more information, and I can check with Apple whether the serials are marked down anywhere, but that could take days.'

'Why wipe the drive?' Declan sat in the chair beside Billy, frowning. 'Did Ilse order it done after gaining a copy, or was it wiped beforehand?'

'Your father could have factory reset it,' Billy suggested. 'I mean, he has a secret room and USBs hidden in books, so he was quite security conscious.'

The door opened and Monroe walked in.

'I just had an enlightening meeting with our German friend,' he announced as he placed a notebook on the table. 'Seems that brother and sister aren't quite brother and sister.'

"We need to call everyone in,' Declan suggested. 'I think our list of suspects has increased.'

Billy checked his screen. 'Doctor Marcos and DC Davey are on their way back right now, so they'll be here in a few minutes,' he said. 'Anjli, De'Geer and Jess are in the bar.'

'Drinking?'

'Going over every minute of CCTV that The Olde Bell has,' Billy smiled. 'They're hoping that something new might turn up.'

'Call them in,' Monroe added. 'It's time for a catch up.'

It was a few minutes before everyone returned to the Library. Anjli and De'Geer had come up with nothing when visiting the Brunel family; all they had was confusion why Dotty Brunel would kill herself. They couldn't even fathom how this was a murder case, and so Anjli and De'Geer had quietly diverted the questioning, making it sound more like a simple follow up.

Doctor Marcos also had a similar lack of news; there were no fingerprints on the ratchet, the strap, the buttons to raise the ramp or on the large spanner that had been cast to the floor, and most likely struck the unsuspecting Karl Schnitter. It was as if nobody else outside of Karl had been in there which was exactly as previous victims had been found.

Monroe had explained about his conversation with Rolfe Müller, while Declan had explained about his finding of the empty iMac in Karl's garage, the conversation with the drugged Karl, and the appearance of the hard drive at Nathanial Wing's house. This done, Declan walked over to the portable whiteboard that was usually provided for workshops, and had now been converted into a makeshift crime board.

'I think we need to add a new suspect to the list,' Declan explained. 'We have two timelines we need to think about, and we've been using data from the first for the second.' He drew a vertical line down the middle of the board. 'On the left, we have Red Reaper cases until 2012, and my mum's death five years ago.' He started writing on the left-hand side.

'We know that the killer, or at least the believed killer was male, German, brown haired. He flipped a coin before the murders happened, and that he forced the victims to kill themselves, before placing a calling card on their person, and usually removing the item that caused the death.'

'We also know that Wilhelm Müller did a similar thing with a coin in East Berlin,' Anjli nodded. Declan now moved to the right-hand side.

'Now *here*, we have murders after my mum's death.'

'Why start there?' Jess asked. Declan showed the line.

'Because this is possibly where your granddad killed Wilhelm Müller,' he said. 'And if Müller was the Red Reaper, then this is where the murders by him would have stopped.'

'You've got a subdivision there, then,' Monroe added. 'Because we can't for certain say that Wilhelm Müller is dead.'

'True,' Declan wrote WILHELM on the board. 'There's every chance that my dad didn't execute him, and that he was set free, given another chance. I don't think this is that likely, though. I would have thought that he would have contacted his kids within the years between.'

'Maybe he has,' De'Geer offered. 'Maybe they're keeping that quiet.'

'I'm not sure,' Monroe said. 'Rolfe Müller seemed quite adamant that daddy hadn't been around for a while.'

'Wilhelm aside, we have two other suspects, both under the copycat heading,' Declan continued, writing both ROLFE and KARL on the board. 'Rolfe could be continuing the mission, as he was in contact with Nathanial Wing and had every opportunity to kill him. He also, as Wilhelm's son may have known about his father's hobby, and even knew where the calling cards were kept.'

'The *reaper* in Karl's pocket was the same cardstock as Wing's,' Doctor Marcos added. 'Which means it's the same as the earlier murders.'

'The problem with Rolfe, though, is that he wasn't around a couple of months back when my father died,' Declan added. 'Which means we have a discrepancy there.'

'I'm checking his passport right now to see if he hadn't popped across with his sister,' Billy was typing as he spoke.

'Sister?' Anjli asked, Declan nodded.

'We'll get to that in a minute,' he replied, tapping at the KARL written on the board. 'The other suspect is Karl Schnitter. Wintergreen fancied him for the original Red Reaper but wouldn't say why, and he has his own supply of secrets. He could easily have been the killer, and could have been the person who met with my dad and arranged for his crash.'

'Apart from the fact that someone tried to kill him today,' Billy said.

'True, but there's still something going on here,' Declan said. 'For a start, he had what looks like my dad's stolen iMac in his garage. And second, he met with Ilse Müller a couple of months back.'

'Ilse was in the village before?' Jess rested an arm on the table as she turned to look at her dad. 'Why?'

'Well, that's where the soap opera aspect of this tale starts,' Monroe smiled. 'Seems that Rolfe and Ilse are only half siblings. One of them results from an affair between Mrs Müller and *A N Other*, a few years before the fall of the Berlin Wall.'

'When Karl Meier worked under Hauptmann Müller,' Anjli noted. 'Christ, is *he* the daddy?'

'Possibly,' Monroe replied. 'Now, Rolfe reckons they decided to not test themselves, as that way they'd never have to face who wasn't the legitimate Müller, but to be honest they don't seem to be best friends, and there's every reason to suspect that Ilse might not have kept to the same memo there.'

'Ilse visited Karl Schnitter a couple of months ago,' Declan said to Anjli now. 'He told me while in hospital. He didn't say why, but it gives us two possible leads. First, that Karl might be Ilse's dad, and we need to know how that works into things. But it means that she was around Hurley the night my father died.'

'Ilse worked for a pharmaceutical company before she joined Rolfe,' Doctor Marcos was writing on a sheet of paper as she spoke, working through a list of compounds. 'She would have been working for them two months ago. We don't know why she was fired, but it could be because of stolen supplies.'

'Like what?'

'Potassium chloride is a possible,' DC Davey suggested. 'It causes heart attacks.'

'That's on my list too, but you'd need about half a kilo,' Doctor Marcos agreed. 'There are ways to concentrate it though, and if she met with Patrick at the Dew Drop Inn, she could have spiked his drink. Add the rain, the roads...'

'But surely the Red Reaper is a man?' Jess asked now. 'The witnesses—'

'Are all before Wilhelm's possible death,' Declan replied. 'You said they heard a German speaking to Nathanial Wing, and we assumed it was the same person, but that could have been a call related to Rolfe's hiring of him to hack the hard drive. There're no witnesses for any of the murders after your grandmother.'

'Also,' Anjli mused, 'there's no reason the killer couldn't be a woman. Ilse's not exactly a wilting flower, and the deaths have been psychological. No struggle, no fight, and Wing killed himself.'

'And they struck Schnitter from behind,' Monroe sat back in his chair. 'Unconscious, it's very easy for a victim to be dragged to a ramp, have the ratchet wrapped around his neck and then a button pressed. Could easily have been a woman.'

Declan took the pen and wrote ILSE under the other two names.

'We need to find out what Ilse's game is here,' he ordered. 'She told Wing to delay telling her brother about this hard drive. Why? She visited Karl a couple of months ago, without Rolfe knowing. Why?'

'Reconnect with her real dad?' Billy offered.

'Then why try to kill him?' Anjli countered. Billy smiled.

'Looking at my family, I can totally feel her vibe there,' he said.

'Tonight we'll consider this.' Declan finished. 'Go home, or to your rooms, whatever. Take a break, we've done some outstanding work here today. Tomorrow DCI Monroe goes to Berlin—' he looked to Monroe as he continued '—and I think we need to know why Ilse was fired, whether Rolfe is AWOL from the force, and whether we can find out anything about an extra murder before the wall fell.'

'Another murder?' DC Davey asked.

'We're still missing a murder, I'm sure about it,' Declan explained. 'Nathanial Wing wasn't placed on the sixteenth green for convenience, as he could have walked to any of them without a problem. Sixteen is a message, and we just have to decipher it.'

'I'll work with Joanna to see if we can deduce which of the kiddies is the bastard,' Doctor Marcos said. 'We can't use DNA of Wilhelm, but we now have a lot of Karl's. If both don't match, we'll know that's a dead end.'

'Good plan,' Declan nodded. 'Let's get as much as we can before we start the next wave of enquiries. Until then, stand down.'

'You heard the man,' Monroe rose from his chair. 'Let's go grab a drink. I have a flight tomorrow and there's no way I'm flying completely sober.'

17

DARK BEFORE DAWN

It was late by the time Declan and Jess returned to the house. They'd stayed at the pub for dinner, but it had been a long day and so they'd left the others and walked back through Hurley. It was a quiet, cool night, but the sky was clear and the wind was light as they walked down the half-lit streets.

'Dad,' Jess asked after a few minutes of silence. 'How do you do it?'

'Do what?' Declan asked, looking at her.

'Compartmentalise this,' Jess answered. 'I mean, I've seen crime photos. I've watched films with gory scenes—'

'And how have you done that, considering you're not eighteen?'

'Look, I'm being serious. I've seen terrible things out there, but this afternoon I had a tightness in my chest, like I was having a panic attack.' Jess looked at Declan, and he could see the trouble etched deep into her face. 'I had to get some air outside. When I calmed down, I realised it was connected to the case. To Nate.'

'That's why you're feeling this,' Declan said as he opened the door to the house, allowing Jess to enter first. 'He's not Nathanial Wing to you anymore. He's 'Nate'. The friends that you spoke to humanised him, gave him a personality, a past. He's not just a statistic now.'

He walked into the kitchen, flicking the kettle on as Jess followed.

'Yeah, but you do the same,' she said. 'You speak to the parents, you gain an idea about how the victim lived, you enter their head when working out what happened. I mean God, dad, look at Kendis Taylor. She was your first love!'

Declan paused as he placed tea bags into mugs. One normal bag for him, one herbal for Jess.

'Yeah, Kendis and I were close,' he replied, not looking at Jess as he spoke, forcing his emotions back down. 'And that was hard. I was ill, violently ill when I saw her body. I had an anger; when I knew that Malcolm Gladwell was her killer, it took every piece of self restraint that I could muster to stop myself killing him.'

'What happens when we solve this case?' Jess asked, walking to the counter and taking over tea making duties. 'Because you're going to be facing the man or woman who killed your parents. My grandparents.'

'What would *you* do?' Declan turned the question onto Jess now. 'What would you want *me* to do to them?'

Jess sat silent for a moment as she thought about the question.

'I'd want you to flip the coin,' she whispered. Declan nodded at this.

'And that's the problem,' he replied. 'I want justice. You, however, want vengeance.'

'And you don't?' Jess stirred the mugs now, allowing the

tea bags to soak into the hot water, keeping her attention fully on the task. Declan could see however that she was shaking as she did this; whether from shock or anger, he couldn't tell.

'Of course I do,' Declan passed Jess her mug and took her by the shoulder, grabbing his own mug as he did so, leading her back into the living room and the sofa. 'But you have to remember, you're fifteen—'

'Almost sixteen.'

'You're almost sixteen, and you've not seen this world properly before. All you saw are crime documentaries and old case notes. I've been living this life since I was eighteen and in the army. That's over twenty years of this, both in the Military Police and in the Met and City police.' He sipped at his own tea as he tried to frame his next response.

'You granddad hated it so much that he quit,' he continued. 'I almost quit too, several times over the years. '

'You were almost fired several times too,' Jess forced a smile. Declan joined her.

'A lot of that was because of my frustrations,' he admitted. 'And if you follow the family path and join up, you'll likely have those frustrations too.'

Jess nodded silently, staring into her herbal tea as she gently blew on it, sending small ripples across the surface.

'Mum doesn't want me to become a copper,' she eventually replied.

'Your mum's an intelligent woman,' Declan leaned back, sipping his own tea. 'And I think tomorrow you can have a day off.'

'You're benching me?' Jess almost spilled her tea as she spun to face her father. 'Come on! That's crappy!'

'No,' Declan stared at the ceiling. 'I'm just limiting your exposure to all this... all this police shit,' he muttered. 'You're still a girl, Jess. You shouldn't be traipsing around crime scenes and talking to friends of the victim, you should be playing console games or watching TikTok videos.'

'I'm going to join up when I pass my A levels, dad.'

'You haven't even done your GCSEs. And then you'll be at University.'

Jess shook her head. 'I'm doing A Levels and then, when I've passed I'll do a Police Constable Degree Apprenticeship.'

Declan knew about the PCDA. Before they recently introduced it, any potential police officers had to complete a learning and development programme over two years before being signed off as ready to patrol the streets. In fact, this is what De'Geer had recently done. However, any wannabe constables could instead complete a three-year apprenticeship, the PCDA, which was equivalent to a bachelor's degree, with apprentices awarded a degree in professional policing practice and designated as fully qualified constables at the end. Which meant that in six years, Jessica Walsh would be a serving police officer.

Declan was a little proud of that.

'If you do, I'll ensure you get some glowing recommendations,' he said.

'I'd get better ones if I actually caught a serial killer,' Jess sulked.

'And your mum would murder me if I allowed that,' Declan laughed. Jess shrugged.

'Then I'll just solve that one then,' she replied.

Declan and Jess sipped at their teas silently.

'You can stay in the Library with Billy,' Declan eventually offered. 'Learning cybercrime is probably easy for you, anyway.'

'I'd rather be with Morten,' Jess muttered.

'I know,' Declan patted his daughter on the head. 'That's why you're with Billy.'

BILLY AND ANJLI WERE IN THE OLDE BELL'S MAIN BAR, HAVING recently finished their immense pub dinners. Doctor Marcos and DC Davey were back at Maidenhead going over forensics, De'Geer had gone home for the day and Monroe had returned to London to pack for his early morning flight to Germany.

'Tell me you don't miss this,' Anjli leaned back in her chair. 'I saw you on the computer today, asking questions and making suggestions. Why the hell would you go to Rufus Harrington?'

'It's a good job,' Billy protested. 'It's got stock options, and I'd be making a lot more than what I did as a Detective Constable.'

'You'd also be a lot more bored,' Anjli replied. 'Is this because you think it'll make your family like you again?'

'That boat's long sailed,' Billy sipped at a whisky and American ginger ale. 'I think I might enjoy boring, anyway.'

'Nobody enjoys boring.'

'They do if they don't die—' Billy stopped, mid response.

'Is that what this is?' Anjli asked, leaning forward now. 'Is it fear?'

'So what, I'm a wussbag now?' Billy looked away.

'Christ, no,' Anjli placed a hand on Billy's arm. 'It means you're probably suffering from PTSD.'

Billy nodded. 'Probably,' he whispered. 'I have a dream, a recurring one, where I'm being shot at. It's changed recently, but it's always the same locations. I'm outside Devington

House and I'm facing SCO 19. I'm in a warehouse and Frost and his guys are there. We're even in that training exercise.'

'All stressful situations,' Anjli admitted. 'And then what happens?'

'Declan appears,' Billy looked to the drink now. 'Declan appears and then he shoots me.'

Anjli sipped at a wine as she tried to work out what the hell she could say to that. Luckily for her, Billy continued.

'I know, he's the one that saved me,' he smiled faintly. 'Without him leaping in front of me, Frost would have killed me a week ago. But somewhere, deep in my subconscious, I blame him for this.'

'That's PTSD talking,' Anjli replied. 'It's looking for someone to blame. When in the end—'

'I should blame myself?' Billy snapped. 'Great talk.'

'You should,' Anjli snapped back. 'Take responsibility. I mean, you did when you were almost fired, so why not now? *You* did these things. *You* chose to be the Judas before I could offer. *You* ran in front of the SCO 19 response on your own accord at Devington House. You did these things because you're a good man, Billy. A genuine hero, and a credit to the badge.'

Billy nodded, but his expression still looked conflicted.

'Computers are safer,' he said.

'Tell that to Nathanial Wing.'

Billy looked to Anjli, but stopped.

'Remember, I'm just the tech guy,' he whispered.

Anjli went to ask what he meant by this, whether this was more of the argument they were having, but then saw Ilse Müller walking over to their table, a half pint of lager in her hand.

'Would you mind if I joined you?' she asked. 'My brother's

working and it's boring alone in my room.' She looked at Billy as she said this. Anjli hid a smile.

So barking up the wrong tree, love.

'Sure,' Billy was all smiles now. 'This is Detective Sergeant Kapoor. She's one of the officers doing the case in the Library.'

'Anjli, please,' she held out a hand. Ilse shook it.

'I'd give my own name, but I assume you already know it,' she smiled.

'As you probably knew mine.'

'Actually, I didn't,' Ilse's smile never slipped. 'My brother's the one for all of that.'

'You work for him, right?' Anjli asked. 'I have a sister, a couple of years older than me. The thought of working for her breaks me out in hives. A rash.'

Ilse nodded. 'It's not the easiest of jobs,' she replied. 'But I was a PA before this, and I've dealt with worse.'

'Police PA?'

'Pharmaceutical firm,' Ilse sipped from her lager. 'I prefer this though. Less travelling.'

'Ilse and her brother are hunting a war criminal,' Billy said excitedly, as if never having mentioned this before. Anjli raised her eyebrows.

'Really?' she asked, but Ilse's smile dropped.

'Please, let's not play these games,' she asked. 'You know why we're in Hurley, and I know why you're in Hurley. We should be helping each other, not hindering.'

'Okay, in that case, maybe you could answer a question for me?' Anjli asked.

Ilse nodded. 'Of course.'

'Why did you tell Nathanial Wing *not* to pass on his hard drive findings to your brother a day before he died?'

Ilse shifted uncomfortably in her chair. 'I didn't know the boy would kill himself.'

'Technically he didn't, but go on.'

Ilse looked around the bar, as if checking for her brother. 'Rolfe, he has a... what do you call it? A bee in his hat.'

'Bee in his bonnet?'

'Yes. He's obsessed with his father.'

'Hauptmann Müller.' Anjli asked.

'Yes.'

'The Reaper of the Berlin Wall.'

Ilse shook her head. 'I know the rumours, the stories,' she said. 'Wilhelm Müller wasn't the Reaper. These were lies, spread after the fall of the wall.'

'Why should someone do that?'

'Why would someone do anything?' Ilse shrugged. 'It was a terrible time. We were nothing more than babies, children even. We didn't see the people spitting at him, laughing at him, hating him for doing his job. Do you know what the Staatssicherheitsdienst, the Stasi, our secret police would have done to him if he hadn't followed his orders, no matter how abhorrent?' She shook her head. 'Wilhelm was a broken man. He was torn between honour and duty. When they burned the files he stole them, used them to ensure that terrible people were captured and punished. But he made enemies and had to leave. That's when Rolfe began this hero worship. He believed that Wilhelm Müller was out there hunting a killer, a noble quest in a way. But I worried what'd be found, if the hard drive he wanted opened revealed the truth.'

'Was it Patrick Walsh's hard drive?' Billy asked. Anjli knew Billy had already confirmed this, so looked to Ilse. To her surprise, the German woman nodded.

'Rolfe was consumed with hatred for one man. And that man was friends with Walsh.'

'Rolfe hates Karl Schnitter, doesn't he?' Anjli asked softly. 'He told my Detective Chief Inspector today that he believes that Karl's the man that had an affair with your mother.' She took a calculated gamble. 'The man that's your actual father.'

'How do you know that?' Ilse asked, genuinely surprised by this. Anjli shrugged.

'You mention your mother, but when you mention Müller, you say his name rather than call him father,' she explained. 'And, we know that a couple of months back, you visited Karl here in Hurley, without your brother. But I was under the assumption that you'd both kept it a mystery?'

Ilse nodded. 'I learned by accident,' she said. 'I found I had breast cancer, or I should say a tumour. It was removed, and I'm healthy, but I was told that it was the BRCA2 gene, and that it was hereditary, from either my father or mother.'

'But neither had it,' Anjli mused.

'No,' Ilse replied. 'And in doing the testing, I learned that although a DNA match of my mother, I wasn't a match of my father.'

'So why come here?' Billy asked. 'I mean, when you came the first time.'

'I needed permission to gain Karl Schnitter's DNA,' Ilse explained. 'I needed a... paternity test. And, as BCRA2 is a hereditary condition, I wanted him to get checked. It was never to bond with a stranger, to call him *Papa*.'

Anjli nodded at this, while a sliver of ice slid down her spine. Her own mother had been fighting breast cancer recently, and Anjli had also wondered whether the gene had passed on to her as well.

'So you learned Karl is your father, I'm guessing,' she said.

Ilse nodded. 'And I'm assuming that Rolfe meanwhile is on a vendetta against him.'

'I was a fool,' Ilse replied. 'I mentioned to my brother that I'd travelled to England with my company, but I'd forgotten he's a good detective. He learned I met with Karl, the man he had hunted for as Karl Meier, a guard who destroyed our family with an affair. Rolfe looked deeper into this, saw the same Red Reaper cases as you had. We call it a different name, but the result was the same. Rolfe came to England to face him and gain his revenge.'

'So why wait?' Billy asked. 'It's been two weeks.'

'Because my brother is thorough, and when he arrived, we learned that Patrick Walsh was dead,' Ilse sighed. 'Rolfe wanted concrete evidence. He believed that this'd be found on the hard drive.'

'Which he stole.'

'No,' Ilse shook her head. 'I don't know how he found it, but he didn't break into your friend's house. On the day of the theft, he was in London, following another lead.'

Anjli frowned at this. *If Rolfe Müller didn't steal the iMac, then Karl Schnitter was lying.* 'So why keep the information from him?'

Ilse turned and looked Anjli directly in the eye; it wasn't a power play, or a way to hide anything. In fact, it opened her up like a book as she spoke, the raw emotion showing in every word.

'Because if he knew what was on that hard drive, if he knew that Patrick Walsh and Karl Schnitter claimed they killed his father, I don't know how many people he would hurt, or even kill. But I know he would definitely take revenge on Karl, your Detective Inspector Walsh and his teenage daughter for Patrick Walsh's crime.'

MONROE HAD RETURNED HOME AND GATHERED TOGETHER enough items to last him a couple of days in Berlin, and the following morning he'd arrived at Heathrow Airport Terminal 5 bright and early for his morning flight to Brandenburg Airport. As he was only using hand luggage, his trip through check in and security was quite simple, and apart from a quick stop in the departure lounge duty free to buy some water and chocolate, he made it to the departure gate with plenty of time to spare.

A woman was waiting for him.

In her late fifties or early sixties, her short blonde hair peppered with flecks of grey, she wore a navy blue suit worn over a white blouse, a small cabin bag beside her and a neck pillow already in position.

'Thanks for coming,' Monroe smiled, shaking her hand. 'I'm probably okay and all that but with the concussion, I'm a little worried about being alone in a foreign country if I have a... well, you know.'

'Not a problem,' replied DCI Sophie Bullman, checking the departure gate screen. 'I'm between jobs now anyway.'

'Fired?'

'Christ no,' Bullman snorted. 'Promoted. But enough of that. Tell me, Alex... What damn fool adventure have you got me into *this* time?'

18

BERLIN STATION

IT WAS MIDMORNING BY THE TIME THAT MONROE AND BULLMAN reached Berlin; the Flughafen Express had brought them to downtown Berlin Hauptbahnhof, and from there they had paused on checking into a hotel, instead moving straight on to the headquarters of the Bundeskriminalamt, the federal police, on Treptower Park, a street lined avenue around four or five miles southeast of the train station.

The flight itself had been eventless, and was a chance for Monroe to explain what they had discovered so far during the case, as Bullman noted down the salient facts. Once done, Monroe had leaned back in the seat and watched out of the window. He'd offered Bullman the window seat, but she'd taken the aisle seat instead, saying that she had a hatred of having to ask people to move if she needed to stretch her legs. Monroe smiled, saying that he understood, while secretly wondering if this was because Bullman had a hatred of asking people for anything. Looking back to her, he cleared his throat, nervous to the question he was going to ask.

'Just get on with it,' she muttered while closing the book

that she was reading. 'I can just feel the urge to talk flowing out of you.'

'I just wondered how you were doing,' Monroe asked. 'I heard they had the DI White inquest.'

Detective Inspector White had been one of DCI Bullman's team in Birmingham, but had turned out to be corrupt, and had been the officer that gave the unconscious Monroe to Macca Byrne; a transaction that cost White his life and ended with Monroe waking up in a basement of a Manor House near Milton Keynes. Bullman had been unaware of this betrayal, but there had to be an investigation by an Anti-Corruption Unit to ensure there were no unseen connections between Bullman and White. And, when Malcolm Gladwell had been arrested, Bullman had returned to Birmingham to be interviewed.

'Just a formality,' Bullman leaned back in the seat. 'They had brought me in to cover maternity leave, so there was no connection between White and myself.'

'Good,' Monroe replied. 'You're too good an officer to lose.'

'Glad you think that,' Bullman replied, but the tone seemed off somehow, as if Bullman knew something that Monroe didn't. He almost went to reply, but decided that discretion was the better part of valour here.

'How are the headaches?' she asked, returning to the book, as if not that important a question to her. Monroe knew better though; she wasn't asking about his wellbeing, she was checking on how effective a partner he was going to be while in Berlin.

'Barely noticeable,' he admitted. 'Not the crushing pain that they used to be. Top of the bonce is still tender, and it weirdly hurts to wear a hat, but I've not had a crippling migraine in a week.'

'When do you have your next medical?'

'In a week,' Monroe looked back out of the window again, ensuring that Bullman couldn't see the concern on his face. 'If they see no improvement, there's a chance I'll be benched until retirement. Or, maybe even given early retirement on medical grounds.'

'Is that so bad?' Bullman placed a hand on Monroe's arm to bring his attention back into the plane. 'You could retire with honour, Alex. Take it easy.'

'I've seen retirement,' Monroe grumbled. 'Patrick Walsh told me it was the worst mistake he ever made. That and promotion.'

'What do you mean?' Bullman frowned. Monroe smiled, but it was faint, bittersweet.

'Admiral Kirk,' he replied.

'Oh, that.' Bullman crossed her arms as she stared at Monroe. 'Rosanna told me about this. Never liked *Star Trek*. Too fictional.'

'But the point still stands,' Monroe replied. 'He was never happier than when he was out there. And it's the same for me.'

'What if they offer you the role?'

Monroe laughed at this. 'Christ, I'd ask if they were that short staffed,' he said. 'Besides, they already spoke to me about this. I told them that if I *was* medically cleared I didn't want it and gave them a suggestion who they should speak to.'

Bullman stayed silent at this for a moment.

'You'd make a good Detective Superintendent,' she eventually said. Monroe shrugged.

'Not my path,' he replied, looking back out of the window. After a minute of staring, he looked back to Bullman, trying to get a read on her reaction to this.

She was already reading her book, their conversation already forgotten.

THE HEADQUARTERS OF THE BUNDESKRIMINALAMT WAS immense; more of a compound than a building, it comprised a series of three-storey red bricked buildings laid out in what felt like a small campus, with roads spider-webbed between each building, and a more functional concrete office block in the middle of a collection of long, narrow red ones. But the layout of the federal offices wasn't that important, as Monroe realised incredibly quickly, when the gate guard barred their entrance.

They would never see it.

'We have had orders to stop you entering the premises,' the guard explained with no hint of apology.

'But we're Detective Chief Inspectors in the United Kingdom Police Force!' Monroe exclaimed. 'We have a working relationship with the German Police! Who told you to bar us?'

'An order from the main office.' The guard tried not to, but the hint of a sneer crossed his face. 'It looks like your working relationship is not as close as you seem to think so. Things are not so smooth here after Brexit, eh?'

Monroe was about to argue the point when movement to his side distracted him; a woman had emerged from the building to their left and was now walking over to them. In her thirties, she was Asian, with short, spiky hair that completely contrasted with her black suit, while making her look twice as cool as either Monroe or Bullman. As she reached them, she held out a hand.

'Kriminalkommissar Margaret Li, of the Schwere und Organisierte Kriminalität,' she said as she shook Monroe's hand. 'I work with Rolfe Müller.'

'I'm guessing he's the one who told you not to let us in?' Monroe asked. 'Sounds about right, especially if you've got a guilty conscience.'

Margaret nodded.

'Actually, he said you are actively harassing him, while interfering with his case,' she explained as she lead them away from the gatehouse and back to the street. 'My superiors listen to every word that he says, and they believe what he says. Me? Not so much. Especially as he is not assigned to any cases right now.'

'So he *is* AWOL?' Monroe smiled. 'I bloody knew it.'

'Not so much that, more on duty but with his own autonomy,' Margaret explained. 'We did not realise he was in England until he called us.' She pointed north, up the street. 'Schlesischer Busch is just up there. It is a nice, small park, and they have a street van that sells coffee. It is a sunny day, good for a walk.'

'So we can't discuss the case?' Monroe muttered with exasperation. Bullman however nodded to Margaret.

'I think we are, Alex,' she said. 'In the only way she can.'

SCHLESISCHER BUSCH WAS ONE OF SEVERAL SMALL STATE PARKS in the area, and on paper was nothing more than a square of park with office buildings to the south and west, a busy road to the east and a canal to the north. However, once you entered the park, you could see that it was a warm, green area, with flowing paths and tree lined corners, a place where families could gather, and children played; but the first thing that Monroe saw when he entered it was a grafitti covered watchtower that loomed over the rest of the park, a stark reminder of a time long passed.

'That's the *Führungsstelle Schlesischer Busch*,' Margaret explained as she pointed to it. 'All of this, the park, the streets, even the offices we came from were within East Berlin back when the wall was up. That was a watchtower on this side of the wall which would have run through the middle of the park, although back then there was no park here, just warehouses, train tracks and gatehouses. There would have been a small space between the inner and outer wall, which was built up beside the Flutgraben canal.'

Monroe stared towards the watchtower and the canal, almost envisioning what things would have looked like a generation ago.

'However, it has all since been removed, and the Schlesischer Busch now houses art exhibits,' Margaret continued. Monroe couldn't take his eyes off the watchtower as he nodded. Margaret was already making her way towards a small coffee truck, and Bullman followed, dragging Monroe with her.

'So what couldn't you say at your offices?' she asked.

'It is policy not to speak badly of our detectives,' Margaret replied as she ordered an espresso. 'I am sure you have the same?'

'Ours is less a policy, and more of a vague guideline,' Bullman replied.

'One we don't follow that much, either,' Monroe grinned

as he pointed to a latte on the menu. Margaret thought about this for a moment and then nodded.

'Well here, it is a little more official, than as a politeness. And I have known Rolfe since I started here.'

'And when was that?' Monroe asked. Margaret glared at him.

'What,' she said, 'you think that because I don't look like a German I'm not one? I was born in West Berlin, Detective Chief Inspector. I am as German as anyone else.'

'I meant, how long have you been working together?' Monroe replied calmly. 'I don't care about your heritage.'

Margaret seemed to soften at that. 'Six years,' she answered as she waited for her coffee. 'I know him better than anyone in there.'

'So why do you think he went AWOL?' Bullman asked. 'And don't tell us he's on a mission or some kind of secret arrangement. That he phoned in to ask his superiors to help in barring us from our enquiries gives us a ton of doubt on that.'

'You have not yet explained your enquiries,' Margaret accepted a small cup of espresso, paying with her credit card via a contactless reader. 'I do not know how relevant they are.'

'We're looking into the Müller family,' Bullman answered, grabbing a bottled water. 'In particular, his father and his sister.'

'His sister is a conversation all on its own,' Margaret sipped at her drink as Monroe paid for his latte.

'We've time for both conversations,' Monroe replied. 'So why is Rolfe in Hurley?'

'He is on leave,' with their drinks now purchased, Margaret walked over to a bench, sitting down on it. 'There was a case, a violent one. Gang related, and incredibly traumatic. He was sent home, medical leave until he was allowed back.'

'I know how that feels,' Monroe muttered. Margaret either didn't hear this or ignored it as she continued.

'His sister, she visited him while he recovered. Next thing I know, she has then been hired as his assistant and he travels to England with her.'

'Do detectives usually have assistants?' Monroe asked. Margaret shook her head.

'I believe he was helping her,' she replied. 'Ilse was fired by Bayer Ingelhelm, a pharmacy company in Munich. There was no severance pay, no period of transition. She was escorted out of the building the same day and was left with nothing.'

'Do you know why she was fired?' Bullman pulled out her notebook at this.

'I heard rumours, nothing more. Something about unauthorised use of a trial medicine. She worked with products that were not yet released, and many that had side effects.'

'Do you know what the name of it was?' Bullman was writing into her notebook.

'I am not psychic,' Margaret smiled. 'That is a question for Bayer Ingelhelm.'

'Aye, we'll get someone on that.' Monroe was still staring at the watchtower as he sipped at his latte. 'What do you know about the Ampelmännchen Killer?'

'That it is a case that Rolfe cannot let go of,' Margaret sipped at the espresso as she thought. 'That it is a case that he believed his father had been connected to in some manner. Hauptmann Müller had not been a kind man, you see.'

'Yeah, so we've been told,' Monroe admitted. 'In fact, we need to look into that while we're here.'

'I thought you might,' Margaret reached into her handbag, pulling out a notebook. 'This is the reason I suggested we talk here. If my superiors were to see me giving you this, I could lose my job.'

'What is it?' Monroe took the offered notebook, opening it to see pages of German writing.

'Rolfe's notes on his father's work before the fall of the wall, and anything he's discovered on the Ampelmännchen Killer,' Margaret explained. 'Including the names and addresses of the surviving guards who worked under his father.'

Bullman took the book from Monroe.

'Impatient, much?' he asked, annoyed.

'I did German Language to A'Level,' Bullman replied, already flicking through the pages. 'Did you? Do you even know what these words mean?'

Monroe didn't know and so he decided not to reply, instead turning back with a sulking expression to Margaret who, her espresso finished, was already rising from the bench.

'I do not know what Rolfe is into, but it needs to stop, detectives. If you can hasten this, find what he needs for closure, then I am happy to help.' She passed a business card to Monroe.

'My number, if needed. And *only* if needed.'

Monroe nodded at this, placing the business card in his pocket. And, with a curt nod to Bullman, Margaret Li left the two detectives in the park.

'One address for an old guard is less than a mile from here,' Bullman said, checking a map app on her phone, ignoring Li as she left, engrossed already in the hunt. 'I think we need to have a chat with them, see if they can corroborate what your German mechanic said about Müller.'

'Agreed,' Monroe rose from the bench, still obsessed with the watchtower. 'And I need to drop Billy an email, get him to check into Ilse Müller's sacking from Bayer Ingelhelm.'

'Do you want to play tourist for a moment?' Bullman asked, noting Monroe's attention. He shook his head at this.

'It's just that it's a reminder of a far worst time, and far worse people,' he replied. 'One of which still reaches out across the years to right now.'

'God, man, can we stop with all the waxing poetical and just solve the case?' Bullman grumbled. 'No wonder people keep trying to kill you.'

'That's fair,' Monroe replied as they left the park, on their way to find a one-time border guard.

19

FEMALE OF THE SPECIES

ANJLI AND DE'GEER ARRIVED AT THE DEW DROP INN ON De'Geer's motorcycle; she'd told Declan that there were no cars to requisition, but in all honesty Anjli hadn't even looked into it, far happier to ride on a police motorcycle. It was way more invigorating than pootling about in Billy's Mini. And considering that De'Geer was built like a tank, Anjli also suspected that if anything actually hit them, it'd crumple against his torso.

'I thought DI Walsh came here already?' De'Geer asked as he removed his helmet. 'Aren't we doubling up?'

Anjli shook her head.

'They examined the crossing, down the road,' she replied. 'The pub was forgotten.'

'Looks like it isn't open anyway,' De'Geer said, pointing. Following the finger, Anjli could see that the pub was covered in scaffolding, a couple of construction workers on the upper levels. One worker however had noticed the police motorcycle, and was making his way over to them, pulling off his hard hat as he did so.

'Can I help you?' he shouted as he approached. Anjli nodded, stepping forwards. She didn't pull out her warrant card; the vision of a police motorcycle arriving and ridden by a police officer in full uniform made that point blatantly clear.

'I'm looking for someone to talk to about a night a couple of months back,' she shouted back. 'Any staff on site?'

'I'm the manager,' the man said as he reached them. 'Kenny Styles. What's this connected with?'

'Car accident,' De'Geer said, pointing back up the path. 'Blue car, hit a tree, spun out of control.'

'Sure, I remember that,' Kenny nodded. 'I wasn't on shift that day, but I heard about it. Old man, right? Heart attack at the wheel?'

'That's what we're checking into,' Anjli replied. At this, Kenny's face fell.

'Are we being blamed for it?' he asked. 'Nobody came to us and we hid nothing.'

'Do you think you should be blamed for it?' De'Geer responded angrily, but Anjli held a hand up, stopping him.

'At the time we believed he was driving south, from Hurley,' she explained. 'We've now learned that there was a slight chance he was in your pub before the accident.'

Kenny nodded. 'He was, but we didn't do anything that could have caused it,' he replied. 'We overwrite all CCTV though, so that footage is long gone.'

'Is there anyone we can speak to who worked that night?' Anjli looked around the car park as she spoke, as if expecting a member of staff to magically appear out of nowhere. Kenny shook his head apologetically.

'New management,' he explained. 'When we closed for refurbishments, we knew that we'd be closed for a good month or more, Most of our staff were casual, couldn't take that much time off. I think Lisa works at the Rising Sun now, she might have been on shift that day, but that would have been about it.'

'Thanks anyway,' De'Geer replied, already turning back to the motorbike as Anjli passed Kenny her card.

'If you hear anything, could you call us?' she asked. Kenny nodded.

'I don't think I'll be able to help much more than you already know, most likely,' he admitted. 'The guy didn't really stand out apart from the age difference.'

'What do you mean?' Anjli stopped at this.

'I mean we're an out of the way pub,' Kenny replied. 'We get ramblers and cyclists, dog walkers, all that sort of thing; but at night there's a small group of regulars that turn up and the rest are people who...' he paused as if not sure what to say here.

'The rest are people who pick us because we're out of the way,' he finished. 'You know, clandestine meetings, usually between couples who have other halves, if you get my drift.'

'And you think Patrick Walsh was here for a meeting like that?' Anjli looked to De'Geer, who shrugged.

'His wife died years earlier, maybe he was.'

'He definitely met with a woman, but she was much younger. I remember someone mentioning that they even thought she was his daughter until they heard her speak.'

Anjli looked up from the notebook, finally connecting the dots. 'She had a German accent.'

'That's right!' Kenny exclaimed. 'See? You do know as much as we do. Anyway, from what I was told they shared a drink, had a row and then he left. About half hour later the bar staff heard the ambulances down the road. Went down there, saw the crash.'

'Do you know what they had a row about?'

Kenny shook his head. 'As I said, Lisa might know more. I wasn't there.'

'Well, that definitely helps us,' Anjli smiled. And help them it did, as now they had concrete proof that Patrick Walsh came to the Dew Drop Inn before his fatal accident, where he met with a woman who could only be Ilse Müller. They needed a more reliable witness, though. 'We'll see if we can find Lisa at the Rising Sun.'

'Tell her she's welcome back when we open,' Kenny was already walking back towards the pub, and the contractors. 'We should be done in a couple of weeks and the regulars loved her.'

'One last thing,' Anjli shouted out. 'I get Mister Walsh left in his car, but you're pretty out of the way here, even for a local. Do you know how the German lady got home?'

'No idea,' Kenny said, looking back. 'I heard she left with another man, but that's it. Apparently the same age as the other guy, but likely her dad.'

Anjli nodded. 'Because he was German as well.'

Kenny smiled. 'See? You had it already.' And the conversation finished, he entered the building. Anjli looked to De'Geer, who had already reached the same conclusion.

'Karl Schnitter was in the pub when Chief Superintendent Walsh met Ilse,' he said. 'The question is whether Walsh saw him.'

'We also have two more leads here,' Anjli was pulling on her helmet. 'We know Patrick lost control after leaving and crashed. He either had the heart attack before or after that. And Karl is the village's mechanic. He could have easily fixed the brakes while Patrick was inside. Or, Ilse spiked his drink which caused the crash.'

'Or both,' De'Geer started up the engine. 'Spiked drink causes him to overcompensate, and if the brakes aren't working...' he let the thought hang in the air as Anjli climbed onto the bike behind him.

'We need to speak to Lisa at the Rising Sun,' she said. 'We need a witness who can confirm for sure if the Germans were indeed Karl Schnitter and Ilse Müller. And if they were, I think we can pretty much confirm Ilse's tale last night that Karl's her father, making Rolfe the legitimate child of Wilhelm Müller.'

JESS HAD INTENDED TO KEEP HER WORD TO HER DAD, TO STAY away from the case and let him carry on, but at the same time she wanted to help, and sitting with Billy, watching a CCTV feed while he coded on another laptop was a little dull, even if she was impressed with his computer skills. And so she decided that finding out anything else about Nathanial Wing, information that could help the case while staying away from the case, was a good idea.

Within twenty minutes of deciding this, she'd explained to Billy that she had urgent homework to do back at home, caught the bus to Henley and made her way back to the Regal Picturehouse cafe on Boroma Way, hoping that some of the teenagers that she'd spoken to before might still be there. As it was, only Prisha sat at a table, working on a laptop, a green juice of some kind by her side. She had the same hooded jacket on, and this was enhanced by a large pair of Bose over-ear headphones, most likely to drown out the cafe's own music. Walking over, Jess ensured that Prisha saw her before she made any movements or said anything. The last thing she wanted was to spook a possible asset.

Of course, Prisha wasn't an asset. They'd only spoken once, but at the same time you *used* an asset. Jess wasn't sure if she liked the idea of manipulating anyone.

Prisha looked up from the laptop and smiled when she saw Jess. Pulling off the headphones, she indicated for Jess to sit.

'Wasn't expecting to see you back so fast,' she said, closing the laptop.

'I'm not interrupting you, am I?' Jess asked, nervously.

'Nope, just finishing an essay,' Prisha grinned. 'In a way, you're saving me, so thank you. You still trying to get your money back?'

Jess swallowed. 'Look, I wanted to speak to you, well all of you, really,' she explained. 'I lied to you when I said Nathanial had owed me money. I needed to get some kind of 'in', and that worked.'

'Yeah, we guessed that,' Prisha nodded. 'No offence, but you're like twelve. Nathanial only asked people for money when he didn't think they were opening their piggy banks to get it.'

'I'm almost sixteen!' Jess exclaimed angrily.

Prisha laughed.

'I knew that'd get a rise from you,' she said. 'But the fact still counts. He'd only ask students he knew. And you're what, two years below us?'

'Maybe,' Jess admitted. She was one year into her GCSEs, while Nathanial had just started the equivalent of six form college that year. 'Yeah, I suppose so.'

'So why the lie?' Prisha leaned back, observing Jess. 'You

don't seem the type to be a thrill seeker. And I can't see a school newspaper being into this.'

'My dad's running the case,' Jess replied. 'I suggested I speak to Nathanial's friends because a forty-year-old man doesn't get far, you know?'

Prisha frowned. 'What do you mean, case?' she asked. 'I mean, Nate killed himself, right?'

Jess stopped. She couldn't really say anything about this, as it still wasn't public knowledge, but at the same time, she'd used the friendship that these people had with Wing to her own advantage. Nervously, she swallowed.

'Look, I could get into trouble for telling you, but it's likely to hit the news soon, anyway. We think Nathanial Wing is one of more than a dozen people who have been forced to kill themselves by a serial killer,' she explained. 'We were trying to link Wing to several suspects that we had. The news I gained about him owing money to a German helped us lead to a stolen hard drive which linked us to a possible German man.'

'A man?' Prisha was surprised at this. Jess nodded, confused.

'Yeah,' she replied. 'What am I missing? Leon said that he heard the voice.'

'Yeah, I was here, remember?' Prisha leaned closer. 'But Leon never mentioned a dude.'

'Sure he did—' Jess started, but then, clear as day, she remembered the moment.

'Voice on the phone had a strong accent. Couldn't miss it.'

He'd said *voice*. At the time, they were looking at a male suspect. She'd simply assumed they were the same.

'It was a woman's voice?' she asked softly. Prisha nodded.

'After you left, Leon was a little *bigged up*,' she said.

'Having you believe him made him cockier, so he told us more about it. Seems that Nate met a German woman a couple of weeks back, who promised to pay him money for a job. Real *James Bond* stuff. But Leon never learned what it was, and half of what Nate said was always bollocks, anyway. We just took it that Nate owed her money, but he was trying to make a thing about it.'

'And he never mentioned a man?' Jess could feel an icy shiver running down her spine. Prisha shrugged.

'Nope, not to us,' she said, finishing her coffee. 'Just that this woman had contacted him through some shady contacts he knew in Berlin or something.'

Jess looked away as she worked this through in her head. If Nathanial Wing was known as a hacker by people in Berlin, then Rolfe would know of it. And as his assistant, so might Ilse. She'd definitely have access to the reports. And, in the middle of nowhere in the English countryside with a hard drive that needed to be hacked, she'd have been overjoyed to find a hacker in the area.

But why did Rolfe meet with Nathanial Wing?

Rising from the table, Jess thanked Prisha, already returning to her essay, and ran out of the cafe, hoping to catch the next bus home before it was too late.

BILLY SAT IN THE LIBRARY, BUT IN REALITY THE WHOLE OF THE Olde Bell was his kingdom, as he still had the log in details for the CCTV. And, as he waited for people to return from their various meetings, he couldn't help himself. He flicked through the cameras, very much in a bored voyeur kind of way. There weren't cameras in the bedrooms, so it was mainly the corridors and the bars, but there was a little thrill of being able to watch people as they went on with their lives, unaware that they had a witness to their every action.

He'd stopped in the main bar though; sitting at a side table by the window was Ilse Müller, reading a book. She seemed at peace, but that was likely because her brother wasn't there. It was late morning; Rolfe was probably walking around the crypt at the Priory again. It's all he seemed to do right now. Billy clicked through some more cameras, looking to see if Rolfe was inside or even outside the pub, and stopped as he saw a figure walk up to the main entrance of The Olde Bell, his stride quick, determined and angry.

'Shit,' he whispered as he grabbed his phone, dialling quickly. As he waited for it to connect, he followed the figure through the CCTV cameras as he entered the pub, walking into the main bar and then storming over to Ilse's table to confront her.

'Declan,' the voice down the phone replied.

'Guv, you need to get here as fast as you can,' Billy said, watching the scene on the screen. 'Karl Schnitter's just turned up in the main bar.'

'That's impossible,' Declan replied down the line. 'Karl's in hospital, and they're keeping him in until the weekend.'

'Well then, he's discharged himself,' Billy was rising, half tempted to run to the bar in case something violent was about to happen; after all, there was a good chance that either Ilse or her brother had tried to hang Karl the previous day. 'It's definitely him, Guv. He's in the pub, he's angry as hell, and he's confronting Ilse Müller.'

Declan swore an expletive down the line and disconnected the call. Billy hovered by the laptop for a moment, unsure what he should do; Declan could be a way away,

Doctor Marcos and Joanna Davey were in Maidenhead, Anjli was with the Viking and the Guv was in Berlin. He was the only one who could defuse this.

'Ah, crap,' he muttered as he ran to the door. 'He'd better not have a bloody gun. I'm sick of bloody guns.'

20

JAVERT / VALJEAN

DECLAN HAD BEEN OUTSIDE KARL SCHNITTER'S GARAGE WHEN Billy had called; he'd been patrolling the back of the building, checking for broken spots in the chain-link fence that could have allowed a potential murderer to escape. He wanted to examine the back corridor of the garage again, to see if anything else was there that was connected to his father, or indeed the case against Hauptmann Müller. He'd checked Karl's office too, working through the file drawers, searching for something, anything that could give him some inspiration on what had happened after his mother had been murdered, and whether Patrick Walsh had indeed killed the Red Reaper and hidden the body five years earlier.

The investigation cut short, however, Declan rushed back to The Olde Bell and a potentially explosive confrontation. It was only a ten-minute journey by foot, less than half a mile, but Declan paused on the High Street, beside the village store as he faced an equally surprised Rolfe Müller.

'You need to come with me,' Declan said as a way of introduction. 'Karl and your sister are having it out right now in the main bar.'

'What my sister does with that mechanic is nothing to do with me,' Rolfe said, continuing to walk towards the church and the ruined priory beside it. 'My investigation no longer involves either of them.'

'What does it involve?' Declan asked after him. 'What have you found out?'

But Rolfe Müller had already left Declan in the street. Muttering an expletive, Declan continued to The Olde Bell, bursting through the main entrance at speed—

To find nothing. No Billy, no Karl, and no Ilse.

Dave, working at the bar, noted Declan's arrival.

'Pint?' he asked. Declan shook his head.

'I was told that Karl and Ilse had a confrontation?' he looked around the bar. Dave nodded as he poured a pint for another customer.

'Yeah, you just missed it,' he said. 'Your lad came in at the tail end. I sorted it out, though.'

'You sorted it?' Declan didn't quite understand what had happened. Dave smiled.

'I'm a landlord,' he replied. 'I'm friend, confidant and social worker all at the same time.'

Still confused, Declan walked through the bar and out into the courtyard, walking across to the building beside the pub where one of the function rooms was currently serving as a temporary base camp. Entering the Library, Declan saw Billy at the large boardroom table, avidly watching his laptop screen.

'Where's Jess?' Declan asked, seeing no sign of his daughter.

'Homework.'

'She doesn't have any homework,' Declan *tsk*ed. Jess had thrown a sickie and got out of her babysitter's way. He'd have to check into her in a moment. 'What happened with Karl and Ilse?'

'They're right here,' Billy pointed at the screen. 'Karl turned up in the main bar and confronted Ilse. Claimed that her brother was unjustly harassing him, pretty much stopped right before accusing him of the attempted murder in the garage. Ilse in return started shouting back, claiming that Karl had been hiding proof that Hauptmann Müller was still alive, and then I got there.'

'And?'

'Well, I'm just the tech guy according to them, remember? They both told me to piss off. Then the landlord got involved, told them to take it outside, somewhere else, he didn't care. Suggested they use one of the back rooms. I think it was called the Snug? Small room, four tables in total. They went in there and they've been arguing for the last ten minutes.'

Declan looked at the screen where the room's CCTV showed the Snug. However, only Ilse could be seen in the bottom right-hand corner, sitting at a table and facing off screen as she spoke silently, the camera not having sound.

'I don't see Karl,' he said. Billy pointed at Ilse.

'They're at the table that's under the camera,' he explained. 'Now and then they pace, and come into shot, but you don't get an unobstructed view. Probably deliberately.'

As if on cue, Karl appeared, pacing around the Snug as he angrily gesticulated. Declan walked to the door.

'I'd better step in,' he mused. 'Before one of them kills the other.'

It was a quick walk there, but when Declan arrived, he found the door to the Snug locked.

'Karl, open up,' he shouted as he hammered on the door. There was a scuffle of noise, as if a chair was moved back, and then a couple of seconds later Karl unlocked the door, opening it to face Declan.

'Declan,' he intoned, stone faced and emotionless. 'Now is not a good time.'

'This shouldn't be happening,' Declan glanced in to see Ilse glaring at him from the rear table. 'You shouldn't be alone with her.'

'I am possibly the only man who should be alone with her,' Karl replied. 'I learned recently that she is my daughter.'

Declan nodded. Anjli had emailed him about her conversation with Ilse the previous night, so this wasn't a shock.

'Still,' he said. 'I think—'

'I was your father's friend, not yours,' Karl snapped. 'And yet, when you came to me needing help a week ago, I gave it to you, no questions asked. I trusted you. And yet you do not trust me.'

'It's not you I have a problem with,' Declan replied.

'This is nothing to do with your case,' Karl looked back to Ilse as he spoke. 'And I do not believe that Ilse was the one that tried to kill me. We are in a locked room, with no other doors and barred windows. I think I am safer here than at the hospital.'

'You don't know that—'

'Declan,' Karl whispered, interrupting. 'He got to your mother in a hospital.'

Declan stopped. *Karl was right.*

'Stay on the CCTV,' he whispered back. 'If anything happens, we'll be right in.'

Without replying, Karl closed the door on Declan, and

the sound of the key being turned in the lock echoed along the corridor.

Walking back into the Library, Declan looked to Billy, now leaning back from the screen.

'He locked the door on you and then returned to the table,' Billy explained. 'Ilse's had a bit of a barney at him, it looks like. He walked to the window, staring out as he spoke, waved his hands and then sat back down.'

'Out of sight,' Declan noted. Billy shrugged.

'I didn't place the CCTV,' he said. 'And he knows you're watching, so he's probably being obstinate. We should try to find her brother.'

'He'll be at the church,' Declan replied. 'I saw him before coming here. He wanted nothing of it.'

'Hell of a brother,' Billy muttered.

'That's the problem,' Declan agreed. 'He's only a *half* brother. And his father was *Wilhelm Müller*.'

———

Rolfe Müller stood in the crypt, staring at the wall at the back of it. He'd visited every day since he'd arrived; once before noon and once around three, but apart from one encounter with the British DCI Monroe, nothing of note had occurred while he was there.

Which was a shame. Because the whole reason he had done this was to provide a regular location in a secluded place to meet. And every time he'd stood here, he'd wondered if this would be the time, this would be the day that they reunited.

But no. Every time, there was nobody with him. Not even

the ghostly Grey Lady, the sister of Edward the Confessor, bothered to introduce herself.

But today was different.

From the moment he'd entered the crypt, he knew he wasn't alone. He couldn't see who else was in there, the light was dim and there were many pillars to hide behind, but that someone was hiding, rather than saying hello and going on about their day excited him.

It meant that this could be the person who he'd been waiting for.

'Hello,' he whispered. 'Is it you?'

'That depends,' a male voice, older, and with a German twang replied from the shadows. 'On who you wanted it to be.'

'I'm Rolfe Müller, and I've been looking for you for a very long time,' Rolfe admitted, staring around the crypt, trying to work out where the echoing voice had come from. 'I'm a Kriminalkommissar in the Schwere und Organisierte Kriminalität. I didn't join the army, like you.'

There was a silence that followed the line.

'Is it you?' Rolfe asked. 'I've waited for so long.'

'It is.'

'I need proof,' Rolfe replied, looking around. 'You left us when we were children. Mother was broken, and I had to raise Ilse myself. I was told you were dead.'

'But you know better.'

'I still don't know,' Rolfe admitted.

There was a rustle of movement from the corner of the crypt, and a shadowed figure appeared. It was male, but the darkness of the corner hid the face. In his gloved hand was a canvas bag.

'Here,' he said as he threw it across the crypt to Rolfe, allowing it to clatter with a mechanical, metal clang. Picking the bag up from the floor, Rolfe opened it up, pulling out a gun. It was a squat, black semi automatic, with a brown grip with a soviet star embedded in the side. There was a magazine in it, and from the weight, Rolfe could tell that it was loaded. Along the bottom was a serial number, punched into the metal. It was a serial number Rolfe recognised, on a Makarov 9mm pistol, an East German Border Officer pistol that he'd seen as a child.

'You should not have come looking for me,' the figure stated.

Rolfe was staring down at the pistol in his hand as he replied. 'It is my job,' he said, simply. 'You must come in, if only for Ilse. She—'

'She is Meier's spawn,' the figure hissed. 'Why should I care about her?'

'Because *I* care about her,' Rolfe snapped. 'And I'm sick of hunting ghosts and talking to shadows.'

The figure in the shadows paused, and Rolfe smiled.

'Shadows like you, father,' he whispered.

Wilhelm Müller didn't reply.

'Have you seen the musical *Les Miserables*?' Rolfe asked.

Wilhelm nodded. 'I have.'

'There's a scene I enjoy immensely in it,' Rolfe explained. 'It's called *the confrontation*, and it's when Inspector Javert and Jean Valjean finally meet after his escape.' He spoke the words.

'Valjean, at last, we see each other plain. Monsieur le Maire, you'll wear a different chain.'

'Am I the Valjean to your Javert?' Wilhelm asked, keeping his distance, still hidden in the shadows of the crypt. Rolfe nodded.

'You are my quest,' he replied. 'I've hunted you across the years. I've spoken to the men who worked for you. Who feared you.'

'Men like me can never change,' Wilhelm mocked. 'And I will not give myself up. I have spent as much time hiding as I lived before the fall. Why should I change that?'

Rolfe pulled out a coin, an East German Mark.

'I have an idea,' he said, holding it up. 'Let us play for it. A coin toss. If I win? You give yourself up. If I lose? You can disappear again, and I will not come after you.'

'That is not my coin,' the shadowed figure of Wilhelm Müller replied, pulling another East German Mark out of his pocket. 'This is the coin that I would flip daily on the Berlin Wall. This is the coin that I flipped to decide a man or woman's guilt.'

'Then we use that,' Rolfe replied, his brave face nothing more than an act, as his stomach churned with fear and trepidation. The shadowed figure paused and then nodded.

'How will I know you will keep your word?' Wilhelm asked. 'You could pass the information to another. Walsh's son, perhaps. No, we need a more definite end.'

There was a moment of silence.

'I flip the coin,' Wilhelm stated. 'If it lands on the number? You may take me in, shoot me, whatever you need for closure. But if it lands on the compass and a hammer, you will take my service revolver and shoot yourself in the head with it.'

'You cannot be serious!' Rolfe exclaimed in anger and surprise, raising the gun to aim at his father. 'Why would I do that?'

There was a movement as Wilhelm Müller ducked behind a pillar. 'Two reasons,' his voice echoed around the crypt. 'First, because you knew that your last act would rely on chance. And second, because if you do not, I will kill your sister. Painfully, and slowly. You will not catch me here, you will not shoot me. I have three exits and will be invisible to you before you emerge from here. And I will skin her alive, as well as your partner in Berlin, and the people you care about. I will painfully and slowly kill them all.'

A hand emerged at the end of the crypt, holding a coin.

'Or, you take a chance with fate.'

Rolfe cursed his own stupidity. He'd walked into a trap, convinced that his moral ground was enough to turn the meeting. 'You're my father!' he replied angrily. 'Doesn't that mean anything to you?'

'You have meant nothing to me in over thirty years,' Wilhelm's voiced echoed around the crypt. 'And I will have no concerns when I brutally murder everyone close to you, before leaving you destitute, broken and begging for release.'

There was a long pause.

'Now, let us play a game.'

21

LOOSE ENDS

DECLAN HEARD THE GUNSHOT, BUT THOUGHT NOTHING OF IT. Hurley was in the middle of the countryside, and shotguns and crow scarers were often heard in the fields around. It wasn't however until an urgent and quite shaken Anjli called him five minutes later that he realised that the sound had been so much more than that.

A minute later, Declan and Billy were hammering once again on the door to the Snug. After a moment the door opened again, and Karl once more glared out at Declan.

'This really isn't—' he started, but Declan wasn't in the mood to discuss politeness, and pulled Karl bodily out of the room.

'Listen,' he whispered. 'We just heard that Rolfe Müller's been shot. We're trying to work out what happened, but until then both you and Ilse are potential targets as well.'

Karl stared in shock at Declan.

'He is dead?'

'Still waiting for confirmation,' Declan explained. 'But

until we know, Billy here is going to sit with you, and keep the door locked.'

'You think we are also targets?' Karl nervously looked into the Snug through the doorway, and Ilse stared in confusion back.

'Someone tried to kill you yesterday, so you tell me,' Declan replied. 'Billy will ensure you're safe. And keep in view of the bloody CCTV, yeah?'

Billy nodded to Declan as he led Karl into the Snug, and Declan placed a hand on his arm to pause him.

'Don't answer the door to anyone except me or Anjli,' he whispered. Swallowing, Billy nodded, closing the door and leaving Declan alone in the corridor.

He didn't wait there long though, and as the lock in the door turned, Declan was already sprinting out of the building, en route to the priory, and the crypts.

PC DE'GEER WAS ALREADY WORKING HARD ON CROWD DUTY AS Declan arrived; several people in the immediate vicinity had heard the gunshot, and all wanted to know what was going on. Nodding to Declan, De'Geer waved him past as he stood in front of the main entrance to the crypt, a human barrier to the villagers.

'I swear, if any of you enter this crime scene, I'll arrest you!' he shouted, and with his imposing frame and deep, booming voice, the villagers agreed to keep their distance, already backing away.

Anjli was already in the crypt when Declan entered, standing by the entrance, her blue latex gloves already on.

'Shoes, sir,' she said, holding out a hand to stop Declan

moving in any further. 'I've checked the body, and in doing so have already contaminated the scene. I'd rather we had no more coppers do that.'

'How did you come to be here?' Declan asked, peering into the crypt where, near the end, he could see the crumpled body of what had to be Rolfe Müller on the floor. Anjli pulled out her phone.

'De'Geer and I were at the Rising Sun,' she explained. 'The barmaid at the Dew Drop Inn now works there, but she wasn't on shift. As we came out, we heard the gunshot. We rode up and found people coming out of the church. They said that the shot had come from Old Ladye Place, and we knew Rolfe liked to come here, thanks to Monroe's notes.'

She held up her phone, now open on a photo app. On it was a closeup image of Rolfe Müller.

'Until forensics get here, that's what we have,' she said as Declan took the phone and scrolled through the images. 'Looks like he shot himself in the head with a semi-automatic pistol.'

'Or, he was made to,' Declan was already pacing around the entrance as he considered this. 'Could he be another Red Reaper victim?' He shook his head. 'No, Ilse and Karl were both in the pub, so who else could it be?'

'Maybe your dad didn't kill Wilhelm Müller after all,' Anjli suggested.

'Sure, that's an option, but to force his own son to kill himself?' Declan was appalled by the thought. 'I almost hope it was suicide to never have to think of that scenario again.'

In the distance, they could hear the faint sound of police sirens; Maidenhead would have been contacted by De'Geer, and with luck this was a forensic cavalry force being led by Doctor Marcos herself.

'Did you find out anything at the Dew Drop Inn?' he asked while they waited. Anjli nodded.

'Ilse met your dad in the pub,' she replied. 'And we think Karl was there too.'

Declan turned and stared at Anjli in surprise. 'Both of them?'

'It's hearsay, so we're waiting for someone who was there at the time to confirm what we've been told,' she said. 'Although to be honest, that's probably going to be pushed aside now.'

There was a commotion at the entrance behind them, and a forensics team, in white PPE uniforms, masks and gloves entered, led by Doctor Marcos.

'For Christ's sake, put some bloody protection on,' she snapped at the two detectives. 'And stop hanging around the entrance. It's mawkish.'

Declan led Anjli outside to find that *the circus had come to town*. There were so many officers securing the scene now that De'Geer looked redundant. Sergeant Sweeney was now Scene of Crime Officer, having more experience than the raw recruit, and Declan was actually grateful to the bald, bearded friend of his dad for that.

'Grab a suit and follow us,' Declan ordered and De'Geer, looking to Sweeney nervously before following, picked up a PPE suit, pulling it tightly over his uniform. PPE suits were baggy by design, but this fit his broad frame snugly. Declan had wondered why De'Geer had looked to the sergeant, but then realised that, with Maidenhead police controlling the scene, De'Geer was back to being a minor cog in a far larger machine.

Which was a shame, as De'Geer, when left alone, was a perfectly competent officer.

Now with the white PPE suits over their clothes and shoes, the hoods over their heads and masks over their faces, Declan and his colleagues pulled on extra sets of blue latex gloves before walking back into the crypt.

Forensics move fast, especially when organised; and there was nobody more organised than Doctor Rosanna Marcos. As DC Davey examined the crime scene, Doctor Marcos was already carefully checking the body of Rolfe Müller, while keeping the sanctity of the crime scene secure.

'Gunshot to the temple, close range,' she said, her voice monotonous and methodical as she spoke, years of forensic training keeping the emotions out while the salient facts remained. 'Gunpowder residue looks to be fresh on the hand and going from this I reckon we'll find his fingerprints on the gun.'

'Red Reaper?' Declan knelt beside the body. Doctor Marcos shrugged.

'Too soon, but I doubt it. The M.O isn't right. The gun would be missing if it was a traditional Reaper murder.'

'The gun's a Makarov,' Declan muttered as he saw the pistol on the floor. 'Russian and East German side arm.' He smiled, before realising that Doctor Marcos wouldn't see it through the mask. 'Saw a couple of these while I was SIS.'

There's a serial number on the base,' Davey said as she took a close-up photo. 'I'll send it to Billy, see if he—'

'Send it direct to Maidenhead,' Declan suggested. 'Billy's on babysitting duty right now. Karl and Ilse.'

Davey nodded and walked off, already texting. Declan stared down at the body once more.

'Never struck me as a suicide type,' he muttered.

'They never do,' Doctor Marcos was now, with the help of another CSI officer, carefully going through Rolfe's pocket with a pair of long tweezers. Slowly, and with great care, she pulled a coin from his pocket.

'An East German Mark,' she said as she turned it around. 'Pre 1990.'

'Before the wall fell,' De'Geer replied, passing a clear plastic bag for the coin to be passed into. 'I wonder if this was the coin that Nathanial Wing gave him, that we saw on the CCTV?'

'God, I hope not,' Anjli muttered. 'Then we have to work out where he got it from and that's a whole new can of worms.'

The other CSI officer accepted the now bagged evidence, writing on the bag with a marker pen before placing it into a blue plastic box.

'Wait,' Doctor Marcos started pulling a second item out of the pocket, and as it emerged, Declan saw the familiar card of the Red Reaper.

But it wasn't one card. It was a handful of cards, at least a dozen, and all identical.

'Christ,' Doctor Marcos muttered. 'I think we found the last of the supply.'

Declan stared at the cards as they too were bagged and tagged. *How did Rolfe have them, and why were they on him right now? Had he intended to use them?*

'I've got paper,' the other officer said, pulling a folded piece of notepaper out of Rolfe's jacket pocket. Doctor Marcos gingerly accepted it, opening it up with the careful application of two sets of tweezers. It was a sheet, approximately A5 in size and made up of lined notepaper, as if pulled out of a journal. On it, in what looked to be Rolfe's handwriting, was a message, written in English.

I failed.

I wanted to honour my father, but I'm not the man he was. I tried to follow his teachings, but I couldn't do what needed to be done.

I found his gun, cards and coin after my mother died, and knew then the truth of Wilhelm Müller, that he was the Ampelmännchen Killer, or as you call him the Red Reaper. But I've also had the urges, the need to kill. I killed Nathanial Wing, to see if I could. When I realised it was easy for me, I knew I shouldn't do it again. But I had to, and I tried to strangle Karl Meier, who you know as Karl Schnitter. He had an affair with my mother, and it destroyed her marriage and our family. It's what made my father a killer. The Reaper.

But I'm not him. And I'm haunted by what I've done. I've written this in English so that whoever finds my body can understand this. I can't go back now. I can't face the shame. I thought my father was innocent of this, but now I know he was a monster. And I've become a monster too.

I don't blame Patrick Walsh for what he did now. But now I have to end the life of another monster. I've flipped the coin, and I know what I must do, in a place where ghosts walk the land.

Tell Ilse I'm sorry.

Rolfe.

'Well, that settles things then,' Anjli said. 'Everything we did? All meant nothing in the end. Rolfe was the killer, after all.'

'Something's not right here,' Declan replied. 'The letter feels off.'

'We'll check it against Rolfe's handwriting,' DC Davey

was already folding the letter and placing it away in another plastic bag. 'We've got photos of his journal that DCI Monroe's sent across, we can compare this to those. We'll know soon enough.'

'Did anyone see anything?' Declan looked around. 'I mean there were enough people here gawking when we arrived, did any of them see someone leave the scene?'

'Not that I was told,' De'Geer admitted. 'But then maybe they'll tell another officer.'

Declan rose, walking to a pillar. Leaning against it, he pulled down the mask for a moment. Rolfe *couldn't* have been the Red Reaper. He wasn't in England when Declan's dad died.

But Ilse and Karl had been.

However, they had the perfect alibi; they were being actively watched having a parent daughter fight by Declan and Billy at the time of the murder. Which left one name.

Wilhelm Müller.

Had Patrick Walsh lied when he said that he'd killed Müller? Had Wilhelm escaped, or a deal been made, a deal that Wilhelm Müller had now returned to break?

Declan didn't know where to start next. But as he considered this, it looked like his path was being chosen for him, as DCI Freeman, in full PPE, entered the crypt, walking over to him.

'Terrible situation,' he muttered. 'Someone will have to tell Berlin about this and they'll likely kick up a right royal stink. What do we know so far?'

'Looks like suicide, sir,' Declan felt the words turn to ash as they left his tongue. 'Shot himself with a pistol. Possibly East German police issue, maybe his dad's gun.'

'Did he leave a note?'

'Yes, sir. And a coin, and a collection of Red Reaper cards on his person. Seems he was trying to follow in his dad's footsteps, but the guilt got to him. Flipped a coin on himself.'

Freeman patted Declan on the shoulder. 'I know it's not the result you wanted, but it's still a result,' he said. 'The Red Reaper is dead.'

'I don't think it's that easy, sir.'

'Look, just take the win, Declan,' Freeman snapped. 'This'll go well on your file, and'll likely get you back in City Police's good graces. You chased down a killer and he was so trapped by this, he killed himself.' He looked to the crime scene and pointed angrily at Doctor Marcos.

'What's she doing there!' he exclaimed. 'She knows she's not allowed at crime scenes for another three months! Having her poke about the station's one thing, but I could get into major trouble for that!'

'But you said it's a suicide, not a crime scene,' Declan suggested.

Freeman visibly relaxed at this. 'Pull DCI Monroe back from Berlin, and start closing up the case,' he said. 'If Rolfe Müller was the Red Reaper, then the case is over and we can all have cake for tea as a treat. I want a full report on my desk by end of play tomorrow.'

He shook Declan's gloved hand.

'Your dad would be proud of you,' he said before walking back to some other white suited officers, taking charge of the scene. Declan felt the same as De'Geer had moments earlier; *superfluous to requirements*. The case was apparently closed, the murderer dead, justice had prevailed and the world could sleep easier now.

So why didn't Declan feel good about this?

He knew why. Because Rolfe Müller hadn't killed himself.

Someone was tying up loose ends before moving on, and as yet Declan didn't know who that could be. The only thing that was certain was that Declan had been given strict orders to wrap his case up and provide a report on his findings by the end of play the following day.

Which meant that Declan and his team had twenty-four hours to find the true killer before they escaped forever.

22

OLD SOLDIERS

PETER BANISCH LIVED IN A SMALL, ONE-BEDROOM APARTMENT off Kollwitzstraße that was more of a bedsit, or studio apartment than one bedroom *anything*, as the wall that enabled the apartment to be called as such was nothing more than a wooden and plasterboard frame around a corner of the large living area with a small bed inside. Looking out onto Kollwitzplatz, it was about a mile North East of the centre of Berlin, in an area known as Prenzlauer Berg, a recently added district of Pankow, and known locally by the residents as *Kollwitzkiez*, because of the famous residents Käthe Kollwitz, a nineteenth century German artist and her husband, physician Karl Kollwitz, who shaped the area after his wife's death in 1919, and before the start of World War Two. It was one of the more expensive areas of Berlin to live, which explained why Banisch only had such a small living space; but it was his home, and he was proud of it.

'They know me as an artist,' he explained to Bullman as Monroe sat silently to the side, sipping at a small cup of tea.

'It has been thirty years since the fall. Thirty years since I could leave the border guards.'

Banisch was a small, bespectacled man in his sixties, no taller than five feet four and as thin as a drainpipe. He'd explained when Monroe and Bullman arrived that usually the police wouldn't accept people of his height, something that he'd relied on for getting out of his service, but when he applied, more out of necessity than choice, they'd been desperate for 'new blood', and had accepted him even before seeing him. He'd brought them up to his apartment, on the sixth floor of a large, block wide building, six floors that didn't have an elevator to climb, and had immediately offered them a hot drink. Having climbed the flights of stairs, Monroe now understood how Banisch was so slim.

'Wilhelm Müller was a monster,' he'd explained over small square biscuits. 'We all hoped that he'd be killed, or slip down the stairs in the watchtower and break his neck, but we were part of the GDR, and God didn't watch us as carefully as he watched other people.'

'We've been told that he had a badge?' Monroe asked, noting the previous answer down. Banisch nodded.

'The man with a scythe,' he shuddered. 'We all wore it. He said we were the elite, but look at me. Do I look that elite to you? He was a madman. Believed that he was God's will on the wall.'

'I've heard he flipped a coin,' Bullman added.

'For all the good it did,' Banisch spat to the side. 'We all knew it was doctored, that it gave him the result he wanted. Either two coins, each with one side on both, or some kind of weight that allowed him to flip and gain the result he wanted every time, it didn't matter. Whenever he pulled it out, we knew someone would die. He dropped it once, and I picked it up. Before I could check it, he had his pistol out, aimed at my head, screaming that I'd changed Gods will by touching it. I pissed my *ficken* pants that day!'

'Ficken?' Monroe asked.

'Slang for, well, you know,' Bullman replied. 'When a mommy and a daddy love each other very much. It even sounds like fu—'

'Thanks for the lesson,' Monroe interrupted.

'How do you not know any German?' Bullman sighed. Monroe grinned.

'I know some,' he replied. '*Ich bin ein Gummibaum.*'

'And what do you think that means?' Bullman asked patiently.

'I like gummy bears.'

'No,' Banisch shook his head. 'You just told me that you are a rubber tree.'

Monroe looked from Bullman to Banisch and then back.

'I'll keep quiet,' he grumbled, returning to the notebook.

'What do you know about the affair?' Bullman tried to return the conversation back on track. 'Müller's wife?'

'It was a scandal,' Banisch nodded. 'We all knew that she had been unfaithful, she was very vocal in her unhappiness with her husband's... abilities there.' He grinned. 'She was beautiful. She could have any man she wanted. And we believed the rumours.'

'Rumours?'

'That she did have any man she wanted.' Banisch rose from his chair, walking to the wall where, in a small photo frame, was a picture of three guards, helmets on, smiling as the photograph was taken. Pulling it off the wall, he brought it back.

'I took this in 1988,' he explained, pointing at it. 'I am on the left, and then there is Meier and on the right is Johann Hoffman.'

Monroe took the photo, staring at it. Meier was young here, laughing, his helmet hiding his eyes. It was hard to believe that this guard would end up as a mechanic in a sleepy English village decades later.

'Meier, he was the one that had the affair,' Banisch explained, tapping at the image. 'He always was an idiot. Believed that he was untouchable because he had an uncle in the Sozialistische Einheitspartei Deutschlands.'

'Socialist Unity Party,' Bullman translated. 'Known as the SED.'

Banisch nodded. 'Although Hauptmann Müller was a terrible man, he was an efficient captain. The superiors loved him, and they gave him more men, but this meant that he controlled several watchtowers. Meier would wait until nights when Müller and he were on different towers and then visit Müller's wife. Or, he would arrange to have his days off when Müller was on duty. He didn't love the woman, but he enjoyed the risk, the danger of it.' He sniffed. 'Idiot.'

'What happened when she became pregnant?'

'Nothing,' Banisch replied. 'Why would anything happen? Müller believed it was his. All was good. But we all knew that Meier was the father. And when the baby was born, we waited daily for the deutschmark to drop, and for Müller to realise that he was, how you say, cuckolded.'

'But he never was,' Bullman confirmed.

'There was no proof,' Banisch. 'That is also why I never told Rolfe of this when he visited.'

Monroe nodded. He could see why this could be a dangerous situation. 'And so Ilse grew up not knowing that she was a cuckoo,' he muttered.

'Ilse?' Banisch looked confused at this. 'Ilse wasn't Meier's. *Rolfe* was.'

'Rolfe Müller was Karl Meier's illegitimate child?' Monroe leaned forward. 'You're sure of this?' He looked to Bullman. 'Did this mis-translate?'

Bullman shook her head as Banisch pointed once more to the photo.

'Karl Meier was the father of Rolfe Müller,' he explained. 'Whether he knew, though, I don't know. You'd need to ask Johann. They were like brothers.'

'Do you know where we can find Johann Hoffman?' Monroe asked, already pulling out his notebook to take the information down. 'He's not in Rolfe's notes.'

'That's because Rolfe never asked about him,' Banisch replied scornfully. 'Arrogant little scheiße thought he'd gain everything he needed in life because of who his father was, and the deals he made. We never told him he was a bastard. He'll learn it soon enough.'

'Deals?' Bullman frowned.

'Wilhelm Müller was industrious after the fall,' Banisch admitted. 'He had information that he sold to both sides, and in doing so ensured that he had no repercussions in life. Rolfe never understood that this didn't apply to additional generations.'

Monroe's phone beeped, and he glanced down at it, paling as he did so.

'Funny you should mention him,' he replied. 'Because with unnerving accuracy, I've just received information telling me that Rolfe Müller's dead.'

Banisch stared at Monroe for a long moment.

'Well, *I* didn't do it,' he said.

IT WAS EARLY EVENING BEFORE THE CSI REOPENED THE SITE TO the public, and the Maidenhead officers returned to base. Declan was ahead of them, already sitting in DCI Freeman's office as the case was officially closed.

'I just need a day,' Declan pleaded. 'Cross the t's and dot the i's. Nothing more.'

'You don't believe it was suicide,' Freeman complained. 'You're just going to make things difficult.'

'You don't believe it was suicide either,' Declan replied. 'If you believed *any* of this was cut and dried, you wouldn't have allowed me to take on the case.'

'Rolfe admitted the murders,' Freeman insisted. 'The coin they found on him also had Nathanial Wing's prints on it.'

'We have footage that shows Wing giving it to Rolfe the day before he died,' Declan replied. 'That doesn't mean that it was used in his death.'

'It doesn't mean that it wasn't, either!' Freeman sat back in the chair as he rubbed at his temples. 'I didn't realise I was going to have an international police issue on my desk when I woke up today.'

He looked up.

'Talking of police issue, that Makarov gun's serial matched Hauptmann Wilhelm Müller's ID,' he said. 'If Rolfe *was* murdered, how was it by the gun that Müller owned while on the Berlin Wall?'

'Maybe my dad took it from Wilhelm?' Declan asked.

'We don't even know if your dad *met Wilhelm!*' Freeman barked back at him. 'It's nothing but the word of a German car mechanic! One who turns out used to be a guard on the same bloody piece of wall!' He rubbed at his temples again.

'You need to be reinstated in the City police, Declan,' he muttered. 'My ulcers can't deal with you full time. I told you I'd heard you have a reputation for killing your suspects.'

'I didn't kill Rolfe,' Declan argued. 'You just said he killed himself.'

'Maybe he did this because of you, I don't know. Who was the last person to speak to him?'

Declan paused. 'Um, actually me, sir.'

'*Christ on a cross, Walsh!*' Freeman exploded. 'What did you say to him?'

'Just that his sister was in the pub,' Declan replied. 'I swear!'

'Twenty-four hours,' Freeman snapped, bundling his scattered papers back together. 'I expect a report on my desk by then. After that, the matter is closed. Until then, you can do what you want. But in twenty-four hours, this ends.'

Declan watched Freeman for a moment.

'What aren't you telling me, sir?' he asked.

'What do you mean?' Freeman wouldn't, no, couldn't look Declan in the eyes.

'You were fine with me looking into this, but the moment I mentioned Wilhelm Müller, stated that he might still be alive, you're trying to close the case down. Why?'

'Twenty-four hours, Declan. Find an answer that doesn't have people returning from the dead. That'd be nice.'

'There is something, isn't there?'

'Of course there bloody is,' Freeman muttered. 'I'm keeping it from you to ensure you have the smallest sliver of plausible deniability.'

Declan rose from the chair.

'Thank you, sir,' he said. Freeman grimaced.

'My debts, *all* my debts to your father are wiped with this,' he said. 'No more.'

Declan nodded. In all honesty, he hadn't expected this much.

'Don't make me regret this,' Freeman muttered, more to himself as Declan left the office.

ILSE MÜLLER WAS SITTING IN THE MAIDENHEAD POLICE canteen, stirring a mug of lukewarm coffee absentmindedly when Declan entered, walking over to her table and quietly sitting down to face her.

'Are you—'

'Okay?' she interrupted. 'No, Mister Walsh. I don't think I'll ever be okay again. I've had to identify my brother's body, while learning that he was...' she drifted off, staring down at the mug. Declan knew what she was saying.

That he was the Red Reaper.

'Do you have someone who can come and be with you?' he asked. 'We have officers who are trained in this—'

'Do you?' Ilse asked, looking up at him. 'You have officers trained in talking to witnesses who find that not only are they illegitimate, but that their fathers and brothers are *serial killers?*'

Declan didn't reply. Ilse's face softened.

'Sorry,' she mumbled. 'It's been a long day.'

'I understand,' Declan nodded. 'And I hate to do this now, but I need to ask a couple of final questions. So we can close the case down.'

Ilse nodded silently. Declan looked around the almost

empty canteen before continuing, as if making sure that he couldn't be heard.

'I understand you were with my dad the night he died.'

Ilse nodded. 'Karl took me to meet him,' she replied, still stirring. 'I needed closure on whether Wilhelm Müller was alive or dead.'

'And what did he say?'

'He wouldn't answer my questions,' Ilse admitted. 'In fact, he was angry at Karl for bringing me under false pretences, as Karl hadn't mentioned that I'd be there. He was angry and left. We only learned later of his death.'

Declan nodded, visibly swallowing as he kept his emotions in check. 'Do you think that Wilhelm Müller is alive or dead?' he asked. Ilse looked away, across the canteen as she formed a reply.

'I think he lives somewhere, I don't know where,' she whispered. 'I don't think your father was a killer.'

'Hypothetically, could he have learned of your arrival in England? If he still lived?'

'Possibly,' Ilse nodded. 'Hurley is a small village. I was the only German visiting.'

'Could he have followed you to the Dew Drop Inn?'

Ilse looked at Declan in horror now. 'You think I could have led him to your father?' she asked, her voice only a croak now. 'I never considered it. But sure, I suppose...'

There was a moment of silence as Declan watched Ilse. She seemed genuinely concerned by this thought.

'One last thing, I need to discuss your contract termination,' he said softly. 'Our DCI is in Berlin, and he spoke to a friend of Rolfe's who informed us that Bayer Ingelhelm let you go, after you took some stock of an untested trial medicine.'

'Margaret Li,' Ilse muttered. 'Bitch never liked me. I'll bet she gave this information happily. And yes, Bayer Ingelhelm fired me. But the trial medicine wasn't what you think. It was to do with my parentage.'

'DS Kapoor mentioned that you'd spoken to her about that,' Declan nodded. 'That you found Karl was your real father.'

'No,' Ilse stated determinedly. 'That's incorrect. I said that I came to England to learn *if* he was. To arrange a paternity test. But I knew Rolfe couldn't be told, and he'd learn through official channels if I did such a thing. I learned that my company had a drug that could detect the BRCA2 gene in DNA samples, and so I tried to pay off a technician to test Karl's DNA. My bosses found out, and I was fired. And after that, Rolfe, learning everything, came to England. I agreed to work as his assistant, to stay close by and warn Karl. After all, he was possibly my father.'

'Was he?' Declan pulled out his phone, reading an email recently sent to him. 'DCI Monroe emailed this afternoon, telling me he spoke to a man, a guard who worked with Karl and Wilhelm Müller.'

'There were many guards.'

'This one claimed to be there at the time, and said that *Rolfe* was the illegitimate child, not you.'

Ilse sat silently for a moment, her mouth opening and shutting.

'I can't—' she stopped, her eyes filling with tears. 'It can't be, I would never—'

'Doctor Marcos can organise a proper DNA test for you, to answer the question once and for all,' Declan suggested, looking to the door of the canteen where Karl Schnitter now stood. 'I'll leave you alone now.'

'Rolfe wasn't an evil man, Mister Walsh,' Ilse muttered as Declan rose from the chair. 'Whatever he did at the end.'

Looking across the canteen, Declan nodded to Karl and left through the other door. There was something that wasn't connecting here, and he still needed to find out what it was.

More importantly, if Rolfe was the illegitimate child, was he murdered by the *real* Wilhelm Müller?

23

GLITCH IN THE CODING

THERE WAS SOMETHING WRONG WITH THE NOTE.

Billy couldn't work out what it was, but there was something there, just out of reach, that he wasn't seeing properly. It was like a line of code that had a mistake in it; he knew there was a mistake, and he could see how the code should have worked, but for some reason it wasn't visible.

There was a motion at the door to the Library as Declan and Anjli entered the room. Anjli's eyes widened when she saw Billy at the table.

'I thought you'd be long gone by now,' she said. 'The case is over and you're off the clock.'

'Is it though?' Billy shrugged. 'I don't think it is. And besides, I booked the room until tomorrow so I have until eleven to check out. Thought I'd make use of the spa for a change.' He leaned back, stretching. 'These chairs aren't ergonomic, and I've been staring at a monitor for the last two days.'

'Why do you think it isn't over?' Declan asked as he

walked over to the screen, seeing a photo taken of Rolfe Müller's suicide note. 'You think it's fake?'

'I'm not sure,' Billy admitted. 'It's not fake, but at the same time it feels it, yeah?'

'Go on,' Declan sat down beside him. 'Work through it with me.'

'The note, it's off.' Billy zoomed in on it, showing the handwritten letters on the page. 'There's a glitch here in the coding. Something that passes as right, but isn't right.'

Declan stared at the screen as Billy continued, reaching to the side, where he had a sheet of photocopied paper.

'I've examined Rolfe's notebook and the handwriting and ink matches,' he explained. 'Well, I was told by DC Davey that the ink matches. The handwriting though, although similar, is different because it's in German. I needed something better to compare it against.' He held up the sheet of paper. 'When they arrived in Hurley, Rolfe contacted Maidenhead nick to let them know he was here, and asked for copies of all data related to Patrick Walsh's investigation of the Red Reaper. They never replied to him, but that's irrelevant, as we now have an example of Rolfe writing in English.'

'It's pretty much identical,' Anjli said, comparing the two pieces. 'Are you sure these aren't both written by him?'

'No, I'm not,' Billy admitted. 'But as I said, There's a glitch in the coding and it's annoying the hell out of me.'

'Say that again,' Declan looked to Billy.

'What?'

'What you just said.'

'There's a glitch in the coding and it's annoying the hell out of me?'

'*It's* annoying the hell. Not it *is*.'

'I don't get you,' Billy looked to Anjli, to see if she understood where Declan was going with this. Declan, undeterred, carried on.

"Look,' he pointed at the sheet sent to Maidenhead. *'I am not taking no for an answer.'* Now compare that to the suicide note. *'I wanted to honour my father, but I'm not the man he was'.* And here, *'But I've also had the urges',* while on the report he says *'But I have decided to pursue.'* Even here, where on the note he says *'I can't go back now',* in the report he says *'I cannot be stopped in my belief'.* They're contractions. *It's. I've. I'm.* All the way through the suicide note, but not the request to Maidenhead.'

'It's because English is a second language,' Anjli exclaimed. 'You learn it correctly. Contractions like these are like slang. They're corruptions of the language, something you pick up over the years.'

Declan thought back to his first conversation with Rolfe Müller, when he introduced his sister.

'Ilse is here because she has a much better grasp of your language than I have. She is here to ensure I make no communication mistakes when talking to your police.'

'Ilse was better at English than Rolfe was,' he muttered.

'And she always spoke in contractions,' Billy nodded. 'I remember that.' He stopped as an idea came to him. Moving to the side of the keyboard, he rummaged through a small pile of discarded papers, eventually pulling out the note that Ilse had given him after their lunch together.

'It's the same paper source,' he said, comparing it to the one on the screen. 'Same lines. Joanna will have to confirm that, but—'

'But Ilse had access to the same paper stock that Rolfe used for his suicide note, and spoke and wrote English in a style that fit the language in it,' Declan replied. 'And I'm assuming she could have learned how to mimic his style, especially if she'd spent days up in her room alone.'

'Okay, so let's say that Ilse wrote this note,' Anjli leaned back as she considered this. 'How does that help us? She was in the Snug with Karl when Rolfe died. We have CCTV of them.'

'Unless there was another killer out there,' Billy suggested. 'We'd already mentioned that Müller senior could still be around.'

'There's an easier answer,' Declan slammed his hand on the table as realisation hit him. 'Billy, when you got down there during the fight in the bar, did Dave suggest the Snug, or did Karl?'

'I think it was Dave,' Billy thought back. 'But that said, I can't be sure. They were talking about a quiet place. Out of the way. Dave mentioned the Snug... they could have led him to suggesting it though.'

Declan rose from the table. 'Both of you, come with me,' he said. 'It's time to see if an old legend is true or not.'

JOHANN HOFFMAN WAS A GRUMPY OLD MAN WITH NO HAIR, A thick handlebar moustache and an arrogance that made him almost insufferable to speak to, as Monroe and Bullman faced him across a table in a small, dank and well past its prime local bar.

'I am here because Peter vouched for you,' he grumbled. 'I will not be coerced by you though.'

Monroe nodded. Peter Banisch had warned them about Johann; although he was a friend, possibly the best friend of Karl Meier, he was also a staunch believer in the Socialist

Unity Party of Germany, believed that the fall of the wall was a mistake, and more importantly believed that Berlin post-wall was a joke, an eyesore and a shame for the whole country. Apparently he wasn't the only one who still believed this, and ten years earlier had moved to a small community in the north-east quarter of Berlin, where he and many others around him mourned the collapse of the SED, discussed leaving this weaker state, and worked as volunteers for the far-right Nationaldemokratische Partei Deutschlands, or National Democratic Party of Germany.

Monroe hated Hoffman from the moment they met.

'We only have a couple of questions,' Bullman smiled as she spoke, as if a woman smiling might actually help Hoffman warm to the two detectives. It wasn't working so far.

'You want to speak about Hauptmann Müller,' Hoffman replied. 'He was a good man. A misunderstood man. And Karl took advantage of that.'

'How do you mean?'

'By having an affair with his wife,' Hoffman replied haughtily. 'He was not even careful about this. He openly mocked Müller.'

'I thought you were supposed to be like brothers?' Monroe responded. 'This doesn't sound brotherly.'

'Brothers don't have to think the same way,' Hoffman retaliated. 'I loved him, but Karl was a fool, right until the very end.'

'The end?'

'The fall of the wall,' Hoffman replied. 'It was a terrible day. There was chaos. People in the streets cheering. We were the villains of the story. We were hunted, beaten. And debts were settled.'

'What sort of debts?' Bullman wrote in her notepad as she spoke. 'Debts between Müller and Meier?'

Hoffman nodded. 'That is what people believe.'

'Hold on laddie, I think we're going a little off piste here,' Monroe muttered. 'We were told that Karl Meier ended up buying a new identity from Müller. So what do you mean when you say *people believe?*'

'Karl was given a new identity by Müller, that is correct to say,' Hoffman chuckled. 'But it was not the identity he wanted.'

'Because he was named Reaper?'

'No, because his identity went from alive to deceased!' Hoffman laughed, but there was no humour in it. 'They found him dead outside a small warehouse, half a mile from the watchtower!'

Monroe and Bullman stared at each other for a moment.

'Karl Meier is dead?' Monroe replied, slowly.

'Yes!' Hoffman almost shouted this. 'Are you stupid? Deaf perhaps? Protesters killed him during the riots that followed. He was stabbed through the heart, right here.' He tapped his chest. 'Right through the Reaper badge we were all made to wear. Sure, people wondered whether it was Müller that did this, that perhaps he learned that the small child he called *son* was a bastard, but we would never know.'

'Why?'

'Because he disappeared the same day, too.' Hoffman crossed his arms as he finished. 'He had friends in the Stasi. I believe that he feared retaliations from families of dead border crossers, and so he forced the Stasi to give him a new identity, so he could leave.'

'Why would they do that?' Bullman frowned. 'Surely they'd want him close by, to ensure his silence?'

'The Stasi had no say in what he did by then,' Hoffman replied. 'As soon as he was away from them, he turned on them all. Made a deal with other people, Americans in grey suits.'

'You saw them?'

'We all saw them during the fall,' Hoffman spat. 'Trying to put out the flames of the folders the Stasi burned. People like Müller, who'd saved many files, were a Godsend to them. To the CIA.'

'He turned informer? Made deals with Langley?' Monroe was surprised. Hoffman sniffed.

'He gained privilege,' he replied. 'Wilhelm Müller was immune to all prosecution. He could have stayed under the name, but although the people he now allied with were happy to give him a kind of... what do you call it? A *Diplomatic Immunity*, the families would still hunt him down. His marriage was over after the news of the affair came out, and so he had nothing to stay for. And meanwhile, we buried Karl Meier at Zentralfriedhof Friedrichsfelde.'

Monroe pulled out his phone, already typing as he spoke.

'Thank you for your time, Mister Hoffman,' he said, still typing as he rose from the chair, nodding to Bullman to follow him out. And, once on the street, he took a deep breath.

'Christ,' he muttered.

'What kind of case *is* this?' Bullman asked, reading her notes. 'If Karl Meier is dead, who the hell is Karl Schnitter?'

'I think, Sophie, that Declan's friend Karl might be the given, new identity of Wilhelm Müller,' Monroe replied. 'And if that's the case then everything we've ever been told about the Red Reaper case is a lie, in particular how Karl and Patrick were supposed to have captured and killed Müller several years ago. But there's something worse at stake.' He stared at the buildings around him as he worked through the issue in his head. 'If Wilhelm Müller is found guilty of any crimes in the UK, he could call on the CIA, reminding them of old debts, and they could have him out of the cell and disappeared within minutes. He could literally get away with murder. No wonder Emilia wanted us on this. It's some kind of spook pissing contest.'

'Who's Emilia?' Bullman asked, slightly behind the curve here.

'Ex-wife. Long story,' Monroe sighed. 'We need to let everyone know that we've been going the wrong bloody direction here.'

———

THE SNUG WAS EMPTY WHEN DECLAN BROUGHT ANJLI AND Billy into the room, making his way over to the corner under the CCTV camera. There was a small table with two chairs there, and the wall beside it was half panelled with mahogany.

'There was a legend about this building,' Declan said as he moved the table away from the wall. 'That there was talk of an underground tunnel being used during the Bloodless Revolution of 1688, when the anti-Catholic Lord Lovelace helped William of Orange to take the throne. They said that Lovelace would plot this in the crypt at Old Ladye Place, and his fellow aristocratic conspirators would enter through underground tunnels that led from the river and the Olde Bell to the crypt to avoid detection. '

'Stories, or facts?' Billy asked.

'Definitely facts,' Declan pulled at the wood panelling.

'They even had people go down and look into it, but it was unsafe and boarded back up.' The panelling came off with a crack, and Declan faced a small cubbyhole in the wall above a crudely made hole into the ground.

'Looks like someone didn't get the message,' he said as he pulled out his torch and, with a small grin slid his legs into the hole, sliding through, landing in the rough hewn beginning of a small, stone tunnel only four feet in height. Doubled over, Declan shone the torch down the tunnel itself.

The fallen rubble seemed to be removed.

'According to the old folk tales, this leads directly to the crypt,' he said as he climbed back out of it. 'We need to get forensics to check this before I contaminate any more of it.'

Billy was looking at the camera as Declan climbed out. 'We kept seeing Ilse as she walked around the room,' he said. 'She was distracting us, pretending to have a conversation with Karl while he slid into the tunnel, made his way to the crypt, killed Rolfe and then returned, blocking up the hole before we arrived at the door.'

Declan nodded.

'Rolfe didn't kill himself,' he replied. 'Karl Schnitter and Ilse Müller worked together to kill him. The question, though, is *why?*'

———

JESS WAS IN THE LIVING ROOM WHEN THE DOORBELL RANG. Rising from the sofa, she walked to the door, opening it to find Ilse Müller standing in the doorway.

'Is Declan Walsh here?' Ilse asked. 'It's important.'

'No,' Jess replied. 'I could call him if you want?'

'I've already tried, but the phone goes to voicemail,' Ilse said. 'May I come in? I'm... Well, I think I'm being followed.'

Jess thought for a moment as she looked past Ilse, out into the street. At the end of the opposite row of houses, she could see a shadowed figure watching them, half hidden behind a hedge.

'Sure,' she said as she stepped back, allowing Ilse to enter the house. 'And I'm sorry about your loss.'

'Thank you,' Ilse said as she closed the front door.

'Would you like some tea?' Jess asked. Ilse smiled at this.

'That would be very kind,' she replied, looking down at the laptop on the coffee table. 'I hope we didn't interrupt you from something important?'

'I'm just writing up some notes for dad,' Jess walked into the kitchen. 'Actually, you might be able to help. I spoke to a friend of Nathanial Wing today, and they said that it was you, and not your brother, that contacted him to unlock—'

She stopped as Ilse's last line pinged a warning bell in her head.

'*I hope **we** didn't interrupt you...*'

Carefully, and making no noise, Jess reached for her phone, cursing when she realised it was still on the table, next to her laptop. Changing tack, she pulled open a drawer, turning back to the living room.

'Sugar?' she shouted out, using the sound of her voice to muffle the slight clatter of cutlery as she pulled a carving knife out of the drawer.

'No, please,' Ilse replied. Jess, now armed, moved to the door carefully, worried that the slightest sound would give her away. She opened it, moving into the living room—

To find nobody there.

Knife still in her hand, Jess stared in shock for a moment,

but it was a moment too long as, from behind, an arm clamped around her shoulder as she felt the pinch of a needle entering the side of her neck. Pulling away, she turned to face Ilse, an empty syringe in her hand.

'Please, be calm,' Ilse said softly, pointing at the sofa. 'You should sit down, before you collapse.'

'I don't understand,' Jess slurred, staring at the blade in her hand as her fingers, no longer able to grasp onto it, loosened, the carving knife tumbling to the floor. 'Why are you doing this? Your brother just died...'

'I know,' Ilse nodded. 'I helped kill him. Now please, sit on the sofa before I do the same to you, Miss Walsh.'

Jess went to reply, but found that her vocal cords weren't working. The room was spinning slightly, fading away into blackness, as she stumbled around the room, knocking items to the floor with her flailing arms, unable to control them as she sunk deeper into darkness...

Ilse stared at the unconscious girl on the floor of the living room and smiled.

There was one last Red Reaper card in the deck.

And tonight, one last person would face the coin as it flipped.

24

I CAN SEE CLEARER NOW

DECLAN STARED AT THE PHONE IN HIS HAND AS THE CALL ended. He couldn't connect the dots that he'd just heard; he couldn't fathom the news that he'd just been told, the revelation that the entire room had just heard through the speaker. Slowly, he disconnected the call and stared out across the table at Anjli and Billy.

'Did you hear that?' he asked, his voice cold and emotionless. Anjli nodded. They'd all listened to the call from Monroe. And the information he'd gathered from Johann Hoffman actually helped them understand what had happened that day.

Karl Schnitter wasn't Karl Meier, for he was dead.

Karl Schnitter was *Wilhelm Müller*.

'Well, at least that clears up the issue we had with Rolfe and Ilse,' Billy muttered. 'Ilse was Müller's kid. Rolfe was the bastard child.'

'Which means that technically she didn't lie, because if he *is* Müller, then she was correct when she told us that Karl was her dad.'

'Bullshit. We've been bloody well lied to every step of the way,' Declan stated. 'They used us, Anjli. They played us. We were even set up for their bloody alibi, knowing that we were watching them. Her entire conversation with you, last night? Purely aimed at placing us in the line of fire. She knew you were a detective,' Declan now said to Billy. 'Karl knew you were part of the Last Chance Saloon team, so I think we can assume that Ilse did.'

'Does this mean that I never have to be undercover again?' Billy asked hopefully. 'I can live with that. What I can't live with is the two of them using us to kill a police officer.'

Declan nodded. Rolfe might have been a right royal pain in the behind, but he was a police detective, and in the end was killed by the murderer he was hunting. And that was a debt that needed to be paid.

'So what now?' Anjli asked. 'We bring them in? How do we convince Freeman to reopen this? All we have is a border guard who changed his name. If there's no evidence at the crime scene, then Karl, or Wilhelm, or whatever his bloody name is will just walk away again.'

'Nobody's walking away from this,' Declan hissed. Anjli walked over to him, turning him to face her.

'I know he killed your parents, and that alone deserves vengeance, but you need to back down here. We need to find a way to arrest him. It's the right thing.'

'Why?' Declan snapped back. 'Just under two weeks ago you were saying the same about Malcolm Gladwell for killing Kendis. And what happened there? Nothing. His solicitors are trying to arrange a deal for him. He'll be in the cushiest cell possible, he'll write his memoirs, and then he'll sell them for a seven-figure deal, and do a bloody TV redemption tour when he's released. Karl's killed sixteen people—'

'Seventeen,' Billy interrupted. 'He most likely killed Meier too.' His face brightened.

'Hey!' he exclaimed. 'That's why Nathanial Wing was on the sixteenth green! Meier's death makes it correct!'

'Read the room, Billy,' Anjli snapped.

There was a moment of awkward silence in the room, interrupted when the door opened and De'Geer entered.

'Something I missed?' he asked as he looked at the faces that turned to him. As succinctly as he could, Declan explained how Karl Schnitter had used an ancient tunnel under the pub to kill Rolfe Müller, how he wasn't Karl Meier but was instead Wilhelm Müller, and how this meant that not only did Patrick Walsh *not* kill him five years earlier, but that the whole story that Karl had told them, a story that they'd been led to believe as gospel, was likely to be nothing but lies and stories invented to keep Declan away from the truth. And that the moment he was arrested, there was a whole legal can of worms that opened on whether Karl, once outed as Wilhelm Müller *could* be charged with any crimes, or whether he'd simply be extracted from a police cell by whichever CIA department owed him the most and given a new identity, or extradited back into Europe by whichever German politicians he had blackmail information on.

'So Ilse and Karl are working together on this,' De'Geer muttered. 'That concurs with the manager at the Dew Drop Inn, as he said that both met with Detective Chief Superintendent Walsh before he crashed.'

'How long for, though?' Declan asked, pacing around the table. 'And what do we do about it?'

'Go to DCI Freeman,' De'Geer suggested. Anjli nodded.

'Great idea,' she said. 'Small addition to that though, what exactly do we tell him? Everything Declan has just said is hearsay, told to a DCI on administrative leave by an old man in Berlin who's angry at the world. Sure, we can state that Wilhelm Müller and Karl Schnitter are the same person, but we can't conclusively confirm this. Müller disappeared thirty-plus years ago. They didn't have DNA back then, and if the Stasi or the CIA gave him a new identity, they'd have fixed the fingerprints as well. And if he's been giving information against the GDP, you can be damn sure that the Americans won't be helping us here.'

'There's no way to prove any of this,' Billy muttered. 'Karl Schnitter can simply claim that Meier was Müller, killed in the confusion and was buried in his grave by accident, and that Karl didn't know this as by then he'd already left.'

'But Müller is the Red Reaper!' De'Geer protested. 'He has to face justice!'

'I agree,' Anjli continued. 'But how? There's a reason the deaths have all been seen as suicides. You can't prove that Karl, or Müller was near any of them. Even Patrick Walsh's death was deemed an accident. Sure, we've found a nice conspiracy, but you know other nice conspiracies? Moon landings. JFK's death. Paul McCartney walking barefoot across Abbey Road. They're not evidenced facts, and those are what we need here.'

Billy leaned back in his chair. 'So we let them get away with it? That's bullshit.'

'Find me something to use!' Declan screamed out in impotent fury.

The room was silent.

'We're on your side, sir,' De'Geer said gently. Declan nodded, looking to Billy.

'Sorry,' he said, forcing a small, apologetic smile as he did so. 'It's been a hell of a day for revelations.'

Billy nodded at this. 'We've caught bigger people with less,' he replied. Declan shook his head.

'None of them had *get out of jail free* cards before. We need to play clever on this,' he said. 'We need to get Karl, and fast. If he realises we know, he'll cry out for his immunity and ask for a new identity now he's outed. And he's shown for the last thirty years that he's real good at starting new lives under fake names.'

'If we can find any DNA in the tunnel, or even the crypt...' Billy suggested, but De'Geer shook his head.

'The tunnel isn't new. People have examined it or even visited it for years. Karl could simply say he had a look around any time in the last few years and we'd not be able to prove him otherwise.'

Declan nodded. 'Go see Miss Randall again. See if anything we've learned here helps. Meanwhile, let's bring him in for questioning.'

'On what charge?' Anjli asked.

'On the charge of being a lying, murdering piece of shit,' Declan snapped. 'And then we'll move on from there.'

———

DECLAN HAD HEADED TO MAIDENHEAD AFTER THE DECISION had been made, leaving De'Geer to liaise with a squad car that had been sent to pick Karl Schnitter up at his home, as the thought of Karl being arrested and brought to the cells on the back of a motorcycle gave opportunities for too many bad results. Anjli and Billy had stayed behind, however, waiting for DC Davey to arrive back at the hotel with a forensic kit; there wasn't likely to be any evidence in the tunnel, but

Declan had to ensure that they left no stone unturned, even the ones in centuries old crypts.

Arriving at the building, Declan found Doctor Marcos waiting for him outside of the main entrance.

'I heard from Alex,' she said as he approached. 'Are you sure that you want to do this?'

'What choice do I have?' Declan asked. 'If we don't bring him in, he walks. Rolfe's death is a suicide.'

'Technically it was,' Doctor Marcos walked with Declan into the building. 'He killed himself. All the evidence proves this.'

'So you think I should just leave it?' Declan stopped in the hallway. 'I expected different from you.'

'I don't think you should leave it,' Doctor Marcos replied calmly, 'but I do think you should consider what you're doing here. If you can't nail Karl Schnitter for the murders of Nathanial Wing or Rolfe Müller, it doesn't matter who he was in a past life. Your father's death was an accident. Your mother died in hospital of a terminal illness--'

'*You know that's not true!*' Declan exclaimed.

'Do I?' Doctor Marcos snapped back. 'That's what's on the coroner's reports, Declan! If you accuse him of these deaths as well, we have no proof on it!'

Declan nodded.

'I know,' he whispered. 'But if I don't try, then all of this has been for nothing.'

'And there's this whole immunity thing,' Doctor Marcos added. 'If he's an asset, or has been in the past, this could really bite you on the behind. It's not like Whitehall isn't looking for a reason to get rid of you, and they'll value the CIA's special relationship way higher than the Walsh family. And unless we have conclusive proof on all of this, none of it will matter. He'll be whisked away under a new identity before we can even call him out.'

Declan nodded. He knew this was risky.

'Expect flak from Freeman on this too,' Doctor Marcos replied. 'He's not been happy seeing me taking this over, and he sure as hell won't be impressed with you bringing Karl in. Freeman's a provincial copper, Declan. He's not used to the adrenaline filled days of London, or other cities. His is a slower, more rural world. A more comfortable world that doesn't involve this kind of political gameplay.'

'And I'm throwing chaos into it,' Declan nodded once more. 'I get it, I really do. But let's be honest, Rosanna. Karl's not going to hang around after this. Talking to him here might be the last time we speak, the last chance I get to prove my case.'

'And if you can't? If it becomes your word against his?'

'Then I'll step back and let him walk,' Declan looked to the end of the corridor where a furious-looking DCI Freeman waited to speak to him. 'But with luck, I'll cause him to slip up.'

'You'd better,' Doctor Marcos turned and walked the other direction, away from Freeman. 'Because you're throwing a Hail Mary here.'

Sighing, Declan walked to the end of the corridor where DCI Freeman glared at him.

'I understand you've arrested a popular, local mechanic,' he said. 'Bloody hellfire, Declan. I said to take the win. Not this.'

'You said I had until the end of tomorrow, sir,' Declan replied quietly. 'You said I'd used up all my debts for this.'

'You were going to find Wilhelm Müller.'

'I have done, sir.'

'*You found Karl Schnitter!*' Freeman exploded. 'Karl Schnitter! I think everyone in here's used his garages to fix their cars! He's been here longer than I have!'

'He's still Wilhelm Müller,' Declan insisted. 'And I'm going to question him and get him to admit it. Then I'll get him to admit to the murders of Nathanial Wing and Rolfe Müller, to start with.'

'And how will you do that?' Freeman shook his head. 'You going to beat it out of him? You're known for punching suspects almost as much as killing them!'

Declan bit his tongue.

'I've seen Monroe's report too,' Freeman muttered. 'I know he has friends in high places. Kept in the loop, remember?'

'You gave me a day,' Declan reminded.

'A bloody mistake, it seems!'

'My mistake to make,' Declan replied. 'Not my teams. You just saw Doctor Marcos advise against it.'

'You're risking your career for this?' Freeman was genuinely surprised. 'Because that's what you're doing here. If Schnitter raises a complaint, or if some agency kicks off about us harassing an asset for murders he didn't commit, or can't be proven to have committed, you're finished.'

'Let's see what happens by the end of the interview,' Declan gave a smile, but it was an uncertain one, mainly because Declan wasn't confident that he could do this. Freeman muttered to himself, half-mumbled words that sounded more like expletives, and nodded.

'Last ball, Declan,' he said. 'One more strike and you're out.'

And with a final shake of his head, Freeman walked

through the doors at the end of the corridor, leaving Declan alone.

'A baseball reference?' Declan muttered. 'You could have at least made it bloody cricket.'

———

KARL SCHNITTER WAS SITTING IN INTERVIEW ROOM 3 WHEN Declan entered through the door. He was relaxed, smiling even as he leaned back in the chair, feet on the table, whistling to himself. PC De'Geer was standing by the wall, but when he saw Declan enter, he nodded and left the room, leaving Declan and Karl alone.

'You're pretty chipper for a man who just heard of a violent death,' Declan said as he sat down in the chair facing Karl who took his feet off the table, straightening up in his chair as he faced his opponent, as if starting a chess game.

'The man was hunting me,' he said. 'Why should I not be happy?'

'What about the fact that Wilhelm Müller may have killed him, meaning that not only is Wilhelm still alive, but now may be targeting you?'

'That is indeed a concern,' Karl replied with the face of a man who didn't seem concerned. 'But I am sure you will save me.' He smiled. 'You save all the innocent people.'

Declan looked to the recorder at the end of the table. 'The moment I turn that on this becomes official,' he stated. 'So before I do that, is there anything that you want to get off your chest?'

'I am fine, Declan. Let us get on with this. Anything I can do to help.'

'Is that you offering your help as Karl Schnitter, or as

Hauptmann Müller?' Declan asked, happy to see a flicker of surprise on Karl's face. 'We've been talking to some old soldiers. They had quite a few stories.'

'I'd like to hear them,' Karl said, the surprise now gone. Declan smiled.

'Good, because I've got a great one for you,' he replied as he pressed record. 'Although you might really hate the ending.'

25

INTER-VIEWED

'THE TIME IS SEVEN FIFTY-FIVE, DI WALSH INTERVIEWING KARL Schnitter, AKA Karl Meier, AKA Wilhelm Müller.'

'Alleged,' Karl smiled.

'Are you saying that you're not Hauptmann Wilhelm Müller, formerly of the *Grenztruppen,* and stationed in Berlin before the fall of the Berlin Wall?'

There was a long moment of silence, as Karl considered the question. Declan wondered if he was working through scenarios in his head, deciding what the best option was to take, again like a chess player in a competition.

'For the record, Mister Schnitter is not replying.'

'I am thinking,' Karl replied, and for the first time Declan heard irritation in his voice. 'It is something I have hidden for a long time, my actual name, and I am aware of the diplomatic, or legal ramifications I create by admission.'

'Is that a confirmation?' Declan pushed. He wondered if this was the play Karl had to try for; to give up the truth of his identity while avoiding anything to do with The *Red Reaper*.

Karl nodded at this. 'I thought you would find out,' he

replied. 'I forget how good a detective you are. Much better than your father.'

'You don't get to mention my dad,' Declan hissed. 'You don't get to say his name ever again.'

'He was my friend, Declan,' Karl replied, calm once more. 'No matter what you think of me, he understood.'

'You told him you were Müller?'

'Yes,' Karl said, looking directly at Declan as he spoke. 'He asked for my advice when Dotty Brunel committed suicide. He recognised the symbol of the Ampelmännchen, and when I saw it, I recognised the symbol of my old unit.'

'A symbol that you designed, after they named you the Reaper, correct?'

'No,' Karl shook his head. 'Command created it, to strike fear into dissidents. *The Reapers, the Wolves, the Inquisitors,* all units named to scare.'

Declan stopped, watching the completely calm Karl. *He was creating a new narrative right here, right now. One that made him into the victim.*

Doctor Marcos and Freeman had been right. Declan was out of his depth here.

'Why did they call you the Reapers?' he asked.

'Because we killed escapees,' Karl admitted. 'It was our job. But I always tried to save them. I would flip a coin, give them a fighting chance. In fact, over a dozen people escaped because of that coin.'

'I heard you had a fake coin, one that always benefited you.'

'Lies, spread by a guard that hated me.'

'Meier?'

Karl nodded. 'He wanted me removed. He was sleeping with my wife. Having me moved or even arrested for atrocities I never committed would have enabled him to be more open.'

'From what I heard, he was pretty bloody open.'

'Only at the end,' Karl replied. 'When Rolfe was three, maybe four years old, I learned of the indiscretion.'

'Ilse was yours?'

'I hoped so. But in those days it was hard to confirm.' He smiled. 'If Meier had been black, it would have been easier.'

Declan declined to answer that, moving on.

'When we spoke, you claimed you had taken the name Karl Schnitter when escaping Berlin in 1989.'

'That is true.'

'And that your name was originally Karl Meier.'

'I never said that,' Karl frowned, as if confused at the question. 'I think you must have been confused as to what I said.'

Oh, you bastard.

'Was it all a lie?' Declan asked. 'I've known you since I was a kid. How much of that was real?'

'All of it,' Karl replied. 'Yet none of it. I was told by agents of your own government, and also by the American CIA, that when I turned informant against my old superiors, although I would have a blanket amnesty for all crimes I had committed under my real name, to stay known by it would create reprisals. Better to run and hide in a lie.'

'Convenient answer, when there's no way to prove the truth.'

Karl nodded.

'I am sure there are official records of my agreements in many places,' he smiled. 'But then again, what is truth?'

'The truth is that you're a monster,' Declan snapped. 'Sixteen, seventeen bodies, all by your hand. My mum.

Nathanial Wing. Karl Meier. Craig Randall. The list goes on.'

'I know the list,' Karl replied. 'I helped your father with it. But all we found was the truth, that these were just suicides, of people who wanted a way out, and who found a death cult that they could follow. The Red Reaper.'

'I have a witness that says Craig Randall wasn't alone before he died.'

'His sister. A child. From a distance, a decade ago,' Karl nodded. 'Your father saw her testimony, even though then-DI Freeman never took the statement seriously.'

'So she's a liar?'

'No, Declan. She's a child.' Karl leaned back in the chair and seemed to be genuinely enjoying this. 'Craig Randall was a rapist. Dotty Brunel killed animals for sport, Nathanial Wing a liar and a debtor, and Rolfe Müller a murderer.'

'Murderer?'

'Of course,' Karl nodded. 'Did he not confess to Wing's murder? And he tried to hang me also, remember?'

'So the others were murdered?'

'I believe they were, by Meier,' Karl replied, holding up a hand. 'Yes, I know he is dead and buried, but it was a confusing time. People were rioting. There was confusion everywhere, records being burned. If I escaped, then so could he.'

Declan was getting flustered now. He could feel the vibration on his phone; a message. Pulling it out, he looked at the words on the screen.

Your daughter is very sweet when sleeping.

He looked up to Karl who smiled, placed a finger to his

lips and pointed to the recorder.

The bastard knew what the message said.

'Do not make these people into martyrs,' Karl continued. 'And do not continue on this Quixotic quest like your father. You have me on my true identity, and I have admitted that. However, that is not cause for arrest, and more importantly at best can only cause me to be extradited home, or given a new identity elsewhere. Do you know the definition of a criminal?'

'Someone who commits a crime.'

'And how is that decided? That they did indeed commit that crime?'

'They're found guilty.'

'Exactly,' Karl clapped his hands together. 'A criminal is a man who is *proven* to have committed a crime. Which, dear Declan, has not happened.'

'Monster,' Declan whispered. 'All this time, you've lived in plain sight.'

'Because I have had nothing to hide,' Karl shrugged, looking up to the camera. 'Although I am concerned with this continual harassment. Is it anti-German? Something from your time in the army? I heard from Ilse that you called Rolfe a Nazi in the middle of a bar.'

'I did no such thing!' Declan rose from the chair now, furious.

Karl smiled wider now. 'What would your superiors say?'

'I'll keep hunting you,' Declan hissed. 'Even if they close this down, I'll find a way to make you pay.'

Karl nodded at this, as if expecting it. 'And others will suffer for your arrogance,' he replied. 'How many more will lose their jobs, following you down this rabbit hole? It's over, Declan. Allow it to die.'

He smiled.

'Just like your father did.'

Declan moved forward at this, his hands reaching out, but the door opened, and DCI Freeman stormed into the room.

'This ends now,' he said, turning off the recording and facing Declan. 'I gave you a chance because you said you had something. All you have is a man who changed his name.'

'A war criminal!'

'*Not our war!*' Freeman shouted back. 'If Berlin want him so bad, they can get him!'

'They tried,' Declan hissed. 'Rolfe Müller, remember?'

'Your own people proved that Rolfe Müller was acting on his own cognition and was AWOL from his post.'

Karl coughed; a polite one.

'I have no issues with Declan,' he said as Freeman looked to him. 'I would be the same. It is a testament to his skill and his ability, his passion for justice that he has got this far, even if he has lost his way.'

'Thank you for your understanding, Karl,' Freeman replied. 'I hope that this doesn't cause any problems down the line.'

'Not at all,' Karl smiled. 'I wondered if I could have a private word with him? Maybe a conversation without recording devices and cameras may be more fruitful? I would like to explain my situation with your government, explain how I am, as you say, *untouchable*?'

'Of course,' Freeman nodded, looking to Declan. 'When this is over, you can go home, back to London, whatever you want, but you're barred from this Command Unit. Understand? All debts are paid.'

Declan nodded as Freeman left the room.

The CCTV camera's red light winked off.

'And they were all alone,' Karl muttered with a sly smile. 'Did you really think I would give in so easily? That I had not spent thirty years ensuring that my life was beyond reproach? I can return to Berlin as Wilhelm Müller whenever I want. Maybe I will go tomorrow. Nobody cares about the fall of the wall anymore. They want the world to move on. And you should move on, Declan. You have a beautiful daughter and a wonderful life. I have always envied your family, that and your father's. Maybe I can find one of my own now I have reconnected with Ilse.'

'Did Ilse send me the message?' Declan asked. Karl shrugged.

'I am not psychic,' he replied.

Declan balled a hand into a fist, his anger rising.

'I would not do that,' Karl interjected. 'My daughter is waiting for me to return, and if she believes I am in any way compromised or hurt, she will skin your beautiful daughter Jessica alive, with a potato peeler. A blunted one.'

For a moment, though, genuine emotion crossed his face.

'I am sorry, Declan,' he continued. 'I truly am. We could have been firm friends, if this had not happened. But sometimes the urge strikes me, and I must *feed the beast,* as they say.'

'Was that why you killed Nathanial?'

'Nathanial Wing killed himself,' Karl shrugged. 'It was sad. But it was his own doing. As were all of them. Even your mother. Who was sick and dying, Declan. In a way, I gave her mercy.'

'I won't give you mercy,' Declan hissed. 'If you've touched a hair on her head, if you've even shouted at Jess, I'll find you and I'll end you.'

'You will do nothing of the sort,' Karl said, shaking his

head sadly. 'We both heard your DCI. You have nothing on me. Your case is dead. Your team and yourself are finished here. I will be gone tomorrow, and your own government will provide my new identity, on behalf of either America or Germany; whoever contacts them first. I am, as they say, a belle of the ball, even after these years. You will send your colleagues home, and you will write your closing report on this case, stating that Rolfe Müller killed himself, unable to live with failure, and the guilt of murdering Nathanial Wing.'

'And if I do that?'

'Then you will go for a drive. Don't use your car, I know there's a tracker. Use the same car you borrowed from me. It's outside your house by now, and the key is under the wheel arch above the front passenger wheel. Leave your phone in your Audi, and drive to where I tell you to wait until midnight. Do this and I will release your daughter, unmolested,'

Karl walked towards the door.

'It is a shame though, I have really enjoyed this village, and these people. It is sad that people searching for justice must ruin such things. Stop your team, Declan, Stand them down. I have one Red Reaper card left, Declan. It would be a shame to use it on Jessica.'

With that Karl walked out of the interview room, closing the door behind him, leaving Declan alone.

He wanted to scream, to break something, to kill. But none of these would help him right now. *He needed to find a way to make this work.*

But there wasn't a way to do this in the manner he needed. And Karl's last line had shown the truth of the matter.

'I have one Red Reaper card left, Declan. It would be a shame

to use it on Jessica.'

Not that it would be a shame to use it, but that it would be a shame to use it on *Jess*. Which meant that Karl still intended to use it, to leave one last death behind, before he moved on to a new life. And Declan knew without any doubt that *he* would be the next victim of the Red Reaper, likely at midnight tonight.

All loose ends removed.

He knew he could stop his team from searching; the moment they knew Jess was taken, they'd stand down. At the same time though, he needed to make Karl and Ilse pay for their crimes, even if he couldn't be prosecuted in the legal manner.

Which brought him back to the mindset he'd had after Kendis Taylor had been murdered. Declan was an ex soldier and had a soldier's mentality. He had killed before, and knew that if the stakes were high enough, he could kill again. But that wasn't who he wanted to be. He was a Detective Inspector, and that meant something to him, even if he wouldn't be one for much longer.

He had to plan this carefully.

He had to plan this *cleverly.*

Pulling out his phone, he dialled Anjli.

'It's me,' he said when she answered. 'Gather the troops back. We're closing this down.'

'De'Geer's gone back to the Randalls,' Anjli replied. 'I know we can—'

'I said *close it down*,' Declan snapped. 'We're done. We lost. Go grab a bite to eat in the bar.' He looked at the clock; it was almost nine pm. 'They should still do food, but only just. I'll meet you tomorrow for breakfast and explain everything,' he lied.

'If you're sure—'

'I'm sure. Close it down.' Declan disconnected the call, and, still holding the phone in his hand, he paused, unsure that the next call that he was about to make was the correct one.

But it was the only call that he could make.

Declan took a deep breath and dialled a number. As it was answered, he looked around the Interview Room one last time. It was probably the last time he'd be in one as a police officer.

'It's Declan,' he said into the phone. 'I think I now understand why you had a problem with Karl. So, I have a favour to ask, and a gift for you. One I think you might like.'

———

DCI Freeman sat in his office, staring at the wall as his phone went. He'd been like this for a good hour now, physically there while mentally miles and even years away.

He'd joined the force to make a difference. But where had that got him?

Returning to the present, he answered the phone.

'What,' he muttered, but then stopped, listening.

'What about the daughter?' he asked, shaking his head at the reply.

'Well you, sir, can go to hell,' he snapped, before slamming the phone back down, and staring at it.

It looked like Karl Schnitter, or Wilhelm Müller, or whatever his damned name was, had played his last card.

The *Americans* were coming.

———

26

CHANGE OF PLANS

It was close to ten PM when Anjli and Billy arrived at Declan's house. His Audi was in the driveway which meant that he'd returned from Maidenhead. Passing it, Anjli hoped that back home now, he'd be more likely to listen to reason.

'I'm telling you, something's wrong,' Anjli said as they walked up to the door. 'You don't just close down something that's as personal—'

'Anj,' Billy interrupted, pointing at the front door to the house; it was ajar. Pushing it gently, Billy leaned in, looking through the doorway and into the house. The lights were off. It was deathly quiet.

'Declan?' He said loudly, walking in. 'Jess?'

Anjli, following, turned the lights on, and the two detectives stopped.

The living room looked like a fight had occurred; books and magazines were scattered on the floor, and a carving knife was on the carpet near the kitchen door, next to a discarded, empty syringe.

'Call it in.' Anjli said softly. 'We need forensics here right now.'

PC Morten De'Geer was in the break room when DCI Freeman entered. He wasn't making himself a hot drink, but just sitting on a chair, staring at what looked to be a local newspaper, currently opened on a middle page.

'Busy week,' Freeman said conversationally, but De'Geer didn't reply to this. Turning, Freeman watched the police officer for a moment before continuing.

'Something you wish to say?'

'No, sir,' De'Geer replied sadly. 'Just considering my place in the department.'

'And what's that supposed to mean?' Freeman asked. De'Geer looked up at him.

'Do you remember when I first met you?' he replied. 'When I decided more than anything that I wanted to be a police officer?'

'I do,' Freeman walked to the table sitting down. 'It was in the campsite. Craig Randall. You were what, seven?'

'Twelve,' De'Geer smiled at the dig. 'I was seeing Ellie Randall at the time. Her parents had taken her away from the crime scene, but I wanted to see what had happened. You came out of the woods holding a card in your hand. It was in a baggie and I didn't know what it was, but I do now.'

'A Red Reaper.'

De'Geer nodded. 'Do you remember what you said to me?'

'You asked me what was happening,' Freeman remembered, looking across the room, avoiding De'Geer's gaze. 'I said I couldn't tell you. Then you asked if I was going to catch who did this.'

'And you said to me?'

'I said that sometimes we couldn't catch the criminal, but I'd make sure that justice was served, no matter what.' Freeman sighed as he leaned back, looking at the lights embedded into the ceiling. 'I was a little more hot-headed in those days,' he continued. 'A little more optimistic.'

'You were passionate,' De'Geer added. 'You were a believer that no matter what, you would find the culprit. But he never was. And Craig Randall was classed as a suicide.'

'That wasn't me,' Freeman replied angrily. 'You can't put that on me or Patrick. We fought to keep the case open, but the powers that be felt that this would only keep the story out in the open for longer.'

He looked to the table. 'He did to me what I just did to Declan,' he muttered.

'Yes,' De'Geer replied.

'Look, I'm as pissed about it as you are,' Freeman snapped. 'The bloody Reaper has been a chain around my neck for decades. But we have no evidence!'

'I visited Ellie Randall again this evening,' De'Geer stated softly. 'I took this newspaper with me. It's a *Maidenhead Advertiser* from 2013. A *Comic Relief* special.' He looked up to Freeman. 'We have them all in the archives. I asked her to look through it, see if anyone in it was familiar.' Now he pointed to the pages that were open on the table. 'She stopped at this.'

Freeman looked at the article that De'Geer was showing. It was an article about local companies holding events for Comic Relief, but the photograph used was clear and visible;

a photo of a garage, the mechanics in fancy dress and smiling.

Front and centre was a younger Karl Schnitter.

'She said that this was the man that Craig was with in the woods,' De'Geer stated. 'I didn't lead her to this, she picked it up herself. And they took this less than a year after Craig's death.'

Freeman stared at the photo as he spoke. 'A twelve-year-old child, at a distance, and over ten years ago,' he said. 'This wouldn't even reach court, especially now we know Schnitter is Müller. By this time tomorrow he'll be somewhere else, under a name provided by our own taxes.'

'*Sometimes we can't catch the criminal, but don't worry lad, I'll make sure that justice is served, no matter what,*' De'Geer almost spat the words. 'That's what you said to me. Word for word. I never forgot it.'

Freeman sat silent for a moment.

'Karl Schnitter is Wilhelm Müller,' he muttered. 'But that's not enough to convict him of murder. And to ensure justice is served here smacks of vigilantism, not police work.'

'As you just said sir, by tomorrow Karl and Ilse will be gone,' De'Geer rose from the table, closing the newspaper up as he did so. 'They'll have escaped, again, and we'll be telling the press that a good German police officer killed a teenager and then took his own life.'

'There's more to this,' Freeman muttered. 'Higher up the chain. Müller is untouchable.'

'And Ilse?' De'Geer stopped at the door, looking in. At no reply from his DCI, he smiled.

'Thought as much, *sir*,' he said as he left.

DCI Freeman sat at the table, staring down at the newspaper. There was nothing he could do about Karl Schnitter. He'd outplayed everyone, and to try anything would just bring down a world of administrational pain and hurt on his department.

But there *had* to be something that he could do.

His phone beeped, a call coming in from the front desk who, unable to gain him on his office land line, would have passed the call over to his mobile phone. Which meant this was important.

'Freeman,' he answered. His face paled as he listened to the call, before disconnecting without another word down the line.

'De'Geer!' he shouted out. After a moment, the officer leaned back around the doorframe.

'Sir?'

'Where is Declan Walsh right now?'

'I don't know,' De'Geer answered honestly. 'He left under a bit of a cloud, and Doctor Marcos mentioned a little while back he hasn't answered his phone since he left.'

Freeman nodded. 'Then get your team together,' he replied, rising. 'We've got a problem. Declan and his daughter are missing, and it looks like there was a fight in his house.'

JESS HAD A KILLER HEADACHE WHEN SHE WOKE UP, STARING around the darkened room in confusion until her vision cleared into focus. She was in what looked like a garage space, a workshop; to the side was a full length cabinet with tools scattered across its surface, and on the floor were discarded pieces of cars and bikes. It was most likely the garage where Karl Schnitter had been found hanging from a ramp, although she couldn't turn to see if the ramp was behind her.

'You're awake,' Ilse Müller smiled as she walked into view, and Jess realised for the first time that she wasn't able to move; her hands and legs were cable tied to a wooden chair placed in the middle of the workshop, a portable arc lamp the only source of light. And she wasn't able to shout either, as Ilse had forced a foul smelling rag into her mouth, and gaffa tape wrapped around her head held it in place. It smelt and tasted faintly of oil, and Jess had to force herself not to puke. At the same time, she had to convince herself not to panic, as this was definitely the scariest situation that she'd ever been in.

Ilse stood silently, her hands in her jeans pockets, relaxed, and completely in control. As if coming to a decision, she walked over to Jess, pulling out a vicious looking folding blade which she locked open. Jess struggled, pulling back as the blade moved towards her face, but Ilse simply cut the tape, pulling the foul tasting rag out of the mouth.

'You scream, shout, try anything? I slit your throat to stop you, understand?'

Jess nodded.

'I worried I had used too much,' Ilse explained softly. 'And I wanted you to be awake.'

'Why?' Jess tried to keep her voice calm. 'If you're going to kill me, I'd rather I was unconscious.'

'Why would I kill you?' Ilse asked, surprised. 'I've killed no one.'

'Nathanial Wing?'

'He killed himself.'

'After you contacted him,' Jess corrected. 'I know you were the voice he spoke to, not your brother.'

'*Half* brother.'

'Whatever.' Jess shifted in the seat, trying to feel out how much give the cable ties had. It wasn't much. 'And you were out the night Nathanial died.'

'I walk at night,' Ilse admitted. 'That doesn't mean that I was at the Golf Club.'

'Doesn't mean that you weren't, either,' Jess snapped back. 'Did you kill granddad?'

If Ilse was blindsided by the question, she didn't respond to it. 'All we're doing is waiting,' she said. 'When I get a call, I will leave. You will unfortunately stay here until you're found in the morning, but you will be alive.'

'What's the call?'

'To tell me that everything is over.'

'Where's my dad?'

'I don't know, child,' Ilse said soothingly, stroking Jess' face as the teenager tried to pull away. 'All I know is where he will be at midnight.'

'Where's that?'

'Flipping a coin for his life.'

Jess shrugged in the chair, rocking it as she angrily spat out at Ilse. '*You bitch!*'

The backhanded slap was expected, but Jess was unable to lean back from it, and so the impact caught her square on the cheek, knocking both Jess and the chair over. Ilse walked to it, pulling the chair back upright as she glared at the fifteen-year-old girl tied to it.

'One more,' she said. 'One more. Say it. I will *end* you.'

'No, you won't,' Jess fought back the tears of pain as she replied. 'You need me alive. If I'm dead, my dad won't come.'

Her jaw tightened into a line.

'Now, did you kill my granddad?'

Ilse laughed. 'You are a firebrand!' she exclaimed. 'Tied up and in fear for your life, yet you still possess such anger, such passion.' She walked away, but stopped and turned back.

'I do not know if I killed your grandfather,' she replied. 'I doctored his drink that night, I will admit, but whether that was what killed him, or whether it was the impact of his car striking the tree and rolling into a ditch...' she shrugged. 'It's far easier when they kill themselves.'

'But you screwed up,' Jess mocked. 'You allowed Nathanial to leave a note. You didn't clean up as well as your daddy did.'

'And you've not examined the case as thoroughly as *your* daddy did,' Ilse snapped. 'I didn't see the note because it was covered in blood! I trusted him to do the right thing! He knew what would...'

She stopped.

'Oh, you're very good,' she nodded. 'It will be a shame to kill you.'

'Wait!' Jess said as Ilse forced the gag back into her mouth. 'You said I would be—'

'You know too much,' Ilse replied sadly, stepping back from the now re-gagged Jess. 'No coin for you, I'm afraid. No card, either. Just a girl, in too deep, and grieving her father's death.'

As Jess screamed muffled, silenced yells of anger through her gag, Ilse turned and walked away.

'Everything ends at midnight,' she said.

MONROE AND BULLMAN HAD TAKEN THE FIRST FLIGHT BACK TO London, and once through customs had called in a couple of favours from the local police; within half an hour of exiting the terminal, a police squad car pulled up outside The Olde Bell, turning off its flashing lights as Monroe and Bullman climbed out, nodding a thanks to the driver as the car returned towards the M4 and London.

Making their way to the Library, Monroe opened the door and stopped in surprise. He'd expected to find Declan, Billy and Anjli there, maybe even Rosanna Marcos, but what he faced was a little more than that.

'You're here. Good,' DCI Freeman nodded as he turned back to the others in the room; Billy, De'Geer, Anjli, Doctor Marcos and DC Davey. 'DCI Monroe and DCI Bullman will also assist in the operation.'

'What's going on?' Monroe said as he entered the room. 'Can't help but think we're missing something.'

'That's because you are,' Anjli replied to Monroe before nodding to Bullman. 'Ma'am.'

'Catch us up,' Bullman said as she glanced down at the newspaper on the table. 'We're still on German time.'

'Declan's missing,' Billy explained. 'And so is Jess. We think Karl and Ilse did it.'

'Karl Schnitter is our person of interest, but he's clever,' Freeman explained. 'He was in the bar of The Olde Bell on the night of Nathanial Wing's death, seen by multiple witnesses and, until we can prove he used a secret tunnel to kill Rolfe Müller, he has an alibi for that too. However, we have a witness stating that she saw him in 2012, and your work in Germany has gained us intel that shows that he was a

US government sponsored informant, and given immunity from all crimes committed.'

He grimaced.

'The same US government that is sending someone tonight to pick him up and whisk him away to a new identity, and who have tied my hands on getting anyone else onto this case.'

'You're here, and that's what matters,' Monroe replied. Freeman nodded a *thanks* to this as Billy took over.

'Also, hospital records show that Karl was the only other person who visited Christine Walsh the night of her death, and we have witnesses claiming they saw him in a pub with Patrick Walsh the night that he died,' he said.

'With Ilse Müller,' Anjli added. 'Who had personal contact with Nathanial Wing before his death, and no alibi for her whereabouts that night. Whose handwriting and notepaper matches the suicide note that we found in Rolfe Müller's pocket—'

'That has contractions that match her own writing style,' Billy added. 'And who was also with Karl Schnitter and therefore is his alibi for when Rolfe Müller died.'

'We also had a report from the detective you chatted to, Margaret Li,' Doctor Marcos interjected. 'Patrick Walsh's blood work on the night that he died showed no major drugs in his system, but there was some erroneous data. A substance that couldn't be recognised until Bayer Ingelhelm contacted her in relation to this. Ilse was fired for taking an untrialled medicine to a convention in the UK, two months ago. The medicine was however taken off trials because of severe side effects.'

'Heart related ones?' Monroe offered. Doctor Marcos nodded.

'It's a proprietary medicine, so we're having issues getting a sample, but we learned of some of the substances in it.'

'And these are the mystery ones in Walsh's blood?' Bullman asked. Doctor Marcos nodded.

'Extensively.'

'So now we have a link to Ilse and Patrick Walsh.'

'A possible one,' Freeman said, bringing attention back to him. 'None of this is solid. It's all circumstantial. We have enough here to bring her in for questioning, but not for anything concrete. We can't prove she gave Patrick Walsh the drug. Even if she did, we can't prove it's the same substance that he had in his body. We can't prove that she was there when Nathanial Wing died, but we have her leaving The Olde Bell on the night in question and turning right.'

'Why's that important?' Bullman was confused here. 'I mean, I've only seen your village for five minutes...'

'Ilse claims she would walk along the Thames at night, ma'am,' De'Geer explained. 'If she was, she would turn left. Turning right leads you south out of Hurley.'

'And it's the direction you go when heading to the Golf Club,' Monroe added. 'So the plan is to bring in Ilse. Nice. So why isn't Declan here?'

'That's the reason *we're* all here,' Anjli replied. 'We went to the house and found it trashed. The door open, and neither Declan nor Jess are there; Declan's phone is still in the Audi, on the passenger seat. But we found this.'

She looked to Doctor Marcos who picked up a clear bag from the table. Inside it was an empty syringe.

'It's a strong sedative,' she replied. 'We don't know if Declan, Jess or both were taken, and the doorbell footage from across the road didn't pick up motion. But neither of them are contactable, and if Karl and Ilse are intending to disappear, they'll want to settle all their scores first.'

'Basically, there's a very strong chance that Declan, Jess or both are about to become the last victims of the Red Reaper, before the bloody CIA gives him a new identity.'

27

TWO MINUTES TO MIDNIGHT

DECLAN HAD DONE EVERYTHING THAT HAD BEEN ASKED OF HIM. He'd returned to the house, leaving his phone in the Audi when he swapped cars, and clambered into the Peugeot 308 that was parked outside, taking the key from the wheel arch and climbing in. On the passenger seat was a single piece of notepaper, with four words written on it.

DO DROP IN, DECLAN

So it was the Dew Drop Inn. That made sense. Anjli had mentioned that it was closed for renovations, and the contractors wouldn't be there so late in the evening.

It felt strange being back in the car again; he'd used this to drive to Woking and then to London, all while hiding from the police, wanted for a murder he hadn't committed, and a claim of treason that wasn't warranted. And in a way, he was hiding from the police again.

Except this time, he knew the police would work out what to do. He trusted his team to save Jess.

He'd entered the house briefly and had seen the mild carnage inside. Jess had been taken, and from the looks of things had put up a small fight while this happened.

Good girl.

Christ, Liz is going to kill me when this is over.

That said, the door had been closed and locked, and from the outside nothing looked out of place.

When he left, he made sure that the front door was left ajar. That way if, or even *when* Anjli, Billy or whoever it was arrived at his house, they'd be able to enter, and see that something was wrong. He'd placed his phone in a visible location, too; they'd know that something was amiss, even if Karl didn't realise Declan had passed a message. It was the best he could do, as he still didn't know what Karl's plan was. For all he knew, Karl could have been watching him the entire time, so it was better to make these look like casual mistakes than a planned revelation.

He'd arrived at the car park of the Dew Drop Inn at fifteen minutes past ten that night; a good hour and a half before Karl was likely to arrive. But again, there was no proof that Karl wasn't there already. Looking around to make sure that he wasn't being watched, Declan reached carefully into his pocket and pulled out a small mobile phone. It was a burner phone, and one that Karl wouldn't have known that Declan owned, one that only had one number in it. He hadn't used it since he'd been on the run, but it had been the only thing he picked up from the house as he left. And he only sent one text on it right now.

Dew Drop Inn

This done, he leaned back in the seat, closing his eyes.

Nothing was going to happen for a good hour or more, and he needed to be at his best. But the moment he did, visions of Jess; captured, tortured, even killed crossed his vision. Opening them again, he sighed, turning on the car radio, allowing the sounds of *Classic FM* to enter the car, as he mentally prepared himself.

After all, this might be the last time he ever heard classical music.

———

ILSE WAS PACING AROUND THE WORKSHOP NOW, SILENT BUT obviously irritated. Jess glanced at the clock on the wall; it read 11.30pm. Half an hour before whatever was supposed to happen, well, happened.

Ilse stopped, turning to face Jess.

'It wasn't supposed to end this way,' she muttered. 'Rolfe was meant to give up. We could have lived in peace.'

Jess snorted, the only thing she could do while tied up. Ilse went to reply but then stopped, looking towards the main entrance.

'It'll all be over soon,' she cooed softly, as if to herself. Jess said nothing, but kept completely still. In fact, she didn't want to draw any more attention to herself, as in her right hand, hidden from view was a sliver of snapped metal hacksaw blade, no longer than four inches in length and grasped by Jess when the chair went over on the garage floor. It cut into her own hand, but Jess hoped that by gently sawing it against the plastic cable tie, she might break it. Or at least she might weaken it enough to snap the cable tie with her own strength. This way, if she could mostly cut through both cable ties, and that was a large if, as it relied on her being able to pass the blade from hand to hand, both tied to different arms of the wooden chair, she'd be able to burst free, surprising Ilse and taking her down.

That's how it was planned in her head. The facts of the matter were a lot more complicated. To actively attack, Jess would have to leap up and attack Ilse, but with her arms free and her ankles still secured, all that would happen was that Jess would tumble to the floor.

No, better to free one hand. There was every chance that she'd be left alone as Ilse became more jumpy, the right-hand arm of the chair wobbled after the fall, and could maybe be removed, used as a baton and she'd be able to break more bonds before the German madwoman realised.

In fact, Ilse was distracted now; staring out of the main door.

'I think I saw a car pass us,' she whispered. 'Your father's friends must have realised that you're missing. Or maybe it was just someone driving past, and I'm paranoid.'

Jess said nothing, using Ilse's distraction to saw harder, feeling a gentle snap as the cable tie gave way. When Ilse looked back to her captive, she didn't see the tie, hanging loosely on the other side, and so walked over to a side table, grabbing a can of cola and drinking from it.

'We could have lived in peace,' she repeated. She hadn't seen Jess pass the sliver of blade from one hand to the other, nor did she see Jess flex her legs, pulling at the cable ties around her ankles.

And she certainly hadn't seen Jess pull at the arm of the chair, her hand now freed, working the wooden armrest out of its socket with a little force.

BILLY LOOKED TO ANJLI AS THEY CARRIED ON DRIVING. 'Anything?'

'I don't know,' Anjli replied, looking over her shoulder, back at Karl Schnitter's garage. 'We can't just pull up, anyway. If they are in there, then things could get messy if they see us arrive.'

Billy nodded. 'They've found nothing in the Maidenhead garage or Karl's house. There aren't that many more places to look. And to be honest, they might not even be in Hurley any more.'

'True, but they didn't have time to work something out in detail, and they probably haven't realised we're looking for them,' Anjli replied. 'Pull over here, now we're out of sight.'

Billy pulled his Mini to the curb where it stopped, the lights turning off as he switched off the engine. 'Now what?'

Anjli looked down at her watch. 'It's half-past eleven,' she replied. 'I think we have a little time for a look around, yeah?'

Climbing out of the Mini, Billy and Anjli carefully stalked back to Karl Schnitter's garage. They could see a faint light emanating from inside, but the view wasn't that good from where they stood.

'We need to get closer,' Billy whispered. 'I told you that this sort of thing was why I didn't want to be a copper, right?'

'Shut up,' Anjli mocked as she crept towards the side window of the garage. 'You live for this shit.'

Now at the door, Billy carefully tried the handle. To no surprise at all, the door was locked. He turned to tell Anjli this, only to find that she was no longer outside the garage, having slid down the alley to the side, most likely intending to find a way in from the back of the building.

Which of course meant that Billy could either join her, or stay here and act as a distraction, as bait. He weighed up both options and was about to move towards the alley where the faintest of clicks paused him, stopping the breath in his chest.

The front door was opening.

ILSE LOOKED BACK TO JESS AS SHE MOVED TO THE FRONT DOOR. Through the glass, she could see the faint image of a man on the other side, lit from behind.

'You make any sound, you die,' she hissed. Jess struggled at the other cable tie as she sat there, worried that this could be her dad, about to walk into a trap. She needed to free herself quicker, but the blade was blunt now and the plastic was denser than she'd hoped as, picking up a vicious-looking wrench, Ilse slowly turned the lock in the door, clicking it open as slowly she turned the handle, raising the wrench to strike...

BILLY STEPPED BACK FROM THE GARAGE DOOR AS IT OPENED, THE back lit figure of a woman appearing in the doorway, some kind of weapon in her hand.

'I'm unarmed!' he exclaimed in fear as Anjli, a length of pipe in her grasp, emerged from the garage.

'Good job I'm not,' she laughed. 'Christ, Billy, you weren't joking. You really are terrible at this.'

'I'm guessing that there's nobody here?' Billy asked, leaning past Anjli to look into the garage.

'I don't think anyone's been in here since we were,' Anjli replied. 'There's still forensics tape everywhere.'

Billy sighed. 'Well, that's the last place empty,' he moaned. 'What the hell do we do now?'

———

ILSE STEPPED BACK FROM THE DOOR AS KARL SCHNITTER entered, quickly closing the door behind him.

'I thought you were the police,' she said. Karl smiled.

'They're too busy looking for any place I owned in Hurley,' he replied. 'Standard practice. Start where you know and work outwards. By the time they think of coming here, we will be long gone.'

'Is it done?' Ilse placed the wrench back onto the table as Karl nodded.

'I spoke to some old friends,' he replied. 'They will ensure we are well looked after. We will stay long enough to fix up some new identities and then we will be extracted.'

Ilse smiled. 'Will we be father and daughter?'

'Of course,' Karl replied. 'You might not be a Müller again, but I have lived with that for decades. A name is just a name.' He placed a rucksack on the counter as he watched out through the window on the door. 'There is a ferry leaving Tilbury at first light. It will take a couple of hours to drive there, and we will have to hide while it goes to Le Havre, but once it departs there, we will be free until we reach America.'

Ilse looked at Jess, now watching them. 'Should you have said that in front of the girl?' she asked. Karl shrugged.

'Who will she tell?' he replied, opening up his rucksack and pulling out a medical bag. 'Nobody listens to the dead. Once her father has taken his life, we will arrange it to look like he killed his daughter first.'

Jess didn't move, staring in horror at the two Germans.

'Do not worry, little one,' Karl smiled. 'It will be quick.'

BILLY WAS ABOUT TO START THE CAR WHEN HIS PHONE WENT. Looking at the screen, he frowned.

'We need to hold for a moment,' he said. 'I've got an automation that's ended.'

'And that means what exactly?' Anjli asked. 'Or is it some kind of tech thing that I'm too stupid to understand?'

Billy grinned. 'I need to remote access the computer at the Library,' he said, holding his phone sideways and using it as a small tablet. 'I need to see what—' he stopped.

'Oh.'

'Oh what?'

'I'd left the hard drive attached, to see if there was anything on it that could be retrieved,' Billy explained. 'There's one file. It was corrupted somehow, so the wiping must have kept it in some kind of stasis, not allowing it to be fully deleted, while not showing it.'

He turned the screen of his phone to Anjli. On it was a scan of an order note.

'I can't read it,' she complained. 'Go on.'

'Patrick Walsh must have got hold of a scan of a hire contract a couple of months back,' Billy was using his fingers to zoom in on it. 'Ilse must have heard about this, and that's why she had the iMac hard drive wiped. But it wasn't a document, it was a corrupted image.'

'An image of what?' Anjli was getting exasperated now.

'When Ilse Müller was here last time, she rented a workshop off the Thames, about half-a-mile west of Hurley, off Frogmill Lane.'

He looked to his partner.

'Nobody knows about it,' he said. 'Nobody would think to search there.'

IN THE LIBRARY, MONROE STARED IN HORROR AT THE LAPTOP AS it burst into life.

'I told you,' he muttered. 'The bloody things are sentient.'

'It's a remote login,' Bullman said as she watched the screen. 'Likely Fitzwarren. He's found a receipt on Patrick Walsh's drive, tracking it through his phone, most likely.'

'You don't mean car drive, do you?' Monroe replied as he paused, a sudden thought coming to him.

'Tracking. We can track Declan's car.'

'It's still at the house,' Freeman replied. Monroe shook his head.

'We have that doorbell camera footage from across the road, right? Can you bring it up?'

Bullman nodded. 'He seems to have logged off again,' she replied as she brought up the image. It was a doorbell camera from earlier that night. Declan's car wasn't in the drive, so before he arrived. However, there was a car on that side of the road, parked in front of the house.

'There,' Monroe tapped the screen. 'He's in that car.'

'How do you know?' asked Freeman. Examining the screen, Bullman nodded.

'When Declan was on the run, Karl loaned him a courtesy car from his garage. A Peugeot 308. That's the same car.'

'Okay, but that doesn't really help us.'

'It does, actually,' Monroe smiled. 'A lot of garages put trackers in their courtesy cars, so they can ensure they're not nicked. And if Karl had Declan take this one, I'd bet a month's salary that he's got some way to track it, to make sure Declan didn't do anything he shouldn't. All we have to do is find the tracking signal, and we find the car. And when we find the car, we find Declan.'

IN THE CAR PARK OF THE DEW DROP INN, DECLAN WATCHED AS Karl Schnitter drove in, parking up on the opposite side before exiting his vehicle and walking towards Declan's car, lit up by the headlights of the Peugeot 308. Looking to the dashboard, he saw it was just shy of midnight.

Always punctual.

Climbing out to face him, Declan walked in front of the lights, casting a shadow across Karl as he stopped about twenty feet away.

'I did what you said,' Declan said. 'I didn't alert the police. I told them to stand down.'

'Good man,' Karl replied.

'So let Jess go, yeah?'

'In good time,' Karl nodded. 'First, we must do something together.' He pulled out a coin from his pocket, holding it up, allowing the headlight to catch the face as it glinted in the lamplight.

'First, we must dance with the Red Reaper one last time,' he finished.

28

MIDNIGHT

DECLAN STARED ACROSS AT KARL WITH AN EXPRESSION OF frustrated annoyance.

'You're bloody kidding,' he snarled. 'You want to play a suicide game with me? After all of this?'

'I felt it would be the fitting way to end this,' Karl replied with a shrug. 'The end of the chase, so to speak.'

'You can go to hell,' Declan snapped. 'All I want is Jess.'

'She is not here,' Karl waved a hand around the car park. 'But my daughter is with her still, and she is waiting for a message from me. One that says to either release her, or execute her.'

Declan shook his head. 'You were our friend,' he muttered. 'We broke bread with you.'

'That is on you,' Karl replied. 'And for what it is worth, I am sorry, Declan. Your parents were good people. But they needed to move on. Their pain was simply too much to bear.'

'What, so you were helping them? Like an angel of mercy?' Declan laughed bitterly. 'You're insane. And you're going to pay for what you did.'

'Oh, I am well aware of this,' Karl replied. 'But not right now.'

Declan looked around the empty car park.

'Fine,' he said. 'I'll play your stupid bloody game. But first, you're answering some questions.'

'I am an open book,' Karl nodded. 'Whatever you want.'

'Did you kill Karl Meier?'

'Yes. He thought he could cuckold me. I proved he was wrong.'

'Why pretend you were him? Why all these lies?'

Karl shrugged. 'When you spend so long pretending a lie, you believe in it,' he explained. 'For a while, I forgot I had been Wilhelm Müller, and genuinely believed that I was Karl Meier, reborn as Schnitter.'

'Bullshit,' Declan snapped. 'You always knew who you were. A murdering sociopath.'

'I murdered no one,' Karl protested. 'I gave them a choice.'

'You gave them no choice!' Declan shouted back. 'You placed them into a corner! Told them that if they didn't do this, you'd kill their loved ones slowly!' He spat the words out at Karl, furious. 'You may not have pulled the trigger or used the blade, but you killed every one of them.'

'Not quite,' Karl looked around the car park, still not fully comfortable about the setting. 'I do not know if it was I or Ilse that helped Patrick to pass, and Ilse was the one to stand vigil over Nathanial.'

'Stand vigil?' Declan was appalled. 'Is that what you call this? Watching a terrified teenager slash his own wrists open rather than see his parents die?'

Karl's eyes darkened in the headlights.

'I knew you would never understand,' he said.

Ilse was pacing now, nervous, muttering to herself. Jess chuckled through the gag.

'What are you laughing at?' Ilse snapped, looking to her captive. 'What do you possibly see as funny here?'

Jess continued to chuckle, shrugging before looking away, effectively dismissing Ilse with her eyes. Unable to accept this, Ilse stormed over to Jess, ripping away the tape, pulling the gag out of Jess's mouth.

'Tell me!' She ordered. Jess looked up at her.

'You're supposed to kill me,' she said. 'But you've never done it before, have you?'

'I killed Nathanial Wing,' Ilse said proudly. 'I helped—'

'Did you though?' Jess raised her eyebrow at this. 'I mean, I saw the reports. He killed himself, right? You just watched like some sick voyeur.'

'Shut up,' Ilse muttered, but she didn't replace the gag. 'You don't know.'

'I don't know what?' Jess laughed now. 'How to scare someone into killing themselves, rather than doing the job itself?'

Ilse glared at Jess now, her eyes not moving from her gaze as she pulled out the sharp, folding knife once more, opening it up.

'I'll show you just how good I am at killing,' she snarled. 'I'll slice up your pretty—'

She didn't finish the statement because at that exact moment, as she leaned close to her captive, Jess swung her right hand, now gripping the loosened and pulled free wooden arm of the chair as a weapon up and from the side, a solid right-hand blow that connected hard on Ilse's head, busting it open, and sending her tumbling to the ground. Quickly grabbing the fallen blade with her also-free left hand, Jess moved down to her ankles, using the far sharper edge to quickly snap through the bonds. Then, rising up, she kicked the chair aside as she looked down at Ilse, still on the ground.

'You picked the wrong Walsh to play with, bitch,' Jess snarled. 'You're under arrest. A *citizen's* arrest.'

There was a noise outside of the workshop; it wasn't much, most likely a cat, or maybe a fox clattering past, knocking aside a metal tile, but the sound distracted Jess for a split second—and that was enough for Ilse to attack, blood streaming down the left side of her face as she rose from the floor in a charge, spearing Jess hard in the midsection, almost folding her in two as she followed through, the two of them crashing back onto the floor.

Climbing back to her feet, Ilse spat to the side.

'My turn now,' she said.

DECLAN WALKED CLOSER TO KARL NOW.

'So how do we do this?' he asked. 'We've got your gun, but there was no knife by Nathanial, so I'm assuming you still have that.'

Karl reached into his pocket and pulled out a syringe, filled with some sort of liquid. This shown, he placed it onto the floor between them.

'Heroin overdose,' he explained. 'They have accused you of many things over the years, Declan. I am sure *junkie* won't be a surprise to anyone.'

'You seem sure that you'll win,' Declan smiled. 'But I suppose the coin always favours the tosser.'

Karl went to reply, unsure on whether this was an insult or not, but Declan continued.

'Why did you give Nathanial a coin?' he asked. 'I'm guessing that Ilse gave him it to pass to Rolfe?'

'No, I gave it to him,' Karl admitted. 'I intercepted him outside the inn, and said that it was Rolfe's, that he'd dropped it outside. I then followed him in to watch and left when Ilse did.'

'You wanted Nathanial's prints on the coin,' Declan nodded now. 'When it was found on Rolfe, forensics linked the coin to Nathanial Wing's death. It validated the letter.' He smiled. 'Shame you didn't think of the CCTV watching this happen.'

'I am not some kind of master criminal,' Karl shrugged. 'I cannot think of everything.'

'No, you're just a murdering scumbag, like all the others,' Declan replied. 'Who has an urge, every two years.'

'That's how you beat the urge,' Karl explained as he backed a little away from Declan. 'I could do this every day, there are so many people out there that need to be removed. But I gave myself boundaries. I could only serve justice on an even year.'

'Serve justice,' Declan snapped. 'What bullshit you speak, Karl. And my parents?'

'Your father was a good detective,' Karl looked to the ground. 'Your mother was sick, and I knew I could help her. Nobody else would, and the pain would be unbearable. And your father? He was following Ilse, he was learning the truth about her, and me. I could not have that happen. I am truly sorry about Patrick, Declan. We could have done great things together.'

Declan stared down at the syringe filled with heroin. 'Tell me about the CIA,' he breathed. 'Tell me why they'll save you, no matter what.'

'When the wall fell, the files were burned,' Karl replied. 'The Stasi, they didn't want the West to know what atrocities they had committed, or who they had in various gulags under faked names. There were, shall we say, rotten apples in the departments, and they needed to be stopped.' He shrugged, as if embarrassed at this. 'I had friends in high places. I could go into rooms that others couldn't. The day the wall came down, there was confusion. Nobody knew what was going to happen, but I did. And I went to headquarters, went into these high places with a holdall bag, and I filled up with every secret I could find.'

'And nobody stopped you?'

'Of course not. Everyone there was trying to save their own skins. But, on the way back I bumped into Karl Meier. He'd followed me, wanted to kill me. But he did not realise that I had been waiting. Before he could do anything, I had stabbed him in the chest and moved on. It was liberating. I had ended evil.'

Declan shook his head. 'You're truly a monster.'

'I took these folders and walked to the American Embassy,' Karl continued. 'Offered to trade for certain privileges. One was to keep me safe if they ever placed me under trial.'

'Your *get out of jail free* card.'

'Yes. And at the same time, I hid other folders, ones on politicians that I knew would escape the wall's fall unscathed. And, as the years went on, I would contact them, letting them know that I kept their secrets safe for them. This way if the Americans decided not to play, I had powerful friends to remind them of the promises they made.' He looked out of the car park, up the bridleway towards Honey Lane.

'In fact, my American friends will be here soon,' he said. 'We should wrap this up now.' He pulled out a coin; it was a one mark piece, similar to the one that Rolfe Müller had held.

'Heads or tails?' he asked.

JESS KICKED OUT WITH HER LEG, CONNECTING HARD WITH ILSE'S shinbone, sending it backwards and Ilse back to the floor as Jess clambered back up, grabbing a wrench from the sideboard.

'My dad trained me in self defence since I was six,' she said, moving her head around, loosening her shoulders. 'But I've never needed to use it before. But don't think that means I don't know how to.'

Ilse rose, her nose now joining the bleeding cut on her temple.

'I'm going to skin you,' she hissed. Jess backed away a little at this.

'You have to catch me first,' she said, tossing the wooden arm rest at Ilse. As the German ducked to avoid it, Jess ran for the door, pulling at the handle in frustration as she realised it was locked from the outside. Turning slowly, she faced Ilse again.

'Okay, so maybe that wasn't such a good idea,' she said.

'Child, you know nothing about me,' Ilse spat. Jess nodded.

'True,' she replied. 'So show me what you've got.'

And with a scream she took the attack onto the offensive, rugby tackling Ilse hard at the knees, taking her back down to the floor with a resounding crash as the wrench went clattering into the toolbox to the side.

ON THE THAMES TOWPATH, ANJLI LOOKED TO BILLY.

'Did you hear that?' she asked, turning her head to see if she could narrow down the noise. Billy nodded, already running towards one of the buildings at the end of the small lane.

'They're in here!' he cried out. 'I can hear them fighting!'

Anjli pulled out her extendable baton and, preparing herself for a fight, she ran with Billy towards the workshop door.

ON A COUNTRY LANE JUST SOUTH OF HURLEY, DOCTOR MARCOS had her foot down as she drove her Mercedes A Class like a maniac. In the back seat, thrown around like a pinball was Freeman, the seatbelt he wore doing nothing to assist him against the sharp turns along the road, while Monroe held tight to the dashboard with one hand while he stared at his phone, held in the other.

'The signal's south of Honey Lane,' he said, looking up. 'It has to be the Dew Drop Inn.'

It had only taken them a matter of minutes to locate and contact the company that had installed the trackers into Karl Schnitter's cars, and only a matter of seconds to convince the company to provide them with what they needed; Doctor Marcos had arrived while they were doing this, and between them, Bullman and Marcos had made quick work of it. This done, Monroe and Doctor Marcos ran for her car in the hotel car park, while Bullman took a call from Billy which gave the likely location of Jess as a lockup west of Hurley, and as they arrived at the Mercedes, they saw Bullman join De'Geer on his police motorcycle.

Personally, Monroe thought that Bullman just wanted to have a go on it.

The motorbike roaring off, Monroe and Doctor Marcos had clambered into the car, but paused when Freeman joined them, stating that this was his patch, and he'd be the one to represent Maidenhead.

Monroe was actually grateful for this; Freeman was probably the only legitimate, non-suspended officer they had in the car right now, and the last thing they wanted was to arrive, arrest Karl Schnitter and then see him released on a technicality.

As the car screeched to the side to avoid a badger crossing the road, he screamed.

'Don't be a girl,' Doctor Marcos chided as they continued. 'It's three minutes until arrival.'

'I DON'T REALLY CARE,' DECLAN SAID, MOVING TOWARDS KARL as he held the coin in the light of the Peugeot. 'You call.'

'Tails it is then,' Karl said, as he flipped the coin—

Only to be caught mid air by Declan, who stepped back, throwing the coin with all of his might into the woodlands beside the car park.

'Not that coin, though,' he said, pulling another coin out of his pocket. It was still in its clear plastic bag, an item of evidence he'd pulled from Maidenhead before leaving. 'Let's make it a fair fight, yeah?'

He opened the bag and slipped the one mark coin, the one that Rolfe Müller had in his pocket when he died into his hand, flipping it across the car park towards Karl, who caught it, ashen faced. As Karl stared at the coin, Declan smiled.

'Have a good look,' he said. 'No trickery, just a fifty fifty chance of success or failure.'

'We cannot—'

'Cannot what?' Declan asked with mock innocence. 'It's the same coin you threw a minute ago, isn't it? Slightly newer perhaps, but with the same equal chances you gave everyone else?'

He smiled; a dark, vicious one.

'Unless you've never believed in the coin's luck, and you're just a lying piece of shit.'

Karl went to speak, thought better of it, and then threw the coin back to Declan.

'You can throw,' he said, the bravado returning to his voice. 'I choose tails.'

Declan nodded, but then paused.

'Can you do me a favour first?' he said, softly. 'Could you phone your daughter, so I can say a goodbye to mine?'

Karl nodded, pulling out the phone, dialling.

'No funny tricks, or she dies,' he said as he waited for the phone to answer. 'Come on, where are you...' he disconnected and redialled, still to no answer.

'Oh dear,' Declan replied. 'Looks like things aren't going well there. The question is, did my daughter beat the snot out of your daughter, or did my team get in there first?'

Karl looked around the car park, as if expecting armed police to leap out at any moment.

'Don't worry,' Declan continued. 'I didn't bring anyone. It's just us. And the coin. You said tails, right?'

And with that, Declan flipped the coin high into the air.

29

HEADS OR TAILS

KARL, OBVIOUSLY MORE NERVOUS ABOUT THIS COIN FLIP THAN any other he'd flipped in the past, watched the coin as it lazily turned in the air, reaching its peak before falling.

He wasn't however watching Declan, who, having never cared about the coin's result, took this moment to charge in heavily, slamming into Karl, sending them both to the muddy car park floor as the coin landed, unseen in the darkness.

Declan was military trained, but so was Karl; he might not have used it over the last three decades, but the German was a killer; cold, calculating and fighting for his life for probably the first time in years. *This would not be as easy,* Declan thought as—

Karl rolled up quickly, slamming his elbow towards Declan's stomach; but the move had been telegraphed, and Declan managed to desperately block it with his forearm, smacking it aside as he grabbed at Karl's arm, turning it into a hip toss, sending Karl flying onto the bonnet of the Peugeot with a crunch.

'That was for dad, you wanker,' Declan hissed as he

charged back in, only to catch a boot in the face, Karl kicking out and sending Declan staggering back as Karl tore the windscreen wiper off the car, whipping it at Declan's face like a rapier, catching his cheek, the vicious cut welling up with blood as Declan blocked another attack with his shoulder, letting the momentum carry him into a wicked sidekick that caught Karl square in the midsection, the air expelling with a *whuff* as Karl crumpled to the floor.

'Careful, Declan,' he chuckled. 'You break me, you might have nothing left to arrest.'

'Who said anything about arresting you?' Declan snapped back as he moved in for the kill.

'I'm *ending* you.'

———

The door to the workshop crashed open as Billy slammed his foot against the door handle, and Anjli ran in, brandishing the baton.

'*Armed police!*' she shouted. 'On the floor now!'

Jess and Ilse were in the workshop's corner; Ilse had the better of Jess and was pushing her backwards over the counter, a length of chain pressed against her opponent's throat. However, as the door crashed open, she momentarily glanced towards it, and Jess grabbed hold of a cordless drill on the worktop and swung it hard, the battery base of the drill connecting hard against Ilse's skull, sending her tumbling to the ground, disorientated.

'Get up,' Jess hissed, sweat dripping from her face as she wiped at it with her arm, the drill still in her hand. 'I haven't finished with you.'

'Yes you have,' Anjli replied as she grabbed the confused

Ilse from the ground, pulling her hands behind her back and cuffing her. 'You've done enough. Stand down.'

'Have you heard from dad?' Jess asked, leaning against the wooden counter, gulping in large, thankful breaths as she placed the drill back on the worktop. Billy shook his head.

'We think we know where he went, but it's a cellular dead zone there half the time,' he replied. 'The bosses are all on their way though.'

There was a roar of a motorcycle engine, and the door lit up with a mixture of headlamps and bright blue flashing lights.

'Cavalry's finally arrived then,' Anjli mocked. Moments later De'Geer and Bullman ran in, ready for a fight, but stopped as they saw the scene on the floor.

'Ah. We're not needed then. Good show,' Bullman said to Anjli, who smiled.

'Girl did it, not me,' she said.

Bullman looked at Jess, her breathing now back to normal.

'I see no girl,' she stated. 'All I see is a highly competent woman.'

Jess smiled. 'Thanks, ma'am.'

'It doesn't matter that you have me,' Ilse muttered to Jess. 'My father will kill your father, and then we will both walk free.'

'Yeah, about that,' Bullman walked over and knelt in front of Ilse. 'He did without you for thirty years. You think he'll risk everything for a daughter he barely knows? Who's on charges of kidnapping, accessory to murder—'

'Attempted murder of a minor,' Jess added.

'That as well,' Bullman smiled, looking back to Ilse. 'Face

it, love. Even in the remote chance he wins, he's not risking his freedom. Men like him never do. You're screwed.'

De'Geer moved in and grabbed Ilse, pulling her to her feet and pulling her outside where, in the distance, more police sirens could be heard, more backup from Maidenhead as Jess walked over to Anjli.

'Armed police?' She enquired. Anjli grinned, showing the extendable baton.

'A technicality,' she replied. 'And it always makes them look, doesn't it?'

Billy was working through messages on a phone that he'd found on the worktop.

'They're at the Dew Drop Inn,' he said as he looked up. 'But Karl doesn't intend to walk out with Declan still alive.'

'That's fine,' Jess forced a smile. 'Dad probably has the same idea. Does anyone have...'

And without finishing, Jess' eyes rolled back into her head as she finally passed out, collapsing to the ground in a heap.

KARL PARRIED A FOOT TO THE HEAD AND SWEPT DECLAN'S LEGS out from under him, sending his opponent to the floor. Now up and moving, Karl ran back to his car, a slow, limping run which showed that the German was feeling the injuries.

'Running away?' Declan cried out as he climbed to his feet. 'You goddamn *coward*!'

Karl reached into the glove compartment of his car and pulled out a folding cut-throat straight razor. Straightening up, he started back towards Declan, the blade now out.

'I used this on Craig Randall,' he said. 'And Michael Bose, back in Paris. What do you say? Third time's the charm?'

He slashed at Declan, who staggered back, trying not to overbalance as Karl kept moving in, the straight razor glinting in the car headlights. Declan darted right, towards the Dew Drop Inn and the scaffolding around it as Karl moved after him like some kind of insane, German Terminator.

'Where are your funny lines now, Declan?' Karl shouted. 'Where are your arrogant beliefs in yourself? All those times I pretended to be your friend, and not once did you think I was lying! I even came into your house after I stole your father's computer and offered to stay with the glazier! Me! Alone in your father's house! What would he have said!'

He slashed again at Declan, who retreated behind a skip, looking for something he could use as a weapon.

Slash. Slash.

'And then, you come to me through the back garden!' Karl continued. 'That was a clever idea, to use the back fence, it meant the police could not work out how you escaped. I used it tonight, when we removed your daughter from the house without that bitch of a neighbour across the street seeing!'

Slash. Sla—

Declan swung hard with a piece of plywood, a torn scrap of framing, but large enough to do some damage. Karl ducked away from most of the blow, but the torn edge of the wood slammed him hard in the forehead and now, bleeding from the cut he stumbled back.

'Just shut up,' Declan said, moving in once more. 'Shut up and damn well die.'

Karl's face was ashen now as he realised that this could actually be a fight he was going to lose.

'Your daughter by now is arrested or worse,' Declan continued. 'Your CIA friends haven't turned up, and the police aren't here to finish this. *I'm* here to finish this. Here—'

He pulled a business card out of his pocket. It was one of his Temple Inn ones, and on the back was a stick man with a scythe, drawn in blue ink. He tossed it to Karl.

'Pick it up,' he hissed. 'Let's start a new cult. The *Blue Executioner.* Doesn't have the same ring as yours, but hell, I only intend to use it *once.*'

Karl raised up his straight razor, but Declan kicked out at the hand, sending the blade clattering across the carpark tarmac. Walking to the syringe, Declan picked it up, turning back to Karl.

'Time for an overdose, you son of a bitch,' he snarled as he walked back towards Karl, now trying to back away while still in a sitting position.

'Wait!' Karl begged. 'We can talk about this!'

'Did the others beg?' Declan asked. 'Did you hear their pleas? Did you ignore them? Force them to die?' He tossed the syringe over to Karl, where it came to a rest against his thigh.

'Your American friends aren't coming,' Declan smiled darkly. 'I called in a favour. You're more good to them gone than still around.'

'I will make sure they—'

'*Stop!*' Declan screamed. 'Don't you get it? I'm *not arresting you!* The name Karl Schnitter will never be *spoken again* after tonight! You're *gone, forgotten, removed!*' He pointed at the syringe.

'That's your only honourable way out. To do what others did before you. To accept the ruling of the Red Reaper and kill yourself.'

Karl stared at the syringe, at the death within it, and shook his head.

'No,' he whispered as he tossed it aside. 'I will not play this game. Arrest me and let us get this over with.'

From the bridleway there was the sound of a car arriving at speed, and Doctor Marcos' Mercedes skidded into view as almost before it stopped, Monroe, Freeman and Doctor Marcos emerged from it, running towards the two men.

'Don't do it, Declan!' Freeman shouted. 'We've got Jess. She's safe. And Ilse is under lock and key.'

Declan turned back to Karl to see him smiling.

'And now the police are here, and normality returns,' he said gratefully, climbing painfully to his feet, holding his hands out. 'Please, arrest me.'

Monroe went to walk forward, but Freeman halted him.

'We can't,' he muttered. 'The CIA has claimed him the moment we place handcuffs on him. He won't see a moment of prison time.'

'Then what do we do?' Monroe snapped as Karl laughed.

'You could let me go free?' he suggested. But Declan simply smiled again as, in the distance, they could hear another vehicle approaching.

'Not happening,' he said as a grey van pulled into the car park, looking remarkably like the one that had abducted Declan a couple of days earlier. It pulled up beside Karl and stopped, the side doors opening and three men leaping out, grabbing him by the arms.

'Wait!' Karl cried out. 'What are you doing?'

'I second that!' Monroe joined in. 'What the hell is this, Declan?'

The driver's side door opened and Tom Marlowe emerged, nodding to Monroe.

'It's justice, uncle,' he said simply. 'Justice for all that were killed, in particular Christine and Patrick Walsh.'

He turned to the terrified Karl.

'Hello, Wilhelm,' he said with a relaxed grin. 'We have some people who want to chat to you in a deep, dark, government black site. And we have some German buddies who are mightily pissed that you shot one of their own. They've asked for some pounds of flesh, too.'

'When my friends hear what you've done to me—' Karl started, but stopped when Declan put up a finger to stop him.

'How will they hear?' he asked. 'Seriously. Tell me. I won't be telling anyone about tonight. As far as I'm concerned, and as my report will state, you escaped and left your daughter to rot in prison.'

He looked to Freeman.

'We'll leave the case open, the CIA won't be able to argue it, and justice will be served.'

Monroe also looked at Freeman. 'You okay with this?' he asked. To his surprise, Freeman nodded.

'I don't have to be okay with it,' he replied calmly. 'Because when we got here, Declan was alone. Isn't that right, DCI Monroe?'

'I don't think I'll be DCI much longer,' Monroe said. 'But, if I'm going to be kicked out for doing something against the rules, this is a pretty solid one to do.' He looked at Doctor Marcos. 'You?'

'I'm only happy with this, if you send me pictures of what you do to him,' Doctor Marcos said to Marlowe, who nodded.

'That can be arranged,' he said, nodding to the three men who pulled the kicking and screaming Karl into the van. Declan walked up to the door, facing his one-time friend.

'You helped me when I needed you, so I will never forget

that,' he said. 'That's the only reason I didn't kill you tonight. That, and that the amount of pain and suffering you'll endure for the rest of your life will be punishment enough for the people you killed.'

He looked to Marlowe.

'Make sure it's a long life,' he ordered. 'I didn't give him to you, to make Ilse an orphan.'

Marlowe nodded, climbing into the van and, with a last wink to Monroe, he started up the engine.

'Laddie,' Monroe walked up to the window. 'Tell her... tell her I hope she's happy, and if she is, I'm glad.'

Marlowe grinned.

'I don't think I've ever seen her happy, but I'll tell her,' he said as the van drove away into the Berkshire night.

There was a moment of silence in the car park.

Declan stretched, feeling his shoulder, wincing at the pain.

'Gunshot wound opened?' Monroe asked as Declan nodded. 'Well, it serves you right for being a bloody martyr, then.'

'How did you find me?' Declan looked up to all three officers. 'I didn't tell anyone.'

'Tracker in the car,' Doctor Marcos smiled. 'It's always the tracker, Declan. God, you still have so much to learn.'

'Jess?'

'Being taken to St Mark's hospital now,' Freeman patted Declan on the arm. 'You know how you've been a pain in my neck on this? I'm afraid I had to return the favour, and I called her mum. Sorry.'

Declan nodded. To be honest, having Lizzie angry at him while Jess was safe was the best of the outcomes he'd envisioned for this night.

'We should get out of here too,' Doctor Marcos continued. 'We need that shoulder looked at, and we need to confirm the story that we're telling everyone.'

'It's simple,' Monroe nodded to Declan. 'Karl and Ilse kidnapped his kid, he went to negotiate, our guys saved Jess and realising this, Karl ran, never to be seen again.'

'That works for me, as long as you're all okay with that,' Declan nodded, but then stopped, looking out across the car park.

'Have any of you got torches?' he asked.

'What now?' Monroe muttered. 'Did you lose your car keys?'

'More a fatal overdose of heroin,' Declan replied, scanning the floor. 'Thought it might be an idea to pick it up before we leave.'

And with their smartphones out as torches, Declan, two DCIs and a Divisional Surgeon played a midnight game of *hunt the syringe,* while in a van three miles to the east, the Red Reaper was taken to face *real* justice.

EPILOGUE

It took another week before the fallout finally settled.

Declan had returned to the hospital to face a furious Lizzie; he'd expected this, and although Jess was awake and explaining that she'd only passed out due to shock, the bruises on her wrists and around her throat gave the true story that she was trying to gloss over with bravado and, when Lizzie grabbed him by the arm and dragged him into a corridor, he was ready for whatever words she had to say.

He wasn't however ready for the words that she did say.

'I'm speaking to a solicitor later,' she hissed at him, pushing him against a corridor wall. 'We're going to petition to have you removed from custody for Jess. I don't want you near my daughter ever again.'

'Lizzie, you can't—'

'I can't what?' She snapped back, tears welling in her eyes, tears of anger and fury. '*Jess almost died,* Declan! She almost died, and you put her into that situation! She's fifteen!'

Lizzie looked away, taking in deep breaths to calm herself.

'I don't know what's happened to you, but you're not the

man I married, fell in love with. You've thrown yourself at every opportunity to kill yourself ever since your bloody dad died. And I'm sick of it, Declan. And I'm sick of you trying to drag our daughter with you. If it's not men stealing her bag, it's women trying to murder her.'

She looked away.

'Not anymore, Declan. You're toxic. You destroy everything you touch. And I'll be damned if I'm losing Jess to that.'

Declan stared at Lizzie for a long moment before speaking.

'I agree,' he whispered. 'You don't need to spend money on a solicitor, I agree. I didn't think this would happen, and I didn't look after my daughter enough.' He looked through the window at her, currently laughing at something PC De'Geer, who'd been with Declan since he arrived to have his own wound stitched up, was saying.

'Just tell her I'm sorry,' he continued. 'That I'll call her—'

'You'll do no such bloody thing,' Lizzie interrupted. 'You're a ghost, Declan. I don't expect to hear from you apart from birthdays and Christmas, you understand?'

Before Declan could answer, Lizzie turned from him, walking back into the ward where she embraced Jess. After a moment of conversation, Lizzie and Jess left together; Lizzie staring straight ahead, while Jess managed a brief nod to her father, standing alone in the hospital corridor.

Karl Schnitter, or Wilhelm Müller rather wasn't the only one to lose a daughter that day.

After that, things had been a little more normal around the village. Declan still received glares from some villagers, and he understood that. To some of them, people who didn't know the full story, Declan was involved with one of their own, and the result was a missing, popular local mechanic. There were even rumours that Declan had murdered him, hiding the body in the woods near the Dew Drop Inn, but rumours were just rumours. The truth was far wilder, and Declan had ensured that nobody would ever learn that.

Billy gave Declan back his dad's iMac, now reunited with its hard drive, but the only thing on it was the image of a receipt, the one that Billy had deduced the location of Ilse Müller on. Declan had shivered at that; he'd had faith in his team to come through, as they always came through, but for the first time he realised just how close they came to failing.

How close Jess was to dying for his own mistakes.

Lizzie was right to keep her from him.

Later the same day, Declan had taken a sledgehammer to the fake wall in his dad's study, making sure not to re-tear his shoulder wound, and by the end of the day he'd removed a chunk of framing wood and plasterboard, and beginning a long route to removing the secrets and lies that had ended Patrick Walsh's life. He didn't know what to do with all the rubble though, so he placed it in his Audi and drove to the Dew Drop Inn; the contractors were still there, working on the place, but didn't mind Declan dumping a few more pieces into their skip. There was no crime scene tape, as according to DCI Freeman, there'd been no crime scene there. And therefore forensics hadn't bothered to visit.

As Declan walked back to his car, he stopped, noticing something glinting on the gravel floor. Walking over to it, he saw it was the coin that he'd thrown, that Karl had been too busy watching to realise that it was nothing more than a lure. The number 1 faced upwards on the surface of the coin.

Heads.

Declan almost laughed at this. Even without the fight, Karl had still lost and, no longer rigged, the coin toss had fallen in Declan's favour. Picking it off the ground, he placed it in his pocket as he continued to the Audi, climbing in. His phone, left on the passenger seat, was flashing. Picking it up, he saw he had a new message from DCI Freeman.

As he read it, he smiled.

———

Billy was sitting in a booth at the Eight Club when Rufus Harrington arrived, all smiles.

'William!' he exhorted as he sat facing his new hire. 'I see you're in your suit and tie? Not needed, old chum. We're far more casual in the office.'

'Thanks for meeting with me,' Billy replied. 'I wanted to say this face to face, as you've been so kind.'

Harrington leaned back, staring at the ceiling in mock despair.

'Dear God, you've returned home, haven't you?' he said. 'That's why you're in your best Savile Row.'

Billy smiled. 'I'm a copper, Rufus,' he replied. 'I just needed to be reminded of it.'

'You sure you're making the right decision?' Rufus looked back at Billy now. 'You're losing a lot of money, of stock options here.'

Billy smiled. 'It was never about the money,' he said. 'Thanks for the opportunity.'

'Hey, it's always there, for when you realise this was a big mistake,' Rufus grinned as Billy rose from the booth and walked to the entrance. 'But at least this way I know my parking fines can be squashed.'

'Dream on,' Billy laughed as he left, looking at his watch.

He was late for work.

WHEN THE TEMPLE INN OFFICES HAD FIRST BEEN OFFERED TO the City Police, they were part of a reciprocal deal for police security. The deal had been long forgotten now but the premises, grandfathered into the deeds meant that in this maze of barrister chambers and dinner halls, of courtyards and of pillared walkways there was a part of a small red bricked building off King's Bench Walk that were City Police offices. Used as nothing more than file storage for the last fifteen years, it had been left 'as is', meaning there were no upgrades to the networks or the wiring, and the furniture was two decades out of date.

It was home.

But recently it had been renovated as The City Police, realising that they had a good thing here had renegotiated the deal with Temple Inn, or to give the official title, The Honourable Society of the Inner Temple, one of the four 'Inns of Court' in London, four professional associations for Barristers and Judges in the city, and an area of land set up by the Knights Templar almost a thousand years earlier.

The Knights Templar were gone now, but the Last Chance Saloon hadn't, *yet*.

Declan had parked his Audi in its usual spot and stared up at the red bricked building. From the outside, nothing had changed, but the last time he'd entered it, he'd been hand-cuffed, and the last time he exited it had been via the roof. In part, showing these flaws in the structure had been one reason for the refurbishment; he just hoped that things hadn't changed too much.

He'd also expected not to return here, but the message from Freeman had been pretty convincing; Declan and the team, working on their own initiative, had solved a vicious murder enquiry, and were due for a commendation. There was no mention of the fact that Karl escaped, as Whitehall most likely knew the full story, anyway.

Taking a deep breath, Declan entered the building. Before, when he walked in, he found himself in a narrow corridor, with forensics to the side; now he found himself in a police waiting room, a desk sergeant, a sturdy-looking woman in her fifties, grey hair pulled into a bun, watching him from behind a glass windowed counter. He didn't recognise her, but she obviously knew him as she buzzed the door to the side, which opened.

'This is new,' he said, opening it.

'Your ID will open that once you receive it,' the desk sergeant replied. 'There'll be a sergeant on shift here during working hours. The rest of the time, it's keys and passes only.' With that she looked back to her paper, introductions seemingly not needed. Shrugging, and not keen to continue the conversation himself, Declan continued down the corridor. To the side, he could see three rooms, one of which had the door open, revealing a morgue table.

At least some things don't change.

Walking up the stairs, Declan found himself on familiar ground now; the offices were still open plan, but the briefing room was double the size, the interview room now missing. Besides this, there was a new office next door to Monroe's one; a larger corner office, too. Declan had heard that the department was gaining a Detective Superintendent, and he wondered how Monroe felt about this, considering the Last Chance Saloon was his baby.

There were still desks in the middle of the office, but now there was a section of wall that seemed to be built out of monitors. This had to be the new and updated cyber crime section; Declan hoped that they'd at least updated the fibre optics and the cables, as Billy had always been complaining about the lag. Declan also wondered who they'd convinced to join them to run it, with Billy now gone.

'Good, isn't it?' Monroe said as he emerged from the briefing room. 'Feels like a real department.'

'Where's the interview room?' Declan asked. Monroe pointed upwards.

'Next floor up,' he said. 'They knocked through to that staircase you found, and now we have the floors above us too.' They walked towards the briefing room, which currently had the blinds pulled. 'Top floor is just storage, but we've got interview rooms and a couple of shift cots upstairs, in case we're pulling all-nighters.' He grinned. 'No more sleeping on sofas.'

'Any news on the new Guv?' Declan asked, hastily adding 'of course, you'll always be the *Guv*, Guv.'

'All good things to those who wait,' Monroe pointed at the briefing room door. 'Come on, we started a few minutes back so you haven't missed much.'

'There's a desk sergeant downstairs, didn't seem to want to talk to me,' Declan replied. 'Are we gaining uniforms?'

'A few,' Monroe winked. Declan, unsure what that meant, walked into the briefing room and smiled.

DS Anjli Kapoor sat at a desk, chatting to DC William 'Billy' Fitzwarren. Behind them, currently arguing whether

Harley Davidson's were better than Triumphs, were DC Joanna Davey and PC Morten De'Geer. By the wall, eating a cornetto and grinning at Declan was Doctor Marcos.

'Find a seat, laddie, there you go,' Monroe pointed at a spare chair beside a table at the front. 'You can sit at the *teacher's pet* table.'

Refusing to comment on this, Declan sat down as Monroe faced the team.

'So, new day, new start,' he said. 'And now mister Walsh had graced us with his presence, we can begin.' He cleared his throat, and Declan could see that he was nervous.

'We made some big enemies, and also some influential friends,' he started. 'And because of that, they've given us a larger scope and remit, including new uniforms,' he nodded to PC De'Geer who grinned at everyone, 'and a new boss.'

He stopped, and looked to the door where Detective Superintendent Sophie Bullman entered, a small, faint smile on her face, as if concerned what people would say.

'Before anyone says I was parachuted in, or that I took someone's job,' she said, pointedly looking at Monroe, 'he didn't want it. Some bollocks about Captain Kirk and being in space. Personally, I think we should put DCI Monroe out to pasture, or shoot him.'

'Hear hear,' Doctor Marcos raised her cornetto.

'Been tried before,' Monroe smiled as Bullman continued.

'Apparently, the devious bastard convinced his superiors that the one person he didn't want to command here was me, so here you go. I know all of you, although some of you are lesser known, and I've seen what you can do. But that was yesterday, and all the bosses care about is tomorrow. So have a look around our new offices, make use of the new kitchen upstairs before Doctor Marcos eats all the ice creams, and settle in. If I've learned anything about this unit the last three times I've worked with you, it's that normality is more a guideline than choice.'

'Welcome to the Last Chance Saloon, Guv,' Anjli grinned, looking back to De'Geer. 'To both of you.'

There was a smattering of applause, and with the meeting now over, Declan rose and walked to Monroe.

'You okay with this?' he asked.

'I wouldn't have worked well with the suits,' Monroe replied with a faint smile. 'Bullman is a far more political animal than I am. She'll let us work on the cases, and I won't have to deal with all the touchy feely bullshit anymore. And I won't have to deal with explaining your screwups to Chief Superintendent Bradbury anymore.'

Declan laughed as he walked into the office, looking around. For a split second, it reminded him of Section D's modern style office, and so he walked over to Billy, currently still connecting devices in his new setup.

'Greatest IT team in London, they said,' he moaned as he reconnected a USB-C connector. 'Idiots have already screwed up the network. It'll take me all day to fix it.' He looked to Declan and smiled.

'Thanks, sir. For getting me involved in Hurley. For reminding me why I do this.'

'You never need to thank me again,' Declan replied. 'I owe all of you.'

'How's Jess?'

'I don't know,' Declan stated mournfully. 'Her mum has banned her from contacting me. All I know is that she's home and safe, and I can deal with that.' He pulled out a USB drive, the small one that Tom Marlowe had given him a week earlier.

'But as you claim you owe me, I could do with a favour,' he explained, passing it across. 'Off the books.'

'Christ, I haven't even settled in!' Billy lamented.

'Just check it over, ensure there're no viruses or anything,' Declan replied. 'Wintergreen wanted me to have it, and I'm untrusting of gifts these days.'

Billy nodded, taking the drive, and Declan walked over to De'Geer, currently standing at a bit of a loss in the middle of the office.

'Transferred or sent?' he asked. De'Geer looked towards the offices of Monroe and Bullman.

'Requested,' he replied. 'Seems someone here felt I was being under-used in Maidenhead.'

'Hell of a commute, though,' Declan said. 'Trust me on that one.'

'Not on a motorcycle,' De'Geer chuckled. 'You should try it.'

He looked up as DC Davey waved him over, their bike argument unfinished. 'Sir,' he said as he left Declan alone once more.

He walked over to his new desk, seeing that his items, packed away by the contractors, were beside the keyboard, waiting for him to unpack. On the top was the *British Bobby* Funko that he'd had on his desk since Tottenham North; a gift from Jess almost a year earlier. Pulling it out, he saw that in the packing and subsequent movement, it had been broken and hastily fixed, a long broken scar running across the face where the two parts had been glued back together. Holding it up in his hand, he stared hard at it.

I hope to Christ this isn't an omen.

And then, placing it on his desk, he unpacked his things, preparing for work.

He looked up, watching everyone else hard at work doing the same thing. Anjli was placing a photo of her mum on a desk, Billy still struggling with network wires, even Monroe was finding the right placement for his yucca plant, all getting the little things out of the way, all knowing that they had to be organised and ready for anything as quick as they could.

Because you never knew what the *next* case would bring at the *Last Chance Saloon*.

DI Walsh and the team of the *Last Chance Saloon* will return in their next thriller

TO HUNT
ᴬMAGPIE

Order Now at Amazon:

http://mybook.to/tohuntamagpie

And read on for a sneak preview...

PROLOGUE

THIRTY YEARS AFTER THE BOOKS HAD BEEN FIRST RELEASED, THE *Magpie* series of children's detective stories were almost forgotten in the contemporary book market. Set at the start of the nineties, the novels were simple and quick to follow; Agatha Christie for the pre-teen generation, a series of adventures with titles like *The Adventure of the Drowning Duchess, The Adventure of the Missing Prince* and *The Adventure of the Broken Clock,* all stories that showed how a small and clever team of teenage sleuths could defeat grown up criminals, with detective skills and good old fashioned *gumption.* More contemporary than their *Enid Blyton* related peers, the *Magpie* series however had one major difference to the others.

They were based on the *truth.*

The official story was as old as the novels themselves; that author Reginald Troughton had learned of the *Magpies* and their crime solving through a report in a local newspaper, and had written their adventures as stories, never expecting the interest that they would generate. In fact, he wrote seven novels in total involving the adventures of *Tommy, Luke,*

Tessa, Jane and *Daniel*, and their group mascot and crime solving spaniel *Dexter the dog,* finishing when the *Magpies* themselves disbanded after a distinguished teenage crime solving career.

The books had sold on for a few years more, but in the same way that many other book franchises suffered, they were overtaken by new trends, new technology, and eventually faded into the realms of nostalgia.

But the *fans* never forgot them. And, as the years passed, and the *Magpies* moved on with their lives, the fans still supported them.

Well, some more than others.

Thomas Williams, or as he was known back then, *Tommy* wasn't a teenage sleuth anymore. Now he was in his midforties but still looked a good few years younger, his brown hair short and styled with the slightest hint of bottle-dye, a *Ted Baker* suit over a pale Eton shirt, his tan brogues shined to perfection and his stubble carefully curated. He looked like a cross between a television presenter and a self-help guru. Which, actually, were two of the many roles he'd played over the years.

Today however he was there, not as Thomas, but as *Tommy* once more. The fourth floor of *Waterstones'* Piccadilly branch had been converted from bookstore to event venue for the night, with folding chairs in rows facing a clearing at the front where a lectern had been hastily placed, a table to the side piled high with newly released editions of the *Magpies* books. Beside that a sign had been tacked onto the wall, the same poster that had been strategically positioned around the store; a photo of the *Magpies* in their prime, above a line of text that read

MEET THOMAS WILLIAMS - 'TOMMY' FROM THE MAGPIES - 7PM!

Thomas hated the photo; he hated that Daniel had got to sit beside Jane for it, while he had to place a brotherly arm around his 'cousin', Luke, who was being an absolute prick to him at the time.

Nothing changes.

He looked across the floor at the chairs from his hidden 'backstage' area, which was in actuality a small, closed off space made from repositioned bookshelves. It wasn't exactly a West End dressing room, but he'd had worse.

The audience was primarily female; it always was for these events. Thomas assumed it was the same for teenage heartthrobs when they attended events years later, but he had never been a heartthrob in any sense of the word, and these women only wanted him now because he was a reminder of their youth—

He stopped scanning the audience as he spied a lone woman in her forties in the fourth row, her blonde hair pulled back. Slim and still as stunningly attractive as she was as a teenager, Thomas grinned on seeing her, and straightened his jacket.

Ah, Jane. You couldn't stay away from me.

Now, Thomas Williams had an audience that he gave a *damn* about.

As the audience mumbled and muttered excitedly to each other, a small, stocky woman in her late thirties walked to the lectern, tapping the microphone on it to check that it was working, silencing the audience's conversations as they turned to face her with expectant gazes. When he'd arrived an hour earlier, she'd told Thomas her name, and he seemed to remember that she was the manager of one floor, but there were so many managers and store owners over the years, that in the end they all merged into one. He never remembered the names.

Well, only the pretty ones.

'Thank you everyone, for attending tonight,' she began, her face beaming with pride. 'When I was a girl, I loved the *Magpie* books. I'd even dream of one day solving cases with Tommy Williams, Luke Ashton, Tessa Martinez, Jane Taylor, Daniel McCarthy and Dexter the dog. Anyone else do that?'

There was a smattering of hands and a chuckle of approving laughter. Validated, the manager continued.

'One reason the books sold so well, apart from the excellent writing of Reginald Troughton, was that the five characters—'

'And the dog!' a voice called out. Thomas, listening, cringed. He had *hated* that bloody spaniel.

'And the dog, yes,' the manager replied. 'One reason the books sold so well was because unlike so many other 'teenage detective' stories, these were *true*, written by Troughton, based on notes and interviews given to him by the *Magpies* themselves.'

Thomas moved into position for his entrance, and the audience, seeing this, fidgeted with excitement as, unaware of this, the manager continued.

'And tonight we're very lucky to have with us one of the original *Magpies*, a man who has written new introductions for the upcoming reprints, celebrating the thirtieth anniversary of the group's first adventure,' she gushed. 'He's here today to sign them for you, but before we put him to work, let's hear it for 'Tommy' from the *Magpies*, Thomas Williams!'

As the audience applauded and cheered, Thomas walked

to the lectern, waving to the crowd and nodding to the manager as she backed away to give him space. Now at the lectern, he gave a second brief wave to his adoring fans and then spoke, a prepared speech that he'd spoken at events around the world for over twenty years; one so well rehearsed that he could alter it on the fly.

'When my cousin Luke and I started the *Magpies*, it was to prove that our milkman wasn't a killer,' he explained. 'We couldn't even conceive the global phenomenon that it would become. But Reginald Troughton did. He believed the stories he would write about us would become famous. Would make *us* famous.'

He went to motion towards the back of the room, but paused, thrown for a moment.

There was a gap at the back of the crowd that shouldn't be there.

And a cryptic message he'd had earlier that day suddenly made sense.

'Uh... Unfortunately Reginald can't be with us today as he's suffering from a head cold in Scotland,' he continued on, recovering. 'But he sends his regards to all of you.'

He looked at Jane who, realising what he was about to do, started shaking her head.

'But that's not to say I'm the only celebrity here today,' Thomas smiled, pointing to her. 'I'd like to introduce to you another member of the *Magpies*, my good friend Jane Taylor!'

As the audience, surprised at such a person in their midst, looked to Jane and applauded, Thomas took a deep breath, grateful to her for the distraction.

Because Reginald Troughton wasn't in Scotland and didn't have a cold.

He was supposed to have appeared, out of nowhere, from

the back of the audience. It was a 'surprise appearance' skit that he'd performed for years, and one that was as far from a 'surprise' as you could get these days.

So where the hell was he this time?

REGINALD TROUGHTON SAT IN THE OFFICE OF HIS APARTMENT IN Temple Inn, facing his desk and MacBook Pro with an air of frustrated irritation. He was on a deadline, and he was failing it. He remembered some kind of anecdote by Douglas Adams about *deadlines* and *whooshing noises,* but it didn't really help that as far as he was concerned, Adams was a hack who could write a novel in a week, while he, the great and lauded Reginald Troughton couldn't write a sodding children's book in a month.

His agent had called earlier that day, passive aggressively demanding the finished manuscript by the end of the week, or else the advance was being taken away. Reginald had taken the scolding before pointing out that *he only heard from her when she needed something,* and *where the hell was the auction for his adult thriller series she'd been promising.* However, as he'd already spent the pittance *BadgerLock Publishing* had sent him months earlier, and after Michael's funeral expenses, he didn't have the cash around to give back.

He would in a few days though, a windfall was coming his way; but that was his retirement. There was no way that he'd be using that to pay back Julia Clarke and her band of merry marketers, and this meant that he had to buckle down and finish the bloody thing, which meant he couldn't go to the *Waterstones* event.

Which was fine by him; now in his mid-sixties, he wasn't

interested in fanboy totty anymore. Also, Thomas Williams was an insufferable bastard to be around, a little snivelling shit whose only income was milking people's nostalgia for *pennies*. He'd passed the message that he wasn't attending tonight down the line, but he'd left it vague in case he managed to actually make it.

He hadn't.

And now he was finishing up the 'lost' *Magpie* adventure, trying to work out how to say what he wanted to say without shitting the bed too much. It was supposed to be called *The Adventure of the Blacksmith's Apron*, and was possibly the most made up bollocks he had ever written, but halfway through he'd had a revelation. He was going to write the *truth*. And so the book had been re-titled *The Adventure of the Stolen Innocence*, and instead of some bullshit about a blacksmith in a Devonshire village, the book was now the truth about the bloody *Magpies*, why they'd been formed and, more importantly, why they'd *ended*. He knew it'd piss people off, but frankly he didn't care. The contract didn't state what the novel had to be about, and they didn't pay him enough to keep silent anymore.

There was the sound of a sudden *crack* in the other room, as if someone had thrown a stone at a window, breaking it, and Reginald rose wearily from the chair. The bloody teenagers were buggers for smashing windows in the Inns of Court—

He didn't finish the thought as, to his left, a man entered the doorway to the office. That was, it looked like a man because of the full-head latex mask of a bald man that the figure wore. The black clothing; a hoodie, gloves and cargo pants were shapeless and could have been of either sex, but the one thing that was obvious was the intention, shown by the brand new tyre iron that the bald man held in their left hand, likely the item that had made the glass cracking noise, as they'd forced entry through the glass in the front door.

Reginald swallowed nervously.

'So,' he whispered. 'Which one of you finally had the balls to face me?'

The 'bald man' didn't reply as they moved in, striking down hard with the tyre iron.

———

THE AUDIENCE LAUGHED AS THOMAS FINISHED READING ALOUD from the first of the books, *The Adventure Of The Rusty Crowbar.* He'd learned many years ago that they'd eat up anything he said, and it was easier to read books they knew by heart than to actively work on something original.

Looking up at them, he grinned.

'I think you all know what happens next,' he finished. The audience nodded and murmured in agreement, before applauding.

Of course they knew what happened next, he thought to himself, as the manager leaned past him, a little *too* close as she brushed his arm on her way to the microphone. *They've read everything a dozen times.*

'And now if you bring your purchased books to the signing table, Thomas will sign them for you,' she gushed with excitement, as the chairs were almost thrown to the side by the rush of hormonal women running to be first in line.

As Thomas closed the book on the lectern and walked across the event space, gingerly picking his way to the table that had been set aside for his signing, a woman moved in front of him, effectively blocking his way. She was in her late thirties or early forties, scarily thin and with her hair scraped back into a bun, giving her the look of a stern governess a good decade older.

'Mister Williams, before you start, can I have a moment?' she asked.

'I have a signing,' Thomas smiled politely. 'I can write whatever you want when—'

'Oh, I'm not one of *them*,' the woman replied, glancing around in disgust. 'I'm doing a piece on Reginald Troughton. You said he was in Scotland?'

'I believe so,' Thomas glanced around for the manager, hoping that she could step in, do her bloody job and move this woman away. He didn't want to move her; someone could always misconstrue such things in this day and age.

'I spoke to him yesterday,' the woman replied. 'At home, in London. And he didn't seem to have any flu-like symptoms then.' She offered a business card, which Thomas took almost automatically. 'Care to make a comment?'

'Well, all I can go on is what my publisher told me,' Thomas really wanted to move on now as he faked a concerned expression for the woman. 'I believe the flu hit him overnight, or he would have made it. I'll check on him tomorrow. I'm sorry.'

'Well, if I can just ask—' *God, the woman simply wouldn't take a hint.*

The smile faded, and Thomas moved closer.

'Look, I've had an endless day, and I don't have time for interviews. If you want to talk to me, you can get me through my talent agent...'

He stopped as he looked at the woman properly for the first time.

'Have we met before?' he asked.

'Yes, we have,' the woman's face was emotionless now. 'I was one of the gang, not that you'd remember, or give a damn about. Have a nice day, *Mister* Williams.'

And as quickly as she'd arrived, the woman left, Thomas now standing alone and confused where he knew her from. The audience were still patiently lining up before the table, each with books in their hands, but before he could move towards them, Jane now marched towards him. Thomas looked towards the manager, nodding apologetically as he did so, and she smiled and nodded back at him in a *'no worries'* manner. The last thing she was going to do was stop two members from the *Magpies* from chatting to each other in her store. This was something that hadn't happened in years, and she could see that the audience, while waiting for the signature, were very aware of the history happening beside them and were eating it up.

'Thanks for outing me,' Jane smiled humourlessly.

'It was the least I could do,' Thomas said, shrugging. 'So what's it been, five years?'

'Seven.'

'Wow. How's—'

'He's fine,' Jane interrupted. 'We both are.'

One fan, a middle-aged lady with a book in her hand, who simply hadn't garnered the basic fact that *you left the talent alone,* walked up to them, breaking the moment.

'Hi, I'm sorry to interrupt, but I was hoping you could sign this?' she said to Jane. 'You're Jane Taylor, right?'

'Actually, it's Ashton now,' Jane replied, glancing at Thomas as she said so.

'Oh, like Luke Ashton?'

'Exactly like that.'

The lady paused at this sudden revelation. 'Oh. *Wow*.'

Thomas forced a smile as he leaned in.

'I'm sorry, we haven't seen each other for a while and only have a moment before I start my signing. Over there. Where you should be queuing,' he pointed at the line of now irritated women. 'Do you mind?'

As the lady finally got the hint and reluctantly left them, Thomas looked back at Jane.

'Can you wait around until after?' he asked softly. 'Catch up?'

Jane nodded, as Thomas grabbed and squeezed her hand before walking over to the signing desk to more applause.

Jane, meanwhile, pulled out her phone and, after reading a text on it, turned it off.

———

THE OFFICE IN THE TEMPLE INN APARTMENT HAD NEVER BEEN tidy, but now it looked like a bomb had hit it. Or, more accurately, that a fight had occurred there; a vicious beating of a sixty-five-year-old man.

A photo frame, one that held the same publicity photo of the *Magpies* that *Waterstones* had used was now discarded, broken on the floor, the glass smashed by the impact of a shoe's heel on it. A red smear of blood had been wiped across the broken glass, covering all the faces in the photo, smeared by the blood covered hand of Reginald Troughton, whose glassy, dead eyes stared vacantly ahead, as he lay face down on the carpet, his arm, stretched out rested beside the frame as if his last act had been to smear the photo with his own blood in some kind of message, or act of defiance.

Beside his body, the killer had also left the bloodied tyre iron on the floor, the end slick with the author's blood.

Reginald Troughton would never finish his tell-all adventure.

And the *Magpies* no longer existed to solve his *murder*.

TO HUNT A MAGPIE

Released 6th June 2021

Order Now at Amazon:

http://mybook.to/tohuntamagpie

ACKNOWLEDGEMENTS

Although I've been writing for three decades under my real name, these Declan Walsh novels are a first for me; a new name, a new medium and a new lead character.

There are people I need to thank, and they know who they are. To the ones who started me on this path over a coffee during a pandemic to the ones who zoom-called me and gave me advice, the ones on various Facebook groups who encouraged me when I didn't know if I could even do this, who gave advice on cover design and on book formatting all the way to my friends and family, who saw what I was doing not as mad folly, but as something good. Also, I couldn't have done this without my growing army of ARC readers who not only show me where I falter, but also raise awareness of me in the social media world, ensuring that other people learn of my books, and editors and problem catchers like Maureen Webb, Chris Lee, Edwina Townsend, Maryam Paulsen and Jacqueline Beard MBE, the latter of whom has copyedited all five books so far (including the prequel), line by line for me.

But mainly, I tip my hat and thank you. *The reader.* Who took a chance on an unknown author in a pile of Kindle books, and thought you'd give them a chance, whether it was with this book or with my first one.

I write Declan Walsh for you. He (and his team) solves crimes for you. And with luck, he'll keep on solving them for a very long time.

Jack Gatland / Tony Lee,
    London, March 2021

ABOUT THE AUTHOR

Jack Gatland is the pen name of *#1 New York Times Bestselling Author* Tony Lee, who has been writing in all media for over thirty years, including comics, graphic novels, middle grade books, audio drama, TV and film for *DC Comics, Marvel, BBC, ITV, Random House, Penguin USA, Hachette* and a ton of other publishers and broadcasters.

These have included licenses such as *Doctor Who, Spider Man, X-Men, Star Trek, Battlestar Galactica, MacGyver,* BBC's *Doctors, Wallace and Gromit* and *Shrek*.

As Tony, he's toured the world talking to reluctant readers with his 'Change The Channel' school tours, and lectures on screenwriting and comic scripting for *Raindance* in London.

An introvert West Londoner by heart, he lives with his wife Tracy and dog Fosco, just outside London.

Locations In The Book

The locations that I use in my books are real, if altered slightly for dramatic intent. Here's some more information about a few of them...

Hurley-Upon-Thames is a real village, and one that I visited many times from the age of 8 until 16, as my parents and I would spend our spring and summer weekends at the local campsite. It's a location that means a lot to me, my second home throughout my childhood, and so I've decided that this should be the 'home base' for Declan.

The Olde Bell is a real pub in the village too, although owned by a hotel chain rather than man named Dave. It was founded in 1135 as the hostelry of Hurley Priory, making it one of the oldest hotels (and inns) in the world. There *is* a secret tunnel, that was used by John Lovelace to overthrow royalty, although it's not as traversable as I've claimed here. It was also used as a meeting point for Churchill and Eisenhower during World War II. The Library in the Malthouse also exists.

Temple Inn Golf Club exists, and my dad used to play many rounds there when I was a kid. The sixteenth hole is exactly where I state it is in the story. The course was designed by the 1887 and 1889 Open Champion Willie Park Jr in 1909, and it was indeed built on land once owned by the *Knights Templar.*

The Crypt at Hurley Priory is real; founded by Geoffrey de Mandeville in 1086 in memory of his first wife, the Priory was central to the life of the village for 450 years until Henry VIII's reforms swept it away in 1536. Believed to also be the site of an Anglo-Saxon church founded by St Birinus as he converted the Thames Valley in the 7th century, Editha, the sister of Edward the Confessor, is rumoured to have been buried in the church, and therefore near the crypt. In the 16th Century the Lovelace family took the manor, building Ladye

Place, and it was here in 1688 that John, the 3rd Lord Lovelace played a significant role in the Glorious or Bloodless Revolution. The crypt became a centre of plotting and its said that fellow aristocratic conspirators would enter by way of underground tunnels that led from the river or *The Olde Bell* to avoid detection. This crypt, which still stands in private grounds on the old monastic estate at Hurley, was also visited by both William of Orange and George III.

Finally, the **Dew Drop Inn** also exists, and was actually a pleasant surprise; when writing book one I had a totally different area for Patrick Walsh's car crash and death, but when revisiting the scene I realised that it wouldn't have worked. Picking the junction of Honey Lane as a new location, I realised very quickly that forensically, the crash could only have happened if he travelled from a different direction, and I decided to use the *Dew Drop Inn* as a location, not realising how important it would become in the tale. The building itself dates back to the 1600's and is steeped in history owing to its reported use by the infamous highwayman *Dick Turpin* and his horse *Black Bess,* who would stable in the cellar. Which is lovely as a story, but Black Bess was a fictional creation used in the novel *Rookwood*, and as such wouldn't have actually been there. There is proof that Turpin did move around Berkshire though, so there's every chance that he (and whatever horse he really rode) visited there.

If you're interested in seeing what the *real* locations look like, I post 'behind the scenes' location images on my Instagram feed. This will continue through all the books, and I suggest you follow it.

In fact, feel free to follow me on all my social media, by following the links below. They're new, as *I'm* new - but over time it can be a place where we can engage, discuss Declan and put the world to rights.

www.jackgatland.com

Subscribe to my Readers List: **www.subscribepage.com/jackgatland**

www.facebook.com/jackgatlandbooks
www.twitter.com/jackgatlandbook
ww.instagram.com/jackgatland

Want more books by Jack Gatland? Turn the page...

THE THEFT OF A **PRICELESS** PAINTING...
A GANGSTER WITH A **CRIPPLING DEBT...**
A **BODY COUNT** RISING BY THE HOUR...

AND ELLIE RECKLESS IS CAUGHT IN THE MIDDLE.

JACK GATLAND

PAINT
— THE —
DEAD

A 'COP FOR CRIMINALS' ELLIE RECKLESS NOVEL

A NEW PROCEDURAL CRIME SERIES WITH
A TWIST - FROM THE CREATOR OF THE
BESTSELLING 'DI DECLAN WALSH' SERIES

AVAILABLE ON AMAZON / KINDLE UNLIMITED

EIGHT PEOPLE. EIGHT SECRETS.
ONE SNIPER.

THE
B☉ARD
ROOM

HOW FAR WOULD YOU GO TO GAIN JUSTICE?

NEW YORK TIMES #1 BESTSELLER TONY LEE WRITING AS

JACK GATLAND

A NEW STANDALONE THRILLER WITH
A TWIST - FROM THE CREATOR OF THE
BESTSELLING 'DI DECLAN WALSH' SERIES

AVAILABLE ON AMAZON / KINDLE UNLIMITED

THEY TRIED TO KILL HIM...
NOW HE'S OUT FOR **REVENGE.**

NEW YORK TIMES #1 BESTSELLER **TONY LEE** WRITING AS

JACK GATLAND

THE MURDER OF AN **MI5 AGENT**...
A BURNED SPY **ON THE RUN** FROM HIS OWN PEOPLE...
AN ENEMY OUT TO **STOP HIM** AT ANY COST...
AND A **PRESIDENT** ABOUT TO BE **ASSASSINATED**...

SLEEPING SOLDIERS

A **TOM MARLOWE** THRILLER

BOOK 1 IN A NEW SERIES OF THRILLERS IN THE STYLE OF
JASON BOURNE, JOHN MILTON OR **BURN NOTICE,** AND
SPINNING OUT OF THE **DECLAN WALSH** SERIES OF BOOKS

AVAILABLE ON AMAZON / KINDLE UNLIMITED

Printed in Great Britain
by Amazon